Without Consent

Without Consent

by Virginia R Degner

Strategic Book Group
Durham, Connecticut

Strategic Book Group
P. O. Box 333
Durham, CT 06422
http://www.strategicbookclub.com

ISBN: 978-1-60976-400-5

Book Design by Julius Kiskis

19 18 17 16 15 14 13 12 11   1 2 3 4 5

Dedication

In memory of my parents, Margaret Alice MacIntosh and Raymond Stuart MacIntosh and my twin brother James Allen MacIntosh. My mother- and father-in-law, Leonard and Gladys Degner, and their daughter, Linda Moglia. My friends Lisa Defranco, and Barbara Eakle Baker. My twin babies Carol Elaine and David Duane Degner who lived but a short twenty-four hours, but who have not been forgotten. Their births were the catalyst of this novel.

Acknowledgments

With thanks and love to my children, Barbara, Karyn, Michael, and to Terry, and Victoria who love my children, and to my grandchildren, Brandon, Treves, Taylor and Camille, whose lives have touched mine and taught me so much about what it means to be a family. With special thanks and love to my husband, Duane, who has always encouraged me and supported my dreams. To my sister, Brenda MacIntosh Bigongiari, for her steadfast love and to her husband, Vasco. My brother Raymond Stuart MacIntosh and his family and my brother William Daniel MacIntosh and his family. My in-laws, Dennis and Marlene Degner and Frank Moglia. I am thankful to my East Coast cousins who help me to see the continuity of life through their parents whose lives have included such a strong connection to their California cousins.

I have appreciated the encouragement and support in this writing effort by Roy and Sami Davis who opened their almond ranch to me to learn all about how to run an almond farm. Linda Wollenweber for her knowledge of flying airplanes and airport procedures. Elizabeth Moore for her patient editing of the manuscript. There have been many friends who have been supporters of my growth as a writer but who have especially been my life supporters and have had a positive impact on my life throughout my life. Thank you, Kathy Serenello, Jan Romeiser, Lisa Lottie Luck, Ethyl Morgan, Linda Wollenweber, Janet Marquet, Lois Jaffe Preisendorf, Karon Dupre, Sandy Muniz, and Beverly Terrell.

Thanks to all who helped me with technical information. If I got any of the details wrong, it's my error, and I plead guilty.

This is a long list, but all on it have enriched my life and taught me what it means to be a wife, mother, and friend. I wish for them all "golden dreams and happiness.

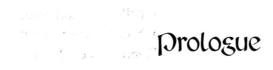

Prologue

Dr. Sarah Frazer stood facing the red-faced, sulking man. His body language was stiff and angry. They had reached a stalemate, and neither would budge.

"I'm going to notify Ariel immediately. Then I'm going to report you to the AMA for unethical and unprofessional conduct." She turned abruptly walked out of the kitchen, straight toward the front door. Obviously, their conversation was over.

Suddenly, behind her, she felt his dark shadow loom over her, as she turned to face him.

The man spat out, "You bitch! You'll not be telling anyone!" He lunged at her. The glint of her long-bladed kitchen knife hovered over her head. She put up her arms to block the thrusting blade, felt it slice into her arms. She turned to run out the front door and immediately felt the blade enter her back. Carefully and exactly, it sliced into her spinal cord and severed it. Her legs buckled. Useless and helpless, she saw the shadow of the knife as it came down a final time. Her scream pierced the air, but the closed-up house muffled it.

The man reached down and felt the still pulsing jugular vein at her throat. In order to reduce the blood trail, he grabbed a light cotton throw, hurriedly wrapped her in it, and carried her back through the kitchen and out the sliding side door to the pool where he dropped her unconscious body into the water. She came to as the water rushed over her head. She was helpless to fight, and as her life seeped away, she thought only of Ariel. There was no way now to warn her.

The man was dripping sweat with the exertion of carrying her body. He leaned over and pushed her body down until all the bubbles stopped, and the water was smooth. He wiped his hands on his pants, returned to the cottage, wiped up the blood spill off the hardwood floor, and put everything neatly in a plastic bag for disposal in the medical waste bag. As he drove away from the cottage, he quickly glanced at his Rolex. It was just 8:30 a.m. He'd be in time for the staff meeting.

Chapter 1

Zoe Clayborn was the first to arrive when the call came in from Sarah Frazer's housekeeper, Julie, to the sheriff's office in Sonora, California. As small a town as this was, she expected that someday she'd run into someone she knew while investigating a murder, but Zoe was stunned to find out it was Sarah. What a terrible thing to happen! The tears welled up. Zoe forced them down, turning red with the effort. Her partner David looked closely at her. The two detectives had worked together ever since Zoe joined the department ten years ago.

Zoe and David worked so well together that they could anticipate each other's thoughts and actions. David was only an inch or so taller than Zoe's five eight and was slim and blonde like her too. He wore his hair in a low ponytail, and sometimes Zoe did too. When they walked into the police department on a day when Zoe had her hair in a low ponytail, their cohorts often did a double take, and they'd laugh when they got a glimpse of David's mustache. Long and lean, they wore black jeans and police tee shirts when it suited them, putting on black parkas on cold days like this January one. Their breath froze in the air as the two finished their investigation at the murder scene and watched as Zoe's best friend's mother was wheeled out by the coroner's office for a post. The autopsy would tell them what the scene hadn't.

1

"You okay?" David asked.

Zoe turned away, walked to the outside patio, and sat down at the glass-topped table as the memories flooded through her. Sarah had been her best friend's stepmother. David sat down beside her and watched her carefully.

"This murder is the most gruesome thing I've ever seen. Sarah didn't have a chance, she must have suffered so. I feel so sorry for Ariel and Lily and Mark." Zoe struggled to get control of herself.

"Are you all right with this, Zoe?" David squatted down beside Zoe and offered her his big white handkerchief. His face registered his concern; Zoe's long-time partner had never seen her so devastated.

"I'm fine David, or I will be. I've got to be."

David and Zoe walked purposefully back to the swimming pool area together. David supported his partner as she would have supported him under the same circumstances.

Sarah's stepdaughter, Ariel Frazer Houston, and Zoe had gone through school together. Though Zoe was five years younger, they were at the same grammar school.

The older students would often tutor the younger ones. When Zoe was in kindergarten, Ariel was her reading tutor.

Zoe looked up to Ariel and because their parents were friends, Zoe was in and out of the Frazer farm small medical clinic during summer vacations with Ariel, answering phones and filing. It was fun to pretend that they were grown-up, and they got to know Dr. Frazer's patients. They especially enjoyed playing with the little ones when their mothers needed to see the doctor. It was a good training for the detail work that she did now. Dr. Sarah didn't let them be sloppy with any chore she gave them, and she'd make them re-file or retype anything that didn't meet her standards. When they did a good job, she was lavish in her praise.

Zoe was often in the office attached to the side of Frazer's comfortable farmhouse, getting her knees swabbed with iodine and bandaged by Sarah.

Looking at Sarah's body being put into the coroner's wagon, Zoe felt the tears well up in her eyes, and she reached out to her partner, David Delangue. He steadied her and asked her if she was going to be able to cover this investigation. She nodded, took a deep breath, squared her shoulders, and took out her notebook.

When they were through processing the scene, she turned to David. "I have to go see Ariel."

She started across the patio and out the side gate when David came up beside her and grabbed her elbow. "I'm coming too."

Sarah had moved out of the main house and back into her little cottage ten years ago when Ariel and Morgan Houston had married. She let them have the use and the care of the big farmhouse.

Ariel, though still working full time as a social worker, enjoyed overseeing the farm, working with Ben and Julie Roberts, old friends of her parents who, when they retired, moved into a small apartment over the barn and helped with the care and maintenance of the orchards and buildings. They were invaluable to Sarah after her husband Paul died. They kept the farm running smoothly, and now they helped Ariel. Ariel, with Ben and Julie, built it into a thriving farm. Fifty acres of almond trees were generating over $170,000 a year in profit that went into a trust funds of $37,000 apiece for the three of them, Ariel, Lily, and Mark, enough for Sarah's children to have meaningful lives through their work, so they weren't dependent on trust fund money only. Paul had been very aware of how easy money could make them dependent and exclude them from having the satisfaction of earning their own way through life.

Julie was invaluable during the years when Sarah was having her babies and caring for Ariel. Sarah had had Lily and Mark, bang, bang, eleven months apart, shortly after she had married Paul Frazer when Ariel was just five years old.

Ariel received an additional twenty thousand a year for acting as overseer. This arrangement worked well, and everyone was happy except for the fact that Ariel and Morgan had been trying to have a baby and finally had resorted to fertility treatments. This was the third attempt, and as far as Ariel was concerned, it would be the last attempt. The drugs were powerful, and Ariel felt weak from them. The last two treatments resulted in miscarriages; she didn't think she could stand it if it happened again. Win, lose, or draw, this was it. She was working as a social worker and that took about all the energy she had. If this in-vitro failed, then her work would have to be enough.

Ariel's brother, Mark, and sister, Lily, were happy with the extra income, but they had no desire to stay on the farm. Mark had become a firefighter in Sonora. Lily had become a physician like her mother and was serving in the navy in the Gulf of Iraq.

By the time Zoe and David were able to leave the scene and go to the farmhouse to tell Ariel, Ariel had already spent a full day out in the field with Jason Pepper, a young sixteen-year old whom she had just placed in foster care two weeks ago. Ariel worked four days a week out of the Sonora office. It kept her busy, and she enjoyed the children. It was hard seeing how difficult their lives were, and even though she kept a busy schedule, she enjoyed doing fun things with the kids to bring a smile to their faces. Ariel smiled as she remembered the afternoon spent with Jason.

Jason had separation anxiety disorder. Though she knew he liked her, he made sure when they went to McDonald's for their weekly meeting that afterwards they went by the pet store for flies and mice for his pet snake and Gila monster. Jason was more attached to the critters than to his foster family or her. It would take time to gain his trust after the trauma he suffered when he and his brothers were taken from his father, because they were discovered all living in a car. Jason's mother, a drug addict, was long gone, out of their lives.

When Ariel took him to be with his father and siblings at supervised visits at the social services playroom, she was startled when she peeked in and saw all four siblings piled on their father's lap, sprawled out on the sofa together watching television. She could see the love that they had for each other and their father, and her heart ached for Jason who didn't have much chance of being reunited with his father and siblings until he was eighteen and out of the system. It was hard being a social worker and having to watch the pain the children had when they were torn apart from their parents and each other and placed in several foster homes, but it was rewarding when she could reunite a family. It was satisfying when she worked with the biological parents who had done the work of getting a job and were getting off drugs in order to regain custody of their children.

Ariel sighed when she saw the red light blinking on the answering machine, but she was just too tired to check her messages. They'd wait until later. If it were an emergency, her supervisor would have paged her. A hot bath was all she could think of.

The hot water filled the tub to the top, and Ariel sank into the bubble-filled tub with a sigh of pure contentment. The room filled with scented steam and a hint of rose water. With her long curly red hair wound up in a bath towel, Ariel lay supine in the bath and put her hand on her stomach, marveling at the brand new life inside of her and wondering whether it was a boy or a girl. They could have asked when the embryo was implanted, but both Ariel and Morgan wanted to be surprised. Ariel lay in the warm soapy bath and listened to her newest CD, a new release of Celine Dion called "Taking Chances." The bathroom was large. It had once been a small sitting room next to the master bedroom but soon after Ariel and Morgan married, they had gutted the room and called in plumbers. The rest of it they did themselves. It had turned out to be charming, and Ariel had insisted on white porcelain and pink tile. A thick white throw rug served as a carpet. There were fluffy white curtains with tiny blossoms embroidered all over them in shades of pink to white. The CD player shared space with bath salts and magazines and a wonderful bar of creamy French soap infused with lavender to soothe and relax her. The bath towel was huge; it would cover her completely once she had enough energy to get out of the tub. The Paper Whites that Ariel had picked and put in a vase by the tub were intoxicating. Ariel breathed in deeply as the fragrance mingled with the steam in the room. She sighed as she relaxed in the hot soapy water.

Suddenly the sound of feet pounding up her stairway alerted her. She grabbed her bath towel and hurriedly wrapped herself in it. Then there was a pounding on the door, and an urgent voice calling her name.

Sofie, her basset hound, was barking deep in her chest. Ariel heard her sniffing at the crack under the bathroom door. Ariel recognized her friend Zoe soothing Sofie. She hurried to the door just as Zoe called her name a second time.

"Ariel, are you in there?" Zoe yelled through the door.

Ariel yanked the door open with a look of surprise and questioning. Why was Zoe yelling at her? Breathless, Zoe grabbed her hand and rushed her into the adjoining bedroom where she seized her bathrobe and threw it to her. Behind her, David coughed discreetly and motioned for Ariel to close the bedroom door and put on the bathrobe.

"What's all the yelling about?" Ariel questioned as she struggled to get her arms in the sleeves of the warm plush robe.

Zoe, standing behind her, grimaced. She didn't know how to tell her that the only mother she had ever known was dead. She took a deep breath and turned Ariel toward her. "Let's go downstairs," she said, as she led Ariel out the door and down the stairway to the living room where David had quietly retreated.

Chapter 2

Zoe sat next to her and held her hand, all the while stunned herself by what she had seen.

"It was instantaneous. Julie found her this morning when she went to clean the cottage. I made Julie go home and told her I'd tell you. Julie and Ben are waiting to see you after we finish." Zoe then poured them all a cup of hot tea and brought it to them.

Ariel suddenly stood up and ran to the telephone. Morgan, she must tell Morgan. The phone rang and rang and finally he answered. "Morgan, I need you, it's Sarah! She's dead." Ariel couldn't talk anymore; all Morgan heard was her sobbing.

"Oh my God, no! Ariel sweetheart, I'll be right home."

Morgan was about five minutes away in downtown Sonora, his law office conveniently located next door to the county courthouse. Zoe had just finished brewing Ariel another cup of tea when he came into the kitchen, slamming the door behind him. Morgan went directly to Ariel and gathered her into his arms. Ariel burst into tears, and Morgan cried too. Soon, Zoe was swept into their huddle, and they all cried together. They sat down around the Franklin stove. Morgan got busy building a fire, carefully nurturing it to a satisfying blaze.

Morgan turned from the fire and looked at Ariel. "You'll

have to call Lily home. And did you call Mark?"

Ariel reached into her pocket and speed-dialed Mark's cell. He answered on the second ring. Ariel handed the phone to Morgan, whimpering, "I can't tell him." Morgan grabbed the phone.

"Mark, we need you here right now." He explained it was urgent, but he found his throat went dry, and he could only say, "It's your mother." Then he broke down and thrust the phone at Zoe.

Zoe took a deep breath and talked into the phone, "Mark, get over here! Sarah's dead."

Zoe could hear Mark barking questions at her. How, why, when?

Zoe, her voice raspy with emotion said, "Just get over here now." As she hung up, she thought, *Lily wouldn't be so easy.* She was in the Gulf on a hospital ship. However, she had given Ariel the number of her admiral's staff in case of emergency.

"I've got the contact number in the desk. I'll get it." Ariel walked over to the roll top and picked up her telephone book. It was only a few minutes as she went through the switchboard and overseas operator. They could patch a call through. Moments later, she was talking to the admiral's staff. They would give Dr. Lily Frazer the message and get her on a transport going back to the states as soon as possible. Ariel hung up the phone. She knew it would be a while until Lily could get back to her. Just then, tires screamed into her farmyard; Mark jumped out of his Wrangler. Taking the front steps two at a time, he was in the house, embracing Ariel. At six feet four, he was a big, solidly built man with the same green eyes as Ariel and with his father's jet-black hair. Sometimes when Ariel looked at Mark out of the corner of her eye, she thought it was her father. They were the same height and coloring; it always startled her. She missed her father keenly.

"Jesus! Jesus, Ariel! What the hell happened?" He hugged her tight to him and looked over her shoulder at the others. Ariel buried her head in Mark's shoulder, shaking her head. Zoe and David filled him in, censoring the details as they talked.

"It happened, as near as the coroner can tell, early this morning. Julie found her when she went to clean the cottage at about ten thirty. She called 911 right away; we got there in about ten minutes. Julie went out to the pool after she didn't find Sarah in the cottage. She saw her car parked in front, so she knew she should be home. There was blood in the living room that the killer tried to clean up--which leads us to believe that this was where she was attacked before being dumped into the pool. The autopsy will tell us more." Zoe stopped as Mark and Ariel grimaced at the thought of an autopsy. Zoe saw their expressions and said, "No way around it; They have already started the procedure, and we will be notified when they have completed it."

The back door opened quietly. Julie and Ben tiptoed in. Julie went immediately to Mark and Ariel, throwing her arms around them both. Ben came up and patted Julie who had dissolved into tears. Finally, Julie got her breath; gulping, she told them what she had found.

"I was surprised to see Sarah's car still in the driveway. I thought she might not be feeling well, but when I knocked there wasn't any answer, so I opened the door and called to her. When she didn't answer, I went to her bedroom, but the bed was made, still no sign of her. It was when I walked out to the kitchen and saw the back sliding door open that I thought maybe she'd be out at the pool. The only thing was that there didn't seem to be any activity in the pool. You know what a vigorous swimmer she was. I found her floating in her business clothes. That's when I called 911." Julie turned and buried her face in Ben's chest as he quietly led her to the couch.

Ariel hurried over to her, sat next to her, and held her tight against her. "I'm so sorry that you had to see her like that. It must have been horrible." There wasn't much to say after Julie's tearful disclosure; the group sat quietly together still in shock.

For something to do, though she wasn't even hungry, Ariel got up and started rummaging in the refrigerator. With Julie and Zoe's help, they got some sort of a meal together. There was leftover beef stew that they heated up with some crusty garlic bread with cheese that only took a moment to broil. Julie fixed a green salad.

Mark stayed with Ariel and Morgan through the makeshift dinner. The stew and cheese bread were delicious; it was an effort for them all to try to eat though.

After eating, Zoe shooed them out of the kitchen; she and David would clean up while Mark went with Ariel and Morgan to McCarty's Funeral Home. Zoe and David were off duty. They had both put in so many overtime hours that a few hours to decompress with their old friends were welcome. If anything more came up, they would be notified by cell phone.

Ariel and Morgan went upstairs to their room to clean up. Ariel's bright red curly hair had dried haphazardly; all she could do with it was pull it back in a low ponytail and secure it with a covered brown hair band. She stared at her pale skin and put a touch of semi-gloss coral lipstick on, using a bit for rouge to brighten her cheeks. Her cat-like green eyes stared back at her, looking so much like her father's that it was a comfort to her. Just then, Morgan came in and did a quick shave. He was as tall as Mark and her father, his hair was thick black, and his eyes were dark brown. The bathroom had twin sinks that allowed them to work side by side without jockeying for mirror and sink space. They stared at each other in the doublewide mirror. Morgan reached over and hugged her.

"Oh Ariel, I'm so sorry. Zoe and David will get the person. I know they'll get to the bottom of this." Morgan held Ariel tightly as she dissolved in tears. Reaching for a tissue, she blew her nose, nodding at Morgan.

Ariel was tall at five feet eight inches but next to Morgan, she felt diminutive. It was the only time she felt so small. Most of the time, she towered over her coworkers and the foster children, many of whom were Hispanic with short stature. They clung to each other. They were both still in shock.

Morgan and Ariel were still holding on to each other as they went down the back stairs to the kitchen to meet up with Mark. Ariel didn't want to see Sarah as she was now but with Mark and Morgan beside her, she thought she could face it.

Zoe and David finished up the dishes and put them away, quietly discussing the murder together. This was only the second murder case they had processed together in the ten years they had worked in the Tuolumne County Police Department. They had a lot of domestic violence cases that were usually the result of alcohol or drug abuse. A big workday consisted of flushing out marijuana growers or overseeing the retrieval of cars that sped out of control into the canyon. Usually there wasn't much to retrieve. Often the cars would go clear to the bottom, bursting into flames.

Ariel took a few minutes to call her supervisor, Meredith Campbell, to tell her of her stepmother's death and that she'd be out for a while. Ariel gave her a rundown on all of her cases that were up for court appearances. Someone would have to go into the files, write reports to the court for Jackie and Jason Baldwin, Roberta Bellows, and a couple more cases that would be coming due before Ariel got back to work. It couldn't be helped. Whenever Ariel needed time off, she would prepare the reports herself, way ahead of time. Sometimes she did all of her cases up to be a little bit ahead of the paperwork, then added any last minute details or changes. Thank heavens for computers!

Meredith would find her reports all ready except the past week's activity. She would update them and have them ready to go when the children's court dates came up. This was why Meredith always let her take some time off whenever she and Morgan could get away. Because she was so efficient, it made it easy to assign a temporary worker who would just add her notes to the child's file. It worked now; Ariel wasn't sure what would happen with Sarah's death and her pregnancy. Right now, everything was up in the air. Ariel couldn't give Meredith an estimated return date.

"Ariel, I'm so sorry. Don't you worry about any of your cases. I'll get Jill Harper to do this week's home visits; she can add her notes to your reports. Right now, you need to focus on your family. Stay well, my friend."

She thanked Meredith, who was a good friend as well, and then she was ready to go to the mortuary with Mark and Morgan.

Ariel had fortunately not been inside the place since her father had died. It was dark by the time they drove up to the mortuary, and it was a solemn group that walked in and waited while Don McCarty went to the back and arranged Sarah's body for viewing. When he opened the blue velvet curtain, Ariel felt her knees buckle. Morgan grabbed her and held her up. It felt like hours, but the viewing only took a few minutes then Don closed the curtain. The medical examiner had finished the autopsy, and results were not available yet. McCarty's had brought Sarah back from the coroner's pathology department only about an hour before Mark, Ariel, and Morgan had gotten there. Sarah was white and waxen with a white sheet draped over her up to her neck--nothing like the vibrant woman Ariel loved. She decided then and there that it would be a closed coffin with no one but the family able to see her to say good-bye. Lily would want to see her, but Ariel couldn't go through this again. Zoe or Mark could come with her to see her for the last time.

"Oh damn it, Ariel! She's so white; I can't believe this is what Mom's life has come to. Mom saved lives! Why would someone kill her?" Mark turned to Ariel; she held him and coaxed him away from the gurney.

Ariel had brought Sarah's favorite dress with her, a creamy yellow dress with chiffon sleeves that Sarah had worn for a dressy medical conference dance. "Here, Don, this dress always looked so great on her. Sarah loved it. Will it do?"

"Sure, Ariel, I'll just take it and put it over here. It will be fine." Don put the dress in a plastic box and wrote Sarah's name on a sticky note. Don ushered them outside the viewing room, walking them toward the casket room to show them what he had available. Mark, Ariel, and Morgan looked over the small selection, chose a simple casket, and made the funeral arrangements. While they were there, they called the Little Red Chapel in Sonora. The after-hour voicemail gave the phone number. Ariel dialed it and got hold of Reverend Ted Bender. He agreed to hold the service the following Saturday morning; he'd meet with them tomorrow to go over the details.

The coffin was inexpensive, the gray fabric-covered plain wood in keeping with Sarah's philosophy of not impacting the earth negatively. The siblings discussed cremation as an option, but her father had already purchased two full-size graves, side by side. Ariel knew he had wanted Sarah to be buried beside him when the time came. Sarah was to be buried immediately after the service in the historical cemetery in Columbia.

Both Paul and Sarah would now be together there in the family plot as Paul had wished. It was a small, old cemetery founded in 1855 and was where Sarah would have wanted to be, next to her beloved Paul. Ariel remembered her father's burial there. She felt better, as if he were with her now, steadying her. His whispered thoughts floated around her head. "White roses." Yes, that would be what he would have wanted to have them put on her coffin. Ariel remembered the white roses he'd given her stepmother every year for Valentine's Day. Sarah always put them in pride of place on the dining room table.

A little over an hour later, they were heading for home. Ariel hoped there would a message from Lily. There was. The e-mail was brief and just said that she was coming home by way of military transport. She asked if Zoe could come get her in her Cessna150 that she kept at the Columbia Airport for her commute to her weekend retreat at Half Moon Bay. Ariel made a note to call Zoe as soon as she could. She'd told Ariel, when they'd said goodnight after dinner, that she'd be at her parents. Ariel knew that Zoe was as shook up as she was, so she'd wait until about 8:00 p.m. to call her.

Zoe was close to her parents, especially after her husband and daughter had died over eight years ago. Zoe had never gotten over it. She spent a few hours each day at her parents' home in Columbia, stopping off for dinner with them most evenings. As a widow, she didn't enjoy going home. Her mother and father doted on her, and she'd been coming over for dinner ever since Howard had died in a car accident coming home from Sonora with their infant daughter when he'd taken Hallie to the pediatrician for her six-month checkup. They'd both died instantly. Hallie would have been nine this coming March.

Ariel would wait and call Zoe at her home.

Lily would be back in the states around 6:00 p.m. tomorrow, she thought.

She started to jot down all that needed to be done to get

things ready for her. She supposed that Lily would want to stay in Sarah's cottage, which was hers now; she'd leave that up to her.

Zoe had just gotten home from filing the paperwork and had started a murder book regarding Sarah. She hadn't gotten to her parents house after all; she settled for calling her parents and telling them about Sarah over the phone. They were as shocked as everyone else was.

Zoe answered Ariel's call on the first ring and agreed at once to go fetch Lily in the plane. She was happy to help her two oldest friends; actually, they were more like sisters than friends. They'd shared so much. Zoe would tell Lily what happened to Sarah so that she would have a little time to deal with the fact that her mother had been murdered, a fact that Ariel omitted in her phone call to the ship. Ariel had just said her mother had died and that Lily was needed at home.

Ariel put down the phone with a heavy sigh of relief. It was a relief to Ariel that she wouldn't have to be the bearer of such news. Zoe would be sensitive and break the news as gently as she could. Ariel walked into the kitchen where Morgan was popping some popcorn. Mark had gone home. Julie and Ben had retreated to their apartment. Only Morgan and Sofie were there. Ariel sniffed the popcorn and went to the cupboard for two bowls. Sofie sniffed the air, waiting expectantly for her share. Morgan finished making the popcorn in the microwave; holding the bag gingerly by his fingertips, he emptied it equally into both bowls. Morgan took Ariel in his arms. The two stood by the granite counter top and hugged. Ariel was the first to speak.

"I got hold of Zoe. She's agreed to pick up Lily tomorrow night at six. They should be back here about nine, because Lily wants to go to see Sarah at the funeral home first. I've made up Lily's old room. That should do for her until she decides where she wants to be. Oh, Morgan, I'm so thankful that I have you."

Ariel looked up at Morgan, accepting his gentle kiss.

"Come on, let's sit down for a bit by the fire. Sofie's waiting for her treat, and you look exhausted."

Morgan, with his arm around Ariel, led them to the brown leather sofa that Morgan's father had given them. Morgan liked to stretch out on it to watch his football games with the iron Franklin fireplace blazing in the family room adjacent to the kitchen. The sofa was used as a boundary to define the open area at the end of the kitchen where the Franklin stove made a cozy spot.

It had been a shock for Morgan, an only child who had grown up in a small professional household and sent to Eaton, a private boarding school in England where his father had gone, to come to Frazer ranch as the bridegroom of Ariel and instantly be part of a large extended family. Morgan's parents had grown up in Columbia but had lost their parents before Morgan was born. They had both been only children; there was no other family but the three of them. Now his parents were dead too--his mother of cancer and his father of a massive coronary while judging a high profile murder case in Sonora. Ariel and the baby inside of her was all that remained of the Houston family line. Morgan was grateful for the Frazer family; they had brought him into their lives, included him, and trusted him totally. Sarah had given him the family finances to oversee, and he had carefully invested all of the Frazer money. The Frazers had lived so simply farming almond groves that Morgan had had no idea that the family was worth millions.

Paul Frazer had an inheritance he'd gotten from his grandfather in Scotland. He'd come to America after Ariel's mother, Kate, had died in a boating accident. Paul, a shrewd Scotsman, had gotten the farm at a huge under-market savings, because the owner wanted Paul to buy it. Old Joe Kraft was pulling up stakes and heading for his daughter's home in Hawaii. Joe felt that Paul would do a good job running the farm. He wanted the farm to continue. That's how it was in the mountain towns. The farms and ranches went to families, but if there wasn't a family member who wanted to run it then it was at the discretion of the owner who bought it. There was no realtor showing the place to strangers. Joe Kraft knew and liked Paul, so that was that. They had met when Joe hired him to manage the farm. Paul had managed the farm well for the two years before Joe had come to him and told him he was moving on. Paul jumped at the offer, and so the deal was done with a simple transfer of ownership at the courthouse.

Chapter 3

Ariel and Morgan were watching their favorite CSI show when the doorbell rang. As Morgan went to answer it, Ariel wondered who could be stopping by at that hour. It was too early for Lily and Zoe to be back. When Morgan didn't come right back, Ariel got up and walked to the front hall to see what was going on. It was Zoe's partner, David Delangue, and another officer. The look on their faces said that their business was serious. Morgan joined the two officers in a huddle by the door. "What's the problem?"

Ariel listened as David turned to Morgan. "I'm sorry to tell you that we have got to take you down to the station. The chief has some questions for you, Morgan, in connection with the murder of your mother-in-law, Sarah Frazer."

Morgan let out a startled breath and before he could respond, the other officer was moving in to handcuff him. David moved in front of Morgan. "Put those cuffs away, Bob; Morgan won't need them, will you Morgan?" David looked at Morgan and then at Ariel.

Morgan saw Ariel's look of panic, turned to her, and said quietly, "It's okay, baby, I'll be right back." He kissed her quickly, turned to David. "Let's get this over with. I've got nothing to hide." Morgan turned back to Ariel. "Call Stan and tell him where they've taken me. I have nothing to hide, but I'm not a defense lawyer. Stan will deal with this."

Morgan was whisked out to the patrol car. Ariel saw David putting him in the back behind the wire mesh. Ariel rushed into the house and looked up Stan Water's number. She punched in the number with trembling fingers. The exchange was on, so Ariel had to explain why it was such an emergency. Ariel held the phone while the operator called Stan. It was only a minute or so before she heard Stan's booming voice. "Ariel, what's the matter?"

Ariel had to sit down on the chair by the phone and explain. "Stan, they've taken Morgan to the Sonora police station to question him regarding my stepmother's murder yesterday morning. Stan, I don't know what to do, and Morgan asked me to call you and put you in the picture."

"Jeez, I'm sorry to hear this, Ariel. Don't worry, I'll go down and see what's what."

Ariel hung up the phone and stood staring blankly through the window out into the dark night. Sofie nudged her, jarring her. Ariel knelt down and hugged Sofie as she cried tears of anguish while Sofie stood patiently next to her, lending her the comfort of a warm live presence. Ariel stood up, wiped her eyes, and picked up the telephone to call Mark.

Zoe was waiting outside the gate when Lily's plane landed and taxied into the gate. It was surprisingly on time; the doors were opened, and the passengers were deplaning.

Lily was the second one out the door, her long black hair flying in the wind from the engines as they shut down. She had a duffle bag over her shoulder and was dressed in fatigues of light brown with olive and brown splotches all over them. She saw Zoe; they both waved at the same time. Lily was to the gate and hugging her in a matter of seconds. Releasing Zoe from her bear hug, she pulled back, her cat green eyes the same as her sister's and brother's bore into Zoe's. "There's more to the story than what Ariel said, isn't there?"

Zoe, caught off guard, couldn't speak and nodded. She put her arm around her as they moved toward the crowd charging down the long airport corridor searching for sustenance before the long ride home.

"Come on, let's go get a soda and something to eat. I'll tell you all I can." Zoe and Lily sat down in the airport restaurant. Each ordered a light sandwich and a soda. When the waitress took their order and left them alone, Lily looked straight into Zoe's eyes.

"Okay! What's going on? I know something horrible happened to her. I've got to know what." She seemed to steel herself, and though her eyes glowed like a green-eyed cat, the rest of her seemed to shrink right before Zoe's eyes.

"She was murdered at the cottage. The murderer used a knife and then threw her into the swimming pool. She was paralyzed and couldn't help herself. There was water in her lungs." Zoe thought that Lily was going to faint. But instead, she reared up out of the chair, and ran to the lavatory where Zoe found her moments later, sick to her stomach.

Zoe put her arms around her and helped her to the sink where she washed her face with a wet paper towel before pressing it behind her neck. Lily stood at the sink, her head hanging low over the porcelain bowl. She raised her head and met Zoe's eyes in the mirror. Zoe's blue eyes were soft with sadness and concern for Lily's loss of Sarah. Sarah had always been there when Zoe, Ariel, Lily, and Mark had spent their summers on the farm. The two old friends stood together in front of the mirror, exact opposites. Zoe had silvery blonde hair and blue eyes, and Lily's black hair was a startling contrast. Both Lily and Zoe were about the same height--over 5 feet 8 inches, tall and willowy, with slim hips and long legs. Zoe was Mark's age, twenty-nine, but she had been both Lily and Ariel's friend ever since she was a toddler at nursery school with Mark when she would come to the farm for play dates with him. While Zoe's mother and Sarah had tea, Zoe, Mark, and the girls would splash together in the huge swimming pool that Paul had installed for Sarah after they were married. The summer months in Columbia at the almond farm ranged from the eighties up to one hundred ten degrees. The pool was a godsend with three small children for Sarah. They spent their days around it. As the children grew and became teenagers, the farm became the hub of activities for them. There was always a pack of friends, and everyone was welcome. Sarah would make pizzas and all kinds of cookies that she'd sneak oatmeal into. There was always fresh fruit and almonds shelled and ready to pop in their mouths.

When Ariel met Morgan, the group expanded to include him and his best friend, Riley. Riley and Morgan knew each other from childhood when they'd ride horses all day during their summer vacations. Morgan didn't know Ariel was a friend of Riley's because he had gone away to school and was only home for holidays. Morgan's and Riley's parents had grown up together in Columbia. Morgan's father had been a judge. Ben had only wanted to ranch. They kept their friendship, and Morgan's father appreciated Ben's down-to-earth sensibility. Riley was Julie and Ben's oldest child and only son. Riley's sister, Melonie, was three years younger, and she preferred to spend her summer reading and going with her friends to the movies. Once in a while, if the day was really hot, she'd join the group around the pool, but Melonie was more of a loner than Riley, who thrived at the farm.

Zoe hugged Lily, offering her much needed comfort, and then Lily briskly broke away and said. "Let's go; I have to see her." She started out the door and ran into the waitress bringing their drinks and sandwiches. Thankfully, they were in paper containers. Zoe swept them into her arms, gave the waitress a twenty-dollar bill, and thanked her as she ran to catch up with Lily and take her to the plane.

They climbed aboard. Zoe was busy with the tower. As they waited to taxi out onto the runway, Zoe unwrapped the sandwiches and handed a ham and cheese to Lily. Lily handed back half of it, and they both sat quietly munching the shared sandwich while the air traffic controllers chattered over the radio.

Zoe called the tower. "This is Cessna 2359er. Requesting 32 left," she said indicating the left airfield marked 32. The radio crackled in reply.

"Okay, 2359er. Hold for two." Zoe sighed and bit into her sandwich; they were in line and would be third to take off.

They'd just finished their sandwiches and colas when they got the okay to approach the runway. It would be another fifteen minutes before they could take off. Zoe sipped her cold soda while Lily leaned back in the co-pilot seat and closed her eyes. It was over twenty-four hours since she had left the war in the Gulf; she hadn't slept much. The cargo plane had hard seats and had been packed with returning Navy Seals who were so tired that they slept where they sat.

The tower crackled again. "Cessna 2359er you're cleared for takeoff."

Zoe headed down the runway gaining speed and lifted off with room to spare. The plane felt light. Zoe turned due east--crossing the waters of the Bay, dark and brooding as the little plane skimmed over it.

Zoe enjoyed flying across to Oakland, the atmosphere causing the lights to look like the Emerald City in Oz. In the Central Valley, a light fog was forming, which concerned Zoe, but she'd be down before it obscured visibility at the little airport in Columbia. She looked down as she followed 580 to Highway 99 across the

Central Valley to Highway 120 and over to 49. Lily slept on, and it wasn't until Zoe started her descent, the radio crackling as she communicated with Columbia airport, that Lily awoke.

"This is Cessna 2359er. Requesting permission to land," Zoe spoke briskly into the radio.

"Right, Zoe, you can come right on in. All the sensible folks have already flown in. Visibility is good but don't be a lackey. The ceiling is going to drop with the tully fog rolling in." Barney Hinkle chuckled as he clicked off the mike. Zoe could come into this field with a blindfold on. He watched as the lights on the plane came into view then circled so that the Cessna would be coming down north to south heading on the runway.

When the plane taxied to a stop, Zoe jumped out and caught Lily's duffle bag. Barney watched as a long-legged, slim-hipped vision with long, straight, black hair climbed out of the plane. Lily looked around with her piercing green eyes and stared at the tower. She gathered up her duffle and marched inside. Barney greeted the women with a community hug that brought them both into his meaty arms. He'd known them since they were knee high to a grasshopper.

"I'm sorry about your mom, Lily, we all are." Barney got choked up and couldn't continue. He waved them away and went into the back room to blow his nose furiously.

January 20, 2009 was a cold thirty degrees. As the new president, Barack Obama, danced the night away at his spectacular inaugural balls in Washington D.C., Zoe dealt with arrival details. Lily, impatient to leave, went out the double-front glass doors and stood waiting for Zoe at the Jeep Wrangler.

Zoe got in, started the cold engine, got the heater going, and swung out of the parking lot headed toward Columbia and home. Abruptly, Lily broke the silence, "I want to go see her right now!" I'm a doctor; I'm going to go see for myself what happened."

Zoe nodded, gunned the motor, and spun out of the parking lot, turning right onto the highway headed toward Sonora. Columbia and a warm supper could wait.

The snowplow had been through. The road was icy; the jeep's snow tires held fast to the road. Sonora didn't get snow very often, but when it did, the civic folk were right on top of it and whisked it off the roads efficiently.

"Lily, I wish you would leave this alone and let us handle the investigation. What good will this do for you to go see her like she is now? Wait for the funeral. You're exhausted." Even as she spoke, Zoe could see by the hard stubborn look of Lily's jaw that she was bent on doing this; nothing was going to stop her. Zoe sighed as she pulled into McCarty's. The lights were still on. Don didn't go home early either.

When the jeep stopped, Lily jumped out and took the steps two at a time, reaching the building before Zoe got her seatbelt off. Zoe followed her. She saw that Don wasn't willing for Lily to examine her mother's body; she nodded to him. Reluctantly, he went around and opened the door to the morgue. Lily marched behind him and barked orders.

"Get me a gown and gloves," she barked as she stripped off her jacket and grabbed paper booties off the shelf.

Don went to the steel drawers and pulled out number 17. The body was covered in sheets, but no one could mistake the flowing red hair that had escaped the confines of the shroud. Zoe tossed a gown and gloves to Lily and stood back to watch that she didn't do more than look. "Now Lily, just look, don't be touching anything. Ask Don to do any moving that needs to be done."

It was eerily quiet in the icy cold room. Lily said nothing, just kept her eyes on the sheet as Don pulled it away from Sarah. He stopped just above her breasts and modestly folded the sheet over them. Lily motioned for him to bring the sheet down to her hips. The Y incision from the autopsy was uncovered as well and made Zoe suck in her breath. It was terrible to see Sarah like this. In front of Zoe's eyes, Lily became a seasoned physician that could put aside her feelings for her mother and examine her clinically and with professional detachment. Zoe, who had known both women most of her life, struggled to keep from crying and almost succeeded. When Lily motioned for Don to turn her mother so that she could see the wounds to the spinal column, Zoe, a seasoned cop, felt tears flow down her cheeks. She looked up at Lily and was shocked to see the rage on her face. She reached, put her hand on her shoulder, and coaxed her away from the lifeless body of the woman who was no longer a vibrant, loving mother. Lily let her move her out of the room, and she sat on a chair in the office. Don covered Sarah and then slid her back into the drawer.

"This was a vicious, cold-blooded killer, and if it's the last thing I do, I'm going to find him. When I do, I'm going to blow him away." Lily ripped off the booties and gown covering her and grabbing her coat, she stomped out of the mortuary.

"All right, I'm all right. I've got to go see Ariel and Mark." Lily got back into the jeep, staring straight ahead as Zoe swung the jeep back toward Columbia to the yellow farmhouse waiting for her to come home.

The jeep swung into the farmyard, spewing mud from the tires behind them as Zoe lurched to a stop at the back of the house. They were out of the jeep and climbing the back stairs to the deck when the back door burst open. Mark hurdled himself into Lily's arms. Ariel and Zoe huddled in the doorway. "Lily! I'm so glad to see you. Oh, Lily, Mom's gone! I saw her. That wasn't our Mom lying so still and quiet." Mark hugged Lily tight, as the two siblings cried together.

Then Ariel and Lily stood facing each other. The wooden structure of the door framed Lily so she looked like some photograph that someone took four years ago. Ariel's memory had made her taller. It made her body more like a reed, her bones prominent, her jaw sharper, and her eyes greener, but then she merged with the image Ariel had been carrying around in her head, and the two became imperceptible. They stared, and then Lily held her hand out. Ariel stepped toward her. Lily wrapped her arms around her sister. Lily looked at her siblings and chided them.

"Mark, you're too thin, and, Ariel, you look exhausted. Ariel, you look like you haven't slept for a month."

"Lily, I'm so glad you're home." Ariel began to sob, and all Lily could do was hold her and gently move them, arms entwined, into the warm kitchen. Lily stood with Ariel until she composed herself enough to look at her without blinding tears getting in the way. Ariel held back from blurting out about Morgan's visit to the police station. Right now, Lily needed them to be there for her. There was time enough when they settled down.

"Oh, Ariel, you don't know how much I've missed you." Lily sighed as she held her sister in her arms and comforted Ariel as Mark had comforted her. The three of them moved apart and with tears still streaming, smiled wistfully at each other, so glad to be together. They sat together on the sofa in front of the Franklin stove. The fire had been dying, but Mark reached down and added fresh kindling and a good log of almond wood from the wood box. When old almond trees were past their prime and under producing, they were cut down, and new trees planted in their place. This assured a hearty, healthy orchard. The wood smelled so fragrant when burning.

Ariel looked at Zoe. "Zoe, David and another officer came to the house and took Morgan to the police department for questioning."

"What! Why wasn't I informed?" Zoe grabbed her cell phone and jabbed her partner's cell number fast and furiously.

When all she got was David's voice message, she jumped up and grabbed her jacket.

"I'm going in to see what's happening. Don't worry, Ariel, this is more common than you know. It doesn't necessarily mean anything at all. Sit tight. I'll get back to you." Zoe walked purposefully to the front door, took the steps two at a time, jumped into her jeep, and sped away.

After Zoe left, the three siblings clung to each other. Not only had they lost their mother, now Ariel's husband was being questioned. It was all too much.

Zoe drove fast from the farm, through the town of Columbia, and straight into Sonora. She was at the station within minutes and walked quickly inside. Her heart ached for the family. She didn't think Morgan's detention would amount to anything, but it was a terrible ordeal for him and Ariel. Zoe spotted David grabbing a cup of coffee and went to meet him.

"David, what's happening?" Zoe sat on the edge of his desk and waited.

"Well, right now it's not looking so good for Morgan. There are witnesses who heard Morgan and Sarah arguing in her office at the clinic her last night just before five o'clock. They say that when Morgan came out of her office, he was scowling, and he slammed the door and sped off in his car with his wheels screaming. It doesn't look good. He was apparently the last person to speak to her. Sarah left the office right behind him, and she was in a foul mood as well."

Zoe felt a hard pit of fear knot in her stomach. Fear for Ariel. If Morgan had something to do with Sarah's murder, it would be terrible for her friend. David saw the look on Zoe's face and knew what he had to tell her would devastate her as well, but it had to be done.

"Zoe they've taken you off the case. You're too close to the family. I'm sorry."

Zoe looked up at him, clenched her teeth together, spun on her heel, and walked out of the station. She was furious, and yet she knew they were right. She was too close to the family. It was suddenly all too much, and it brought back her own painful losses. She drove back to the farmhouse and joined Ariel, Lily, and Mark.

"Listen up! David told me that they are questioning Morgan because an argument between him and Sarah was overheard at the clinic. Did he say anything to you about it, Ariel?"

Ariel thought back to the last time she had seen Sarah and Morgan together on Sunday when they had her along with Julie, Ben, and Riley over for barbeque chicken.

Morgan and Sarah had gotten along fine. Sarah was a little withdrawn, but Ariel thought she was tired. The clinic was a very hectic environment, and Sarah was beginning to think of retiring and going back to the little clinic on the farm.

"No, Zoe, Sarah, and Morgan got along fine on Sunday. Sarah seemed kind of tired, and she left shortly after dinner, but everything seemed okay between them." Ariel worried her fingernail, just as she did when she was upset as a child. She looked up at Zoe with her huge green eyes. She looked like a waif.

Zoe felt so sorry for Ariel. She knew what it was to lose someone so suddenly. Her mind went to the call she received when her husband, Howard, and their infant daughter had died together in that car crash on their way home from Haley's doctor visit. Howard had taken her when Zoe's work scheduled a mandatory meeting, and Zoe couldn't get out of it. It all came back to her as she saw the Frazer siblings huddled together. Zoe was an only child. Her parents did their best to be there for her, but she was alone with her grief and guilt.

Zoe sighed as she looked at Mark. She wanted to go to him, pull him into her arms, and kiss his pain away. Zoe shook herself and chided herself for thinking such a thought. It was silly to think of Mark as more than a buddy. Pie in the sky, her mom would say. But Zoe couldn't deny the increasing feeling of wanting more than being a best buddy from Mark. Zoe calmly told the Frazer family that Morgan was being held; there was nothing they could do tonight.

"Tomorrow, he'll go before the court, and they'll either arraign him or let him go. His lawyer was doing everything he could to get him released, but nothing more was happening tonight." Zoe withheld her anger that she wasn't part of the investigation. They had enough to worry about without adding her frustration to their plate.

It was midnight when Ariel finally started picking up empty cups and carrying them to the kitchen. The others agreed when she said she had to get to bed.

"It's getting late, and I've got to get some rest. I don't know what will happen next. This is crazy to think that Morgan had anything to do with Sarah's death. Just crazy!"

It was morning. Ariel was at the courthouse talking to Stan Waters. Morgan was brought in, and Ariel couldn't talk to him. He was being arraigned. Stan stood with Morgan as the judge refused him bail, and Morgan was led back to his cell. Ariel looked on horrified as Morgan looked at her and shook his head.

Ariel grabbed Stan's arm. "Stan, what is going on here? What's Morgan got to do with Sarah's death?"

Stan took her arm and led her to a chair in the corridor. "Ariel, there are witnesses who say that they saw Morgan and Sarah arguing the Friday before her murder. They haven't any other suspects. Because Sarah is such a prominent physician, and Morgan is a lawyer, there is pressure to find someone to blame. Morgan doesn't deny that they argued, but he's holding client-lawyer confidentiality, and he won't say what they were arguing about. Unless he tells Judge Harper why they were arguing, he's going to be held over. I have a meeting with the judge and the prosecutor to try to get him released. Don't worry, Ariel, they'll release him. They're just going to make him sweat it out for a while. I've got to go now. Go home, and I'll call you as soon as I can."

Ariel drove home in a daze. Her world was breaking apart right in front of her. She couldn't believe that Morgan had anything to do with Sarah's death. Ariel drove into the farmyard and was met by Ben.

"Ariel, I'm so sorry, come into the kitchen. Julie's got fresh coffee, and her cinnamon rolls are just coming out of the oven." Ariel was grateful for Ben and Julie's support, and she let them fuss over her. Lily joined them and as Julie poured her a cup of coffee, Mark slammed in the back door.

"Ariel! What happened? Where's Morgan?" His questions were fast and relentless. Ariel struggled to give them all the information she had.

"So I'm waiting now for Stan to call to let me know when or if they will release Morgan. Morgan had told me that he was going to go see Sarah to sign her new will paperwork. That's all I know. He was upset when he got home Friday, but he shrugged it off and wouldn't talk about it. Unfortunately, Morgan left the house earlier than usual that morning. He said he had to finish up some paperwork for a client who was going before the judge in a divorce case at ten o'clock. There wasn't anyone else in the office when he got there. Since he left here at seven thirty in the morning, he doesn't have an alibi for the time he was alone in his office until his staff got there at 9:00 a.m." Ariel went over to the sink and got a drink of water. When she turned to the others in the room, she was brisk and all business.

"Look, guys, I can't do anything until Stan calls, so let's get busy and get the stuff together for Sarah's funeral. It will help me to keep my mind off Morgan. We need to get things organized."

Lily got up and the two went to the dining room where a box of photos was waiting. Ariel, Lily, and Mark worked together picking out pictures for the memory board.

The morning flew by with no phone call. Ariel's face was grim as she focused on getting everything together for the funeral. Ariel had them all hunting up pictures and choosing the ones for the memory board. Finally, when they were done, Ariel got up and stretched. "I'm exhausted! I've got to go lie down. If Stan calls, come and get me immediately."

Reverend Tom would be by to discuss their plans in the afternoon. Reluctantly Lily and Mark left Ariel to rest. Lily had been persuaded to stay at the big house at least until the police released Sarah's house as a crime scene and let them get in and clean it up. Lily and Mark walked over to his house, and the two sat watching an old Laurel and Hardy film. They both fell asleep, Mark in his lounge chair and Lily on his comfy leather sofa, before the first commercial was over.

Ariel was up and making lemonade when Mark and Lily came back to the house just in time to greet Reverend Tom.

Ariel smiled at Lily as she handed her a glass of lemonade with ice. The three were sitting quietly together in the kitchen sipping their drinks when the doorbell rang. Mark went to answer it.

Ariel handed Lily the paper as they waited for Mark to return. "Did you see the paper?" Ariel motioned to the still-folded *Union Democrat* that she'd walked out to get from the metal holder on the road. She pointed as Mark grabbed it up and opened it. The headlines LOCAL PHYSICIAN MURDERED jumped out at them.

Lily quickly skimmed the paper and read aloud, "Dr. Sarah Frazer, prominent physician, was killed yesterday at her home outside of Columbia. The body was discovered by her long-time housekeeper, Julie Roberts. There were multiple stab wounds, and her spinal cord was severed. She appeared to have still been alive when her murderer dumped her into her backyard swimming pool, the coroner said." Lily threw the paper down on the table and stood up, breathing heavily. She wiped her eyes and turned toward her sister.

"Why!? Why? I just don't understand why anyone would want to hurt Mom like that; nothing will ever make me believe that Morgan had anything to do with it!"

"Want more lemonade, Lily?" Ariel said as she poured herself another glass. Lily shook her head.

"Ariel, I examined Mom last night. There is more to this than a random act. What was done to Mom was deliberate and cruel." Ariel stood up and started to gather the glasses and load them in the dishwasher. Meaningless activity was the only thing holding her together while she waited for Stan's phone call and her husband to come home.

"Zoe told me that there is something going on at the clinic that Mom was upset about. Zoe said that they had found some notes in her office, but she didn't tell me what was in them. She did warn me not to go to the clinic for any more prenatal visits and that I should find another doctor. Lily, what do you think?"

"That sounds like a good idea, Ariel. We don't know who may be involved. God, I'd like to kill someone right now!" She slammed her fist against the counter and smarting from the pain, rubbed her hand absentmindedly as she looked out the window to where Ben was working. The two of them watched Ben and Sofie. Ben had bent down and was stroking Sofie's ears she lay down on her back and let him scratch her belly. As he scratched, the puppies inside Sofie rolled and moved around, creating bulges all over her belly. Pretty soon, Sofie got a worried look on her face. She tried to see her belly and figure out what was happening inside her. Finally, she'd had enough of Ben's teasing, rolled on to her belly with an indignant snuff, and went to sleep.

Ariel remembered a conversation she had had with Riley Roberts, Julie and Ben's son. Riley had examined Sofie, pronounced her in good health, and predicted the pups would be born in early March. Riley told her a little bit about the basset breed. "You know, Ariel, basset hounds are not a breed to be ignored. Serious huntsmen have long been aware of the merits of this deliberate scent hound who tracks his quarry with sureness, in his own way, and in his own time. See that big nose and how short her legs are. Sofie here, she's been bred for foraging in deep brush. She's low to the ground, so she can push through shrubbery and dense bushes that other dogs would have to go around. Small animals like foxes, rabbits, or pheasants would head for these spots, and Sofie here can track her quarry with sureness, easily going through heavy ground cover and with her deep bark, she gives plenty of tongue."

When Ariel looked puzzled, Riley explained. "Tongue is a loud-barking basset in the heat of the hunt." Riley had patted Sofie, lifted her ample tonnage down off his exam table, and handed Ariel the leash. He gave her vitamins and food portions for the mother to be, and Sofie looked back at Riley with a sorrowful look as Ariel led her out of the exam room.

Ariel chuckled as she watched Ben rubbing Sofie's growing tummy and called to Sofie from the back porch to come to her. "Sofie, Ben isn't giving you any respect, and you are almost royalty in hunting circles. Really, Ben, you ought to be ashamed of yourself."

Ben smiled sheepishly at Ariel and then turned and called Sofie to follow him back to the barn.

"Come on, girl. Ariel doesn't know our little game, does

she?" Sofie wagged her tail and trotted beside Ben, rubbing up against him as they walked.

It was a peaceful scene. No one would have thought that a tragedy had visited the farm, touching them all deeply. It was certainly one none of them would ever forget. Mark and Reverend Tom had been talking on the porch and walked into the kitchen as Lily and Ariel were watching Ben and Sofie.

The rest of the day went by in a blur. Rev. Tom was from the Anglican church that folks around Sonora called the Little Red Chapel, though the church's official name was St. James. Ariel, Lily, and Mark had listened to Reverend Tom, and together they planned Sarah's funeral. It was almost five o'clock by the time the reverend had gotten up to go. "Well then, that's that! I'll have the order of service typed up, and all that's left is to see if Mary Turner can sing. I'll call her when I get back to the church. God bless you all. I want you to know I'll be praying for Morgan, that he is home free soon. Good-bye, my dears."

Ariel saw him to the door and sighed heavily after seeing him out. Everything was done that could be with the pictures of Sarah and Paul holding Lily and Mark as newborns, Ariel as big sister always lurking in the background or beside her with a wide smile on her face. They had their pictures for the storyboard chosen by the time the Most Reverend Tom Bender had said goodnight, and he agreed with their decisions for the funeral.

The reverend was just getting in his car when Zoe drove in. "Hi, Rev. Tom!" Zoe visited with him for a few minutes before he drove off, and Zoe climbed the front porch stairs and knocked gently. Ariel opened the door wide for her and invited her to join them for a glass of Chablis. Ariel had a Seven Up.

Ariel looked Zoe straight in the eye. "Well, Zoe, what have you found out?"

"Whew!" Zoe said as she drank the cold wine. "I'm bushed."

She looked at both Ariel and Lily and running her finger around the rim of her glass, she spoke.

"I can't tell you much. I've been taken off the case because of my friendship with your family. The investigation isn't done yet, but it looks like she discovered something wasn't right at the clinic. It was bad enough that when she confronted the person, she lost her life. There were notes in her office that lead us to surmise that someone had done something very unethical at the least and possibly illegal as well. She was looking at all the patient records, and the nursing staff said she appeared to be very, very angry when she left for home Friday evening."

"But, Zoe, Sarah never told me anything like that. She just seemed distracted and was quieter than usual on the weekend. We'd had her over for dinner, and she ate like a mouse. It really wasn't like her at all, but she didn't say a word about anything underhanded going on. I know she would have been up front with me if she was really concerned." Ariel sipped her soft drink and frowned. "What about Morgan? Why are they questioning him and not letting him come home?"

Ariel rubbed her face with her hands and when she looked up at Zoe, tears were streaming down her face. Zoe felt so sorry for her that she wanted to gather her in her arms but until Morgan was released, Zoe couldn't tell her anything. Being off the case made it difficult to have up-to-the-minute information, and David was so involved in the interrogation that she hadn't seen him at all since Morgan's arrest.

Zoe couldn't say any more to them, and so she changed the subject to the police presence that was planned for the funeral.

"We are going to have several undercover officers at the service Saturday morning to pick up whatever we can from casual conversations. So just act as normal as you can and if you hear anything unusual, let me know right away. We'll take it from there. Just be careful. Someone who would kill to keep her from ratting them out would do it again."

Just then there was the sound of a car crunching up the gravel road to the farm. Ariel looked out and opened the door to Riley. He had called as soon as he had gotten word of Sarah's death, but he had been out with a foaling. It took most of the day and all night before the cute little filly finally entered this world. Being a vet of both small and large animals gave him scarcely enough time for anything but the animals. It had been one of the main reasons for the breakup of his marriage. His wife, Rachel, didn't like playing second fiddle to a cow or a horse. She'd just got up, driven away one morning when he'd been on another all-nighter, and had a lawyer contact him for a quick divorce. She didn't want anything but her freedom. Riley had never seen her again. It had put him off relationships, and now he just kept his nose in his work. If anyone seemed interested in more than a quick role in the hay, so to speak, he'd stop seeing her.

Riley burst into the kitchen and put his arms around Ariel and Lily. "I'm so sorry to hear about Sarah. Gosh, she was such a wonderful woman; I just can't understand someone killing her like that." Riley hugged Mark and then went to his parents in the kitchen. He asked if they were all right. Everyone talked at once; they were all so glad to see Riley. He was such a solid, caring man that everyone felt comforted and safe as soon as he came into the room.

Julie had made her famous fish chowder in a white sauce. There was plenty for all of them, and with the White Zinfandel that Riley had brought, the simple dinner took on the flavor of a party. The old friends gathered around the big oak table and talked long into the evening. It was a comfort to be together. It helped ease the pain that was so close even while they laughed and joked together.

Chapter 4

When Ariel turned off the kitchen lights and went upstairs to try to sleep after shooing everyone out, it was after midnight, a very late evening for her. She was so worried about Morgan. Nobody was telling her anything, and she was desperate to know why they'd detained him. She was exhausted and after a quick wash of her face and the ritual brushing of her teeth, she crawled into bed, afraid for Morgan. She tossed and turned and finally fell into a fitful sleep.

At around two that night, Ariel dreamed of Morgan. In the dream, the sky was a deep blue and there was snow so dazzling that the sun created prisms of crystals that shimmered and made it difficult to see. She was skiing. The black pines of the Sierras were stark against the snow. Then, emerging from the pines, she saw Morgan far ahead of her. She knew the skier was Morgan. She wanted him to know that she was there, so she called to him to wait for her. But Morgan hurtled down the slope away from her. She could hear her voice blown away by the wind and the sound of her skis on the crusty snow.

"Morgan," she cried, but he was gone. Then she hurtled over a rise and saw that he had heard her call and stopped and waited for her. Ariel skied as fast as she could but when she got almost to him, she saw that it was not Morgan at all, but another man with a sneer on his face and eyes hard as steel. The sky suddenly turned from deep blue to storm black, and she was afraid. Then the phone was ringing, forcing her out of the dream.

Finally, she opened her eyes and grabbed the phone. "Hello, Ariel, it's Sam. They're going to release Morgan this morning. Can you be here by nine thirty?" Ariel listened as Sam explained that Morgan finally agreed to tell the judge that the argument with Sarah was over the new will he had had written up for her. Without disclosing the details, he was able to satisfy the judge who then released him. Morgan had been cleared of any charges, and the court was satisfied that he didn't have anything to do with Sarah's murder.

"Oh, Sam, that's the best news I've heard since this nightmare has happened. Yes, yes, I'll be there at nine thirty." Ariel put the phone down, jumped out of bed, and hurried into the shower. The phone call had wiped the residue of her dream from her mind, and she was focused on seeing Morgan.

The drive to the courthouse took only minutes. Ariel was waiting in the hallway when Morgan walked out with Sam. Ariel stepped into his path, the two embraced, and the world was centered again for Ariel.

"Ariel, I'm so sorry you had this on top of Sarah's death to deal with. I swear that I had nothing to do with Sarah's murder. Come on, let's go home." Ariel and Morgan walked quickly out of the courthouse after shaking hands with Sam and drove directly home. Ariel brought him up to date on the happenings at the ranch.

"Lily's here, Morgan, she got in just after they took you away. She's anxious to see you." As soon as they got to the farm, the door burst open, and Lily was opening the car door. "Morgan, Ariel, thank heavens you're here! Come in. The coffee's hot and fresh. I want to hear everything.

The three sat in front of the Franklin stove as logs crackled and snapped, making the room warm as toast. Morgan told Lily and Ariel exactly what had happened in Sarah's office. "I went there to show her the updates to her will, and we got into a discussion about the way she wanted the property to be handled. I felt that she was not being realistic, and I guess I did argue with her, but I never dreamed that they would use that to point suspicion at me. I'll be showing you everything as soon as we get together for the reading of the will."

Lily and Ariel barely had time to think of what the will contained, and the two put it out of their minds as they rushed to finish the arrangements for the funeral. Morgan had to go to his office and catch up with his clients. Thankfully, they'd been able to keep Morgan's visit to the police station quiet, at least for the moment. Finally, all the arrangements were done. They'd notified everyone they could that the service would be held at the Little Red Chapel Saturday at 10:00 a.m.

The caterers had been called, and they would be bringing a light luncheon to the house of cold cuts and salads with cookies, cakes, and their signature cheesecakes, as well as coffee and punch.

Morgan would set up the bar in the front living room. They expected about seventy-five people to come to the house after the funeral. Julie had been through the house with her lemon-fragrant dust clothes and the vacuum. The clutter had been tucked away, and the house would be overtaken Saturday morning by the caterers who would be bringing their own dishes, glasses, and silverware. They would take everything thing back with them to be washed at their facility. All that was left to do was get through the service. Mark would say a few words and so would the girls. Then anyone who wanted to could say a few words too.

That evening, when the house was quiet, Ariel turned to Morgan. "Morgan can you remember anything Sarah might have said that could have been worrying her that she didn't tell me?"

Ariel lay next to Morgan and spooned against him, exhausted from all of the upheaval that was part of a death in the family, not to mention Morgan's detention.

"No, Ariel, I don't remember a damn thing, and I sure wish I could. I just remember how tired and out of sorts she was Sunday. She just seemed terribly distracted. I just thought she'd had a bad week." Morgan turned to Ariel and kissed her gently. Settling together closely for comfort, they both fell into an exhausted sleep.

As Zoe drove back to her little house in Columbia, she thought of Mark and Lily. They were Sarah's blood children and though Sarah was always loving and kind to Ariel, Ariel had been Paul's before the rest of them had come. Zoe remembered that occasionally Ariel would get very quiet when her father and Sarah excluded her from what they were doing, and she occasionally felt like she had been pushed aside when her father married Sarah. They were so much in love. They couldn't help but exclude her without the least intention of doing so.

Zoe was Ariel's friend and knew her pain at being the odd person out. Zoe hurt for Ariel, and she remembered that she would call her up and invite her to stay overnight with her as often as her parents would let her. Now Sarah and Paul were both gone, and Ariel, though an adult and married with her own child on the way, had never really felt like she belonged. Zoe knew that Mark and Lily loved Ariel and needed her more than they knew. She hoped that the three would bind together and keep their family close as Sarah and Paul would have wanted them too.

Saturday morning dawned bright and clear. The Frazer and Houston households were relieved that finally it was time to let go of Sarah and bury her next to Paul. It was time to come together and celebrate her life with her friends and patients. Today they were sharing their grief with the entire town, and they were all up early to meet this day, united as Sarah and Paul's children. Julie had the coffee pot percolating and fresh hot cinnamon buns waiting for them. No one could eat much, but the coffee was delicious and helped to fortify them against the cold morning. It would soon be over. It was a relief when they all climbed into the shiny black Lincoln that the mortuary provided and were driven to the little church five miles away in Sonora.

The sunlight streamed into the little chapel. Though it was a blustering cold morning, the tiny chapel was warm with all of the bodies crowded into it. The casket was draped in white satin and a huge spray of white roses with green ferns blanketed the simple gray casket. The family sat in the front pew, rigid in dark suits, with Ariel and Lily in black suits that, instead of looking somber, were the perfect foil for Ariel's red hair and Lily's jet black. Lily had her hair up and rolled into a chignon fastened with a mother of pearl hair clip. Ariel had let her hair riot over her shoulders and cascade down her back. Morgan, Mark, and David sat shoulder to shoulder next to them. Zoe squeezed next to David. Ben and Julie were at Ariel's left. Julie wore her good black dress with little white polka dots. She looked slim and tall next to her Ben, who almost looked like her brother--they looked so much alike, same dramatic silver mane and ruddy complexion.

Ben glowed with health and energy, and Julie was thankful. Ben held his red cap, so much a part of him that he even wore it with his suit, respectfully off his head and on his knee for the service. Julie looked around the church with a worried expression on her face. Where the heck was Riley? Her only son was always sauntering in late, and it frustrated Julie no end. The animals were Riley's first priority, and if an animal was in pain, then people would have to wait. Riley was the only vet in this small community, and Julie didn't know how he kept up with everything. Julie had been after him to get a partner, and he finally was looking into it, but it took time to find the right match. In the meantime, Riley did the best he could. Julie spotted him walking up the side aisle looking for them. She raised her hand, and he headed their way, nodding to friends and clients as he went. Riley had gotten his blue eyes, dove brown hair, and long legs from her, but he got his ruddy complexion from Ben. Riley slipped quietly into the pew next to his parents and gently put his arm around his mother, giving her a firm shoulder hug.

When they stood for the prayers, Julie stood shoulder to shoulder with Ben; both of them boasted six feet in height with Riley easily four inches taller. The trio watched who came in to the chapel. They wondered who among them might be the killer. Their clear blue eyes didn't miss much, but no one was acting suspicious or inappropriately. The Roberts stood together next to the Frazers and Houstons. One in spirit, they surrounded the family, using their own bodies to protect them from the curious eyes of the congregation, Ariel, Lily, and Mark had come to feel they were like family. Ariel smiled at the Roberts. She was so grateful to them. It was the best thing Sarah had ever done when she offered Ben and Julie jobs at the farm.

When Ben retired, and he and Julie had come to live at the farm, Sarah was happy. Riley and Melonie were on their own, and this way they would not have to deal with a mortgage. They sold their house in Sonora and invested the proceeds, providing them with a comfortable retirement. Sarah paid them both comfortable salaries, and they took a month off every year to travel and visit their daughter's family, especially their granddaughter, one-year-old Callie. Ariel looked across the aisle. In the pews across from them on the right side of the church sat the co-workers of Sarah's from the clinic. The name of the clinic was the Wilson Clinic, but nobody called it that. It was just called the Clinic by everyone in town. Ariel watched the rest of the town file in and sit down. There were patients and members of the community of both Columbia and Sonora. Everyone had loved Sarah, and the turnout showed it. Ariel looked at every face, knowing that the odds were that one of them didn't love her at all but had in fact murdered her. But which one?

The Most Reverend Tom was walking to the pulpit when he spotted Riley Stuart Roberts sitting next to his parents. His long legs in brown denim were sticking out of the end of the pew. It was cold in the chapel, and Riley wore a brown leather jacket that stretched across his shoulders. Riley nodded to the reverend with a sheepish grin. He knew that he'd been caught sneaking in almost late for the eulogy. Ariel smiled at the reverend and nodded for him to begin. The church became quiet with the low murmur of voices. Zoe, too, smiled as she watched Riley, all six feet four of him, squeeze in next to Ben and Julie. Zoe had known Riley as long as she'd known Ariel. He was a boy from school, and now was a grown man. Zoe had a lot of respect for Riley, as she did for Morgan and Mark. She'd known them all through school and especially remembered the summers at the farm where they'd always met. Sarah was a special woman, and it didn't seem possible that she was sitting here at her funeral. This moment today brought back all the memories of her childhood.

Ariel looked over at Zoe and smiled at her as if to say, "I know, I'm thinking the same thing." Zoe smiled back, sending silent support to Ariel and her family. Ariel turned her attention back to the pulpit.

The room quieted as the Most Reverend Ted Bender rustled his notes on the pulpit and began.

"We are gathered here today to honor the memory of one of our own. Sarah Frazer was a talented physician and supportive wife and loving mother. Today her children are here to remember their mother. Sarah's life was cut short before she could experience the joy of the upcoming reunion that she was planning for when her daughter Lily was home for good from serving in the war in Iraq, a physician, as she herself was. Her life was cut short before she could hold her much longed for grandchildren in her arms or see her son Mark married. She wanted what all mothers want for their children--their happiness and the fulfillment of all their lives. Sarah joins her beloved husband, Paul, and leaves us to mourn her. We do mourn her, but through the risen Christ, we know that she is with her beloved Paul and that we will one day see her again in eternity."

The church became silent as the reverend started the familiar Burial of The Dead. "Oh God of grace and glory, we remember before you today our sister Sarah. We thank you for giving her to us to know and to love . . . "

The message drowned on, and Ariel lowered her head and leaned into Morgan's strong shoulder, listening anxiously as the Most Reverend concluded with intercessory prayers for Sarah's soul. The reverend looked at Mark and nodded, turning the eulogy over to Mark, who walked with his head straight ahead. Mark spoke lovingly and briefly about his mother and what her loss would mean to him. Then it was Ariel's turn.

Ariel looked out at the crowd and took a deep breath.

"My mother was not just ours; she belonged to all of you too. She nursed you when you were ill and birthed your babies and bound your wounds as she did ours. I was looking forward to her birthing her grandchild in July, but I know she will be there. She will be there!"

Ariel walked down from the pulpit, laid her hand on her stepmother's coffin, and bent and kissed it. Lily motioned to her sister that she couldn't say anything, so Ariel invited others to come up and speak, and they did. It was over an hour later before all of the friends, neighbors, and Sarah's colleagues were finished. Finally, it was done, and the invitation issued to come to the house for lunch. Then it was time to escort Sarah on her final ride. Mark, Morgan, David, and Riley lifted the casket and slowly carried it out to the waiting hearse. Ariel, Lily, Zoe, and Julie quietly followed.

Ariel and her family got into the black limousine and followed the hearse down Highway 49 to the little town of Columbia. They turned up Cemetery Lane and made a right on Pacific Road. The hearse turned up a short street, and then they were going through the tall, white, arched gate. The freshly dug grave was under an oak tree in the back corner of the cemetery, overlooking the town of Columbia. Ariel, Lily, and Zoe, with Ariel's arm around Julie, followed the casket carried by Mark, Morgan, Ben, and Riley to her father's grave. Sarah would be with her Paul. Ariel always knew that once Paul and Sarah met, something had shifted in her relationship with her father. Paul and Ariel had been content with each other until Sarah showed up. Ariel had felt the abandonment of her father. However, seeing them together in the cemetery, Ariel knew that her father had always loved her, but he needed Sarah in a way a child would not understand. All the old resentment Ariel had felt toward her father and Sarah totally dissolved, and she cried for the loss of both of them.

The commitment service was short, and as Ariel, Lily, and Mark each took their turn throwing the traditional clod of dirt into the grave, they all felt the sobering awareness that they were truly orphans. Never again would they have their parents to listen to them and create the safe haven that was their home. Now they would have to create it for each other.

Chapter 5

A riel had just said good-bye to the last mourner who had come to the reception after the service for Sarah and had stayed until the rest of the family had gone home to rest after a huge lunch catered by Sarah's favorite caterers, Conrados. Even the lunch was somber; it was difficult to keep a smile on her face, and her feet hurt as well. She sighed as she slipped off her heels and padded around the house picking up cups and little plates. Someone would be by later to collect all the dirty dishes, but she still had to get them into the containers the caterers had left for that purpose. Mark and Lily were destroyed, and Ariel shooed them out of the house and over to Mark's to rest. Mark was proud of his new house. He had had it built to suit himself, and it did. It was only five minutes away. He had taken the northwest corner of the farm--just enough property for the rustic home. It was an open-floor plan living room and kitchen all in one with a loft bedroom. The house overlooked the deep canyon that was carved out of the earth millions of years ago by the South Fork of the Stanislaus river. The river was still viable, and it swept down the canyon swollen with the winter rains. In May, it would be even bigger when they let the water out of the damn above. Then the water would be shut down. The river would empty rapidly into New Melones Reservoir, leaving little more than pools of deep water, along with swiftly flowing water that carried the gold from above to settle in the cracks and crevasses of bedrock, just waiting for the whine of the dredges to suck out the precious gold, new money that had never been in circulation before. The miners below were unaware that there were forces in Sacramento trying to shut down the dredging in the river. They thought that the dredging would destroy the salmon fishing. Mark knew that in some of the northern rivers, the lobbyists might have a point. However, here where there was no salmon, the threatened moratorium would just eliminate miners from access to a river that benefited from the aeration of the river by the dredges. The river's stagnant waters were refreshed and renewed, and the brook and brown trout feasted on the food the dredges suctioned up and spewed out the back of the dredge as food for the fish.

The views of the canyon at sunset were spectacular, and Mark and Lily now stood admiring the orange orb as it sunk below the horizon. Lily hugged Mark, and the two walked in to the house from the deck. In the kitchen at the farm, Ariel was thinking of the future. Mark had his own home, and Sarah was gone. Lily would own Sarah's cottage. It would do for her for now. If she wanted it bigger, Mark and Morgan would help with a remodel, maybe a big country kitchen with a family area at the end, like the big house, maybe another bedroom, or two also. Ariel was lost in her thoughts. Already she could see how much more livable the cottage would be with a simple remodeling.

At Mark's house, Mark was lost in his thoughts when Lily interrupted them. "Mark, I love what you've done to your house. I'm green with envy."

Mark smiled at her. "Hell, Lily, you can enlarge Mom's cottage any time you want. With you still in the navy, I thought you'd want to wait, but if you've a mind to add on, let's talk it over with Morgan. I'm sure he could find the money for a contractor and an architect too, if you want."

Lily leaned against him and smiled wistfully. "Things are a bit unsettled right now, and if you promise not to breathe a word to any of the others, I'll let you in on a little secret." Mark nodded, mystified as to what Lily was up too but so darn curious he'd agree to anything she said.

"I've met a man that I'm angling to get to marry me. Don't worry. He's interested, but he just hasn't gotten around to popping the question. With my tour of duty over in September and his in December, we might be talking a Christmas wedding. When I go back to Iraq at the end of the month, I think we will be making plans for a life together."

Mark looked stunned. "Who is this guy?"

Lily laughed at the expression on his face and teased him. "What's the matter, little bro, worried he's not good enough for me?" She giggled as she told him that Matt O'Connell was a physician with a private surgical practice in Maine. He had a partner who was running the offices right now, but he planned to go back to Maine and plunge right back into private practice. Lily had met him and assisted with him on the nasty gunshot wounds he'd been treating for his whole tour of duty. Lily had admired his skill as a surgeon, and their relationship just came naturally as they shared late-night coffee after a long night of surgery. Matt loved her, she had no doubt at all about that, but until they were free of their responsibilities on the war front, they didn't talk about anything farther ahead than making a date for their day off. They'd enjoyed several furloughs together, one all the way to Hawaii where they spent two wonderful weeks together, snorkeling and swimming in the Pacific Ocean.

Mark hugged her tightly to him. "That's wonderful, sis. I can only wish you and your Matt the best of luck. Does this mean that you'd be living in Maine year long?"

"Well, for most of the year, but we'd come back to the farm every year for the summer. Of course, we haven't gotten that far in our discussions, but what's great about a surgeon is that if you have a competent partner or two, you can choose when you want to practice and take off as much time as you want. With a surgeon's income and mine, we wouldn't be hurting for money and could create a lifestyle that would suit us both."

Lily and Mark hung out in front of his roaring stone fireplace and talked about their plans. Lily quizzed Mark about his lack of female companionship, and it was his turn to dodge and keep from letting Lily know anything about his love life.

"Don't worry about me, sis. I am not a monk, and right now, I don't have any intention of strolling down the aisle. I'm only twenty-nine. I've got lots of time before I make a commitment to anyone."

Lily had to bite her tongue from blurting out that she had always felt Zoe would be perfect for Mark. "Well, don't wait too long. I don't want a crotchety old bachelor uncle when Matt and I decide to have kids. I want you to be as happy as I am." She smiled at him and busied herself with the popcorn.

Lily and Mark popped popcorn the old-fashioned way in a wire basket over the fire, and Lily fixed butter in the microwave and tossed it with salt to top it off. The two ate the popcorn instead of bothering about dinner. The reception had filled them up, and besides with their mother just buried, they really weren't hungry. The talk turned to Ariel and Morgan."

"I'm so happy for them. I really hope this pregnancy ends with a healthy infant. Ariel and Morgan don't deserve anything less." Lily looked out the window at the last dredges of the sunset and sighed. "Oh, Mark, why did Mom have to die? She would have loved to have had a grandchild, and she was looking forward to helping with the birthing in July. It just doesn't make sense that someone could do something so terrible to her. I just can't think about what she must have gone through in her last minutes. Damn it, Mark, what is Zoe saying about who killed her?" Lily pounded her hand on the arm of the stuffed chair and looked up at Mark, her green eyes flashing and filling with tears.

"Right now, nobody is saying anything official. It's all rumor and suspicion. Zoe suspects that it had something to do with Mom's work at the clinic. She was furious when she left the clinic Friday evening. Her staff has been very helpful with everything but opening their patients records. Patient confidentiality you know."

Mark put away the popcorn basket and washed up the greasy bowls. His cat, Marmalade, a big orange female, he'd had for over seven years, was nosing in the kernels, and Mark didn't need an emergency visit to Riley's clinic for a cat with a tummy ache from eating the hard kernels. He'd already been that route, and Riley had scolded him about leaving the kernels in the bowl where Marmalade had access. A couple wouldn't have hurt her, but that night there had been a lot of kernels in the bowl, and she ate them all. Mark was afraid they'd pop inside her and blow her up. Riley reassured him that Marmalade's body temperature wasn't warm enough to pop the corn, but there had been a few days of giving the cat doses of cod liver oil to smooth their exit. Marmalade had been so miserable that Mark was more aware and cautious about leaving anything out that she could get to.

Mark turned on an old black and white movie with Ingrid Bergman and Humphrey Bogart, *Casablanca*, and the two watched the movie and dozed off before the ending. Mark had taken the precaution of turning on the kitchen alarm for two hours, so that if they did fall asleep, they'd wake up in time for the meeting with Morgan and Ariel.

Zoe and David were back at the station. Zoe watched David

and her replacement going over all the information they had gathered from Sarah's staff. From the family statements, Sarah seemed distracted lately, but they didn't think anything about it. Sarah often brought her difficult cases home; she sometimes had difficulty with boundaries and worried a case until she came up with a solution that would solve it. After she had, she would be apologetic for being distracted, but she never told them what she was working on or what was upsetting her.

David, sensitive to Zoe's position, tried to keep her in the picture. "I think that something is going on at that clinic. That doctor who was her partner, Dr. Hillerman I think his name is, seemed very evasive when I talked with him. He said that he hadn't worked with Sarah for a while on any cases, and he didn't have a clue what she was upset about. His story checked out. He hadn't done anything with Sarah since October." David ran his hands through his hair and dropped them loudly onto the desk. "I don't know, Zoe. This case is a puzzle."

David looked up at her with a worried expression. He was a quiet man who didn't react with frustration like Zoe did. It was what made them good together. Zoe had a lot of energy and imagination, and he just plodded along, but he was thorough and painstaking with his observation. "I think we ought to lean harder on the good Dr. Hillerman. There's something about that guy that feels slimy. I can feel it, but so far, nothing comes back to him. He was everywhere he said he was, and no one noticed any nerves or tension, such as you'd assume someone would show who had just done such a vile act." He paused, such a long speech unusual for him, and suggested that they go back to the clinic on Monday and go through her office with a magnifying glass. The answer was in the clinic; he'd bet his life on it.

It was almost seven o'clock when Ariel padded into her cozy yellow kitchen, designed farm style with black and gray granite counters. There was a great bouquet of dried sunflowers in a cheery yellow vase on the island.

Everything had been put away, slipped into the big French-door refrigerator in case Ariel needed food for family. She sighed and opened the refrigerator door where there were platters of cold cuts covered in plastic wrap, enough for sandwiches for a week. Mark and Lily would be back soon. Then everything would be pulled out for a snack later. At least she needn't think about getting anything together to eat. It was all there.

Ariel glanced into the mirror hanging over the buffet table as she walked back into the dining room. She sighed and stood looking at her image in the glass.

Her green eyes were dull with fatigue. Her skin was honey hued, and her cheeks were brushed with apricot blushing across her cheeks, enhanced with peachy silver gloss covering her full, lush lips. Her nose was perky and was sprinkled with a scattering of small copper freckles across the bridge. *In spite of her fatigue, she looked okay*, she thought.

Ariel had on a soft black sweater and black wool pants. The sweater tapered to her once trim, tiny waist, and her hips hugged the pants clinging over her still slim hips. Her legs were so long they went on forever, with a hint of power in the well-toned thighs. The sweater held ripe, but not overly large, breasts. Her hair swept her shoulders each time she moved her head, and the fiery red, with a riot of unruly curls, moved with it glinting gold in the evening lights. Ariel rubbed the fatigue from her face and sighed as she thought about the months ahead of her when her body would change so drastically. She was determined to lose any post pregnancy weight as soon as possible. Her figure wouldn't be ruined; she wouldn't let that happen. Sighing again, she brushed her fingers through her hair, glanced quickly in the mirror, and then moved on to her roll top desk.

Ariel opened the desk and started looking through the papers and bills she'd gathered from her mother's mailbox just that morning. The envelope with Morgan's law firm's return address on it lay unopened among them. She snatched a letter opener from the jar of pens on top of the desk and opened it. There was a quick step on the front porch, and Morgan, who had walked Mark and Lily to Mark's house and stopped to talk with them, was just back from a quick walk around the farm before returning to Ariel. He needed some time to reflect on this horrible day and brace himself for the reading of the will. Sighing, he turned the door handle and opened the heavy plank door, shutting it softly behind him.

She jerked her head up and frowned at him, still reeling from what she had found in the envelope from his law office. She stared up into the blackest eyes, feathered by the thickest lashes she had ever seen. His nose was slender and finely shaped like his mothers. His mouth was full and wide; the lips were smooth and sensual. His jaw and skin were taut and at that moment stubborn and male but saved from arrogance by deep dimples near the corner of that intriguing mouth.

"Morgan Houston!" she sputtered. "How could you?"

"How could I what?"

"You were Sarah's lawyer, how could you let her do this?" She thrust the papers containing her stepmother's last will and testament into Morgan's hand. Morgan's eyes narrowed, and he shrugged. "Why did she do a new will now?"

"Well now, it was her wish, and she felt that you were entitled to it. The update is understandable. She hadn't done anything since Paul died. His assets have increased, and her desires for the farm have become clearer. When Paul died, she wasn't thinking of the same things as she was now. You know Sarah; she never wanted to leave anything hanging." Morgan set the fat envelope down on the dining room table, brushed his thick black hair out of his eyes, and slid past her. Ariel, still seething, followed behind him as he walked to the back of the house and straight into the huge farm kitchen.

As Ariel moved to the Franklin stove, a log was burning to hot coals, and it let in welcome heat on this foggy, winter day. Morgan reached the refrigerator in two long-legged strides and reached inside for a cold soda. He gulped a big slug, snatched a piece of ham from the cold cut tray in one smooth motion, and looked at Ariel. "Ariel this is what she wanted!" Morgan slid into the kitchen booth, chewed up his ham, and swallowed it down with his soda.

This was just too much! Ariel had just buried Sarah that morning, and now discovered that Sarah had left the entire farm to her with the stipulation that the income of the farm continue to be shared with Lily and Mark, and Ariel would continue to receive an additional $20,000 for the manager's fee. Ariel was shocked. "What about Mark and Lily?" she said, turning to face Morgan. "What are they going to say?"

He shrugged and took another huge drink of his coke. "They're well provided for, and this farm has always been your baby. With their careers going in such different directions-- Lily's gone into medicine like Sarah, though her practice is as a navy doctor, and Mark is happy as a fireman--Sarah felt that this would be a fair decision. I'm going to get you three together and go over this with you all tonight. Let's wait and see what they think. If they're not happy with it, then we can look at other options. I tried to tell Sarah that you would be upset with how she was arranging things, but she wouldn't budge." He scratched his head and sighed. "I'm beat. I'll go grab a quick shower. Lily and Mark will be back here in a few minutes." He took the stairs two at a time and left Ariel standing in the kitchen.

She slapped the papers on the old round oak table that Sarah had brought with her to this farmhouse, sat down, and let the tears pour down her cheeks. The table triggered memories of when her father was alive.

It was thirty years ago. Ariel was four and a motherless child, and her father, Paul Frazer, was a widower, half out of his mind trying to deal with the death of Ariel's mother, Kate, and care for a tiny little girl, as well as run the farm with no help. Truth to tell, he thought he was doing pretty well with Ariel until the fine morning when he was distracted. He had been in the barn fiddling with the tractor, and Ariel, bored waiting for her dad, had gone exploring in the almond orchard. Sarah had found her fast asleep under a blossoming almond tree right behind her cottage. Her face was dirty, her hair tangled, and the little yellow shirt and Osh Gosh bib jeans looked like she had slept in them, and she had. Paul had done his best, but he didn't see any need to be overly clean and pressed all the time, especially when no one was expected. Paul was doing the best he could, and he didn't give a darn what anyone else thought.

Sarah gently woke up the sleeping child, coaxed her into her little cottage, washed her face and hands, and offered her fresh-baked cookies and a well-watered cup of warm tea. When no one came to claim her, she asked Ariel where her mother was, Ariel burst out crying, saying she was with the angels, and she wanted to see her very badly. Sarah soothed her as best she could and then asked where her daddy was. Ariel was so upset that she looked around blankly and then pointed toward the almond trees. Sarah took Ariel by the hand, and the two of them walked through the orchard and toward the tall yellow and white wood-frame farmhouse, surrounded by blossoming almond trees, and a big old barn that had lost its paint. Ariel led Sarah into the barn, and she was prepared to confront Paul, her Irish temper more than ready to let loose, when he stood up and looked her in the eye with the identical green eyes that Ariel had. His jet-black hair was a little long and due for a trim. He'd let his beard grow, and he looked like a rumpled, unkempt miner, but his eyes saved him, riveting, as he stared right back at Sarah.

Sarah sputtered and with her mouth gapping, tried to regain the temper that was so close to the surface, but tongue tied, she just stood and stared. Ariel broke away from her and ran to her father, climbing up into his arms, and breaking into sobs.

"What's going on here? Why is Ariel crying, and who are you!" he shouted.

"I'll ask you the same. What's this little girl doing all alone in the orchard fast asleep under my almond tree?"

That was the start of it and before long, feathers were soothed all around, and Sarah agreed to have Ariel during the days, so that Paul could keep the farm together. It was less than a year later that she also agreed to be his wife and a mother to the now five-year-old.

They married in the spring under the blooming almond trees in the circle of the standing stones. The stones were all that were left of the 49er's gold dredgers. When the river failed to spill forth more gold, the miners switched to hydraulic mining, which used great gushing water pouring out of huge nozzles trained on the surrounding ancient riverbeds. They aimed the hoses on the soil and stripped it away from the earth, leaving huge formations of bedrock ten to fifteen feet high. The bedrock was at one time molten rock that twisted into strange shapes and designs deep under the earth. It reminded Paul of the standing stones in Scotland with their mystery and legend. Paul would tell Ariel stories of the fairies that lived among the stones. The Most Reverend Ted Bender stood in the center of the stones with Paul while Ariel, in a spring green, light, short shift that went straight from the shoulders to just above the knees and with white leggings and white patent leather Mary Jane slippers, held a basket full of almond blooms that she scattered before Sarah. Walking behind Ariel was Sarah in a soft white dress of fine silk that draped over her shoulders and into a peak just above the mounds of her breasts. Her strawberry blonde hair was long and silky, her blue eyes shining only for her Paul.

Paul was as shy as a new bridegroom in a rented tux of white with a deep green cummerbund the color of his eyes. The jacket was short and fitted and showed off his slim hips and broad shoulders. Their wedding day was sunny and warm; the twenty-five guests sharing in their happiness toasted them and wished them a happy life, and it was.

Just a few short months later, Sarah graduated with her medical degree and walked up, hugely pregnant, to receive her diploma, her new family smiling broadly.

Sarah, Paul, and Ariel greeted first Lily, now thirty and then Mark, twenty-nine.

The family prospered with the twice-yearly almond harvest, and as soon as Mark was in first grade, Sarah started her medical practice on a small scale, seeing her patients after the school bus had picked up the three Frazer children and closing for the day when the bus deposited them in front of the farmhouse.

Sarah and Paul loved the farm, and their love spilled over to their three children and their friends who crowded into the kitchen during the warm summer days of school vacation. It wasn't easy being a busy physician, farmer's wife, and mother of three, but Sarah managed to juggle the three roles easily and gave her full attention to whoever needed it the most.

This idyllic life continued until Ariel was eighteen and a half, Lily thirteen, and Mark twelve. Ariel had just graduated from high school. She was planning on going to the university at Davis, California to learn the latest agricultural techniques, but one evening, just after the August harvest, Paul suffered a massive heart attack and died in Sarah's arms. It was almost instantaneous, and Sarah's attempts at resuscitation and CPR were futile.

Suddenly, Sarah was a widow with three half-grown children and a farm to run. Ariel changed her plans and instead of going away to school, she stayed home to help her stepmother cope with the second harvest in late September. Sarah closed her small practice and became a partner in a new clinic that dealt with fertility and gynecological conditions. The salary was twice what she had made on her own. The salary, though nice, wasn't the reason she closed her home practice; it was too difficult to stay all day at the farm she had shared with Paul. Sarah had often stopped for lunch and brought sandwiches out to the orchard to share with Paul. Now Sarah couldn't bear to be alone in the big rambling house without Paul. The small practice she had developed over the years was just too close to the memories, and she needed a new work environment in order to keep her sanity.

Ben and Julie moved in, and Ariel learned from Ben how to manage the farm. She was good at it and knew that this was what she wanted to do, but she'd also dreamed of going to college. With Sarah at the clinic for such long hours, someone needed to keep an eye on the farm. Ariel learned to drive tractor and spray and irrigate the orchard. She also learned how to get the best price for the almonds. Every year since Ben and Ariel had been running the farm together, they had gotten premium price for their almonds. Mark and Lily took over caring for the farm animals, anything to keep busy and stay out of the once laughter-filled house that was now silent and lonely for them too. When they were out of school, Lily joined the navy and went to college, and then to medical school to become a doctor and Mark joined the local Sonora fire station. They both worked hard at their training, and now Ariel knew that they didn't want to work the farm. Finally, she was able to do both, though it was the local college for Ariel. Ben and Julie encouraged her to get her degree. Ariel was too young to bury herself on the farm. Ariel was able to go to school and get her master's in social work. Ben and Julie were such a big help that Ariel wasn't needed as much as before and could indulge her love of going to school. Ariel, it seemed, was the only one who seemed comforted by the farm. When she thought of her father, it was a feeling that he was still there, working a corner of the property, just out of her sight. She felt like he was watching out for them all.

Ariel wiped her eyes, put down the will, went over near the Franklin stove, and curled up in the La-Z-Boy chair. A throw rug was handy, and she grabbed it and draped it over her body. She stared into the fire as the tears welled up into her eye again, blurring her vision. She missed both her parents so much and as she watched the fire dancing in the fireplace, she felt exhausted from the strain of the day. Yawning hugely, she let the desperate need to sleep claim her.

She didn't wake up until she heard the quiet knocking, and Morgan's firm step walking to the front door. Lily hadn't changed and, still in her same black suit, with her long black hair and Paul's eyes, came in, followed by Mark, a spitting image of Paul with the green eyes that all three of the Frazer kids had inherited. They came back to the kitchen and all flopped around the Franklin, replenished with a fresh supply of logs.

Ariel hugged them both. "Anyone for a glass of wine?" Mark voted for a beer and Lily a white wine. Ariel quickly brought drinks for her sister and brother, a diet cola for herself, and beer for Morgan.

Morgan presided over the meeting just as if this was a formal will reading of any of his clients. He read the will quickly, and when he finished, he looked up expectantly and guzzled down his beer.

"All right now, anybody have anything to say? The floor's open for discussion."

Lily put down her glass of wine. "What happens if Ariel doesn't want to farm anymore?"

Morgan answered, "I can't see that happening anytime soon, but if that were the case, you and Mark would then have the option of taking over the manager's position if you wanted to. If you didn't want the responsibility, then a manager could be hired, and you would all three receive your money equally. The stipulation that Sarah had made was that the farm not be sold but that family members would retain the deed until there were no more living descendants of Sarah's and Paul's. Then the farm would be sold, and the money given into a charitable trust. Sarah always wanted a place that meant any member of the family would always have a place to stay. There is money set aside for building additional cottages when necessary. I know it's unusual, but Sarah knew that land and housing was going to be scarcer, and young people will have difficulty getting into their first home." Morgan paused, looked at the three gathered in front of them, and then dropped the bombshell. He looked at first Ariel and then Mark and Lily. "I want you to know I tried to talk her out of this. I felt that this tied your hands too much, but Sarah was stubborn and refused to be talked out of it." He sighed. "You could all appeal this if you wanted too."

Morgan continued, "The money comes from Paul. In addition to the farm, Paul had money invested that his grandfather left him and when he died, his estate was worth over fifty million dollars. Paul's parents have Brindle Hall and still get the income of the hall in Dornoch, Scotland. They both were happy for Paul and encouraged him to start fresh. When he met Sarah, they were overjoyed. Sarah left everything intact and instructed me to give you each five million apiece."

The three siblings just stared in shock at each other. "My God, I never knew Dad had money like that." Mark took a deep breath. "Hell, this is quite a deal. I just don't know what to say except you got my vote!" So the children of Sarah and Paul Frazer toasted their parents and marveled that they could have kept a secret like this from them. It meant that there would always be enough money and a place to come if the want or need arose, but that it could never be taken from any of them, at least in their lifetime.

Chapter 6

The next morning at breakfast, Ariel and Morgan were seated at their breakfast nook when the phone rang. It was Zoe.

"Ariel, I'm just checking in to see how you're doing." Zoe paused.

Ariel sat down on the hall bench where the telephone had always been and sighed. "Oh, Zoe, I was just about to call you. How could this have happened? Do you have anything new to tell us?" Ariel wiped her hand over her eyes when tears began to well up and overtake her. The phone went silent as Zoe weighed whether to tell her what she knew. She took a deep breath and began.

"Listen, Ariel, we've been checking out Sarah office, and we've come across some information that leads us to think that this was someone from the clinic. Sarah discovered some irregularities in the in-vitro process that she was upset about. She made notes about it. Did she ever say anything to you about anything going on?"

"About what?" Ariel spoke hesitatingly. Sarah had hinted recently that maybe Ariel and Morgan should go to another ob-gyn rather than Dr. Hillerman, but she stopped short of insisting. "No not really, only that maybe we should not use the clinic for our baby's birth. I just thought she was being overly protective since she saw the inside of how things were run there. But we haven't made any decision about it yet. Why?"

"I'd like to advise you to take her advice as soon as you can find someone, Ariel. Things don't look on the up and up at the clinic. Look I've got to run, just think about it, okay?" Zoe hung up the phone and made a note in her notebook that Sarah was concerned about something at the clinic that she felt was unethical. What could it be?

Sipping her coffee, Ariel thought back to the memorial yesterday. Most of the clinic staff had come, and they had appeared very sad at the loss of their cohort. Dr. Hillerman had expressed concern for Ariel's pregnancy and had insisted that she get off her feet and let others do the hosting.

"You've had a very bad shock, and I want you to rest as much as you can. I'll want to see you in the office very soon, to make sure your baby is doing well." He talked quietly but with urgency in his voice, and Ariel agreed to make an appointment. Thinking back on it, he was the only one who seemed stressed, but Ariel shook off feelings of foreboding. Taking another sip of her decaf coffee, she grimaced; it was cold. She must have lost track of time. The morning sun was warm, and you'd hardly think it was January! Ariel had a meeting scheduled with Ben to discuss the upcoming almond season.

Hurrying, she donned jeans and a flannel shirt over a snug turtleneck and walked to foreman's office in the back of the big weathered white barn. Ben had been with the family for years, and he and Julie had a comfortable apartment above the barn, overlooking the orchard of almond trees. Right now, the trees were bare of leaves, but come spring there would be blossoms covering the trees, and Julie loved to look out on the fifty acres. It looked like a field of snow then. Julie had served as Sarah's housekeeper in the cottage back of the orchard. She also did a weekly clean up in the big house that Ariel was grateful for. It was a big help during the season. Ariel gave Julie and Ben a month off in November, and they'd hook up their Allegra motor home and go down to the Bay Area to have a visit with their daughter and her family. They'd have a couple of weeks to do some traveling and loved to go to Arizona, so off they'd go, waving all the way to the road. They were always back the week after Thanksgiving, after filling up with turkey with their daughter, Melonie, and her husband, Greg. The first thing they did when they got back was download all of the pictures of their first grandchild, Callie. She was a year old, and her grandparents were very proud of her. Greg, Melonie, and Callie Foster came to the farm in the summer, and Greg enjoyed helping his father-in-law fertilize the orchard. Julie enjoyed Callie and was a willing babysitter when Greg and Melonie wanted go out to dinner and a movie. There was always lots to do on the farm, and extra help was always welcome.

It just took a few moments to reach the farm office in the big white barn. Ariel opened the door and turned to Sofie. "Sofie girl, I'm right inside, come lay down." Ariel knew her words were not being heeded and, exasperated, Ariel let herself into the office, leaving Sofie to her own devices.

Sofie wasn't in a hurry this morning. She'd sniffed every leaf and rock on the way to the barn. Ariel let her nose around while she let herself into the office. Sofie would wait patiently by the open door once she satisfied herself that all was well on the farm. Ariel grinned at her and gave her an extra pat on the head, and a dog biscuit as a treat. After all, she was eating for three or more pups as well as herself. This would be her first litter. "Just like me," Ariel said to the slow-moving basset. It took just about sixty-three days for a dog to whelp, and Riley had said Sofie was about three weeks along, judging from the stud date. That would mean that the big basset hound would have her puppies sometime in late March. She had been bred to a champion male, and her puppies were already spoken for. Ariel hoped this first litter would be easy for her, but first litters, like first babies generally, took longer and could have complications. Ariel put up a prayer for both Sofie and herself that her baby and Sofie's pups would go easy on them both.

Ben was at his computer ordering bees and a beekeeper for the orchard. They had to have them in place before the February bloom started. Three hives per acre and with fifty acres that would be one hundred and fifty hives at $150 per hive, a whopping $23,500 for the month. The bees assured good cross-pollination, which made the difference of a good crop of almonds, but whew, Ariel whistled through her teeth as she looked over Bens shoulder at the figures on the computer. This was just the beginning of the expenses of running the farm. After pollination, a crew had to be hired to help with irrigating every four days as well as flooding the orchard twice in July. They'd be spraying nutrients of zinc and copper starting at the first of March, and the weed spraying took place every six weeks from February to October when the last almonds were harvested. Leaves would be analyzed two or three times from the first of March by a field man sent from Union Chemical Company, who supplied the liquid fertilizer that Ben applied every four days--over one thousand gallons a year.

"Old Henry will be here with the bees by next week. Do you want me to call Denny and Curt Miller to help Henry put out the hives?" Ben asked, stretching in his chair. The brothers had worked for Ben whenever he needed them to help with the almond trees farm labor.

"Are they finished on the Taylor farm with the spraying?" She sat down in the only extra seat, a lumpy old recliner that had seen a lot better days, but Ben liked it. He called it his thinking chair. Ben nodded.

"Okay then, give them a call. I want to get them before Harry Slater does." It was always a race to beat the other farms since they all used the same pool of workers. These men were born and raised on farms, and though they still lived on them, they had sacrificed much of their land to the encroaching housing market and hired out to the local farmers to keep their hands in farming. It worked out. Ariel was glad that at least in her lifetime she needn't worry about having to sell off the farm that was officially called Frazer's Acres.

Sofie was whining at the door. Ariel reached across the threshold, snapped her fingers, and the big basset sauntered in, making a big production of walking in a circle and plopping down right in the middle of the room where everyone would have to walk around her if they wanted to look at the computer screen again. "Well, Ben, it looks like you have a good plan for this year. I know that we just got finished pruning in October right after the harvest and did the winter spraying in December of copper and oil, so it looks like you've done a fine job of it."

Ben grinned from ear to ear and got out a huge pipe, thumping it on the ashtray overflowing with several previous pipe cleanings. He thumbed his favorite Cherry Granger tobacco in the deep bowl, lit it with a stick match, and sat smoking quietly.

"Well, sugar, we should be okay, but I don't know how this year is going to be. We haven't had much rain, so I can't factor in the cost of irrigation yet. If we have a real soaker in March or April, that will help a lot." Ben turned back to the computer and was soon deep in concentration as he went over the last few years to see if the irrigation expenses could be averaged, which would help him to estimate his water costs for this year's crop. The water costs were different every season, and it was only by averaging them that he could get a ballpark figure.

Ariel left Ben to his pipe and his figuring. Sofie and Ariel walked along the border of the farm. Frazer Acres was an impressive acreage, and she and Morgan walked the perimeter daily, putting in a solid three miles before they arrived back at the house. Riley, Ben, Julie, Morgan, Zoe, and Sarah would enjoy a before-supper walk around evenings in the spring through the fall as their schedules permitted. It gave them an opportunity to survey the progress that had been made during the day and was a chance to catch up and make plans for the next day. Not unlike a corporate board meeting but much more satisfying. Without Sarah, it just wouldn't be the same. Sofie and Ariel ended up at Sarah's little cottage and taking a deep breath, Ariel unlocked the door and walked inside. Ariel wanted to clean out the refrigerator and change the sheets on Sarah's bed. Lily wanted to stay there for the rest of her leave.

The crime tape was gone and surprisingly, Ariel didn't feel at all depressed coming in like this. Sarah had made the place so light and airy and cheerful with lots of yellow and white that Ariel was able to walk through the quiet--too quiet--cottage. Ariel's mind went back to that first time she'd seen the cottage as a tiny four-year-old. Even then, the cottage had been warm and friendly. Sarah had put a new open-style kitchen in that gave her a feeling of spaciousness. The rest of the cottage was about the same. It was only when walking into her bedroom that the sweet smell of her lavender oil sachet forced Ariel to turn and walk out abruptly. It was overwhelming! She seemed to be still here, as if she only just stepped out of the room. Ariel hurried Sofie outside and instantly vomited up her breakfast. She wiped her mouth and took a drink from the garden hose. She wasn't going to go back in that cottage alone.

Ariel didn't go into the cottage again. She sent Julie to empty the refrigerator and make up the bed with fresh clean sheets.

Julie, with the help of Lily, worked all through the week and by the end of the week, Lily was settled in the cottage. They had moved all of Sarah's clothing and personal things out and stored them in the barn until they felt like they could make a decision about them. Now, though everything was familiar to Lily, there was no longer a shade of Sarah in the house. It was clean and smelled of lemon polish. Lily bought a few things for snacks as well as fresh fruit but ate the majority of her meals up at the big house with Ariel, Morgan, and Mark when he was off his shift at the fire station. Zoe and Riley often showed up as well, so Ariel was busy cooking large pots of stew and hot crusty cheese bread. On Thursday, Riley showed up with a big pot of chippino that he had made the night before, and all it took was to warm it up and put a bottle of zinfandel to cool. Ariel made a salad and toasted French bread with garlic and butter under the broiler. It was a close and healing time for the siblings and their long-time friends, Zoe and Riley.

That night a raging storm batted the farmhouse, and after dinner, the lights flickered and suddenly went out. Riley headed for the drawer with the candles and matches, still in the same place as they were when he visited here as a boy. Laughing, he picked up a handful of candles while Ariel gathered candlestick holders together and placed them in the middle of the table. They soon had a soft, flickering centerpiece of blazing candles to cheer them. They finished the fish stew and dumped their bowls in the sink to be rinsed and put in the dishwasher once the electric water pump and the lights came back on. The candlelight and warmth of the Franklin stove made them drowsy and after talking well past midnight, Riley got up, stretched, and slapped his hand against Morgan's knee. He had been dozing, and Riley's slap woke him up.

"What the hell, Riley!"

Riley grinned and put on his jacket and scarf. "Ah ! That was delicious if I do say so. But I have surgery tomorrow on old Mary Smith's dog, Duke. He has a growth in his stomach that I don't like the looks of. Duke's only two years old, so I'd like to try and fix this. Otherwise--" He stopped talking, and grabbing his coat, he pecked Ariel, Lily, and Zoe on their cheeks and gave Mark and Morgan a bear hug as he opened the door and bent his head to the storm.

Zoe left a few minutes later, and it was only Mark and Lily left. They took a few more minutes to straighten the kitchen up with Ariel before they grabbed their coats, trudged out on to the porch, and got into Mark's jeep. He'd drive Lily to the cottage and then head over to his place.

Chapter 7

The following day was Friday. Ariel drove into Sonora in the Silverado pickup. It was a 2009 silver blue model 250, new and with the automatic transmission, easy to drive. She had to get groceries for the farm and also enough to take to the little mining claim that she and Morgan owned on the South Fork of the Stanislaus river. Morgan had suggested that they spend the weekend away from the farm. "Just let's go and let Lily and Mark fend for themselves for a night." Ariel was exhausted and the thought of spending a weekend with Morgan and nothing to do but relax was a relief, and she agreed. They were going immediately after Morgan got home from court. As Ariel went up and down the grocery aisles, the persistent feeling of fear and anxiety that had been with her since Sarah had been brutally murdered gripped her, and she just couldn't shake it off. Sighing, she dumped the groceries in the back of the truck, climbed in, and headed back to the farm. She'd have to go through Columbia to get to the old Yankee Hill Road, so she decided to stop at the historic park and grab a hotdog from Larry Clark.

Larry had a vender hotdog stand that he set up on Fridays, and the farm people all made a point of stopping by for a big fat Polish sausage with all the trimmings. The little, covered steam wagon was set up in front of the Wells Fargo stage office where a line of tourists was waiting in the frigid air for their ride in the coach. It was a perfect place for the steaming hot dogs and hot coffee Larry made. Business was brisk because historic Columbia had school trips all year long and over seven hundred children a day learned of the events of the 1849 gold rush and its impact on California. Ariel happily waited in the line still three deep to sample this local fare. Finally, it was her turn, and she was starved.

"Hey, Larry, give me a Polish with everything on it and lots of sauerkraut." Ariel smiled at Larry. It was funny. She had gone all through school with Larry. He'd been in the service, and when he got out, he lived at home with his mother and had this little business. It actually was quite a going concern, and Ariel knew that this was all Larry had wanted to do when he got out of the army. Desert Storm and Desert Shield were all the excitement that he wanted. Give him a small quiet sleepy town like Columbia, and he was happy.

After chatting with Larry and getting the news of the town, Ariel finished off her sausage, waved good-bye to Larry, and headed back to the parking lot. She glanced at her watch. She'd have to hurry because Morgan would be home any minute if court let out early, as it usually did on Fridays. The judge and all the participants had mining claims, and they all tried to get out and up to their claims before dark to stretch the weekend as much as possible. This was the price of living in a gold mining town with much of the gold still in the ground and river.

The house was quiet when she stepped into the kitchen. Ariel remembered that Lily was going to go get her hair trimmed and nails done. It would be good for her to get back into the life of the town. She had been going to see Sandy Miller since she was old enough to get her nails done and tagged along with her mother. The Millers were old timers in Columbia, and they knew everyone. Having her hour a week with Sandy was like going to visit an old friend. Sandy knew so much about her, and she would pamper Lily. After the last four years away in Iraq, Lily needed to be pampered. Ariel frowned when she opened the refrigerator and put away orange juice, bacon, and eggs. Lily was strung kind of tight, and Ariel was worried about her. She finished putting away the groceries and packing up the supplies, clothes, and treats for the mining cabin.

Ariel was just finished packing and was dressed in her jeans and a flannel shirt when she heard the back door slam, and Morgan's heavy footsteps coming down the hall. "Hey, all set?" Morgan grabbed her, gave her a big hug, and kissed her soundly before shedding his suit and stepping into the shower. Ariel picked up the cast-off clothing and hung the jacket and pants neatly in the closet. She sighed as she looked at the crumpled pants. Morgan thought nothing of leaving his clothes where they lay. She had learned to just go ahead and hang them up, or he'd wear them wrinkled.

It was just a little after three o'clock when they finished packing the truck and headed out, tooting their horn at Ben and Julie as they passed the barn. As the road climbed, and they headed toward Italian Bar Road, Morgan switched on a CD of Celine Dion. Her "All By Myself" filled the cab as they pointed the truck east on Italian Bar Road. They'd be at the claim in about twenty minutes. The view on the left side of the canyon was spectacular. The trees, bare of their leaves, let them see more of the canyon than they could ever see in the spring. It was warmer than she thought it would be, probably in the low fifties, but tonight it would be hovering in the thirties. Often there would be ice crystals on the ground in the morning. The cabin was insulated and with the little Franklin stove fired up, they would be toasty.

As the truck turned into the mining camp complex, Ariel waved at the camp caretaker and looked around to see if anyone else had arrived yet. There were twenty some cabins. Most were small one- or two-room dwellings that hugged the side of the mountain and faced the river. It was a busy, fun place in the summer when families came with their kids and dogs, and even the grandparents, and stayed the season from June to October, if they didn't have school-age kids. The social hall was filled every Saturday night, and Texas Hold'em was the game of choice. Both Morgan and Ariel enjoyed the game and the camaraderie of the group. But this weekend the social hall would be shut tight, and no one would be playing cards. January was just for the hardy, and most folks who came for the weekend were nesting and enjoying their cabins, rarely venturing out further than a daily walk about to get some exercise after all the pancakes and sausages they ate for breakfast. This was what Ariel and Morgan planned.

They drove up to the snug cabin and began the routine of opening it up and airing it. They brought in wood and turned on the propane for the gas range. Morgan soon had a fire blazing in the stove, and Ariel had the kitchen supplied and a homemade soup simmering on the range. She'd add hot crusty bread with cheese broiled on top to go with the soup. It was relaxing as they went through the familiar routine of getting the cabin up and running. The solar panels were enough to supply electricity for lights, and propane fueled the range and hot water heater.

As Ariel and Morgan worked together, the nagging feeling of fear and anxiety that had been with Ariel subsided, and Ariel began to relax. With Sarah's death and funeral, Ariel had been overwhelmed with grief and sadness. Thankfully, the cabin worked its magic, taking them away from the sorrow and giving them peace.

After dinner and a quick clean up of the kitchen, Ariel and

Morgan sat in front of the open Franklin hearth and sipped hot chocolate. Ariel had brought homemade molasses sugar cookies, and she loved to dip them in the hot chocolate just as she did when she was a child. Her father loved the cookies, and Sarah had made them every winter for the holidays and then continued making them into spring. Ariel was so slender that she didn't have to worry about gaining a pound or two. With the baby, she was very protective of what she ate and drank, but these cookies were her weakness, and Morgan loved them too. Yum!

Lights flashed across the front window, and Ariel and Morgan knew that their nearest neighbor, Riley, had arrived. They'd visit with him in the morning when he usually popped in just in time for coffee and pancakes. Tonight was theirs, and Ariel snuggled up with Morgan with the couch throw across their legs. They relaxed together and caught up with their day.

"Remember when we finally got the cabin built and had our first night together, and the skunk got under the crawl space and stunk us out?" Morgan grinned at Ariel. "You told me you'd never come up here again, but you did!" He put his arm around her and wiggled closer.

Ariel laughed and leaned into him. "Well, you enclosed the crawl space, so we wouldn't have a repeat performance from that little bugger. My hero!" Gradually the chocolate warmed and relaxed them and when a half hour later Morgan banked the fire and closed the iron doors on the stove for the night, the two of them headed for the bedroom arm in arm.

Ariel loved the little bedroom, snug with their big king-sized bed taking up most of the space. There was a door that opened off the deck in the back, giving them a wonderful view of the river in the spring when the water was at its highest. The river roared until June when the upper dam shut down the flow so that the miners could start dredging. Until then, the camp was quiet and more like a resort, but come June 15, the whine of the dredges pierced the air, and from morning till dusk, the miners dredged the river, making holes eight to ten feet deep in places. The river was forgiving, and come winter would fill the holes with silt and boulders it pushed down stream. The fish enjoyed the new food source from the bottom dredging that stirred up the silt and all manner of tidbits for the fish to eat. The miners were used to fish elbowing their way in for the food. Even as they were dredging, the fish weren't afraid of the dredges or the men in the river and spent their days darting to and fro to grab the flies, crickets, and mosquito's that settled in the silt when their life cycle ended.

Morgan turned off the lights as Ariel climbed into to bed, and in the dark, he pulled her toward him. Ariel welcomed his warm body and clung to him. It soothed them of the past week of terror they'd experienced to cling together and begin to make slow sweet love together. Morgan stroked Ariel's back and kissed her deeply. Ariel reached out to him, and Morgan gently cradled her in his arms. With the baby, both of them were a little afraid of being too amorous, but Morgan gently but insistently opened her legs and, barely controlling his urgent need, slipped inside her. Taking his time, his fingers wound around her hair.

"Soft, much too soft to resist, hmm you feel so good, I love you, Ariel," he said quietly into her ear. He seemed to need to touch and taste all of her but so slowly, so thoroughly, Ariel felt like she was floating safe and warm.

Suddenly his mouth grew greedy, and he pressed his body down, trapping Ariel's hands under his chest. He began to move deeply within her. Ariel moved with him, her hunger matching his and gentleness was forgotten, all that mattered was they were together as one. Ariel moved with him, urging him more and more deeply. She cried out against his mouth and surrendered into him until their hunger was spent.

Afterwards, Ariel spooned against Morgan, her eyes closed, breathing steady at last. Lazily, possessively, Morgan ran his fingers over her arms and stroked her gently. He hugged her and held her and together, wrapped in each other's arms, they slept.

Chapter 8

It was pitch dark when Ariel woke with a start. She couldn't get any air. The room was filled with thick smoke.

"Morgan, Morgan! " she screamed, and coughing, she reached over and shook him. "Wake up! The cabin is full of smoke! Oh God, Morgan, wake up!" Jumping out of bed, she threw on her robe and raced over to Morgan's side of the bed.

As she dragged him toward the edge of the bed, he awoke, startled, as he started to fall to the floor. "My God, Ariel, get out on the deck!" He got up and pushed her out on the deck. She looked back just as the bedroom door burst in, and a man stood there with a blowtorch.

Morgan turned and faced him. "Run, Ariel, run!" he shouted. Ariel raced out of the cabin and down the steps leading to the side of the cabin. She kept running until she reached Riley's cabin and started pounding on his door, screaming his name. It seemed like an eternity before a light went on, and the door opened. "Riley, help! Morgan is in the cabin, and there is someone there trying to burn us up."

Riley in boxer shorts and nothing else, raced out of the house toward the flame-filled cabin. Ariel went as fast as she could behind him and when they reached the deck, Riley could see the cabin was fully engulfed in flames, and Morgan was nowhere to be seen.

"Ariel, go ring the fire bell now!" he barked. Ariel charged across the compound, reached the fire bell, and started striking the heavy iron triangle with the iron bar attached to a rope. She didn't stop ringing it until she saw people coming out of their cabins. She hollered at them to go help get Morgan out of the cabin. In minutes, hoses were lowered to the deepest pool, and the men had the hand pumper going, squirting water from the river on the cabin. Ariel ran to the cabin just as Riley came out carrying Morgan. He laid him on the ground and started artificial respiration. Morgan didn't respond. Riley kept it up until finally one of the campers touched him on the shoulder and said, "He's gone, Riley."

Ariel stood there as Riley searched for a pulse. When he turned his face up to look at her, Ariel dropped to her knees beside her husband. "Morgan, Morgan. Oh God, no!" she screamed. Riley reached up and just held her. The look in his eyes told her that the still form of her husband would never move again. Her mind shut down, and as she fell into a black, black sphere of nothingness, she lost consciousness.

Riley picked her up and carried her back to his cabin. She regained consciousness as he laid her down on the sofa. Ariel grabbed his arm. "Why, Riley, why? Oh, Riley, Morgan didn't deserve to die." She collapsed into sobs against his chest, and Riley held her tight against him while she sobbed.

Riley had used his truck's On Star to call the fire department, but by the time they got there, the cabin was a smoldering mass of charred wood. A fireman covered Morgan, and an ambulance took him to Sonora Regional. Riley kept Ariel away in his cabin, and somehow Mark was there holding her. Zoe too. They both had gotten called out when the fire department was called. The man who started the blaze was found later when police and firemen walked through the sodden embers. He was burned beyond recognition.

Zoe heard that his truck had been found about a half mile

from the camp, and they were putting out a trace on the license plate now. She stared at Ariel, and even as her cop mode kept the pain of the loss of her friend's husband detached, she was shattered inside. It took every bit of her discipline and training not to be wailing right alongside Ariel.

"Oh, Ariel," she whispered, reaching out, taking hold of her friend and holding her tight. Her voice broke and tears welled in her light blue eyes, turning them to steel gray as she felt her friend's pain and vowed she'd catch whoever was responsible for yet another tragedy for her friend.

Riley watched Ariel, anxious for her, and he felt so helpless. Whatever was happening to his best friend's family was sinister and wicked. There was nothing to be done right now except get Ariel to a safe place. Riley took hold of Ariel's hand and looked at the shattered woman, gently squeezing her hand. "I promise you we will end this."

There seemed nothing else to do but to take her in his arms and hold her. Riley could feel the trembling of her body as she leaned into his warm strength. Then the moment was over, and Riley was brisk and efficient, covering the feelings that were enveloping him. Lord God, he had felt a stirring inside of him like a hot flame. There was only one thing to do. He had to get away from her. This was a terrible time to bring up what he had stamped out of himself as soon as he had known that Ariel and Morgan were going to marry. As Morgan's best friend, he could never acknowledge his feelings for Ariel. He had been successful in keeping them covered all these years. Why were they surfacing now on such a horrible night when all Ariel needed was a friend? Riley resolved to keep tight control over himself; Ariel would never know how he felt.

Riley helped Ariel to Zoe's cruiser, and Zoe drove swiftly toward Sonora Regional where they had taken Morgan. Ariel sat next to her and stared sightless into the darkness. Only the road ahead was visible. Zoe took her home to the farm first to get her changed into a sweat suit and sneakers. Lily met them at the door, already up and dressed. She had heard the telephone ring, and Mark yelling for her to get up and dressed. He quickly told her what he knew and charged out of the house. Now she reached for Ariel, put her arms around her, and helped her up to her room. She found some clean sweats for her and helped her into them. Zoe got her shoes out of the closet, and, with Lily's help, got them on her. Then the three of them climbed into the cruiser and headed into Sonora. They saw Riley's pickup already in the parking lot when they got there.

The hospital was at the other end of town and up the hill. Zoe could see the lights. As they drove into the parking area, Zoe saw the ambulance backed into the bay. There was another surprise that greeted them as they crested the hill in the safety of the police cruiser. The front driveway of the hospital was covered with news trucks, and bright lights shown on them.

As Zoe drove up, she gunned her motor, whipped the cruiser around, and headed back down the hill. "Hold on," she yelled. She turned on her lights and drove as fast as she dared. At the bottom, she got on the radio and called her dispatcher to patch her through to the hospital night desk. As soon as she heard the front desk pick up, she barked orders for someone to go to the back entrance and open the door. They'd be going in the service entrance. Zoe drove around to the back service area and waited until she saw a janitor peek out the window. Zoe flashed her lights, drove up, and parked by the entrance. Zoe quickly opened the door for Ariel and Lily, and the trio walked into the hospital.

"I don't know how to help you, Ariel, but I'm here for you. Oh God, it doesn't make any sense, someone make sense of this for us!" Zoe cried.

Ariel and Lily, who had just buried their mother, were now

walking into the emergency room at Sonora Regional again to face the cold, dead body of Morgan. They were directed to a tiny room in the back of the emergency room. Riley was sitting next to Morgan's body. He got up and met them at the door. Reaching Ariel, he leaned down, hugged her, and then kept his arm tight around her as she moved toward the body of her husband.

"Uncover him, please." Ariel stood in front of the gurney and waited. Everyone froze, unable to move. They knew what they'd find under the sheet, and it horrified them to see their friend dead.

Ariel, her face set in a mask of grief, stepped toward the gurney, and pulled down the sheet. Ariel gasped as Morgan's blackened face appeared. He hadn't been burned, but he was black, covered in soot. She reached up, brushed the soot off his face, bent down, and kissed him on the lips.

Ariel then collapsed over him, and Lily and Zoe gently led her out into the corridor. Riley kept her close to him, and they all sat down in the waiting room in a huddle.

Riley quickly told them the situation with the press. "They think there is some connection between Sarah's and Morgan's deaths, and they think it has something to do with you, Ariel."

"Me! What makes them say that? That's a terrible thing to say." Ariel, her face a frozen mask, stared at her friends in shock.

"Come on, let's get out of here, and back to the farm," said Riley, and he led them back through the hospital corridors and out through the service entrance. Lily and Ariel climbed into his truck with him, and Zoe drove back in front of the hospital, showing them an empty cruiser. The press would think they were still inside. They all reached the farm in a short time with no press tailing them, but it would only be a matter of hours before they had the address of the farm. They'd need to make some plans soon to keep them away from Ariel.

Chapter 9

The next morning was spent in a deep swirling fog of listlessness and suspended time. It was cold, and outside the fog lay heavy on the ground when Ariel got up and wandered into the kitchen in her pajamas. She sat at the kitchen table with a steaming cup of coffee. She looked exhausted. She'd slept a little, but when she awoke, it took only an instant for the reality to hit her hard. Morgan was dead! For a second, when her eyes opened, there was a moment of bliss before the memory of the night slammed into her mind--the hideous moment when she remembered. The sweet memory of their lovemaking abruptly shattered into the memory of the man with the blowtorch and of her running, running, running, the whiplash effect shocking her awake.

Ariel sat in the kitchen and felt the comforting presence of Julie and Lily. They urged her to eat something, but all she could manage was coffee. After a while, they left her alone to stare out the window and into the whirling fog. Finally, Lily coaxed her to go get dressed. Ariel moved slowly and managed to put on clean sweats and to comb her hair and brush her teeth. She washed her face in cold water, and she welcomed it—icy and wet, it revived her from the deadened senses that had her walking around like a zombie. Ariel forced herself to go back into the kitchen where Lily, Zoe, Mark, and Riley were gathering for Julie's promised lunch.

It was a little after noon, and Julie had made a clam chowder and hot turkey grilled sandwiches for lunch. Ariel had hardly touched hers, but Riley had gone back for seconds, praising his mother's chowder as he dipped his sandwich into the chowder's white sauce. No one could make chowder like Julie did. She had been making it for Riley and his father since he was a little boy. Riley's sister, Melonie, didn't care much for it, so Julie always made grilled cheese sandwiches for her. Now she made turkey because everyone was trying to keep the fat out of their food. Everyone liked this simple meal. The television was on low throughout the meal. They had just finished eating when a news flash interrupted the television program.

Riley and Lily were with Ariel when the attacker's picture came on the television. He was a complete stranger to all of them.

"Who the hell is Jason Davidson?" Riley yelled at the television. Who was this man who had killed his best friend and for what? The newscaster went on to say that Davidson was a transient who lived in an old abandoned cabin in Arnold, a small logging community off Highway 49. Ariel sat listening, and yet it seemed as if cotton wool was wrapped around her head. She didn't comprehend anything the newscaster said.

"Turn it off, please." Ariel got up off the sofa, went into the bathroom, and threw up. Lily held her head, and Riley got a cold wet washcloth and bathed her face.

Ariel wasn't in any shape to handle Morgan's funeral arrangements, so his oldest friend, Riley, did it. The funeral was set for Wednesday morning at ten o'clock at McCarty's Funeral home. Even though no one wanted to go through another funeral, they decided that they had to make the effort. Morgan was a well-known attorney and Rotarian. He deserved to be mourned by the whole community. A short obituary was put in the *Union Democrat* on Monday. The notice was read by everyone in town by Tuesday morning, and by Wednesday, a huge crowd had flocked to the funeral home. They held the funeral in the largest room McCarty's had, but it was standing room only, and television monitors were put in several other rooms for the overflow crowd. It was an ordeal, but they got through it.

The media wasn't allowed into the funeral, but they were front and center with their cameras rolling when Ariel and Riley arrived at the funeral home. Zoe and David waved everyone back behind the tape that had been designated for the press area, and Ariel and her family were quickly taken inside.

This time the service was short, and there were plainclothes police all through the crowd. Riley did the eulogy, and several friends added their voices of praise for the solid friendship that Morgan had offered them over the years. There was a small reception afterwards. Morgan would be cremated. Thankfully, it was over—neat and orderly as Morgan would have done it himself.

Ariel, Mark, and Lily were driven home by Riley. Zoe and her partner, David, came behind in Zoe's jeep. There was a small gathering at the farm of close family and friends. Ariel was relieved when everyone went home after a light lunch of sandwiches and cold cuts, cookies, and brownies with a huge pot of strong black coffee.

Lily and Mark were her strength, and they stayed close to Ariel as did Zoe, David, and Riley. Ben and Julie were shattered, and Ariel sent them home as soon as she could.

Zoe and David sat with Ariel, Lily, Mark, and Riley and told them what had been uncovered during the police investigation. "Mr. Davidson had over ten thousand dollars in cash in his truck. Way too much money for a man who was known to rummage in dumpsters for aluminum cans to recycle. We think he was a hired killer." Zoe looked hard at Ariel, and sighed. "We think he was after you, Ariel. Morgan was just in the way. This has something to do with you and your pregnancy, but so far, we can't prove it. Your mother knew something, and her papers indicate she was upset enough that she was going to the American Medical Association to report some kind of unethical situation at the clinic, but she didn't say what it was. Her journal refers to unethical embryo transplants of some sort, but no details, and no one is named in her journal. Ariel, I think you should get away from here until we do find out what this is all about."

Zoe looked at Ariel and continued, "Do you have any place you could go that nobody from here would be able to find you? The press has been calling all morning, and I've issued a no comment at this time, but they won't be held off for very long. This isn't your old friends at the *Union Democrat*. This is the national media. They are like vultures when they sense a story."

Lily looked at Ariel and then at Zoe. "What about going to Grandma Frazer's?"

"Where does she live?" Zoe asked.

Ariel spoke for the first time. "She's in Scotland in a little berg named Dornoch. When my mother died, and before Dad and I immigrated here, we lived with Grandma and Grandpa Frazer at her Manse house. Brindle Hall it was called. I was only two, but I loved it there. Yes, I could go there until this is cleared up." Saying this seemed to take all of her energy, and she leaned back on the sofa and closed her eyes.

They discussed this among them and once decided, wasted no time in getting started on the arrangements. It was decided that Lily would accompany Ariel to Brindle Hall and then after a weeklong visit with her grandparents, she would fly back to Iraq to finish her tour of duty. She was to be deployed back to the states the first of September. Riley and Lily called Scotland and explained the situation to Grandma Frazer. A few minutes later, it was all decided. Zoe would take Ariel and Lily to San Francisco, and they would fly to Inverness and then take a taxi that would take them from Inverness to Dornoch. It would be a long, hard trip. Lily and Ariel turned toward Zoe.

Both of them started talking at the same time. Finally, Lily stopped and let Ariel go first.

"Oh, Zoe, how long will the investigation take? When can I come home?" She kept her eyes fastened on Zoe, and Zoe felt Ariel's pain. They were so close, had shared so much of their lives with each other, and knew each other so well that Zoe knew she couldn't lie to her.

"We might never get to the bottom of this, but I can promise you that I'll do my very best to do so." The three women hugged each other and then reached out and grabbed Riley in a bear hug too. With their plans set, they had completely forgotten him.

He reached for his jacket. "Okay, let's call the San Francisco airport and see when the next flight to Scotland leaves. Get your passports." Riley was all business, and he kept Lily and Ariel busy with details to keep their minds off the horror that there might be someone watching and waiting for an opportunity to kill them. He wanted them gone and safe as soon as it could be arranged.

Chapter 10

Scotland

Sibyl Stuart Frazer stood in the sitting room at Brindle Hall, a worried frown on her face. It was a dark winter day. She had just put the phone back in its cradle, and she sat down at the table and poured a hot cup of restorative tea. It wasn't a very long conversation. Sipping her tea, she heard the back door downstairs open and close and knew that Robyn and Joco were home. She got up, leaned over the banister, and called, "Robyn can you come up to the sitting room?"

Robyn Frazer took off his jacket and hat, hanging them on the sturdy hook in the scullery. Joco had already reached the kitchen and his drinking bowl and warm basket snug and warm beside the Aga. The huge stove radiated heat as Robyn walked through the kitchen. He appreciatively sniffed the homemade stew simmering on the back of the stove. It was after five o'clock, and the snow-chilled air and long walk had done him and Joco good. It was Robyn's afternoon ritual to walk Joco.

He'd set out after tea and ambled around the town. Dornoch was a sea town, and today the salt air had been brisk. Robyn would welcome a hot stew with crusty bread for supper tonight. Sibyl met him on the stairs leading to the sitting room, anxious to share her news. She followed him up into the sitting room and poured him a hot cup of tea from the electric teapot that was handy and always ready. The tea was hot and strong, builder's tea, Robyn called it. She laced it with brandy and a spoon of sugar and brought it to him.

Sibyl hesitated saying what was on her mind until he had taken several deep drinks of the hot, restoring drink. She looked out the big picture window that brought the rolling sea close. The sea was crashing against the rocks at the bottom of the cliff. Sibyl could see the gray green water well up for another run and then crash again, endless motion that mostly soothed her, but tonight it just added to her feelings of agitation, and she couldn't wait a moment longer to spill out what had happened.

"Robyn, I've had a telephone call from America. Ariel and Lily are coming to see us. We haven't seen them since Paul died. They want to come and spend the month with us. Lily is home on leave from Iraq. Oh, Robyn, it's Lily's mother; she has been murdered!"

"Then they must come. They belong with us."

Sybil hesitated. "Robyn, it's even worse news."

"What?" Robyn looked at Sibyl.

"It's really unfathomable; it's Ariel's husband, Morgan. Last weekend someone broke into their mining cabin while they were sleeping and set the house on fire, Morgan was killed in the fire. All of this is just too much for the girls. They are both distraught, and I'm afraid for Ariel. There is some suspicion that it was her that the man came to murder, and Morgan fought him off, giving Ariel time to escape out the back door. The police are urging Ariel to leave the country and hide out until they can get to the bottom of Sarah's murder and now Morgan's. This all happened within a week, and they think that it is all connected."

"Oh how terrible! Then by all means, we'll do all we can for them. My word, two murders within a week. That can't be chance. When will they be here?" He looked at her, his gentle face filled with concern.

"I'm not sure. They called to let me know and that when they got to Inverness they would call again. There is packing to do, and of course, Ariel must see to the almond farm. There's a foreman, but she has to put him in the picture. I'll get the extra rooms done up and lay in a food supply, and then I suppose we will just have to wait for their call. I'm numb with fear for them, but it's been so long it will be wonderful to have them here even in such a sad situation. We'll keep a low profile and not have big doings."

"Sibyl, lively company wouldn't do for these girls now anyway. You're what they need and Brindle Hall--it's a healing place.

Chapter 11

riel and Lily were packed and waiting for Zoe to come and fly them into the San Francisco airport to connect with their flight to the United Kingdom. It had taken a little more than a day to make all the arrangements. Ariel had spent an hour with Ben going over his plans for the farm and the timeline for getting the orchard ready for the beekeeper and his hives. They would be there for about a month to cross-pollinate the trees. Ben would be sending e-mails to Ariel, and she had given him signature authorization and Mark power of attorney until she was able to return.

They heard a step on the porch and the clump of boots. Ariel hurried to open the door, but instead of Zoe, it was Riley who stood there about to knock.

"Riley, I was hoping we'd see you before we took off. I just finished talking things over with your father." Ariel smiled up at him with her green eyes and red hair glistening in the bright daylight. "I'm trying to get them to move into the big house where they can keep a better eye on things. Will you encourage them to do it? They can have the new guest suite." Ariel and Morgan had done a bit of remodeling, opening up two small bedrooms to make a larger one with a small bath. So many of their friends spent time with them during the summer and during the harvest that it made it a lot easier to have a bigger guest suite.

"Sure . . . if I have to, I'll come in and move Dad's smoking chair in. He'll follow, sure as shooting." He grabbed hold of both Ariel and Lily and gave them both a bear hug. "You guys take care and keep a look out around you, okay! I wish I could go with you."

The three friends walked to the back kitchen where Ariel had the ever-present pot of coffee brewing. She poured them all a big cup, and they sat down together at the big round oak table. This would be good-bye for a while. Zoe told them there was no end in sight yet for who was behind the murders, and she wanted Ariel away until she could e-mail her an all clear.

"So, you're all set?" Riley asked as he buried his nose in his cup of coffee and looked over the rim into Ariel's eyes. She smiled wistfully at him and shrugged.

"As set as I'll ever be. I just can't believe that this has happened to me!" Ariel raked her fingers through her hair and stared out at the orchard. She looked around the neat-as-a-pin kitchen, and her eyes welled up with tears.

"Oh, here I go again." She sniffed and grabbed the Kleenex that Lily handed her. Riley put his hand on top of hers and squeezed tight. They stayed like that, not talking, just being together, and knowing that life had changed forever for Ariel.

The coffee cups were empty, and the women's bags piled just inside the front door when Zoe's jeep wheeled into the yard with a crunch of tires and a squeal of brakes. Riley stood up and went to the front door to meet her, grabbing black nylon bags under both arms and with both hands. He had all the luggage out by the time Ariel and Zoe had struggled into their coats and checked their purses for passports, tickets, money, and phone numbers for Brindle Hall. Ariel had brought her laptop computer with her as well.

Ben and Julie had seen Zoe arrive so they hurried over from the office and stood huddled next to Riley as Ariel and Lily climbed into the jeep. Ariel got in front with Zoe, and Lily shared space with the luggage. Everything was done smooth and fast, and with a toot of the horn, the jeep sped out of the driveway and onto the highway. Ariel and Lily waved at Ben, Julie, and Riley until they turned the corner. They were really off and, within hours, would be in London. They would be changing planes at Heathrow into a small jet that commuted to Inverness. By about four Thursday morning, they would be in London.

Chapter 12

he little plane taxied into position facing due south. Zoe had Barney Hinkle on the Radio.

"Hi, Barney, I'm ready to fly," she said, knowing that there was only one plane on the tarmac in front of her. In Columbia, they were a might informal, and everyone who flew out of the airport was known to the air traffic controller. "This is Cessna 2359er. Requesting the runway."

Zoe waited until the crackle of the radio with Barney's gruff voice. "Okay, 2359er. You're good to go. Just keep your nose up. There are clouds in the central valley. They recommend that you stay well above them. See you later, Zoe, safe flight, Ariel and Lily."

Barney waved as the little Cessna with Zoe, Ariel, and Lily gained speed and swept into the hazy blue sky. Zoe followed Highway 49 over to 99 and up 120. Within the hour, they were traveling due west above Highway 580. The clouds Barney was worried about had dissipated, and the sky was a crisp cool blue. Temperatures were in the mid 40s, and Zoe watched for aircraft in the Livermore area. In a short five minutes, they were over the Hayward Hills and swooping toward the Bay. The snake-like San Mateo Bridge, straight as an arrow most of the way across the water, turned into a hump back serpent as it climbed and twisted its way across into Foster City.

Zoe made a sharp right and called the control tower, "This

is Cessna 2359er. Requesting to land. Where do you want me?" The tower crackled as a disembodied voice gave her directions to runway 32. The side runway put her well away from the big huge international flights that dropped out of the clouds every fifteen minutes or less. They were quickly on the ground and a small vehicle that would carry both them and their luggage was chugging its way toward them from the terminal.

Zoe kissed them both good-bye and then was back on the radio getting her instructions on flying out of this busy international airport. She had to go quickly while air traffic was light. As Ariel and Lily sped over the tarmac with the driver, she was taxiing out onto the runway, cleared for immediate takeoff. If she had lagged, she might have been delayed for hours. Zoe was next, and she expertly maneuvered the plane over to runway 32 and awaited the towers order to go.

The radio crackled. "Cessna 2359er on 32. Cleared for takeoff."

Zoe zoomed down the runway, lifted up and out headed over Burlingame. She could see San Francisco in the dazzling sunny morning. The Trans-America building was standing like a tall narrow pyramid. Its windows were glistening and sparkling as the little plane moved up and out over the Bay toward Oakland. She could see the Oakland Hills and the Mormon temple standing like a palace on the hillside near the Montclair district, a suburb of Berkeley that looked like an oasis of greenery. The Warren Freeway, a ribbon of black, slid through the town, creating one of the most beautiful and heralded stretches of freeway in California.

Zoe banked southeast and headed back over the central valley, following Highway 580 to 99 back to 120 and finally over to historically picturesque Highway 49. The radio started crackling in welcome. She gave the planes coordinates, level, and speed as she headed back to Columbia and home. After landing and taxiing to her place on the tarmac, she turned off the engine and sighed as she unbuckled her seatbelt and climbed out of the plane. Lily and Ariel were probably in one of those jets far above her settling in for the five-hour flight to New York. Zoe looked up at the newest air stream and said a little prayer for her friends' safety and a healing of their great loss. Zoe felt forlorn herself as she walked into the airport lounge and leaned over the counter.

"What's up?"

Barney was grinning and pouring her a fresh cup of coffee. He shoved it toward her. "Not much, how was that there big city?"

She reached for the coffee gratefully and filled him in on the morning.

Chapter 13

riel and Lily were on board Continental flight 8783. The big plane swooped in a wide sweep from Burlingame toward San Francisco. The seat belt sign was still blinking when Lily looked over Ariel to see the sparkling city where Ariel, Lily, and their mother would go every Christmas break to shop and spend a long weekend doing all the fun, touristy things that they loved. They always stayed at the Saint Francis and loved going to the little bar for canapés when they were old enough. Lily especially loved going to the top of the Mark Hopkins.

"Remember when we went to the top of the Mark, and it was fogged in, and we couldn't see a thing! You were so disappointed, and so was I."

Lily giggled as she pointed out the famous Barbary Coast. Named after the pirate coast of North Africa, this legendary waterfront area has been hopping since the 1849 gold rush. Gamblers, gangsters, brothels, saloons, and disreputable boardinghouses gave the area a notorious reputation then throughout the world. The entertainment strip was still pretty raunchy and catered to adolescent males, Japanese tourists, and tired and lonely businessmen. Chinatown swung into view. Sarah loved Chinese food, and a trip to San Francisco had to include a trip to the Golden Dragon. The three would pile on to a cable car and drop off in Chinatown, walking through open markets with their smoked ducks hanging from the front windows. The place was mysterious, and Sarah, though a board certified physician, would love to go to the ancient Chinese herbalists and talk shop. She even bought some of the medicines that they recommended for her patients whose rashes weren't clearing up with traditional medication.

Ariel glanced down and was just in time to see the Golden Gate Bridge before the plane turned a sharp eastern course. "Look, Lily, there's Fort Point! Remember when we went there and froze in the cold, damp buildings? Sarah always wanted to give us a history lesson. Boy, I remember that place. Brrrr!"

Fort Point nestled under a small arch on the south side of the bridge; it was built during the Civil War to protect California from attack by sea. Ariel looked away as the plane climbed. She settled into her seat, holding a magazine, but not really looking at it. The sisters sat quietly together, alone in their grief, and almost oblivious to the passengers around them. Exhausted, they slept most of the way across the continent and woke up when the steward alerted them to the dinner service. It was a smooth flight and hardly any turbulence at all. It was a little past 6:00 p.m. Wednesday evening when they saw the lights of New York City as the plane came in for a landing at La Guardia Airport.

They waited in the plane as passengers to New York disembarked and passengers bound for England got aboard. Soon the pilot was giving the weather of eight degrees above zero, a cold February evening with snow forecast. It would be ten hours to London.

The women planned to stay at Browns Hotel in London for a day and night before catching a shuttle to Inverness. It would give them a chance to rest and catch a morning flight into Inverness. They didn't want their grandparents to meet them, but they had insisted. They compromised by arriving at 10:00 a.m. on Saturday and were met by Sibyl and Robyn, two eightyish seniors who could out walk and out talk them as they gathered their luggage and headed for the ancient Land Rover.

"Come along, and we'll soon be home and have a nice restorative cup of tea. Robyn, do be careful, you should let the porter take the bags." Sibyl was robust and ruddy cheeked just like Robyn. The two of them were about the same height, though Sibyl was the taller by an inch. At five feet eight inches, she was slim but sturdy, and Robyn had a bit of a roundness about him.

Ariel was exhausted from the stress she was under and was grateful to her grandmother and grandfather for meeting them. She was reassured that the trip wasn't too much for them when they told her they had driven in yesterday. They'd made a day of visiting around their favorite places in Inverness and topped it off by having dinner and breakfast in their favorite pub, the Iron Horse. Ariel watched the countryside slide by as she relaxed in the Land Rover that looked suspiciously like the one they had when she left Scotland as a toddler. Ariel hoped that her grandparents would like the book she had chosen for them while browsing through a shop near the hotel. They'd spent most of the day in their room resting, but Ariel wanted to get them something. Ariel browsed for hours before selecting just the perfect book, a Rosemunde Pilcher book about the town of Dornoch that had been the Pilcher's hometown for ages.

Lily was listening and chatting non-stop and answering their questions. Then finally, they were there. The ancient Rover crept up the hill and inched its way through a cope of trees, finally coming out into the startling beauty of the North Sea glistening like diamonds. Ariel laughed as she looked down into the small town of Dornoch and pointed out all that she could remember to Lily who had never been there.

"Look, Lily, there's the church where I was baptized. Oh, I'm so glad to be here. Thank you, Grandma and Grandpa, for taking us in. I don't know what we would have done if you hadn't been able to have us." Her grandmother reached back across the front seat and squeezed her hand.

"Ariel, you and Lily are most welcome. We talk of you often and wondered what you were doing. The letter at Christmas was wonderful but not nearly enough. I'm so glad you thought to come here." She smiled at both of them and then turned back to direct Robyn to stop at the deli where she had to pick up an order of sliced turkey and bread for their lunch. The stop at the deli just took a few minutes, and Ariel spent the time looking out the window at the little town. It hardly looked any different at all to her, yet she knew they had all the conveniences of the internet and all.

Soon they were turning onto Brindle Drive, the drive to the Manse, and Brindle Hall loomed into view. The imposing estate house stood on a knoll overlooking the sea, weathered by the wind and salt spray into a silver gray stone. It had huge picture windows facing the water, and as the car came to a stop by the front stoop, Ariel could visualize the garden behind, snowed under right now, but in a couple of months the roses would be blooming. Sibyl kept them in big pots with wheels on them that she trundled out of the green house and into pride of place on the top of the stairs that led to the garden terraced below. The house looked just as it did when she was little. After lunch, she'd go visit the roses in the green house, as well as her grandmother's prize orchids that she knew her grandmother was addicted to growing.

Sibyl and Lily put the luncheon together in the warm kitchen around the big scrubbed kitchen table. They had just put the platter of cold cuts and bread on the table when Ariel walked in and sniffed the air.

"Oh, Grandma, you've made that wonderful French onion soup that Dad used to love so much. I hope there is a big piece of cheese in the bottom of each bowl and your croutons." Ariel went over and lifted the heavy kettle lid and peered inside. "Oh good, there's plenty of onions, too!"

Ariel put the big soup bowls on the table with big soupspoons. Everything was in its same place in the kitchen as when she was a tot and was given the job of setting the spoons on the table. Even the tablecloth was the same one, now faded to a soft rose instead of the rich red check it was when she was a child. It all felt so familiar and comfortable. Ariel was surprised that she could remember so much when she'd been so little and especially how thoughts of her mother seemed so fresh in her mind. She sighed as she sat down and cut the cheese that Sibyl gave her along with a sharp knife. She cut generous cubes of Jarlsberg cheese. Lily ladled the soup over the cheese, and Sibyl called Robyn in. He'd been listening to the noon news and arrived breathless to tell them that the forecast was for snow.

"Snow! We just left snow!" Lily and Ariel said together. They laughed and played the old childhood game of scissors and stones like they did as children when they'd spoken at the same time. Lunch was full of laughter and for a while, the whole, sorry, painful past weeks were brushed aside. Ariel was back and nothing could get to her here. She was safe. All of a sudden, she felt extremely tired and yawned mightily.

"Oh, I'm so sleepy. I'll just go lay down for a while." She kissed her grandparents and Lily and made her way up the winding staircase to the top floor and the attic bedroom she and Lily were sharing. It looked the same as it did when she stayed there after her mother had died, whitewashed walls and a light blue woven bedspread. There were twin beds with big fluffy comforters, and Ariel gratefully lay down and wrapped the goose down comforter around her. She was asleep in seconds.

Chapter 14

Lily lifted Ariel's wrist and took her pulse while Sibyl hovered anxiously next to the bed.

"How is she? Should I call the doctor? She's been sleeping for so long." Sibyl brushed Ariel's hair away from her forehead and straightened the comforter.

"I am a doctor!" Lily put Ariel's hand back under the comforter and lifted her eye. With a huge sigh, she straightened and smiled at her grandmother.

"Ariel's exhausted. Her body is forcing her to rest by sleeping. With Morgan's and Mother's deaths so close and her pregnancy, it's a wonder she's been functional at all. So far, everything seems to be all right. I'm going to sit with her, and if she doesn't wake up by—" Looking at her watch, Lily considered the twelve hours she had already slept since yesterday's lunch, "by morning, I'll call an ambulance to take her to the hospital in Inverness. She is well hydrated, and I expect nature will wake her up to use the bathroom, a pregnant woman's bladder and all. Don't worry, Grandma, she's going to be all right."

Sibyl put a warm down comforter over Lily and turned down the reading light so there was only enough light to see Ariel clearly but not strong enough for anything else. "Would you like some tea, dear?" Sibyl said from the doorway.

"No, thank you, Grandma, I'll just sit here and keep an eye on her. If I get thirsty, I'll go down and make myself a cup. Please go to bed now and don't worry. Ariel will be right as rain tomorrow."

With one last worried look at Ariel, Sibyl left the room. Lily could hear her door softly open and close on the landing of the floor below. Robyn had gone to bed about midnight, and Lily could see that her grandmother was very tired. She didn't need two patients.

At dawn, Lily woke to Ariel stirring and getting up to go to the bathroom. Lily jumped up, put her arm around her sister, and helped her into a robe before slowly walking with her down the stairs to the bathroom at the end of the hallway.

"Steady, sis, you've been off your feet for darn near twenty-four hours, so go slow and lean on me till we get you less rocky." Ariel leaned into Lily, and the two walked down the stairs, stopping often to clear the wooziness from Ariel's head.

They trekked downstairs and just a few moments later. Ariel vastly more comfortable, was bundled back to bed. Lily took her pulse, and it felt strong; Ariel again fell back to sleep almost as soon as her head hit the pillow. Reassured, Lily climbed into the twin bed across from her and whispered sweet dreams, knowing that Ariel was already back in a deep sleep. She'd be all right. She had to be!

Chapter 15

S ibyl put the phone back on the hook and immediately started planning the simple dinner that she had just invited Jackson and his mother, Claire, too. It was fortunate that they were both free for tonight. Claire was going to be here today anyway. She was Sibyl's daygirl and had been since Jackson and his brother, James, were small. A pot roast with carrots and potatoes would be easy, and Jackson loved pot roast. Sibyl couldn't wait for Ariel to meet her first cousin. Claire and Ariel's mother, Kate, were sisters.

Sibyl went down to the freezer in the old creamery just off the kitchen and took out her biggest pot roast. She had onions and carrots peeled and ready to add, and with just a few minutes in the microwave, the big hunk of meat was thawed enough to brown in her Dutch oven, a deep pot made of cast iron with porcelain coating. Hers was green with a cream inside. The Dutch oven was the perfect pot for pot roast. Sibyl expertly browned the meat and then layered onions on top. She filled the pot with a beef broth that would make delicious brown gravy. Sibyl had just popped the pot roast in the oven when Robyn stomped in from his walk with Joco out on the beach.

"Ah, that smells delicious! It smells like your wonderful pot roast. I hope that's what we're having tonight?" Robyn stomped the snow off his boots and undid Joco's leash.

"Oh, Robyn, I've a surprise for you. Jackson and Claire are coming for dinner tonight, and Jackson has invited us all over to his farm to see his newest horse. Jackson took in another rescued horse yesterday, and it's a cute little filly. Would you like to come with us before we go into town today and take a look?"

Robyn poured himself a big cup of coffee and liberally added cream and sugar. "That would be a sight to see!" He paused and thought about his projects for the day and decided that the trying out of the new mulch he had bought for the rose bushes could wait until later. Sibyl and Robyn had their coffee and Sibyl's fresh cranberry scones and chatted a while before Sibyl got up and got a tray with cups and tea and muffins to take to the girls.

It was almost ten, and she'd told Jackson that they'd be by around eleven thirty.

Chapter 16

At around 10:00 a.m., Sibyl opened the girl's door and peered in. Both the women were still in the twin beds, but they were awake and looking out the window at the brilliant white landscape.

"Oh look, Lily, at the beach! It's covered in snow, and the herring gulls are all searching and scratching for food." Ariel looked up and smiled when her grandmother came in bearing a tray with tea and scones and three cups. The three of them sat on the beds and drank their tea while Ariel assured her grandmother that she felt wonderful and ready to explore.

Sibyl put down her teacup and smiled at Lily and Ariel. "Girls, I've a surprise for you. Your cousin Jackson and his mother, Claire, are coming over tonight for pot roast. I know you've met Claire because she's in and out of the house all the time. Jackson has been wanting to meet you. Ariel, when you were a toddler, you and Jackson were playmates. I don't expect that you remember that, Ariel?"

When Ariel shook her head, Sibyl smiled at her and continued talking, "Jackson has invited us all over for a few minutes to see his newest horse. I told him we'd stop in before we go to town today and take a look at her. Jackson takes in rescued horses, and yesterday he got a little filly only two days old. The mother had been abandoned and was in such bad condition they had to put her down, but the filly has a chance to make it."

Lily was the first to jump out of bed, and she challenged Ariel to see who could get dressed the fastest.

"Oh, do hurry, Ariel! I'd love to see this filly. Can we feed it?" The two sisters hurried to dress, and by the time Sibyl had the breakfast cups and plates washed, they were ready.

Jackson's farm was just over the hill from Brindle Hall, and Robyn had the old Land Rover to Jackson's gate in about five minutes. Lily and Ariel strained to look at the neat farm and the shed row that looked to be big enough for twenty horses. Robyn drove straight into the yard and down the lane and stopped right at the shed row. Jackson came out and hugged Robyn and Sibyl and looked up expectantly; his cognac brown eyes seemed to zero in on Lily before politely switching to Ariel. The two were introduced to him, and he held Lily's hand a moment longer than necessary. Lily was startled to feel such a strong emotion when she gripped his hand. She quickly brushed the thought away on what a hunk Jackson was. After all, they were cousins. Embarrassed, her cheeks red, she followed Jackson and Robyn into the barn and to a stall in the middle of the shed where it was warmest. There were twenty horses looking out of their stalls at them, their big brown eyes staring and shy. Some of the horses looked very thin, but they all responded eagerly to Jackson's quick nuzzle and apple for a treat. Finally, they got to the filly. Jackson had a bucket with a nipple on it, and he tested the formula to make sure it was warm enough but not too warm. Ariel and Lily crowded into the birthing stall with Robyn and Sibyl and saw the tiniest little roan with a white star and four white stockings. The filly was up on wobbly legs and when Jackson offered her the bucket teat, she eagerly nursed.

Lily was overcome. "Oh, she's so little and so beautiful!" The filly had taken what nourishment the mare could provide and really didn't look too thin. Unfortunately, the mare wasn't getting any nourishment and after the filly was born, she collapsed, and they couldn't get her up again. Lily reached out and took hold of the bucket, and Jackson let her feed the filly.

"Oh, how could anyone be so cruel as to starve its mother and abandon them like that?" Lily looked at Jackson, and he shrugged.

"It's been happening pretty often. Horses take money to feed, and times have been tough for some of the small farms. The farmers, to save face, let them loose to fend for themselves. They get some nourishment from the grass, but with snow on the ground, the horses can't get to it." The filly finished the bucket, and Lily handed it to Jackson. Ariel reached out and petted the filly, and then Robyn and Sibyl took their turn rubbing its head and making soft noises of comfort to soothe the tiny animal.

Robyn and Jackson were the first out of the stall.

"You've a fine bunch of mares here, Jackson! I would never know by looking at them that they were rescued animals. What are you going to do with them all?"

Jackson walked slowly through the shed row and told them of his plans to begin a racing stable.

"Some of these horses are thoroughbreds, and with proper nourishment, I think I can breed them and have a stable of future Derby contenders." Jackson included Ariel and Lily in all of his plans, and by the time they all had walked back to the Land Rover, they were thoroughly impressed with his goals and dreams for these lovely horses. The three of them chatted and made plans to go into Dornoch and visit the cathedral and do some shopping for some silk long john's to wear under their wool slacks. Ariel would need to get hers at the maternity shop in Dornoch. Her stomach was growing so fast, she no longer could button her pants. Coming from California, the sisters hadn't expected snow though it was still considered winter in Scotland, and snow was likely for a month or more.

Chapter 17

A riel was up at first light. She sat drinking her hot tea in the kitchen, still in her warm bathrobe, and chuckled to herself as she remembered last night's dinner with Jackson and Claire and Lily. Jackson was falling all over himself to pull out the chair for Lily, and he was so smitten, he was tongue tied most of the evening. It was a wonderful evening. Ariel made a fresh pot of tea, added a plate of muffins, and took a tray up to Lily. Lily was awake and already dressed when Ariel got to the attic room.

While Ariel dressed, Sibyl went down to make Robyn's breakfast and fry a sausage or two for the sisters, and Lily got online and checked on their messages. She had asked everyone to send her a duplicate of any message they had for Ariel that concerned both sisters and the unsolved case back home. Zoe had written that they had turned the clinic upside down and had found a technician named Gordon Warner who admitted that he had done some experimental work at the clinic. Gordon was an anthologist. Lily knew what that was and it made her skin crawl as she continued reading. She scrolled down the page where Zoe had described his job for Ariel's benefit. He was a lab tech who worked with semen specimens at the infertility clinic. He performed all the procedures on both the sperm and the egg-- storing, freezing, washing, everything required to prepare it for artificial insemination of one kind or another, intrauterine or in vitro. Zoe had painted a clear picture in Lily's mind of what the man might have done to Ariel's eggs and Morgan's sperm. She didn't like what she was thinking. It made her feel kind of sick to think that he had performed some kind of a procedure on Ariel's eggs that maybe wasn't on the up and up. Zoe was talking in veiled terms about cloning. If this was what had happened, then Lily knew why Ariel was in danger. Whoever had implanted cloned eggs into her uterus was jeopardizing his or her medical license. Zoe stopped short of saying that Ariel was carrying cloned eggs, but she did say that they were continuing to investigate and interview all the personnel to see whom he was working for. So far, the man refused to divulge whom he had prepared the eggs for.

Ariel came into the room just as Lily opened up an e-mail from Riley. He was helping Ben and Julie move into the farmhouse and though they thought it wasn't necessary, they begrudgingly acknowledged that it did give them a better handle on who came in and out of the front gates. Lily shared the e-mail with her and then quickly turned off the computer before she could see the message from Zoe. Both of the sisters sniffed the air as they walked down the stair toward the kitchen. The sausages were making their mouths water, and they were soon digging into a plate of over easy eggs, sausage, and hot homemade biscuits

Lily helped Sibyl with the cleanup, and then the three women headed out with Lily driving.

"We're going to Mabel's mom's shop first for you, Ariel, and she'll get you outfitted in some warmer pants and maybe a big cable sweater. They are so big you could probably wear it till spring. Okay, Lily, just turn right at the next corner and then park wherever you can. Mabel's is in the middle of the block on the left." Sibyl pointed to an empty parking slot and sighed in satisfaction as Lily turned off the car motor.

Ariel looked at the shop and all of the obviously pregnant mannequins and laughed! "I just can't see myself with a big belly yet, and I hope I can get away with loose sweaters, sweats, and pants for a while yet!" Lily parked the big old Land Rover, and Ariel got awkwardly out of the car and held the door to help Sibyl out.

It was two hours later that they came out of the shop loaded with packages, and Sibyl proposed that they go down to the little pub on the corner after dropping their bundles in the car boot. Lily seconded it, so the three women locked up the trunk of the car, or boot as Sibyl called it, and headed to the Smokey Lantern. They grabbed the only vacant booth available, and Ariel sighed when she sat down. It was tiring to try on the new clothing, but she was happy with the new warm sweater in a soft pink, the black pants, and a couple of sweat suits that had the cutout with the elastic front of a traditional maternity pant. She could wear the sweats as her around-the-house clothes to keep warm and snug in the big farm manse. Brindle was well built, but there were drafts, and Ariel found that she wore layers of clothes to keep warm. Of course, when they got used to the change of weather, it would be warmer. The waitress came over with menus and took their orders of warm vegetable soup with wide noodles and big turkey sandwiches with cheese on them.

Sibyl was as hungry as they were, and they didn't talk until they had eaten their fill. After the last bit was devoured, and Sibyl and Lily were enjoying a pint of Guinness dark beer while Ariel sipped a coke, Sibyl looked at Lily who had just jumped straight out of her chair when a car backfired out on the street.

"Lily, my dear, your nerves are shot. I thought you were going to dive under the table after that car backfired. I wish you'd put in for early deployment back to the states. You're under too much stress. Heaven knows what you're going to be walking into in Iraq. Promise me you'll think about it. Ariel could use your support too." She put her hand quietly over Lily's as Lily looked down at her liver-spotted hands and squeezed them.

"I'm sorry, but when I'm at the hospital, I duck and cover whenever there is a loud noise. It's instinctual, and I know I will keep doing it for months after I'm finally deployed back to the states in September. I have to go back and help as I've been trained to do. I wouldn't feel right about opting out before the rest of my unit is discharged. We started together, and I want to go home when they all are able to come with me. We've all come together and are so close. I can't explain how close you get to your buddies when you're in a war zone. You're very life depends on it, and, well maybe this isn't the time to tell you, but I have a wonderful friend there. He's a doctor too, and we work together every day. I've missed Matt so much since I came home on emergency leave. He writes to me via e-mail, but it seems that he's as smitten with me as I am with him. Before I left the hospital, he asked me to marry him when he gets stateside, and I'm going to tell him yes." Lily smiled at both Ariel and her grandmother and took a deep swig of her beer.

Ariel was the first to recover and start hammering questions at her, "What's Matt's last name, and why haven't you said anything to me before?"

"I haven't had much opportunity to tell you before this. His last name's McConnell. With Mom's and Morgan's deaths and all the arrangements and then flying straight over here, it's been on the back burner. I couldn't tell you till I knew you were stronger, and we could talk about me leaving you next week." Lily finished her beer and wiped her mouth with a napkin. She smiled at them both and said. "Come on, no long faces, we have almost ten days before I have to leave, and there are things to see and places to go. Are you up to showing me the cathedral?"

"Despite a history of Viking raids and family vendettas that the town of Dornoch endured up to and including the Viking raids in the ninth century, the stately Dornoch Cathedral had been an enduring presence in this tiny Burg since the thirteenth century. The Bishop of Caithness, Gilbert of Moravia, began work on the magnificent sandstone cathedral, and it's a lasting tribute to the achievements of a remarkable man. The Dornoch Cathedral is the most northerly cathedral on the mainland." Lily read the guidebook aloud to Ariel and her grandmother, causing them to laugh at her singsong tour guide manner.

Smiling, Lily stood up and held the chair for her grandmother as she and Ariel got up. After putting her coat back on, Ariel reached over to her sister and gave her a big hug.

"I'm happy for you, sis. I just wish you were coming home with me and not going to a war zone. He better be good to you, this Matthew McConnell. I can't wait to meet him. Will you be married right away or come home first?"

"We haven't gotten that far yet. I'll see to that when I see him. He'll be meeting me at the airport, according to his last e-mail."

The three women walked out of the pub and straight to their car that had an inch of snow on the windscreen. Lily scrapped it off with her credit card, and the three set off with a grinding of gears and a lurch forward. Lily was a good driver but not used to old clutches. She drove automatic transmissions whenever she had need of transportation around the hospital. They used little service cars that were smaller than a Volkswagen and operated with plug-in batteries. Wherever she stopped, she'd just plug it in to a special 220 jack.

The cathedral was close by, and it only took a minute to find a car park, as Sibyl called the parking lot. The names like windscreen for windshield and car park were quaint, but not too different from American terms.

Lily drove in to the Dornoch Cathedral car park and joined one of the last tours of the day. The sanctuary was a lovely soft cream color that with the afternoon light streaming through the leaded stained glass window showed patterns of blue, green, red, and yellow shards of light. There were two huge chandeliers hanging on the side of the altar, and you looked up at a series of arches soaring fifty feet or higher in the air. It drew your eyes up to the front of the church where the arches were built to meet above the altar.

After looking at all of the windows with scenes of the Bible and also some of nature and the animals of the forest, they walked outside among the tombstones in the cemetery. Sibyl led them to Ariel's mother's grave. The stone was polished black and gray granite. It simply read Kathryn Rosemary Murray Frazer, age 35 years. Born 1939--Died 1974. Ariel was startled to see that her mother was exactly her age when she died. She reached out, touched the stone, and put a small pebble that she'd picked up on the stone to show that the grave had been visited. Ariel was quiet for the rest of their tour, until they got in the Land Rover and started back to Brindle Hall Manse.

"Grandma Frazer, what did my mother die of that my father never would talk of it?" Ariel asked, turning in her seat to look back at her grandmother.

Sibyl looked into Ariel's eyes and struggled to keep the control of her feelings from spilling over.

"Kate drowned. Paul and Kate had gone out on his sailboat in the cold of winter, and a big squall blew the boat over on its keel. Kate had just come on deck to bring Paul some hot coffee when she was swept over into the frigid water. By the time Paul got control of the boat and had gone after her and pulled her from the frigid water, she had stopped breathing. He got her to the hospital as fast as he could, but they couldn't revive her. Paul really never forgave himself for taking her out in that terrible storm."

"But where was I? Wasn't I with them?" Ariel voice trembled with emotion as she confronted her grandmother.

"No, you were with me at Brindle Hall. I kept you that day, because you were so little, and they thought you'd be at risk, but for some reason they loved to go out in stormy weather and had gone out this same way ever since they met. I think it reminded them of their carefree courting days, and they used the boat to keep the romance in their marriage."

Lily listened as she drove the car expertly back to Brindle Hall where they could see Robyn standing in the window overlooking the roadway watching for them. He waved as the car turned in the drive and braked to a stop. The wind was fierce as they got out of the car and raced for the front door. Robyn had the door open and a blast of warm heat greeted them.

"I've lit the fire, and I've a hot toddy ready for you all. It's a devil of a day. I knew you'd be frozen when you got back. Come, come, now and let's get you in front of the fire." Robyn grabbed Sibyl and helped her into the house and out of her coat as Ariel and Lily trailed behind. The fire was roaring, and Robyn had pulled chairs closer to the heat. As the women sat down and warmed themselves around the fireplace, Robyn quickly poured hot water from the teakettle simmering on the fireplace warming shelf into huge cups filled with toddy mix and whiskey for Sibyl and Lily and plain toddy mix without the booze for Ariel. Robyn bustled about and informed them that he had prepared his famous chowder in a white sauce with plenty of fish, oysters, and clams. They're would be hot fresh crusty bread dripping with butter to sop up the soup.

Robyn loved to cook, and if truth were told, he was a better cook than Sibyl, often surprising her with a wonderful supper when she'd been out all day in the cold shopping. Robyn listened intently as they described their day of shopping for warm clothes and their visit to the cathedral and Kate's grave.

"Oh, Kate was a one; she was so excited about going out with Paul that last day. I'll never forget her coming to me and giving me a big hug and kiss good-bye, and it was good-bye. In a flash, she was gone, and you were without your mother, such a wee bairn you were. You were just lost without her. We did what we could to help Paul, and the two of you stayed with us for a fortnight until after the funeral, when Paul decided to go to America. Oh, it was with such a heavy heart that we said good-bye to you. We didn't see you again until you were eighteen and then Paul himself was gone, but when we visited the almond farm and met Sarah, we were reassured that you were well-loved by her and your half siblings. We made do with letters and the telephone. Paul called us every month but we should have made the trip. We missed so much of your growing-up." Robyn ran out of words and sat down with a small grunt. It was if he was re-living that dreadful time in his mind, and it disturbed him greatly. They all lapsed into silence and stared at the flames, quietly sipping their toddies.

Lily broke the silence by telling everyone that she had found an ob-gyn for Ariel, and she had made an appointment for her for the very next day. "Dr. Andrea Forbes is the leading neonatal doctor in Scotland, and I've conferred with her on your case. She's agreed to take you on as her patient." Lily took a breath and looked hopefully at Ariel.

"That was wonderful of you, Lily. I know I need to go and establish myself with someone. I'm not sure I'm ready to do that as early as tomorrow though."

"But Ariel, I'm leaving next week, and I wanted to be with

you. Please do this for me. I need to know you're okay, and that there isn't any danger of miscarriage with all you've gone through. I'm worried, and I won't be able to go next week if I feel so worried. Please, Ariel?" Lily reached out, grabbed Ariel's hand, and held it gently as she finished pleading with her.

"Okay, Lily, I'll force myself, but only for you and the fact that I don't want you worrying about me. You've enough to deal with once you get back to your hospital and have to deal with the mess in Iraq." Ariel set down her cup, got up, and stretched.

"Robyn, I'm starved, and your chowder smells wonderful. Let's eat!" Ariel smiled and reached over to her grandfather and helped him out of his chair. Lily, laughing, grabbed Sibyl's hand and helped her up too. The family members walked together to the dining room and sat around the round pedestal table as Robyn did the honors and ladled the soup, hot and fragrant, of fresh chowder into their soup bowls.

Ariel sighed as she sipped the delicious chowder. "Hum, this is wonderful, Grandpa Robyn." Sibyl and Lily looked briefly at each other, and Lily smiled her encouragement that Ariel was going to be okay. After filling themselves and getting out the cards, the sisters taught Sibyl and Robyn how to play Texas Hold'em, a poker card game that was all the rage in California. After a few hands, Ariel yawned greatly, cheerfully folded her hand, and said she was going to bed.

Lily laughed and said. "Now we have three winners; all we have to do is see who comes in first place, second, and third."

Ariel was asleep as soon as her head hit the pillow. She slept straight through the night and was fresh and wide awake early, before anyone else. Ariel got up and went down to the kitchen. She had fresh coffee perking and was frying bacon when Sibyl came down.

"Oh, what a treat, having someone else fix breakfast. Thank

you, my dear!" The two women sat down together with their coffee--decaf for Ariel--bacon, and toast and shared the morning paper together. All you could hear was the munching of toast and bacon and the slurping as they sipped their coffee.

After breakfast, Sibyl started the laundry. Though she had a dryer, she preferred hanging the sheets and towels outside in the fresh air. Sibyl lugged the basket out onto the back porch and proceeded to hang everything up on her pulley clothesline. Sometimes she had to bring them back in still damp, to dry in the electric dryer, but she thought that at least they would smell fresh from the sea breeze that blew from the North Sea. Ariel cleared up the dishes and put more coffee on as she heard Robyn and Lily talking quietly when they came downstairs.

They sat down to fresh bacon and toast, and Lily got a great jar of Limburger cheese out of the refrigerator. The cheese smelled terrible and had the consistency of peanut butter. Lily spread it thinly for both herself and Robyn. They both loved to make a bacon and cheese sandwich with toast. Lily laughed as she saw Robyn add extra cheese to his sandwich and remembered how he had taught her how to make these sandwiches when he came to America for her father's funeral with Sibyl. They were the only ones in the family who could stomach them for breakfast.

Chapter 18

ily drove Ariel to Andrea Forbes' office at eleven o'clock. Andrea was only about forty and was friendly and efficient. The examination was quickly over. Andrea pulled off her gloves and smiled at Ariel.

"Everything looks good, but I'm going to do an ultrasound to check the fetus for size. You either have a very large baby, or there may be more than one." At that, Ariel's eyes got huge.

"What do you mean more than one?" Andrea held her hand a moment and looked into her eyes. "I think that your uterus is too large for a sixteen-week pregnancy, so either the dates are off, or there's more than one baby in there. We will know in a moment."

The ultrasound machine was brought in and set up, and Dr. Forbes rubbed some kind of petroleum jelly over her abdomen. She gently moved the ultrasound wand over her belly and looked at the picture on the screen. Suddenly, two round bald heads appeared on the on the screen, no bigger than a couple of Os.

"Ah, ha! I was right. Look here, Ariel!" Dr. Forbes moved the monitor toward Ariel so she could see. Ariel and Lily both peered closely at the black and white image of two little forms wiggling around in a pool of water like a couple of fish.

"Oh my God, Lily, what in the world am I going to do with two babies?" Ariel looked shocked and stared at her sister speechless. Lily leaned over and kissed Ariel, smiling at her with joy!

"You're going to be a wonderful mother, big sister. Look how you took care of Mark and remember what a little hellion I was, always wanting to get in and explore, causing you and Mom to wring your hands at my shenanigans." Lily patted Ariel and looked back at the sonogram. "Can you tell yet what they are?"

"No, Lily, don't tell me. I want to be surprised." Ariel put her hands over her ears and closed her eyes. Lily peered closely at the monitor and grinned as Dr. Forbes nodded.

Dr. Forbes went over Ariel's diet and gave her some more prenatal vitamins. Just as Dr. Forbes got off her stool to leave Ariel to dress, Ariel asked her a question.

"How do you manage the pain of the delivery? Do you use hypnosis?"

"No, I don't. I haven't been trained in it, so it's outside my scope of practice, but I do use an epidural. My patients tell me that it's very satisfactory. I hope that would be all right with you." Ariel nodded, and Lily looked at her astounded!

"Hypnosis! Where did you ever get an idea like that?" Lily helped Ariel get into her clothes and the subject was dropped when Ariel just shrugged her shoulders.

"I must have read about it at some time."

Ariel was in a daze and dressed herself on automatic.

Ariel was still stunned speechless as they walked out of the doctor's office with her next appointment card clutched in her hands. It wasn't until Lily steered her to the Land Rover, helped her inside, and buttoned her seat belt that Ariel spoke.

"My God, Lily, I just can't believe this. What am I going to tell Grandma and Grandpa?"

"The truth. They'll be overjoyed, and you know they will help you all they can! You're going to be surrounded with love, and we all will do what we can to help. I'll be home in September for a while, and we can manage together. I promise you that you won't regret having them, and they will be a blessing for you."

Lily drove Ariel quickly back to their grandparents' home and sat with her as she explained that there wouldn't be one new mouth to feed but two!

Sibyl looked over at Robyn, and the two turned their faces in unison to Ariel and Lily and smiled.

Sibyl looked right into Ariel's eyes. "Ariel, you're not to worry. We are going to help you however you need it, and I think having two little wee ones is an extra blessing from God. Now, you eat up all of your tea, because you're not just eating for two, you're eating for three!" Sibyl beamed and dabbed her eyes with Robyn's big white handkerchief, then passed Ariel a plate of scones homemade with raisins and orange peel as well as a bowl of clotted cream to put on them.

Both Lily and Ariel retired to their attic bedroom and lay sprawled on their beds, exhausted from the events of the day. Finding out you'd not only be an aunt of one baby but of twins was mind boggling to Lily. She lay with her eyes shut and planned the surprise that she was going to leave for Ariel. She'd be leaving for Iraq in less than a week, and there was so much to do before she left. Lily made a mental list and vowed to go to town early tomorrow morning on the pretext that she wanted to buy herself some new makeup, which she did need anyway. Then she'd go back to the Motherhood shop and buy "her" twins enough layette and diapers to last until she got home in September. By then, they'd have outgrown layette size and be ready for bigger duds. Lily meant to spoil the little darlings good and proper.

The week went by in a whirl of activity. Lily did a mammoth shopping and had everything gift wrapped and squirreled away with Sibyl's help. Sibyl would make sure that Ariel got the packages as soon as the babies were born.

Chapter 19

It was with both sadness and joy that Lily arranged her flight back to Iraq. She hated to leave Ariel and her grandparents, but she was looking forward to seeing Matt, and it would only be six months before both she and Matt would be sent back to the states and free to start their civilian lives again.

Lily was kept busy for most of the week packing and making sure that her business dealings were sound before she went back on duty. She had arranged for her inheritance from her mother to be invested in tax-free municipals that took some overseas phone calls to check on, but finally it was time to leave. The sisters walked around the still-frozen garden and talked.

"Lily, I wish you didn't have to go. It's so dangerous over there, and I need you so much."

Ariel held her sister's hand tightly, and they hugged each other close as well, willing the strength to flow between them. They had always been strong when they were together, but now each one had to face their life without each other.

Robyn came around the front of the hall and tooted his horn. Lily's bags were stacked, ready to pack into the boot of the Land Rover. The whole family was going to go to the airport with Lily. Sibyl bustled around putting on her car coat and scarf. Finally, the three women were settled in the car, and Robyn drove expertly down the lane and turned left toward A-9 highway to Inverness airport. It would take an hour, and the flight would be at a civil

1:00 p.m. in the afternoon. They were leaving at 9:00 a.m. to get there in plenty of time, and they'd have luncheon together at the airport. Lily was quiet and so were the others as they drove along the highway. Big drifts of snow from the plow were piled on either side, making it look like a toboggan racetrack.

Robyn drove directly to short term parking and let the three women off right by the gate. He'd park and then walk over to the terminal to meet them. Robyn had a worried frown on his face that he had successfully hidden from the women, but now alone and in the parked car he let down his defenses and lay his head on the steering wheel. "Lord, protect Lily and bring her back to us safely." The prayer was short but earnest, and he sighed deeply as he got out of the Land Rover and locked the door.

Robyn met Lily, Ariel, and Sibyl inside the airline terminal, and Lily went up to the window and scanned her boarding pass. With everything a go, Lily carefully put her passport and military papers in her backpack and turned to the little group waiting just outside the roped area where passengers handled the details of boarding passes and checking of luggage. She would be flying commercial to Ramstein, Germany and then would board a military transport to Iraq. Robyn gathered the women together, herded them towards the small café, and ordered hot tea and scones for them all. It was hard waiting for Lily to leave, and he knew that Ariel and Sibyl were trying to keep from crying.

Robyn looked at his watch and looked up at Lily. She picked up her backpack, kissed them all, and told them to let her say her good-byes right here where she could picture them all having tea and scones. She didn't want any long faces and long good-byes, so she quickly moved into the corridor and waved gaily as she walked down the corridor and left them at the tea. Ariel and Sibyl quietly sniffed and wiped their eyes with their hankies while Robyn sniffed furiously.

Chapter 20

I was a quiet group that got back into the Land Rover and headed back to Dornoch. When Brindle Hall appeared, everyone sighed with relief. As Robyn took the car back into the big barn behind Brindle Hall, Sibyl and Ariel got busy building a big fire in the fireplace and putting on a supper of sausage and eggs fried on the Aga stove, with fresh coffee and toast. It was a quick supper, and the Aga had warmed the kitchen to a nice temperature. The warm air lulled everyone, and nobody felt much like talking.

Ariel helped Sibyl clear the table and do the dishes before she retired to her room in the attic to e-mail Mark, Zoe, and Riley that Lily had gotten safely off and was headed back to Iraq. Ariel sent a group e-mail to them all and was relieved that the day was over at last. She went downstairs to say goodnight to Robyn and Sibyl, who were having hot chocolate in front of the huge fireplace in the living room. Ariel was too tired to stay up and visit with them, so she said her goodnights and went back up to the now lonely attic room, stripped of Lily's presence. The moon shown in the dormer window, and Ariel was tucked under the down comforter. She said a prayer of safety for Lily as the moon shown across her bed. She closed her eyes and was asleep before 9:00 p.m.

It was almost nine in the morning when Ariel opened her eyes and listened, wondering what had woken her. Then she heard it again. A Herring gull was screaming outside her window, braving the cold snow-covered roof to land with a thud above Ariel's attic room. The gulls were snow white with bright yellow beaks, one of the first birds except the black Rooks to show their faces this early in the year.

The sun was shining, and a feeling of spring was in the air. It was the beginning of March, and Ariel couldn't wait until the earth warmed up and the hothouse roses could be placed in Sibyl's garden. Her grandmother was going to add some American Beauties to her collection, and yesterday morning, Ariel had found her in the kitchen surrounded with catalogs looking for the new varieties, drinking her coffee in sheer bliss. She always had the prettiest roses in the village and won for Best Rose over fifteen times in the last twenty years at the summer fair. Roses were her favorite flower, and she had passed on the love of them to Ariel. Back at the almond farm, Ben and Julie would have already mulched and weeded Ariel's roses. Spring came early to the farm, and it made Ariel homesick to think of her home. Zoe and Riley kept her up-to-date on events at home and Mark too, though he was not as good at e-mailing as Riley was.

Ariel had asked Riley how the investigation was going, and he wrote that Zoe and David were working hard on it and felt that their investigation of the clinic was almost wrapped up. Nothing could be found to indicate a problem at the clinic as her mother Sarah had suggested, and Zoe felt that if things stayed as quiet as they were at the moment that Ariel could come home possibly as early as June. Ariel was fearful and at the same time elated. She was ready to get back to her work and wanted to get her caseload back under her control before she'd have to take her maternity leave. Ariel threw the covers off her body and shoved her feet into her slippers. A warm cashmere bathrobe lay on the foot of the bed, and she wrapped it around her.

Before she went down to breakfast, Ariel started up her computer and went into her e-mail account. There wasn't a message yet from Lily to tell her she was there safe and sound, but Ariel really didn't expect one until sometime after dinner tonight. There was one from Zoe explaining the progress of her investigation into the death of her mother and Morgan. Based on trace evidence taken from both bodies, there were two separate perpetrators involved. The methods of each one was also entirely different. With Sarah, the perpetrator used a knife with expert skill, and with Morgan, the cause of death was blunt force trauma and suffocation from the fire. So Zoe cautioned Ariel to stay away until they could identify Sarah's and Morgan's murderers. It could be anybody, and right now, there would be no way to protect her. Riley's e-mail filled her in on his days and asked her what the doctor had said about her pregnancy. Riley was worried that the trauma of the two murders might cause a miscarriage and warned Ariel to keep her feet up and take it easy. Ariel chuckled as she sent a group e-mail to Zoe, Mark, Riley, and Ben and Julie announcing that she was carrying twins and all was well. Ariel's e-mail described her feelings.

"I guess I'm all right, just absolutely shocked at the idea of twins, but so far the doctor says, I'm doing well, and the sonogram showed two cute, little, bald heads. I wish I was home with all of you, and that Lily was home too. Grandma and Grandpa are wonderful to me, and I can't thank them enough for having me, but I want to come home. I'm giving you fair notice that I'm not having these babies without you, and unless you all come here, I'll have to come home by the beginning of June. I am due about the Fourth of July, and the airlines won't let me fly after eight months. So get cracking and find the bastards that killed Sarah and Morgan. I warn you that I'll be home in June no matter what, and I'll take my chances." Ariel ended the message and sent it quickly before she could change her mind. She was determined to get home as soon as she could, and June was her deadline.

Chapter 21

By the time Ariel got down to the kitchen, Sibyl already had the coffee perking and bacon frying. Ariel made toast and spread it with butter and marmalade, and Robyn joined them just as Sibyl took the bacon off the grill.

"Perfect timing, my dear," she said to him as she gave him her cheek for a quick kiss. Ariel got a kiss too, then Robyn sat down with the paper, and all was quiet except for the chewing of the bacon and slurping of the coffee. Breakfast was simple, and everyone had their special part of the paper they read first.

After Ariel helped clear the table and dry the few dishes and cups, Sibyl asked her if she would like to walk down by the sea with her and Joco. Joco needed a run, and Sibyl wanted company. The March breeze was warmer than it had been, the temperature was in the mid forties, and the sun was shining.

Ariel smiled and hugged her grandmother. "Yes I'd love to walk with you. I'll just go get my sweats on and be right with you." Ariel went up to her little attic room, changed into warm sweats, and picked up her room, swooping all the dirty clothes into a basket to bring down to the laundry and set to washing while they walked.

It was near ten o'clock by the time Ariel and Sibyl, with Joco straining on his leash, set out and down the cliff path toward the sea. There were still some icy puddles, and Joco had to walk across them, cracking them, and sometimes falling right into the ice-cold water. Finally, Sibyl unhooked the dog from his leash, and the bundle of brown fur scampered down and out into the rolling sea, trying to catch a wave with his teeth. By the time Ariel and Sibyl had gotten down to the sand and found a wind sheltered spot to lay out their red plaid blanket, Joco was soaked and tired and came up and flopped down on the blanket, shaking himself as he rolled around, spraying icy water all over Sibyl and Ariel.

"Joco! Stop it, boy, you little rascal. Look at you shaking with cold, and we've only just gotten here. Well, you'll just have to lie in the sun and dry out. I'm not ready to climb up the cliff yet." Joco looked sadly at Sibyl and buried his nose in the blanket with his rear end sticking up. He looked so funny that both Ariel and her grandmother laughed at the naughty dog.

Ariel got comfortable on the blanket and looked out at the sea. It was quiet for a moment, and Ariel loved hearing the rush of the waves hitting the shore. Sibyl put her hand over her brows and pointed out to sea where Jackson Ferguson had his small fishing boat anchored for fishing. Jackson was six feet four and well built with a long slim body that looked like a nice long drink of water. If he wasn't fishing, Jackson was working the farm, growing fresh produce and taking care of his horses. His horses were his relaxation, and he loved to comb and curry them. Someday, he'd have a stable for his secret passion, Arabian horses, but it would take rebuilding the stables and making them first rate. He'd board horses and maybe if luck came his way, he'd be able buy an Arabian and participate in the Derby Race. He had several Arabians that he was excited about. The word was out that Jackson Ferguson was good with horses, and he had a couple of fine horses he was boarding.

Sibyl and Ariel waved at the boat until it went over the

horizon off to deeper fishing grounds.

"That's a fine young man. I don't know what Robyn and I would have done without him. He helped Robyn with Brindle Hall when he was a teen, and he's kept us in fresh fish at least twice a week for years. Claire is real proud of him. He has been so good to her. I've hoped he would find someone who shared his dreams and helped bring some grandbabies for Claire. She's resigned herself that he'd be a bachelor all his life, but he just might surprise her some day. I certainly hope so." Sibyl sighed and smiled at Ariel.

Sibyl brought out a thermos of hot coffee and poured two cups. From inside her car coat, she pulled out a plastic baggie jammed with homemade oatmeal cookies and spread them on the makeshift tablecloth made up of Ariel's head scarf. The two munched and slurped in silence. Finally, Sibyl began the conversation she had been dreading and yet needed to have with her granddaughter.

"Ariel, how are you feeling, my dear? I hesitate to bother you if you'd rather not talk about it, but sometimes it's good to tell someone who loves you deeply what you're going through, much easier to share it together than stand all alone. Now that Lily has gone back to Iraq, I want you to know that we are here to listen and console you."

Ariel reached over and hugged her grandmother and felt her frailness, and yet she was as strong as steel. Leaning into her, she thought of how to tell her grandmother of the pain of the past month when she had lost the only mother she had ever known and her husband in one terrible week.

"It was horrible. I was doing all right with Lily to prop me up, but since she left too, I feel so devastated and alone." She hurried to reassure her grandmother that Sibyl and Robyn had been wonderful, but she felt she needed to be alone for a while to pick up her life and come to terms with Morgan's death and the two new lives within her.

"I thought it was what you were being so quiet about. Come with me, I want to show you something." Sibyl moved purposefully down an overgrown path that moved over the edge of the sand and around a bend on the beach. When the two women were breathless with the hike and Ariel felt she must stop and rest, her grandmother stopped and pointed to a dear little cottage nestled on the edge of the beach. Its windows were blank and unseeing. Sibyl led Ariel to a wooden bench overlooking the sea at the back of the cottage

"This is where I spent a few months after my first husband died. Oh yes, I was married before your grandfather Robyn, but it was during the war, and we had such a short time together before Normandy. He was a pilot for the RAF, and I thought he was dashing in his uniform. He was sent to us for billeting. All of Scotland had airmen living with them. My parents had Charles, and they adored him. He was charming and steady, and I fell deliciously in love with him. Charles Andrew Winslow swept me off my feet, and I was a starry-eyed war bride. We came to the beach house and made it into a cozy warm home with an iron hearth and a wee kitchen and a small bedroom. It was our nest for as long as we had, and it turns out that we didn't have but six months together. I'll never forget him saying good-bye to me in the wee hours of the morning, and then a car arrived, picked him up, and that was that. I received a telegram less than a month later informing me that Charles had been killed in the Normandy Invasion. I was inconsolable, and I lived in the beach house on my own. My parents were very supportive, and they'd draw me up to the house for supper, but I wanted to be alone. But I didn't count on Robyn's persistence. Robyn had been assigned to my parent's home, and when he was off duty, he'd walk the beach. He came upon me sitting looking out to sea and just sat himself down and started talking to me.

"He told me everything that was happening in London and the fierce battles going on during the Blitz when London was being pounded into the ground by the Germans, and yet he also laughed and joked and told me how everyone made the best of their life, just as they were. They'd arrange parties and dancing, and the sirens would roar in the middle of the dinner, and they'd all run down to the basement and huddle together, bringing with them plenty of spirit and spirits with them. The hostess would hand the guests trays of food, and they'd all spend their time down in the cellar, eating by candlelight and sometimes passing the bottle if there wasn't time for glasses. Robyn wormed his way into my heart with no encouragement from me. I held off. I didn't want to lose anyone else, but he was persistent, and when he was away, packages arrived for me filled with sweets and chocolate bars. I still wouldn't be swayed, and it wasn't until after D-day that I began to hope that he'd come back safe and sound. The beach house was a sanctuary for me, and now I offer it to you."

She got up after her long speech and holding Ariel's hand, she walked her to the front door. She had a huge key that turned the lock easily, like it had been kept oiled, and when they stepped into the beach house, though it was cold, it was dry, and the house was snug against the wind. Ariel explored the living room with the fireplace and a load of dry logs and kindling stacked by the hearth. The kitchen was clean, and the appliances hummed softly. When she walked into the little bedroom and flicked on the lights, the room came out of the darkness with a riot of bright red plaid blankets and a feather comforter lay folded at the foot of the bed. She could step right in and live there.

Sibyl smiled at her. "I've always kept the beach house ready for extra company, or sometimes we let it during the summer, but it's sat empty for a while now. I've thought of offering it to you when I sensed that you needed a place to be and heal. This little cottage helped me to heal, and I never thought I would. I would sit on the sun porch and watch the waves pound. When weather permitted, I'd walk. I had a little dog a Terrier mix I called Josh. He was great company and for a long time, that's all I wanted--a quiet little house and nobody to interfere with me.

"My parents were wonderful and would leave me to myself. Mother would send me baskets of fresh eggs and whatever they could get with the ration cards. She kept a few chickens, so she always had eggs, and often that's all I'd have for my supper. After a while though, I helped her with the canning. Mother had a big garden and fruit trees. In the summer, I'd help her can tomatoes, beans, peas, and corn, and we'd pick apples and make apple butter as well as canning pie-ready apples with sugar and cinnamon. I still can the apples that way. Now we have the freezer, and the food is so much fresher. So for vegetables, I put them up in air-free freezer bags. We eat out of the freezer almost all winter." She stopped talking and looked at Ariel hopefully. "Do you like it?" she asked softly.

Ariel smiled her first huge smile since before Sarah's and Morgan's deaths and gave her grandmother a huge hug, tears streaming down her face. "I'm speechless. Thank you for understanding. Would you mind if I moved in right away? It just feels so right, and I'm so grateful to you, Grandma. I never knew about Charles, and I'm so sorry that I didn't get to know him, and that you didn't have much time together before he died. But I know that just as Robyn's perfect for you, that Charles would have been someone very special too." Ariel thought of the short time she and Morgan had been married and discovered that she had a feeling of gratitude that they had had ten years together.

Chapter 22

It didn't take Ariel long to wash up all of her clothes, dry, and fold them. She put them in the Land Rover with a few bits and pieces that Sibyl pressed on her for comfort. It was late that afternoon by the time the clothes were dry, and she'd emptied out the little attic room of her presence. She looked around with mental pictures of Lily lying on the bed sharing her thoughts with Ariel. She'd finally come clean about her fears of working in the hospital in Iraq and described how everyone would tense up when the air raid sirens would go off and the visible relaxation and joking that went on when the all clear was sounded. Ariel was so worried about Lily, and the memories of her here in this little room were so sharp that it would be a relief to go to the beach house. Just as it was a relief to be away from the yellow farmhouse and her life in Columbia with its memories of Sarah and Morgan so fresh and raw. And though Sibyl and Robyn pressed her to stay for dinner, she told them that she'd be fine with the groceries that she planned to buy.

After arranging her clothing in the closet and drawers and making a list of everything that she would need, she got into the Land Rover and went into town to the local grocery. There wasn't a huge choice, but it was adequate, and she soon had a basket filled with Jarlsberg cheese, a loaf of fresh- baked rye bread, eggs, coffee, and tea, as well as fresh fruit and a few tins of vegetables. There wasn't much of a selection of greens just yet, but she did find a nice cabbage and with the apples and raisins, she could make a crispy coleslaw.

By the time she'd driven back to the beach house, turned down the rutted lane that met her grandparents' lane, and passed her cousin Jackson's farm, she was hungry. After unloading the groceries, she made herself a cheese sandwich, munched an apple, and a downed a cup of Earl Gray tea. She felt restored and was ready to go back to her grandparents and return the car. She'd think about a little car of her own that wouldn't be too expensive but that would get her around to her appointments--so that she would be free to roam the countryside. The next time she saw Jackson, she'd ask him where to look for one.

Ariel put her laptop computer on the little desk on the sun porch that overlooked the sea and plugged it in. Thankfully, the little cottage had a telephone line, and she was able to e-mail her friends and family. First, she checked her incoming e-mails and was happy to see a brief note from Lily, "I've arrived, I'm pooped, and I'll catch you later. I'm going straight to bed. I start rounds tomorrow morning at O-five thirty. Good night, sis. I'm glad I could come home, and we could be together."

Ariel smiled and sent her an e-mail telling her of her move to the beach cottage. Ariel yawned hugely and pressed the send button. She was so tired that the rest of them would have to wait till tomorrow. It was just past sundown, and she was ready to go to bed. A quick pick up of the house and kitchen clutter was all she could manage. She slid into the big comfortable bed and was asleep in minutes to the sounds of the waves hitting the shore.

Ariel was up and dressed for the day when the shrill ring of the telephone startled her. Sibyl was already up and solving dilemmas. Jackson had an old Willy's jeep that he could lend her. It wasn't much, but it was fairly easy to drive. He'd bring it around for her to look at if she'd like.

"It was used around the farm until Jackson decided to get a truck. Now he mostly uses it when he goes Grouse hunting. How did you sleep, my dear?"

Ariel was touched by Sibyl's thoughtfulness and knowing just what she needed.

"I slept wonderfully, Grandma! The ocean lulled me to sleep almost as soon as my head hit the pillow." The two of them chatted a bit longer, and then Ariel hung up and sipped on her just-poured coffee. Things were coming together, and she felt hopeful that the time on her own to get used to her new life and the coming of her twins would be just what she needed. To think that in four months she was to be a mother of two tiny infants boggled her mind.

Ariel put a protective hand over her stomach and suddenly something kicked her hand. Surprised, Ariel almost dropped her coffee cup. This was the first real kick that she could definitely say was her babies that she had been able to feel. Lately, she had felt tiny flutters in her womb, but nothing as strong as this. It brought it front and center that there was life within her. Ariel put her hand back on her stomach and spoke to her two babies, cooing at them, and telling them that their mommy was going to do everything she could to keep them safe.

Ariel had finished breakfast and walked on the beach, wishing she'd asked to borrow Joco. It made a walk so much more interesting. Maybe she'd see if Sibyl would let her borrow him for a walk tomorrow.

She had just fixed a tin of soup and was grilling a cheese sandwich when she heard a motor grinding up her lane. By the time the jeep had stopped, and Jackson had climbed out, she'd put another sandwich on the grill. She turned them and turned off the burner to keep them warm while she wiped her hands and headed for the door.

"Hey, Jackson, you hungry? I've got an extra grilled cheese sandwich and tomato soup to share." She grinned as Jackson hurried into the kitchen.

"Well, perfect timing I'd say." Jackson sat down at the table as Ariel placed the platter of sandwiches and two bowls of hot soup on the table. They ate companionably and when they were done, Jackson rose and put the dishes into the sudsy dishwater. Ariel always did the same thing so that when she got around to washing them they just needed rinsing. The two sat at the small kitchen table and drank a fresh cup of tea together. It was fun getting to know each other, as they were virtual strangers.

The two drank their tea, and Jackson filled Ariel in with what his life had been like. Ariel did the same, letting him know he had a family of cousins in America. It all seemed familiar with similar family background but strange too. They were first cousins and had grown up an ocean apart, neither one knowing of the other's existence. The death of Ariel's mother, Kate, had made Paul go into himself, and only Ariel and then Sarah could touch his heart. Paul never discussed his life in Scotland with his children.

Jackson got up from the table, scrapping his chair on the floor as he backed away. He was going fishing and with any luck would have some nice wild Salmon to share come suppertime.

The afternoon was fine with a light breeze and what sun there was peeking out from the clouds. The beach looked inviting, so Ariel put on her warm coat, scarf, and boots and walked over to Brindle Hall to see if Joco needed a walk. Joco jumped for joy to see her and ran racing to the back door. Sibyl and Robyn laughed, and Robyn went to get his leash. Ariel asked if either of them would like to go with her, and Robyn grabbed his jacket and wool hat, and the two were soon on the path leading to the beach. Joco was well ahead of them, having been let off his leash at the start of the path. Ariel and Robyn walked together step for step. Robyn added to Sibyl's account of their meeting and told Ariel what it was like to be an airman in the RAF flying over London to protect the country from the Germany Lufthansa.

"I was scared to death more than once when I was in a dog fight looking straight at a blue-eyed pilot who looked as frightened as I was. But it was war; it had to be done. We were overwhelmed by the Germans; it took skill and daring to go up and engage an enemy that was two to one more powerful than you were. Thankfully, we had good spotters who alerted us to incoming raids early enough that we could get up and attack aggressively. Many a time, I didn't think I'd make it out of there, and once my plane was shot down into the channel. It was always a relief when I'd fly into Inverness, and old Joe would be waiting to bring me to Brindle Hall. I'd arrive usually in the early evening, and there would be Sibyl helping her mum and da set the table or carrying in trays of food. Back in those days, Brindle Hall was quite a show place, but the war had taken the butler and cook. Sibyl and her mum did the cooking and cleaning, and their da planted a huge garden that we maintain today." Robyn squeezed Ariel's hand, and they stopped for a minute, sat on the sea wall, and whistled for Joco. The dog was far down the beach, and he'd turned at Robyn's whistle and stared at them as if to say, "I'm not ready to come in yet."

After Robyn clapped his hands and called to Joco sternly, reluctantly Joco trudged up the beach with his tail between his legs to flop down next to Robyn.

By the time Robyn and Ariel walked up the path back to Brindle Hall, Joco was docile and walked quietly beside them. He had given his all on the way down and climbing up the cliff was an exhausting experience.

The late afternoon was heavy with mist; Ariel couldn't see the sea when they trudged to the top of the cliff. The wind buffeted them and slowed their progress. The purple heather grew on the cliff, and the sweet smell of the heather crushed under her feet released a sweet hay-like smell.

The path led across the heather and as Robyn and Ariel trudged on, their walk took them back down past a salt marsh. Its shallow habitat provided an ideal environment for early spring waterfowl. Ariel and Robyn watched as a Whooper swan, a Greylag goose, and a Velvet scotter shared the marsh. Robyn, marching along beside Joco and Ariel, told Ariel about the prolonged and bloody disputes, political intrigue, and family vendettas that characterize much of the history of the area--from the Viking raids, to a Jacobite orgy of looting and burning the day before Culloden in 1746. Dornoch and the rich fertile lands around it have always been seen as a prize worth fighting for. The MacKays of Strathnaver, the Sutherlands of Duffus, the Earls of Caithness, and the Murrays of Dornoch all played their part in Dornoch's turbulent history, as did the Frazers and the McDonalds.

It seemed to Ariel that the land spoke comfort to her. Hard as the life of the settlers of this historic town was, they survived to build an enduring cathedral town. Their strength seemed to reach out and embrace her, and Ariel felt the deep peace of the land. Come what may, Ariel knew that she would get through the birth of her babies and defy anyone who tried to hurt them. She had no fault in this tragedy and neither did her infants. They were innocent too. Ariel's thoughts went to Morgan and Sarah. It had been two months since their death. Ariel found it harder to bring forth their images without looking at their pictures. Robyn walked quietly beside her and didn't interrupt her thoughts.

The two strode up the trail and over to a bench high on the cliff right in the middle of a field of heather. They watched the wildlife and the rhythm of the ocean peeking through the mist that, in its own way, willed strength to Ariel. She felt Robyn's caring for her and was at peace. After sitting in the wind until even her warm jacket and wool scarf could no longer hold the chill out, Ariel, Robyn, and Joco trudged back to Brindle Hall and sat at the scrubbed pine table while Sibyl poured them both a cup of hot fresh tea. It was hot and sweet and had a dash of cinnamon in it.

Sibyl had finished her shopping list and was filled with accomplishment. Ariel and Sibyl would go into town tomorrow to a small shop called Bits and Pieces. The shop had special ordered a new cashmere sweater for Robyn's birthday from Edinburgh, and Ariel was anxious to see the Scottish gifts and crafts as well as the cashmere and woolens it carried. She needed to do some shopping for Lily's birthday coming up in early September, and it would be nice to bring back something special for Ben and Julie, Riley, Mark, and Zoe as well. The shopping trip promised to be full of everything that a tourist could want. The quality was so good that the locals also bought their gifts there.

The next morning, Sibyl and Ariel were off to town by ten o'clock, full of plans for all they wanted to purchase. In addition to the gifts Ariel planned to take back with her, she decided to take advantage of the shop's ability to provide layettes for newborns as well. Sibyl and Ariel had a wonderful time looking at the tiny miniature sleepers, tee shirts, and nightgowns of light summer weight knit. The shop had everything, including baby lotions, pacifiers, and the tiniest of stockings and caps. Sibyl steered Ariel away from the layettes since Lily had already bought two complete sets, and Sibyl didn't want to give away the surprise. Thankfully, Ariel wasn't obsessed with getting the layettes right that minute, and Sibyl was able to get her out of the store and over to the meat market for some sausage for breakfast.

That evening, Robyn, Sibyl, and Ariel bundled up and went out to dinner. It was a pub dinner of hot meat pasties and pork buns and dark ale for Robyn and Sibyl with hot tea for Ariel. It was a wonderful evening, and they came home stuffed and happy.

Ariel went back to her cottage and e-mailed Riley and Zoe, asking them for an update and sharing her fear of the unknown assailant that kept her from them. Riley's e-mail was full of his latest checkup of Sofie, and he let her know that the pups were expected the last week in March. The sonogram he'd done on her last week showed five big puppies that looked to be about six weeks along. The gestation for puppies was about sixty-three days so that meant that they'd be there within the next two weeks. Ariel wished so much that she could be there when they arrived.

She found her grandmother busy at her desk writing invitations to her friends and neighbors. She was gathering everyone together for Robyn's birthday. Robyn loved a big to do on his birthday, and Sibyl had never failed to delight him with a supper party. Having a March birthday made it difficult to do anything outside because of the still brisk air, but Sibyl had worked out having a buffet with an enormous birthday cake. Claire would help her, and Jackson would help bring in extra chairs and tables. They're would be thirty friends for the Saturday night buffet. They would open up the solarium and move in little round tables and chairs to sit and eat. Sibyl grew orchids, and in March, the first showing appeared. Beautiful big rust and cream, there was always bunches to be placed around the room to bring a garden feel to the dinner. Claire had already washed, starched, and ironed the snowy tablecloths and napkins. The dinner would be in two weeks, and though Ariel wasn't excited to see many people, she'd help Sibyl with table settings and do whatever else was needed to make it a festive occasion.

The next two weeks were filled with getting the house

sparkling clean and helping Sibyl with the shopping and ordering food and wine. There were frequent trips to the store to order the wines and cheeses and anything that could be bought ahead of time. The main part of the meal would be catered, but Sibyl would make Robyn's favorite cake, a huge round carrot cake that could be made a week ahead of time and stored in the freezer. Sibyl had gotten large round pans that filled the oven, and she baked Robyn's carrot cake one layer at a time until she had a three-layer cake that stood ten inches high when assembled. That would come later the morning of the celebration. Sibyl would thaw the cakes and make a huge batch of cream cheese frosting.

Finally, all was ready, and it was the morning of March 20. Robyn turned eighty-five years old. The caterers were there early with prime ribs and hams with gravy and a cranberry orange sauce for the hams. There were pans of au gratin potatoes, and a huge Caesar salad. It was easily enough to feed over fifty people.

At five thirty, Sibyl and Robyn disappeared to shower and dress, and Ariel went back to her beach cottage to take a long luxurious bath. She lay in the water with bubbles surrounding her and moved her hands over her stomach, feeling the small beach ball shape. She was going to wear a light floating caftan of a gray silk and her silver and amethyst necklace that Morgan had given her for their tenth wedding anniversary.

At 7:00 p.m., the first guests arrived and walked straight in and up the stairs. There was a note saying to come right in and that way no one was stuck with answering the doorbell.

Sibyl looked beautiful in a red silk gown, and she wore diamond studs in her ears with a large diamond pendant nestled between her breasts. She had had her silver hair done in an upswept style with a diamond comb to hold it firm. Robyn was splendid in a new suit and crisp white shirt with a matching red tie and gold cufflinks and tie tack. He smelled of Bay Rum, and his face was shiny from his fresh shave and shower. Ariel met him at the bottom of the stairs and walked him into the living room where all his friends and neighbors had gathered to wish him happy birthday.

"Grandpa Robyn, you look smashing, and you smell so good. Grandma Sibyl is going to have to fight off the women wanting to dance with you." She squeezed his arm as Sibyl met him and led the guests in a rousing version of Happy Birthday. Jackson brought him a drink, and Claire, in a new blue dress that brought out the blue of her eyes, came and kissed his cheek.

"Come, Robyn, the guests are hungry. Come lead the way to the buffet." Claire put her arm through his and gathered Sibyl on his other side, and the three led the way into dinner. The buffet was splendid, and everyone ate until they were stuffed. Then Sibyl brought in the huge carrot cake with all eighty-five candles lit on it.

"Happy birthday, my darling." She watched him blow all the candles out with one huge puff. The party was a huge success, and no one could out dance Robyn and Sibyl who did a smashing Charleston, accompanied by hoots and clapping from their guests. Ariel and Jackson watched the two and marveled at their stamina.

"Imagine, both of them are in their eighties and look at them, they're marvelous!" Ariel clapped from the sidelines as they kicked and danced the Charleston.

The next morning everyone slept in and ate leftovers for breakfast--ham with eggs and toast then a late lunch of cold turkey sandwiches. Dinner was prime rib with gravy, au gratins, and fresh green beans. It was even better than the party, because it was all fixed and easy to heat up. Ariel helped Sibyl clear the dishes, and the three of them went upstairs and turned on the television to watch the news in the sitting room. There was great excitement when the newsman read his announcement regarding the troop withdrawal from Iraq by September. There would be twelve thousand American troops withdrawn and four thousand British troops withdrawn. U.S. Military sources said that just after, a suicide bomber killed thirty people in a popular restaurant in Baghdad.

"The U.S. withdrawal will be gradual at first, leaving most troops in place for parliamentary elections at the end of this year. There are currently about 135,000 U.S. troops in Iraq. President Barack Obama has decided to remove all combat troops by the end of August 2010, with the remaining forces leaving by the end of 2011. The four thousand British troops due to leave are the last British soldiers in Iraq."

Robyn switched off the television, and the three discussed their concern for Lily. "The violence and Al Qaida's increasing boldness in targeting Iraqi forces being prepared to take over the country's security so the American's troops can go home is a big concern. It's indicative that Al Qaida feels threatened. They're feeling desperate. They want very much to maintain relevance." Robyn frowned, thinking how different this war was from the one he had fought in. But war is war, and people get killed; it just feels more brutal somehow than the war he fought. He sighed, looking over at Ariel who was white with fear for Lily.

"Hey, what do you say to a game of Texas Hold'em ? I'll see if Jackson and Claire want to play." Robyn hurried to the telephone and dialed. Jackson picked up on the second ring and, with promise of leftover ham and cheese sandwiches and an excellent Zinfandel left from the party for a snack after the game, there was ready agreement. Jackson and his mother were there in just moments; the five moved into the dining room and sat around the old round pedestal table. Jackson took over the first deal--the game was on.

Ariel's mind was still on Lily, and she was slow to pick up the rhythm of the game. "Oh, you beat me with that third queen," she sighed. Taking a big drink of sparkling water, she focused harder on the game. At the end of the game, Jackson came out in first place, and Robyn was second. Ariel was surprised that she had gotten third place. The small remnant of family gathered together in the kitchen to make sandwiches with a rich rye bread and the Jarlsberg cheese with thick slices of ham. Ariel put lots of mustard and pickles on hers.

Talk between bites centered around Ariel's plan to take a trip up A99 to Wick. Ariel had made up her mind to venture out on her own; she was feeling fit and strong, driving somewhere, anywhere, on her own would engage her senses. It was time to get on with her life. A road trip would help her move past her pain. Ariel listened to all of their suggestions and announced that she was going that very next morning.

Chapter 23

Ariel rose early and watched the light of dawn brightening the sky. It was cold. The coffee pot was ready to go, so she flicked the switch. While the brew was steaming into the carafe, she looked out at the leaden sea. It looked cold, gunmetal gray, with a light mist steaming off the water. The waves were low, slow to form. Ariel felt just like the waves looked.

The coffee pinged its readiness. She poured a large cup warming her hands around the hot coffee cup. Ariel sighed; drinking decaffeinated coffee just wasn't the same. Ariel missed the jolt that the leaded kind gave her, but it would only be for a little while more. When her babies were delivered that would be the first thing she asked for. The day looked to be a slow and lazy one. Hopefully it would warm up, and she'd see evidence of the coming of spring. Right now, it looked bleak and cold. The herring gulls flew in large groups over the sea, dipping and diving whenever they saw a small tidbit to eat. It must take a huge amount of food to keep them filled. Their wings flapped as they keened together one large mass of birds and wings, never hitting each other, just perfect union. Ariel looked away, and a sudden pain of loss hit her mid section. She nearly doubled over. She was completely and totally alone. The pain of it sent her reeling, and she sat down hard on the kitchen chair. Morgan was gone, and the finality of it crushed against her heart, causing her to take quick short breathes until she could breath normally again. There could be no more pretending that he was just away on business and would come in with news of a successful transaction. There was just nothing, nothing, nothing.

Ariel shook off the utter despair the only way she knew how, with action. A quick breakfast of toast and peanut butter with a dab of jelly, and she swallowed down the dredges of her coffee and grabbed her jacket and the sandwiches she had made for her road trip. Sibyl had lent her a thermos that she filled with hot sweet tea, and she was off. The old Willy's jeep was filled with petrol, and Ariel tucked her sack of sandwiches and thermos on the floorboards next to her. She ground the gears going down the lane and out to Highway A99. Ariel roared along the highway, driving steadily through Golspie, Lothber Point, Helmsdale, Dunbeath, Lybster, and Wick. She planned on driving until she got hungry and then stopping to be a tourist wherever fancy lead her.

Everywhere she drove, Ariel saw the people. They looked happy and contented, going about their daily errands and maybe some were tourists as she was. The only difference is she sensed that they were at peace with themselves and that, Ariel realized, was what was missing in her. She felt in a turmoil of indecision. What was she going to do? How was she going to keep her babies safe? If she went back to America, she would be risking their lives for her own solace. But everything she loved was in that almond orchard farm. There was work for her there and friends and family. Of course, she had Grandma and Grandpa Frazer, and she loved that she had them in her life again, but it wasn't her home! By the time that Ariel started back, she was already making plans to go home as soon as she could. That would be a start. That would be an action. What awaited her she would just have to deal with and because she knew that there was danger there, she had been forewarned. No one was going to get close to her again without her being totally aware. It would be a plan. It would be all right. It had to be all right. When she got back to the beach cottage, she would write to Zoe, Mark, and Riley, and she'd just tell them that she couldn't hide any more. She was going home.

Ariel drove the jeep straight back to Brindle Hall. She shut off the engine and rushed into the kitchen. Sibyl was putting dinner together. Robyn and Joco were out for a walk.

"Ariel, you're back!" Sibyl was rolling out a piecrust for a meat pasty and had the meat and onions browning on the stovetop in the big black iron frying pan. This was one of Ariel's favorite meals. It made her think of her parents. Paul had taught Sarah to make it just like his mother did.

Sibyl caught a look of strong determination on Ariel's face, and she knew. Busy with the dough, Sibyl lowered her eyes and said nothing, waiting for Ariel to tell her. It didn't take long. Robyn and Joco stomped in the back door; Robyn dropped his Wellingtons. Joco scampered into the kitchen and went straight to Ariel and put his head on her knee. Robyn came in through the scullery and gave Sibyl a quick peck on the cheek, with one for Ariel too.

Tea was made. Sibyl put the huge pie into the oven to bake and brought out some crisp biscuits with crystal sugar on top to go with their tea.

Sibyl sat across from Ariel and looked up at her, meeting her eyes. She felt such love for this granddaughter, but she knew that she was leaving. She braced herself and waited.

"Grandma Sibyl, Grandpa Robyn, I don't know how to tell you how much it's meant to me to be with you this past few weeks. I know that you worry about me. But I'm going to be fine. I've thought it through, and this is the only way. I have to go back, face this threat to my life and future happiness with my children. I can't just sit here anymore not knowing, being afraid of every stranger I meet. If someone comes too close to me in the store, I cringe inside. I know that that isn't good for the babies to be so afraid. I'm sure the adrenalin isn't good for them. So I'm going to write to Zoe, Mark, and Riley and tell them I'm coming home. I expect you all will be worried, but I have to do this. I'm sorry for worrying you, I didn't intend too, but I will be very careful. I won't be rash. Once the babies are born, I know that I will be safe. They're will be no reason for anyone to kill me. I will get to the bottom of this; I promise you I will."

It was a quiet supper. No one seemed to be able to talk, and Ariel was so filled with love for her grandparents and thankful for their support. The meat pasty was delicious. By the time they had topped it off with a dish of vanilla ice cream with hot fudge on it, Ariel was exhausted. She kissed them both goodnight, went to the quiet cottage, and wrote her e-mails.

Chapter 24

Riley and his mother, Julie, put the finishing touches on the spanking new nursery. The pale yellow walls and creamy white woodwork were dry enough that Julie could hang up the sheer white curtains. Riley put the rods up and stood on the stepladder while Julie finished slipping the casing over the rod. She handed the curtain and rod up to Riley.

"Oh, they look wonderful, Riley!" She surveyed the room with the critical eye of an artist. The new paint brought a clean fresh look to the room and the two new white cribs with the matching quilts that Julie had made for them looked perfect. Ben and Riley had refinished the heart pine floors and put several coats of satin finish Polyurethane on them to keep them looking like new for years. Ben had found a child's wardrobe in the barn. All it needed was a coat of fresh white paint to match the cribs. The three worked for several weekends on the project, hoping that they could have it all finished before Ariel returned home. Julie had gone shopping for crib sheets and soft baby blankets as well as a sweet little lamp with the base of a creamy lamb that looked perfect on the wardrobe; it would serve as a soft light for late-night feeding sessions. Julie could picture Ariel rocking the babies in the big old-fashioned rocker that Julie had Ben drag up from the back porch. It looked like new with a coat of white paint and a new soft cushion for the seat and back that Julie had covered in the matching quilt material. The three stepped back and admired the sweet new nursery. It was a cozy room right next to Ariel's bedroom, but there was ample room for toys in the big walk-in closet. In the closet was the big package from Lily that Ariel's grandmother Sibyl had sent over as soon as Lily had gone back to Iraq. The mysterious package was sitting on the otherwise bare shelves waiting to reveal its secret. Since Lily had peeked at the sonogram, she and Dr. Forbes were the only ones who knew the sex of the twins.

The new nursery sat waiting, completely finished, ready for Ariel's twins. Julie started making small, knitted, baby hats and little sweaters with matching booties. There would be no time once the twins arrived. Lily had written to Julie to tell her where to look for Marks's and her christening gowns. Julie found them tucked in Sarah's cedar chest, and with a gentle washing with mild soap and bleach, they came out snow white. All Julie had to do was to rinse them in a light starch and iron them. They were beautiful, delicate lawn with white on white embroidery of little white roses across the bib of the long dresses. Julie knew that Ariel would love them.

Riley had just come from Ben and Julie's after a huge Sunday dinner of fried chicken with mashed potatoes and gravy, a large garden salad with crusty bread, and fresh apple pie with vanilla ice cream. He was stuffed and debating whether to sit in front of the television or go on line and open his e-mails. He wanted to see if there was a message from Ariel; he was looking forward to writing to her too.

Riley opened his e-mail, and he felt a clutch of fear for her as he read it. She mustn't come home yet. Ariel was so stubborn. Someone had to talk some sense into her. Riley made his decision and quickly went online to the airlines and made a reservation for Friday morning. It would give him two days to get his practice in shape, and Jeff Larson, his partner, would understand his need to go. He hadn't taken a vacation since he'd opened the vet hospital; it was time.

His reservation made, Riley picked up the phone and speed dialed Zoe.

"Zoe, I want to go through Sarah's house. Meet me there now. I'll explain when I see you. If David's free, bring him along. We're going to need some manpower."

Riley got into his black Tahoe and gunned the motor. He shot out of his parking lot and whipped the car right toward Sarah's small cottage. This was his only chance; it was worth the effort even if they had to turn the house upside down. Five minutes later, he was pulling into Sarah's driveway. Zoe's jeep was already parked. Zoe and David had the door open and were sitting in the kitchen when he strolled in.

"Riley, what's going on? Why did you drag us over here?"

Riley drew up a chair and looked the detectives in the eye. "Okay, I know you've been all through Sarah's place and went through all her files on her computer and hardcopy files but what if the knowledge she had was so inflammatory that she didn't trust it to her computer or a regular file--what if she hid it somewhere in her house?" Riley stopped and took a breath just long enough for Zoe to jump in.

"What kind of information?"

Riley shrugged, "I don't know, but it got her killed, so someone must have wanted to silence her badly enough to kill her. We don't have much time. You read Ariel's e-mail last night? She's coming home. I made a reservation, and I've told her to wait until I get there. I've got to stall her coming back until we get to the bottom of this. So let's get to work. Where would a person hide evidence? What would be important enough to hide anyway?"

The three started in the kitchen, went through every drawer, pulling them out, and feeling underneath and behind for anything taped to the back wall of the cabinet. The kitchen was clean, nothing. Next, they started in her spare room, looking in the closet and under the mattress. They pulled all of her drawers out of her desk, nothing there either. Zoe walked into Sarah's bedroom and thought like the woman she was. Where would a woman hide something of such magnitude? She looked around the room then went to the closet. Switching on her flashlight, she saw the crawl hole for the attic.

Zoe looked around for something to climb on and dragged the little boudoir chair over to the closet. Climbing on the chair brought her to the height of the crawl space entrance and carefully, she lifted the plywood square up and put it to the side of the attic. A dark hole loomed; she shined her light around, climbing up, to get a better look. She shined the torch all around and over the attic and saw only neat rows of insulation between the rafters. Zoe reasoned that Sarah wouldn't climb all the way in because the insulation was made of spun glass, she would have it all over herself. With that, she narrowed her search and concentrated on lifting the insulation around the rim of the entrance. Nothing! Zoe kept working, moving from the front to the sides; it was when she moved a little farther in to the attic and lifted the insulation from way behind her that she found it. It was in a gallon-size plastic bag filled to bursting with papers.

"David, Riley, I've found something." Zoe scampered down and brought the Ziploc bag with her. She walked into the hallway and collided with both men as they hurried toward her.

The three went back to the kitchen table and began to read the material. It seemed to be in a kind of doctor shorthand. Numbers like case numbers were listed on the first paper. Then next was an address for an institute for stem cell research based in San Francisco. A Dr. Vincent P. Maslow's name and telephone number were prominent on the third piece of paper.

Zoe took the information down in her notebook and looked at David. "Want to take a plane ride?"

The three hurried through the rest of the paperwork and, when they were done, had a plan of sorts. Zoe and David would scout out the institute, and Riley would go to Ariel and persuade her to be patient a little while longer. All three of them would take off in Zoe's Cessna, drop Riley off at the airport, and then Zoe and David would go into the city to visit the institute.

With a plan in place, Zoe and David went back to their office to clear their desks, while Riley went to his clinic to speed through his cases and move up his trip. First thing he did when he got back to the clinic was to move his reservation, so he would leave out of San Francisco tomorrow afternoon. Zoe and David would have him to San Francisco International by one o'clock, and then they had an appointment with Dr. Maslow at three o'clock. It would take them an hour to fly from Columbia to San Francisco and rent a car to drive to the city. The three agreed to meet at eleven o'clock the next morning.

Before Riley left the office, he e-mailed a terse one-sentence e-mail to Ariel in large capital letters. "WAIT, I'M COMING TO YOU. BE THERE SOMETIME TOMORROW. --Riley." He looked at the e-mail before he sent it off and sighed, tired, and yet felt a determination to be by her side. She'd never know how he felt about her except as her friend, but he had to go see her and help her any way he could.

The rest of the evening he packed and cleaned out the refrigerator and took his Brittney spaniel, Freckles, over to Julie and Ben. Sofie had her brood of pups that she had delivered on March 22, and she was a nervous new mother. Riley knew she wouldn't welcome Freckles. It would upset her to have another dog around, but it couldn't be helped. He'd have Ben keep

Freckles in the barn and office with him until he got home. Sofie had whelped the pups in under an hour, shortly after a Sunday dinner that Julie had prepared of ham and au gratin potatoes with a green bean casserole. Dinner had been a bit hap hazard with Riley jumping up every few minutes to check on Sofie's progress, but in the end things had moved quickly, and Sofie's five fat brown and white basset puppies with black ears were snuggled close to Sofie and eagerly nursing.

The pups were almost four weeks old now, and Sofie was getting tired of nursing them. The puppy gruel that Julie fed them relieved Sofie of nursing so often. The puppies were more or less weaned except for little sips during their naptime. Sofie allowed the puppies to nurse then, but she would nip at them if they tried at other times of the day. Most of their day was spent in the puppy pen frolicking with each other and puppy wrestling. Ariel had missed being there, but Riley had sent pictures weekly of the puppies by e-mail. Ariel would write back though Riley could tell that she appreciated him sending her pictures of their growth, she was sad that she couldn't be there to hold them and smell their puppy breath. Riley was holding off advertising the puppies at the veterinary clinic as available for sale, because he hoped that Ariel would be able to see them in person before they were sold.

Riley had everything together and had taken Freckles over to the farm, checked on Sofie, and was relieved that the puppies were growing strong and healthy. Hopefully, they would still be here when Ariel came home. Riley knew how much it meant for her to see them. The moon was rising as Riley got into bed, anxious for tomorrow to come. He had a direct flight from California to New York and after picking up travelers headed for the UK, there was the long flight to London's Heathrow airport. He would get in to Heathrow at about eleven o'clock in the evening, and then it would be a short commuter flight to Inverness, Scotland. He'd probably have to find a place to stay and then rent a car to drive him to Dornoch. It would depend on how he felt and how tired he was. He'd just as soon drive straight through once he landed, and then if he had to, sleep in the car. He'd done it before. Speed was important, and he didn't want anything to go wrong. He must stop her from coming home until Zoe and David said it was safe for her.

Ariel opened her e-mail and read Riley's terse message and frowned. What was going on? Well, she'd give him time to explain himself, then she was going home and that was that. The rest of the day was spent helping Sibyl give Joco a bath, which he hated. It took both of them--one to hold him still in the deep laundry tub and one to lather on soap and put a conditioner rinse over him. He turned out two shades lighter with his tan body and white patches bright clean and soft. Ariel ran a heavy comb through his still damp coat and, thanks to the conditioner, it didn't knot and tangle but combed smooth and effortless through his hair. When they were done, Joco was plump, with his hair standing out all round him. Only his head looked disproportional, small with all of the hair surrounding it. As a reward for his patience, Joco was allowed to lay in front of a roaring fire in the living room while Sibyl and Ariel made afternoon tea, hot Earl Gray with fresh cranberry scones with clotted cream. Ariel always smiled when she compared the "clotted cream" to the American term "whipped cream." Ariel waited till Sibyl and Robyn had had their tea and scones before telling them her news.

"My husband's best friend, Riley Roberts, e-mailed me that he had some news and is coming to share it with me. He said he'd be here tomorrow sometime. I don't know what he has to say, but anything is better than sitting here not knowing what's going on at home. My friend Zoe, who is heading the investigation, hasn't said much except be patient. They are doing a thorough investigation and that takes a lot of time." Ariel sighed and looked out the window at the sea.

Sibyl turned and looked at Ariel and asked her, "What's Riley like?"

Ariel thought a bit, and then she gave them a complete rundown of who he was and how they all went to school together. "Riley was always ambitious, but we were all surprised when he went to school to be a veterinarian. We thought he'd be a regular doctor, but Riley always said he liked animals more than people, because they complained less. Morgan thought the world of him, and his parents both work for me, so he's almost family to me." Ariel trailed off and became silent. Sibyl was busy knitting a blue cable sweater for Ariel, all you could hear was the clicking of her needles.

Robyn got up, stretched, and whistled for Joco. "It's time to stretch my legs. I'll take Joco with me. I want to take a walk around the village. Hank Butler is saving me a new trowel over at the hardware store that I ordered." Robyn clipped on Joco's leash and went over to give Sibyl a peck on the cheek and Ariel too. The dog and his master walked downstairs to the front foyer, and moments later, Ariel heard the door click shut.

Ariel left Sibyl to her knitting and headed out the back door to the path to the beach house. There was a brisk wind, her cheeks were rosy, and her face was cold when she let herself into the cottage. She looked around, saw the small living room with the iron open hearth stove, much like the American Franklin model, and thought about where she was going to put Riley. There was a small cot out on the sun porch that she used as a day bed. This would have to do; he could put his clothes in the tiny cupboard that was at the end of the room. Ariel spent the rest of the day making up the room with fresh sheets and blankets and threw a woven cotton throw of light blue over it. She dusted the small yellow writing desk and found a chair for beside the bed. She surveyed the room and decided it would do. Next, she went through her cupboards and the refrigerator, sat down, and made a list of basic supplies like eggs, milk, bread, fresh fruit, and lean bacon. She decided to buy a big chicken and stuff it with homemade stuffing, bake a few sweet potatoes, and make a big salad that could be pulled out of a gallon-size plastic bag. If they needed anything else, they could go do a shopping run together.

Ariel left the house, drove to the market, and picked up her groceries. The grocer was a friendly fellow, and he brought out a fresh chicken that would be wonderful roasted. It didn't take long to assemble her grocery items, get them loaded into brown sacks and stowed in the Willy's jeep, and, sooner than she thought, she was driving back to the cottage. She lugged the bags into the cottage, unpacked everything, and put it all away. After all the exertion, she decided on just a peanut butter and jelly sandwich and a glass of milk for her supper, which she ate heartily.

The sandwich and milk made her sleepy, and it was well before nine when she crawled into her comfortable bed and pulled the down comforter over her. The babies started bumping her stomach as soon as she lay down, and she smiled as she rubbed her stomach and sang them a melody. Ariel was asleep in minutes, a feeling of peace surrounding her. She was lying in a nest of warm covers, her babies quieting down, and then they all went to sleep.

Chapter 25

R iley arrived in Inverness, went immediately to the car rental, and rented a little Morris that hugged the curves in the road to Dornoch as he sped up the highway. It was easy to find Brindle Hall. All he had to do was ask the postman who was making his daily deliveries, and he found the lane that swept past the hall. He turned sharply and drove up the lane in low gear. The house could be seen at the crest of the hill, as Riley drove steadily toward it.

Sibyl heard the bell chime and hurried out of the kitchen to answer it. She had been washing up the dishes and still held a damp dishtowel in her hands. Through the glass, she could see a very tall man with short sandy blonde hair and piercing blue eyes. He was leaning against the porch post, wearing a chocolate leather coat paired with a blue denim shirt and Levi's that showed off his long lean body. His legs seemed to go on forever.

Sibyl took a deep breath and opened the door. "Hello, Mrs. Frazer? I'm Riley Roberts, Ariel's friend."

Sibyl looked way up at him and smiled. "Hello, won't you come in."

Sibyl bustled around and hoped the house didn't smell of the ham breakfast she'd cooked for Robyn shortly before. Where was Robyn? Why did that man disappear just when she needed him? Sibyl was so busy thinking that she failed to mention Ariel, and Riley asked her with a worried look where she was. "Oh she's not here!" As soon as she said it, she saw his shoulders slump, and it was if the wind was knocked out of him. In that moment, she knew that Ariel meant more to him than a friend, and she felt his keen disappointment. Quickly she explained, "Ariel's living in the beach cottage just down the lane." Sibyl pointed out the half-hidden lane to Riley. Riley smiled with a look of extreme relief. Sibyl was stunned by his beautiful smile; she found herself stammering.

Riley was out the door, in the little Morris, and had turned down the lane before Sibyl could say a word, and she wondered just what Riley Roberts was to Ariel.

Ariel had just finished her breakfast of bacon and eggs with a wonderful whole wheat toast. The coffee pot was freshly brewed, and she was reading a book she had picked up when there was a quiet knock on the door. Ariel got up and flung open the door just as Riley had raised his hand to knock again. The two just stared at each other, and Ariel recovered first, reaching over and giving him a big hug and a kiss on the cheek. She'd had to move her stomach sideways as the round ball in front of her was quite pronounced. Riley looked down at the bulge in front of her and smiled. Ariel's stomach was much larger than a six-month fetus. It was apparent that there was more than one baby inside.

Ariel patted her stomach and grinned. "I'm carrying a litter; it feels like a war going on in there. I'll be glad when it's finally over, and the little rascals are born. My doctor says everything is fine, but twins are usually more active. Trying to find enough room, they move around a lot." Riley became tongue-tied, and Ariel came to the rescue by taking him into the kitchen and pouring him a cup of coffee. She had been slim the last time he saw her, and now her girth was overwhelming to him. She was wearing a gray sweater and gray wool pants. It was still a cool twenty-eight degrees, and though sunny, it was definitely chilly. The Franklin stove was warm and inviting, warming the kitchen to a comfortable seventy degrees. Riley had left Sonora a warm eighty-five degrees and to be thrown back into a crisp, cold, northern spring was bone chilling. Luckily, he'd brought his winter jacket.

Ariel and Riley talked and talked. They couldn't say all of the things that had been going on in their lives. Riley gave her the news from home and conveyed Ben's message that he was just going to plow the orchard and flood it next week. Everything was running well, and Ariel felt like she wasn't needed. It was strange to be hearing about the farm, and Riley had to reassure her that Ben was good, but it was her advance planning that had made her prolonged absence possible. The farm needed her for long-range planning. Finally, they got to the part that Riley had been avoiding telling her.

"There's been another murder!" Riley said it hurriedly, and Ariel's eyes got huge. She said nothing, just stared at him, waiting to hear who had been killed.

"I just got the message from Zoe that that lab tech, Gordon Warner, got his head bashed in, and his apartment was stripped of his computer and anything else of value. Zoe said they're going to get a search warrant and take the clinic apart." Riley stopped and grabbed her hands. "You must stay away a while longer. It's just not safe for you to go back yet."

His blue eyes met hers, unsettling Ariel She turned away and walked over to the coffee pot and poured them both a fresh cup." "I've got to go home. I feel useless here. Oh, Grandma and Grandpa have been wonderful, but it's not my home."

Ariel looked so distraught that Riley turned the conversation to pleasanter things. They'd go back to this again many times before he went home. "I'm beat. I delivered puppies up till an hour before I had to leave for the airport. Do you remember me telling you about Jacqueline, the big Great Dane that Hank Edwards has? Well, Jacqueline had eight whopping pups yesterday morning. Hank called me at two in the morning, and I went out to his farm. Poor Jacqueline didn't know what was going on, her labor was long, and finally the first one started and popped out. I didn't have to do anything, thank God, and the rest came along about five minutes apart. I monitored the pups and Jacqueline, but they were doing well with no distress. I feared she might have to have a C-section, but nature did its work, and mother and babies are doing well." Riley rubbed his face. "I didn't get any sleep. I was happy to get away. My new partner is doing a great job, and it will free me to take some time away."

Just then, the phone rang, and Sibyl invited them to dinner. That seemed to get them started, and Ariel said she'd go into town and get the whipping cream for Sibyl's fruit torte. In minutes, Riley and Ariel were in the car, and Riley was driving them into Dornoch. Ariel pointed out Jackson's farm and told him about her cousin. "Jackson has a horse about to foal, maybe you'd like to go take a look. I know you're going to be impressed with Jackson's stable. He's well respected in these parts, and he has the makings of a fine horse farm. We'll see him tonight at Grandma and Grandpa Frazer's. I think you're going to like each other."

The two drove along with Ariel pointing out the cathedral and directing him to the local market. They'd go sightseeing tomorrow after Riley had a good rest. The dinner tonight would be fun, and Ariel was anxious for him to like Jackson and Claire. There would be six for dinner tonight, and Ariel could count on her grandmother to keep the talk flowing. Sibyl was an excellent hostess, and Ariel knew that Riley would feel warmly welcomed by the time the evening was over.

They walked around the market looking at the specialty items, such as the Scottish shortbread cookies and pork pies that Riley hadn't seen before. Before they knew it, the afternoon had slipped away, and they had to hurry back to the cottage and freshen up for dinner. Riley had bought a bottle of port for her grandfather, and Ariel had picked up a nice lean piece of Canadian bacon for their breakfast in the morning. It was relaxing being with Riley, and Ariel was amazed at how comfortable she was with him.

Chapter 26

Sibyl and Robyn were just finished dressing when the door chimes rang, and Robyn went down to welcome Jackson and Claire. He'd just poured them a glass of Guinness when the chimes rang again, and he heard Sibyl talking to Ariel and Riley in the foyer.

After introductions were made, and Riley was provided with a cold Guinness and Ariel with some Seven Up, the party moved into the lovely dining room. The long trestle table was of ancient vintage and surrounded by six tall-backed, heavily carved chairs. There was a solid red tablecloth freshly starched and ironed with matching napkins in ancient silver napkin rings. The silver gleamed. The big deep plates were white, and a candelabra was lit with eight candles. Dinner was a roast beef and Yorkshire pudding with fresh green beans and warm homemade rolls that Claire had baked for the occasion. The roast was huge, and Robyn carved it expertly. Plates were passed and heaped with prime rib and Yorkshire pudding and generously ladled brown gravy. The green beans were fresh and deep green and steamed to crisp tender.

The dinner was filled with spirited conversation. Ariel listened as Riley and Jackson discussed the horses and Jackson's plans for a future racing stable. Riley and Jackson got on so well that the others were hard pressed to say much more than "pass the salt."

Sibyl listened to the two and then resumed her hostess duties, changing the subject to include Claire, Robyn, and Ariel as well. She was a master of the art of conversation, and she soon had a lively discussion going on America's new president, the first black man in history to hold the position. They talked through dessert and coffee, and then Ariel looked over at Riley and saw his eyes droop. He was dead on his feet. She quickly rose and ushered Riley out the door and into the jeep. They quickly drove home, but Riley was asleep before they got to the cottage.

Chapter 27

Early the next morning, while Riley was still rubbing the sleep from his eyes, Jackson called. He wanted to be off with the boat to troll in the Dornoch firth. He would lend Riley oilskins and sea boots. For the rest, Riley should bring a warm turtleneck sweater and warm wool socks. The wool would keep his feet warm even if they got wet.

Ariel was only half-awake and irritable, which made Riley glad to escape for a few hours. Ariel knew she was not at her best so early in the morning. "Go on, Riley. You and Jackson will enjoy the day." Ariel didn't understand the male bonding thing that said that going out together into the wild ocean and into Dornoch firth would be a an experience to shake the last cobwebs loose from his sleep-deprived brain.

Ariel put a backpack together of hot coffee and muffins with a wedge of cheese, some salt crackers, and a couple of crispy apples. As she handed it to him, she patted his shoulder and smiled. "Here's something to keep your belly full. The more in the belly, the easier it was to keep down, as my father used to say."

Riley took the backpack and kissed Ariel on the cheek. "We'll be back before sunset, and hopefully we'll be eating fish tonight for dinner." Ariel smiled and mentally thought of the ham sitting in the refrigerator "Just in case."

"I hate to leave you on our first day," Riley said as Ariel

wrapped a wool scarf around his neck and gave him a stocking hat for his head.

"No." Her smile was grateful, and her hand was gentle on his. "You need to go. You're over spent; the practice has drained you, and you're long overdue for a vacation. The physical things are what you need while your mind takes a rest awhile. Come back to me laughing and new." Just then, Jackson drove up, and in minutes, they were off heading for his skiff as the sun rose, its warm rays heating up the ancient Land Rover that was older than the one at Brindle Hall.

They did have fish for dinner that night. Riley came home reeking of bait, Jackson with him, and the two men cleaned the salmon and presented them to Ariel with a flourish. Ariel had put an au gratin potato dish in the oven and had made a big, fresh salad to go with the fresh-baked fish. The fish were beautiful, silver with dark iridescent purple on their backs. Each fish weighed over seven pounds. Ariel baked two of them and put two aside to give to Sibyl and Robyn. Ariel prepared a drawn butter and garlic sauce that was delicious with the baked salmon. Ariel, Jackson, and Riley sat at the scrubbed kitchen table long after the last morsel was eaten, laughing and talking together. Jackson entertained them with stories of her father and his as little boys that had been told down through the years until the two close friends' mischievousness had become legend.

The next day, Ariel and Riley dropped off the salmon in Sibyl's kitchen, took Joco, and walked on the beach. It was still cold, and there was a light fog that seemed to make the world go quiet. Ariel sent Joco running to catch the thick piece of driftwood she threw for him. Finally, they came to Ariel's favorite spot on the beach that overlooked Dornoch and the Dornoch Firth. It was a lovely spot, and Ariel enjoyed pointing out the places she and Lily had gone while Lily was here.

"Riley, I'm so frightened for Lily. This damn war is terrible; you can't even go out for dinner without risking your life and limb. Why does she do it? There are lots of people who need her in Columbia. I just don't understand."

"Lily has always craved a larger world than yours and mine, Ariel. I wouldn't be a bit surprised if she would go join the Peace Corps when she was done with this tour of duty. She's so curious about how others live; I think she feels that with Paul's money, she has to give back to the less fortunate."

Ariel and Riley stood up, and Ariel whistled for Joco to come. He was just as reluctant as he was when Robyn was walking with her, and he kept running down the beach until Ariel called to him sternly, "Joco, come now!" He came, dragging his tail and crawling the last few yards on his belly. "Oh Joco, I didn't mean to scare you, but you're naughty to run away when I call you. Come here now, boy."

Joco came up to Ariel and started to jump on her when Riley intervened, snapped his leash on him, and told him to "heel." Joco minded him instantly. The three of them walked back to the beach cottage, and the smell of Ariel's roasting chicken filled the kitchen, mouth watering and almost ready. Ariel slipped the fresh yams in beside the roasting pan and shut the door. "There now, we've just time for a cup of tea or whatever you'd like."

Riley seconded the tea, and Ariel put the kettle on.

The days melted into each other. Riley and Ariel were content to walk the beach and sit watching the ocean every day. They'd take a snack with them that usually did for their lunch. It was a slow easy life; Ariel had never felt as safe as she did with Riley. Some days they'd play tourist, with Ariel showing him around the ancient town. The cathedral intrigued Riley, and he pointed out to Ariel how the arches in the ceiling bore the weight of the building without posts. Riley loved visiting the shops as much as Ariel had, and he selected gifts from Bits and Pieces that he hoped his parents would like. For Julie, he bought a soft Shetland sweater and for his father a beautiful pen set that he knew he'd enjoy using.

The end of his stay was fast approaching, and Riley hadn't budged Ariel from her decision to go home. News of the investigation from Zoe didn't help any. They had gotten a court order to look at the clinic, but it was limited to the lab tech's work. The confidential information between doctor and patient was considered privileged, and even the court couldn't without extreme cause go nosing in patient files. It felt hopeless, and Riley didn't want Ariel to walk into a trap.

Chapter 28

iley and Ariel argued deep into the night, but at dawn, an exhausted Riley accepted that he couldn't budge Ariel's decision and went to the sun porch and turned on his laptop. His first message was to Zoe to let her know that he couldn't persuade Ariel to have her babies in Scotland and that they had made their flight for June 3. It was the middle of May and her babies were due around July 4.

Ariel and Riley, decision made, decided to make the most of their last couple of weeks in the Highlands and go and visit Culloden, the site of the Battle of Culloden on the sixteenth of April 1746. Riley was also interested in following the trail that Mary, Queen of Scots made throughout her captivity and in visiting the various castles where she was held. He hoped to persuade Ariel to come with him, which would further delay their return to America; he'd bring that up later to her.

The day was bright and sunny. Ariel stopped in at Brindle Hall and found Grandma Sibyl in the garden tending her roses. The garden was a riot of blooms of all colors. Ariel stopped just inside the gate and watched her grandmother contentedly working among her flowers. It was a scene from her past and though her grandmother was older and a bit more frail, she looked just as Ariel remembered her when she was a tiny tot of two playing around her while she worked. Ariel sighed and pushed open the gate.

"There you are! I looked all over the house for you, finally I came upon Robyn in the barn, and he said you were here. I wanted to tell you we are off to Inverness. I have my monthly appointment with Dr. Forbes, and then Riley and I will be going sightseeing. I thought we'd visit Culloden first and mosey our way back. We should be getting in late tonight so don't worry about us." Ariel went up to her grandmother and bent over to see what she was doing.

"I'm so happy to see the roses bloom that I'm afraid I've overdone. I'll have to take a salt bath tonight to work out the kinks. Have a wonderful day, my dear, and I can't wait to hear what the doctor says." Sibyl got up and brushed her knees off and leaned over and accepted a hug and kiss from Ariel. The two walked back to the house arm in arm. Ariel was pressed to take some fresh oatmeal cookies that Claire had baked that morning, and she had to hurry to get back to Riley, so they wouldn't be late for her appointment.

Riley drove to Inverness and accompanied her into Dr. Forbes office. When the doctor saw Riley, she paused and then walked forward and held out her hand. Ariel introduced them.

"Riley is a childhood friend come to keep me from going home. He was Morgan's best friend, and he thinks I need looking after." Ariel smiled up at Riley, and Dr. Forbes saw a look in Riley's eyes that made her wonder how Riley really felt about Ariel.

The nurse ushered Ariel into the exam room, leaving Riley to read the month-old *Newsweek*. Dr. Forbes finished her examination and snapped her gloves off. "Ariel, the babies are doing just fine. I think we are on target for July 4."

Ariel sat up, swung her legs around the examining table, and looked straight into Andres Forbes's eyes. "I'm leaving on June 3." Riley has made arrangements, and though he feels I'm still at risk, insists on accompanying me back to California. I want to tell you how much I've appreciated your excellent care and assure you that I will be very careful. I must leave before June 4, to accommodate the airline's regulations. I'll need a note from you that it's okay for me to fly home at eight months pregnant."

"Well you're pushing it, but everything looks okay, and there isn't any sign of premature labor." Andrea Forbes quickly wrote a note on her prescription pad and handed it to Ariel. "Drink plenty of water and keep your feet elevated if you can. Walk around the plane once every hour to keep your veins from forming a clot. Eat lightly and when you get back to America, layover in New York for one night before you take the last five hours to California." Dr. Forbes quickly shook Ariel's hand and wished her well. She was satisfied with Ariel's plans to find another ob-gyn in Modesto that Lily had also recommended. She warned Ariel that twins often came early and suggested that she book a room near the hospital her last two weeks, because it was over an hour drive from the almond farm.

Ariel walked out to the waiting room, and Dr. Forbes shook both Ariel and Riley's hands again and said good-bye. The drive from Inverness to Culloden Moor would take another hour. Ariel suggested that they go to lunch at the Iron Horse, and Riley had a big meat pasty and a Guinness. Ariel found she was hungry and had a fruit salad and a bowl of Scotch broth soup, thick with meat and barley. Ariel showed Riley her safe passage note, and he asked her what the doctor had said. "She wants me to keep my feet raised and get up and walk every hour. If I do that, then she had no objections."

Riley smiled and nodded as he finished off his beer and the huge pasties. "I'll see to you walking every hour, you can be sure of that!" He wiped his mouth and stood up.

"All set? The day is going by, and here we sit!" Ariel got up, stretched, and walked pointedly to the ladies room. Soon they were off and driving with the jeep top down.

The two, at ease, smiled at each other as the Willie's jeep, gears grinding, headed toward Nairn on a leisurely drive through small fishing villages. Ariel spotted an Oystercatcher, black with white strips on the back of his wings, as he soared through the air. The narrow lanes were flanked with wild pink roses and wild flowers dotted the roadside. White daisies and pink foxgloves vied for attention as the masses of wild roses held pride of place along the lane.

They drove into the car park for Culloden Moor and toured Culloden House, not far from the battlefield on Culloden Moor. It was a beautiful afternoon with the sun peeking through the clouds and when it broke through, they enjoyed the warmth of its rays. Ariel and Riley stopped in the visitors' center, which they walked through while taking turns reading the history of the battle aloud to each other as they stopped at each exhibit.

"The Battle of Culloden (16 April 1746) was the final clash between the French-supported Jacobites and the Hanoverian British Government in the 1745 Jacobite Rising."

"Culloden dealt the Jacobite cause to restore the House of Stuart to the throne of the Kingdom of Great Britain a decisive defeat."

"The site where the Frazer Clan fought with many other Highlanders was east of Inverness near Drummossie and around twelve miles before Nairn. The Jacobite pickets first sighted the English Government advance guard at about 8:00 a.m. When the advancing army came within four miles of Drummossie, the Jacobite army formed up about one mile from Culloden House, upon Culloden Moor. As the government forces steadily advanced across the moor, the driving rain and sleet blew from the northeast into the faces of the exhausted Jacobite army who had tried to stage a night attack on the English but lost their way in the dark and decided to wait the one hour till dawn to engage with them. This left them with a night without sleep, and they were fighting against well-rested English government troops. At 11:00 a.m., the troops faced each other on the moor and moved steadily forward. When they were still a hundred yards from Cumberland's right, the orders were given to "Make ready . . . present . . . fire!" About one third of the MacDonalds fell, either dead, dying, or severely wounded. Three times they made to advance in the hope of enticing the redcoats to break formation and attack, and three times they failed. The line held steady, and the MacDonalds died. It was too much, and they fell back in disarray. Panic became widespread, and the tartan tide flooded away from the killing place. The ceasefire was ordered in the Hanoverian ranks. What lay in front of them were heaps of dead and dying where the fighting and gunfire had been most effective. The Bonnie Prince had gone; he left his supporters to their individual fates and made his escape. His commander of Prince Charles Life Guards shouted after him as he departed, "Run, you cowardly Italian!" Lord George Murray still remained; his aides, thinking he might make a solo charge, took hold of his bridle (he had found a remount) and led him from the field in tears."

"The royal dragoons seemed to have been given free rein. Without any kind of order, they scoured the positions previously held by the highlanders. Swords slashing anybody that moved, chasing them to the streets of Inverness; none were given quarter. The infantry was ordered to advance in line to officially take and occupy their enemy's positions, reportedly using their bayonets to see off any wounded highlanders unable to make an escape. The battle was over. The last battle to be fought on mainland Britain had lasted a little less than sixty minutes from the first shot to the cease fire. But the slaughter continued. What occurred thereafter, murder, rape, looting would today be considered a war crime of the worst kind. The official 'butcher's bill' was 50 dead and 259 injured. Of the highlanders, figures are less certain; the dead numbered somewhere between 1,200 and 2,000, almost half of their whole number."

"More than men died that cold miserable day. A dream died, a way of life died, the clan system died, and the highlanders died. An hour was all it took, an hour in which the fate of nations was decided. Scotland would never be the same again."

"The aftermath of the battle was brutal and earned the victorious general the nickname 'Butcher' Cumberland. Charles Edward Stuart eventually left Britain and went to Rome, never to attempt to take the throne again. Civil penalties were severe with new laws that attacked the Highlanders' clan system. Highland dress was not to be worn by the Scots and restricted from use by the British Army."

Ariel and Riley finished reading the self-tour guide description of the battle, and Ariel found herself staring onto the moor with tears streaming down her cheeks. She could almost see the red coats of the English and the ill-prepared and bright plaids of the Jacobites massacring each other with broadswords, axes and bayonets, volleys of musket fire, and artillery rounds of grapeshot. Ariel's Frazer clan and the Murray's joined the Jacobites, largely Highland Scots, and, under the banner of MacDonald clan, supported the claim of James Francis Edward Stuart ("the Old Pretender") to the throne. The government army, under the Duke of Cumberland, younger son of the Hanoverian sovereign, King George II, supported his father's cause. It too included Highland Scots, as well as Scottish Lowlanders and English troops.

Riley handed Ariel his clean handkerchief, and she wiped

her face and leaned into Riley's shoulder. "Oh, Riley, it's our ancestors buried here, and Robyn's and Sibyl's too!" The two walked back to their car in silence, overcome by the tragedy that had taken place on this now hallowed ground. The men were buried where they died in mass graves. Ariel couldn't speak, and Riley helped her into the jeep. It was a solemn pair that made their way back to Inverness. They stopped again at the Iron Horse and had dinner. Ariel looked around the pub at the sturdy Scots and their ladies and marveled that they had overcome such a terrible defeat.

"Oh, Riley, I feel so bad for my ancestors and such admiration for the ones who survived the terrible aftermath of the battle. I heard from my father that many of them landed in prison, and his Frazer patriarch of the future American Frazer's immigrated to America to save his life. There were some who paid his way out of jail but not before he was beaten and almost killed numerous times. Now I can see with my eyes where it happened, and that old Angus Frazer who turned up in Boston in the 1750s was a survivor. I'm going to do my best to be strong like he was when I go home. I'm of good solid stock, and I will not let the bastard kill my babies or me. I will not!"

Ariel pounded her fists on Riley's chest till he reached up and put his arms around her and hugged her. It was meant to comfort her, but somehow his face turned down and found her lips, and the two clung together. It was as if the emotions of the battle site allowed them to let go of the pent up feelings of the loss over Sarah and Morgan. They comforted each other with their bodies and their lips. Riley couldn't let her go, and the kiss lengthened and deepened till they sprang apart in shock.

"Oh, dear God, Ariel, I'm sorry, I'm sorry. I couldn't stop myself." He put his hands up to his face and began to cry. "I loved Sarah and Morgan, and I feel ashamed that I couldn't mourn them without resorting to this. I'm sorry, Ariel, please forgive me."

Ariel and Riley walked in silence toward the car and kept their distance from each. They were both shocked at what had happened between them, and they didn't know what to say to each other. The drove back in silence. Just before they arrived in Dornoch, Ariel reached over and squeezed Riley's hand, and they held hands the rest of the way back to Brindle Hall. They were in shock to discover that they had such strong feelings for each other and were in fact falling in love. Neither of them had had any intention of matters coming to this, but it had happened, and now they had to deal with it.

Chapter 29

It was late afternoon when Ariel and Riley drove into the short driveway that led to the tiny beach cottage. They were exhausted and emotionally drained. They feared that the brief flair of passion would interfere with their friendship, and neither of them wanted to risk that. Riley busied himself reheating some of the rich Scotch broth soup that Sibyl had brought over and left in their refrigerator while Ariel made them thick-sliced sandwiches of ham and cheese. They avoided looking at each other until they couldn't avoid it anymore when they sat facing each other in the tiny cottage kitchen.

Ariel put her napkin in her lap and looked up at Riley with huge green eyes; her bright auburn hair was a mass of curls that fell into her face. She brushed them aside and looked squarely at Riley. "Riley, it's all right. It's just the shock is all. We've been friends since our toddler years. It was bound to happen. With all we have both been through with Morgan's and Sarah's murders, I have to tell you that I really was surprised that I have such strong feelings for you. I am confused and sad, and yet I feel a new feeling of hope for the future. I don't know. I don't know how you feel, and I don't want to risk our friendship, but I'm not upset. Let's just take things a bit slower. We're bound to be attracted to each other. We have so much history between us, but I'm still grieving Morgan, as I know you are too, and I've the twins to think about." The two old friends smiled at each other and ate their dinner in silence.

Riley didn't say anything until the soup was all gone and the last bite of ham sandwich. Then he reached over to Ariel and gripped her hands in his big ones. "Ariel, since my wife left me, I've put all thought of loving anyone out of my mind, and the practice has consumed me. But I have to be honest when I say I always had warm feelings for you and Morgan and a twinge of regret when I'd watch you both when we were out at the mining claim dredging and playing in the river together. Those were wonderful times, and yet they also made me feel my loneliness acutely. I never meant to force myself on you, and I won't again, but I do hope that this is a sign of something unexpected and wonderful for our future. I just know that when you e-mailed me and said that you were going to come home, I was terrified and fearful for you. This is three murders all close to you. I'm petrified that the person responsible for these deaths will stop at nothing to get to you if you go home now. I have a suggestion, and I hope that you will agree.

"My middle name is Stuart, and my mother was a Stuart. I've been told all my life that I was descendant of Mary, Queen of Scots. What I would like to do is take a car ride to all of the castles she was held captive at, in order from the first here in Scotland at the castle of Lochleven to her last captivity in England at Fortherinhay Castle in Northampton. If we took a long week to explore the route that she was taken, I would be very grateful. It's something I've always wanted to do, and it might help us to just spend time together with no expectations of anything more."

He smiled at her, and Ariel smiled back. They kissed then, friends again, careful of the risks of friendship. They were exhausted after their long day of sightseeing, so shortly after dinner, Ariel got up and went over to where Riley was reading the newspaper and quickly kissed him on the cheek. "Good night, Riley Roberts. Golden dreams."

Riley smiled up at her and yawned mightily. "Wow! Is it the Scottish air! I haven't been so sleepy, so early, in a long time. Good night, my dear friend." Riley got up, and the two walked to their separate rooms, turning out lights as they went.

Ariel's night proved restless. She woke a dozen times in the darkness, itching with desire for the man who slept only a few steps away and yet was as far as the celestial stars. For too long she had slept alone but for the bumping of her twins. She hungered for the comfort of warm arms around her, safe. Her body remembered the loving and was rebelling and betraying her steadfast loyalty to Morgan. She switched on the light and read until dawn.

When she heard Riley moving around the kitchen, she crawled out of bed, bathed, and went to cage a cup of coffee in the kitchen.

Chapter 30

Sibyl and Robyn were excited when they heard their plans the next morning at Brindle Hall. Sibyl poured rich thick coffee and nudged fresh baked scones over toward them. "Robyn and I did this same trip for our twenty-fifth wedding anniversary. My mother was also a Stuart, which means that Ariel too is related through my mother's side of the family. It will be fun for you both."

Ariel laughed, "Grandma Sibyl, you are an amazing woman. I never knew that we were of the Royal Stuart lineage. My father never told me anything about his family's history. With you so far away, I didn't get it from my grandparents either. I'm amazed. When we were at Cullenden Moor, the family connections were all there, but I was looking from the Frazer side."

Ariel laughed and for the first time since the death of Morgan and Sarah, was relieved of her deep feelings of grief. It was as if a fresh new beginning was in store for her and her babies. And Ariel couldn't wait to get going and visit Riley's and her joint history. It amazed and thrilled her that they had this in common to focus on. Their feelings could be put on hold, and they could explore as the friends they were. Riley had promised that when they were finished, he would take her home, but this adventure could help them both in so many ways. Ariel and Riley hugged Robyn and Sibyl and agreed to a small dinner with Jackson and

Claire to say good-bye for a while. Ariel knew now that her grandparents and cousin were back in her life, and she would never let the years go by without a visit as her father did. She had already invited Sibyl and Robyn to her farm after the babies were born, and she planned on yearly visits to Brindle Hall with the twins so that her grandparents and her babies would know each other. Ariel was so excited. She danced around the sitting room as her big belly bumped into the furniture. She didn't realize how big she had gotten and when she knocked over a small tea table and looked with shock at her grandmother, a big smile creased her face, and the whole group started laughing.

There was so much to do before they could start. Ariel and Riley were invited over to Jackson's farm to see the mare and her new filly foal that had surprised Jackson the night before. Buttercup had the filly quickly and with little trouble. Jackson didn't even have time to call Ariel and Riley to come over and watch. After a hearty lunch with Sibyl and Robyn, Robyn drove the four of them over in the Land Rover to see the new filly.

Jackson hailed them from the barn. Robyn drove the Land Rover right to the barn doors, and the four got out. After a quick tour of the barns, Jackson led Riley and Ariel to Buttercup and her newborn filly, wobbly legged and nursing eagerly. Buttercup stood patiently letting the little one nurse her fill. Her eyes got big when Jackson stepped into her stall with Riley standing behind him.

"There, there, Buttercup, it's only us, and we've brought a friend." Jackson reached into his pocket and produced an apple and a carrot. He gripped her halter and let her munch the treats out of his hand. Riley, behind Jackson, accepted an apple and stepped closer to the mare. Jackson slipped sideways away from her, and Riley took his place, an apple in his hand.

Buttercup looked at him as he repeated Jackson's cooing

sounds and finally accepted the apple. Riley patted her chestnut head and rubbed his hands over her flanks, whispering soothing words all the while. Riley looked carefully at the filly, watching her nurse eagerly with a clear sparkle in her eyes. She was a beautiful rich chestnut like her mother. After his brief exam of both mare and foal, he stepped out of the birthing stall and turned to Jackson. "That's a fine filly, Jackson. I can see you've taken excellent care of its mother. Look at the sparkle in her eyes, and her coat just gleams. Excellent job, Jackson." The two men stood together, lost in talk of horses and foals. Jackson's chest expanded, and he grinned from ear to ear.

Chapter 31

The morning dawned fresh and crisp, with the promise of a clear warm day ahead of them. Ariel and Riley were eager to start this journey of exploration. Their common heritage was friendly land, a place to focus that would allow them to be together with something other than their feelings for each other to distract them. Finally, they were off. The little Morris car that Riley had rented had been exchanged for a sturdy Land Rover. Ariel and Riley had packed their bags and stowed everything in the trunk. They used the back seat of the car for their picnic fixings and overnight bags that could be grabbed without having to dig through all the luggage. Before they left for the queen's tour of her castles of captivity, they decided to go to the Isle of Lewis and take the ferry across to the Outer Isles. On the Isle of Lewis, there was a little inn in Stornoway, a small village that they found by driving up a single track winding through peat lands and rare small crofts. The road was so narrow that if you met another car, one of them had to pull into a lay-by to let the other pass.

The inn was a lonely place at first look, built of gray stone with sharp gables and narrow dormer windows and rock walls raised high against the sea winds. By afternoon, the weather had changed, and it had begun to rain, a soft, steady drizzle blown in from the western ocean. The clouds rolled low over the hills, making a cheerless gloom. Gulls cried swooped and dived into the sea for their dinner. Ariel and Riley were hungry and cold when they walked inside the inn and asked for rooms. Thankfully, they had two, and they took them both. Leaving each other at the top of the stairs, they agreed to meet in the dining room for dinner in a few minutes. After freshening up and washing the road grime off their hands and face, they met again at the top of the stairs, and Riley gave Ariel his arm as they slowly descended.

The dining room was cozy with a fire in a big stand-up fireplace. The apple-cheeked waitress put them in front of the fire and handed them small menus. Her hand on her wide hips, she scowled at them a look of irritation on her face for having to leave her heavily thumbed paperback.

"You can look at the menu if you want, but I'm to tell you that all the cook is prepared to fix at this time of day is a rich Scotch broth and a pasty filled with ham and cheese." Riley looked at Ariel, she nodded, and the order was given.

It was only a few minutes after they were sipping the strong hot builder's tea that their soup and meat pasties arrived, piping hot and delicious with a fresh flaky pastry made into little turnovers. Riley ordered a Guinness in a mug, a rich dark beer that went well with the Scotch broth and pasty.

After their dinner, Ariel and Riley bundled up in their jackets and walked the sea wall until dusk. Bellies full and completely exhausted, Ariel and Riley trudged back to the inn and straight up the stairs. They paused outside of Ariel's room, and Ariel reached up and kissed Riley softly on the cheek.

"Golden dreams, Riley," she said as she unlocked her door and went into her room, leaving Riley outside her door, yearning to be with her. Ariel closed her door and looked around at the small bedroom with the large feather bed that took almost all the space under the eaves of the dormer windows. In moments, she had undressed and put on her warmest nightgown before slipping under the cover of the great fluffy down comforter. She was asleep as soon as her head hit the pillow. Her dreams were of magic and fairies. Ariel slept the sleep of exhaustion, and Riley was a solid shadow in her dreams. She felt safe tucked in the big feather bed and slept soundly.

It was the next afternoon when they came to the place of the standing stones, a high grassy knoll that falls away southwards towards Loch Roag. The hill lay naked to the sky, and the great megaliths rose out of it, three times the height of man. There were four rows of them and at the convergence of the rows, a circular burial place and a stone, larger than the others, faced the sunrise. No one knew of the men who raised the stones except that they were here before the Celts over three thousand years ago and at this hill, they worshipped the sun and lived their ritual life by it. They left nothing of themselves, no language, and no history. Ariel and Riley felt their ghosts as they stood, hand in hand, under the stone of sacrifice and watched a herring gull fly up and out to the sea. Ariel shivered, and Riley drew her close and kissed her flaming hair. It was then that he had the courage to tell her his heart.

"If it's too early or not to be, I don't care. I'm past worrying about it. I love you, Ariel; I'd like to marry you. I've loved you since we met in high school, but you only had eyes for Morgan, and he for you, and I loved you both. I settled for being your friend, and I always will be no matter what happens, but my heart is so full and aches so much for you and for your pain." He stopped, uncertain, and looked deeply into her eyes, the emerald green of the sea shadowed by her emotions. He feared the look she gave him and yet welcomed it too. Welcomed that they were talking of what stood between them. It was a relief to speak, to declare him and come what may, they would deal with it together.

Ariel reached up and smoothed the hair that had fallen across his face and smiled at him. She patted her enormous stomach, and just then, a foot stuck out and hit Riley full in his solar plexus. Amazed and without permission, he put his hand on the spot and waited for the thrust of foot, a silent communication from within that focused both Ariel and Riley's awareness on the two small people who would soon emerge and take their place in a world that right now felt frightening and tentative to both of them.

Ariel paused and touched his wrist. "My sweet, Riley, I'm glad we're talking; it's been between us for a long time, and I've known. I've known that you loved me; there has always been a place in my heart that loves you, too. I'm so afraid, so desperately afraid, for my babies and my life that I have nothing to give right now. I'm so grateful for your strength and your caring. I must get through this terrible waiting until my babies are born. All of my energy and thought are for them right now. Can you be patient, my dear? Can you let me have this time to gather my strength for their birth and to settle once and for all this menace that plagues me?"

Riley shifted his weight to bring her closer to him. He brushed the windblown hair out of her face and nodded. He realized more than ever that the life they had shared together these past weeks was what he wanted. He was tired of his solitude. But for the moment, there were no other options. Ariel was not ready for more than they had, which was friendship with a possible future passion and romance. She was no way ready for more than that. Riley knew that he had no choice but to wait and see what happened between them, if anything ever did. And if it didn't, Riley winced, if she was never able to reach out to him, then at least he could be a friend to her and her twins. He knew that was a possibility too. There were no guarantees in life. Ariel had ample proof of that.

Riley put his arm around Ariel's shoulders, as they walked through the shrubbery that protected the inn from the winds at the beach. The pathway was narrow and rocky; Ariel had trouble seeing where her feet were with the huge bulk of her stomach filled with squirming babies. Riley's firm grasp reassured her, and they slowly made their way back to the inn. It was getting colder, and a light mist was beginning to fall. Ariel was glad for the warmth of the inn. Its interior was lit with sconces on the wall. Ariel and Riley walked into the dining room and sat before the roaring fire. This time Ariel was starving, and she ordered a prime rib dinner with a baked potato with all the trimmings. There were fresh green beans and hot rolls oozing with butter. Riley had the same. They topped the dinner off with a hot fudge sundae that they shared and steaming cups of hot coffee.

Ariel struggled to explain her feelings to Riley. She loved him, but she was afraid, and she wasn't ready to be with him. Maybe this trip wasn't such a good idea after all. The words were out of her mouth before she could stop them.

"Riley, maybe we should just go home?" Riley looked as if she had struck him.

"No! I'll take you any way I can, and if it's friendship you want, you've got it, but we're not going home until June 3 as planned. Give me that much time to keep you as safe as I can, please, Ariel."

Ariel nodded, and there was no more talk of going home.

Chapter 32

They left the Isle of Lewis the next morning after a breakfast of eggs and bacon and an English muffin with whipped fresh butter and orange marmalade. The day was dark, and a gloom settled all around the Land Rover as it ground its gears up onto the ferry ramp at Tarbert. In a little less than an hour, they were across the Minch and powering into the Loch Snizort on the Isle of Skye, another famous tourist spot. Ariel and Riley pressed on and drove across the island, taking the bridge on A 87 across the Sound of Sleat. Their route took them to Fort William where they found a quaint bed and breakfast at the end of a long drizzly day. Ariel was exhausted, and Riley was worried that the trip was too much for her. The pair parked the Land Rover, walked up to the door of the little cottage, and rang the bell. The door was opened by a small woman who looked almost like a child.

Ariel hesitated and then asked if she had a room available for the night. "Yes, mum, I have a big front bedroom with a king-sized bed. Will that do?" She looked at Ariel's belly and quickly opened the door wide and ushered the tired travelers in.

A quick look at the room was all it took, and Ariel smiled her assent. Riley followed the innkeeper back to the desk and left Ariel to lie down on bed to rest. He was back in no time. "It's the only room she has, do you mind? We could go look for another place if you are uncomfortable." Riley looked at the exhausted Ariel and left the decision up to her.

"Riley, I've seen you in your underwear before. Remember how we used to go swimming in the swimming hole? We'd all hike up, and before the day was done, we'd be in the river. For some reason none of us ever bothered with bathing suits. This will be just fine. I'm so tired I just want to go to sleep." So they did, both of them so tired that they were asleep in minutes, any self consciousness gone as they each lay on a side of the big king with several feet between them.

When Ariel woke in the morning, the space between them had narrowed. Ariel found she had draped her arm around Riley's shoulder, and it felt so comforting. She quickly moved away and was up and in her robe by the time Riley woke up. The two of them dressed quickly and went downstairs to a hot breakfast of coffee and a rack of toast with eggs over easy and bacon. There was also a plate of cinnamon rolls that Riley devoured. They thanked the innkeeper and were on the road again by nine o'clock.

They crossed the Loch Tummel and drove on toward Perth. It was a long drive, but they reached Perth at about four o'clock and found a pub that not only had a hearty dinner in front of a roaring fire, but the innkeeper had a room at the top of the stairs for sixteen pounds. Riley took it. This little room was much smaller and by now, Riley and Ariel were comfortable together. They quickly undressed, put on their nightclothes, taking turns in the bathroom, and got into the big feather bed.

They were soon warm, and this time Ariel reached over to Riley and squeezed his hand. "Good night, Riley, thank you for understanding."

Riley turned toward her, put his big hand under her chin, and smiled. "We'll give it what it takes, my dear." He caressed her face with his big hand, leaned over, and kissed her on the forehead. "Golden dreams, my dear."

Loch Leven Island. After breakfast of a rack of toast and a poached egg with bacon with steaming hot, rich, fresh coffee, Ariel and Riley packed their overnight bags and said good-bye to Mrs. Ross, the innkeeper, who had taken such good care of them. Mrs. Ross was delighted to hear that they planned to visit Loch Leven Island and cheerfully gave them directions from Perth.

"It's a mite past twenty miles, and the road is good interstate straight through. You should reach Kinross by noon, and then the ferry will take you across to the island. It's well worth seeing. My husband was the ferry captain before he died. I used to ride with him and sometimes take the tour. We were given privilege and could tour anytime we wanted for free. I'd get off the ferry, and Daniel would go back for another crossing. I'd love to have my lunch on the side of Kinross lake while he ferried another group over. You'll have a good time, I'm sure." Mrs. Ross walked them to their car and invited them to come back when the babies were born and Ariel would be more comfortable.

Riley drove straight through from Perth, and just as Mrs. Ross said, they were there by noon. The ferry was loading, and they got in line. Ariel was glad she had accepted Mrs. Ross's gesture of sandwiches and sodas. There were chips and fresh crispy apples as well. Ariel and Riley left the car at the car park on the west side of the loch and got tickets for the ferry. The ferry was small and looked a lot like the boats that are used to patrol around cruise ships. It held twenty people normally, but since it was a weekday, they had it all to themselves. The ferry left the pier. Ariel and Riley sat outside and ate the lunch eagerly. When the last crumb was eaten and Riley had finished his soda, they arrived at the castle.

The guide was a young Scotswoman still in her twenties, and she took them on a tour of the grounds and the tower house where Queen Mary was imprisoned. Ariel could feel for the pregnant Mary; she was horrified when she learned that Mary had delivered stillborn twins. The story of Mary, Queen of Scots was tragic, and being in the castle that had housed her during her ordeal was overwhelming. The castle walls whispered, and Ariel could visualize the arrival of Mary to the home of her father, King James V, and his mistress, Margaret Douglas.

Mary had no friend in this castle. Margaret was the mother of the King's bastard, James Stuart, who had been Earl of Mar and had become Earl of Moray. He was the man behind the plot to remove the queen from the throne in favor of her young son, James, who was no more than an infant. The earl could then be Regent and have the sole power of the throne until James was of age. By the time Ariel and Riley had left the castle and were once again seated on the little ferry and headed back to their car, Ariel was almost in tears. Hearing of Mary, Queen of Scots during history lessons was one thing, but walking where she walked, Ariel felt her plight keenly and identified with the ordeal the queen was in.

The lives of the people of history were surprisingly fresh, and Ariel and Riley could relate to the way fate would play its tricks. What one wanted in life was often diverted to something else. It would be that way for Ariel and Riley as well. They were unaware of the wheels of fortune turning their lives to its own end.

Chapter 33

Back in the states, a situation arose that would affect Riley and change his life forever. It was early afternoon; Meredith Campbell had just gotten back from lunch when the call came in. It was from a social worker in San Francisco who contacted Meredith hoping she could help with an investigation that she was struggling with. A woman had died of cancer and had left a ten-year-old son. The boyfriend of Rachel Roberts denied that the boy was his and refused to take any responsibility for him at all. Social services had been called when the nurses had discovered the little boy hiding in the bathroom in his mother's hospital room. They had just discovered Rachel had died, and the nurse heard the little boy sobbing behind the closed door. The message on Meredith's voice mail sounded intriguing. Meredith set aside her other messages to give this one her top priority.

"Hello, this is Meredith Campbell, is this Ashley Harper? I'm returning your call regarding the Roberts child you called me about."

Ashley sounded rushed, and she got right to the point. "Ms. Campbell, we haven't been able to locate any next of kin for Rachel Robert's son. His name is Jonathan Roberts, and right now, we have him in emergency foster care. I've discovered that Ms. Roberts was married to a Riley Stuart Roberts, but she divorced him before the child was born. I don't have any information that Mr. Roberts either knew about the boy or supported him. Jonathan's birth certificate does not have a name for his father, so we are not sure of anything at this point. I would like you to contact Mr. Roberts and see if he knows anything about this child."

"It's Dr. Roberts; he's our local vet up here. I actually know him quite well. I remember when Rachel left, Riley was devastated, but he never mentioned a child. I'll get back to you as soon as I talk to him. I understand he is out of the country for a vacation, so it might be awhile till you hear from me."

Meredith paused, and Ashley rushed in and asked her, "How do you know Dr. Roberts?"

"Columbia is a small town. I went to school with Dr. Roberts, so we all know quite a bit about each other. Rachel was a beautiful woman. I'm sorry to hear she has died. I can tell you though, she was very strong headed, and she didn't like the way the doctor's work interfered with her plans. She was a very selfish person who only wanted things to be how she wanted them. I could see her not telling Riley about Jonathan. Well, we could always get a paternity test done if there is any question."

Meredith hung up the phone and frowned. This was going to be a problem. There wasn't anything to be done except to leave him a message to call her as soon as he got in. Meredith picked up the phone and dialed. The answering machine came on, just as she expected. The social worker raked her hands over her soft brown hair and sighed. Meredith left a brief urgent message on his home answering machine. There was no reason to let anyone at his office in on this. She'd done what she could; now she was waiting on the good doctor.

Chapter 34

Lily

The plane swooped out of the sky and dropped down into Oakland where a scorching hot morning promised to make the trip home hot and uncomfortable. Lily unbuckled her seatbelt, grabbed her small satchel from the overhead compartment, and followed the passengers into the terminal. There was no one to meet her because she had told no one that she was coming home almost three months before she was decommissioned permanently.

Lily looked worn and much thinner than when she had left her sister, Ariel, in Scotland last spring. The war had gotten too close and had killed Matt in a bizarre plot. Matt and Lily had gone to dinner in their favorite tiny bistro. Suddenly a woman came into the restaurant and started shouting slogans in Iraqi. Matt jumped up, pulled Lily to her feet, and pushed her toward the back of the restaurant. Just then, the woman moved toward Matt, pulled the pin out of a grenade, and blew herself up. Matt took the force of the grenade and fell, shielding Lily from much of the shrapnel from the blast. He was horribly injured, and Lily did what she could to stop the blood. Before help arrived, Matt was dead. Lily shut down and when the paramedics arrived, they found her holding Matt in her arms, in shock, her eyes unseeing. In all, thirty people were killed, and many injured. They took her with them to the hospital, and she stayed with Matt until they gently took her arms from around him and took him away.

Lily had shrapnel wounds on her back and legs and was hospitalized for several days. The doctors were more worried about her state of mind than her body. After assessing her and hearing that this was the third death of someone close to her in less than four months, they recommended that she be released from her duties three months early.

Lily recovered at the U.S. military hospital in Landstuhl, Germany. As soon as they released her, and she received her medical discharge, she got on the first plane back to the states. Lily wouldn't let them call her family, and she didn't tell anyone she was coming home. She needed to take her time, so she rented a car, drove up to Marin County, and stayed in a small bed and breakfast she loved called the Pelican Inn near Muir Woods.

Her first morning there, Lily drove down to Muir Woods and walked among the ancient redwoods. The rest of the day, she spent at the Pacific Ocean. She had lunch on Stinson Beach at a little beach shack that had the best fish and chips on the coast. The beach was beautiful. Lily walked out onto the wet sand and removed her sandals. The cool wet sand, firm beneath her feet, helped her to ground herself and to transition from the horror of the war zone to the peace and serenity of the ocean.

Loud noises still startled her. The doctors had diagnosed her with Post Traumatic Stress Disorder and explained that she might have flashbacks of the suicide bombing that took Matt from her just after he had proposed marriage, and she had said yes. Now there was nothing. She felt nothing but a flat line of depression. Her beautiful Matt was gone, and she didn't know how she was going to go on. After two nights at the inn and walking the beach, she steeled herself to go home.

She left the inn at dawn, drove over the Golden Gate Bridge and the Bay Bridge, and pointed the little Honda toward the mountains. It was cool in the morning. She stopped for coffee in Escalon where she traditionally broke her journey and had an early lunch at Cindy's. The last leg of the trip through Oakdale and past Knights Ferry to Jamestown and the turnoff to Sonora went by quickly. After turning onto Highway 49 through Sonora, she drove the five miles into Columbia. The yellow farmhouse looked deserted. Lily drove through the farm gate and down to where her little cottage stood alone and lonely looking. Lily unlocked the front door and walked into the memories--memories of her mother greeting her and smiling at her, memories of her mother's horrible death and Morgan's. Lily collapsed in tears on the big bed and that was where Julie found her late in the afternoon when she returned from her errands in town. She spotted the car parked at the cottage and wondered who was there. She saw Ben on the tractor cutting the long hay that he used for the mulching in the big vegetable garden. Julie waved at him and pointed at the little car. Ben looked puzzled and drove the tractor into the barnyard and shut it off.

"Ben, whose car is this?"

Julie turned and peered into the front window. Ben came up beside her and looked inside. "Beats me, I didn't notice it when I swept this area earlier. Let's go see." With puzzled looks, they climbed the stairs with Ben in front and quietly entered the house.

Chapter 35

Scotland

iley drove fast, and the heavy Land Rover hugged the road. Driving on the left had been difficult for Riley at first, but he had soon gotten the hang of it and drove through the country with assurance. Riley was worried about Ariel; she was tiring earlier and earlier, and Riley decided that they must stop and rest.

The little town of Kirkcaldy was on the Firth of Forth. Riley thought of it as an inlet or a bay, and the Firth was a quaint name to him. They found a tiny inn right on the water, and there was a large room available with a fireplace and big comfortable lounge chairs. Riley tucked Ariel into the one with a footrest and told her to keep her feet elevated while he went out to get them some lunch.

By the time he got back from the fish and chips shop, Ariel had fallen asleep. She woke when he unlocked the door.

"Hey, sleepyhead, are you up for some fish and chips?" He brought in the newspaper-wrapped fish and French fried potatoes and brought out small packets of malt vinegar such as mustard and ketchup came in the states. The malt vinegar was delicious on the potato strips and crisp, fried cod. Ariel and Riley ate the meal in front of the fire with their fingers. Ariel licked her fingers as the last bite was consumed, looked up at Riley, and grinned.

"Delicious. I've never had the real thing before. They say wrapping it in newspaper is what makes all the difference." She paused and then hesitatingly looked up at Riley and asked him the question that had been nudging at her ever since they had left Loch Leven. "Would you be terribly disappointed if we just drove straight through to London and skipped the rest of the locations of Queen Mary's captivity? I am exhausted, and it was more depressing than I realized. I'm just not able to see another woman in such torment. I'm sorry."

"Hey don't worry about it. I've been thinking the same thing, but I didn't know how to ask you. We can drive straight through to London and be there by tomorrow evening. Our reservations are open ended; I can call and get us on a flight by noon the next day." Riley reached over and poked at the fire, renewing the flames by turning the logs.

They spent the rest of the evening watching the boats on the firth from the window of their room and were asleep by nine that evening. They were up and out before dawn, bags packed and tucked in the car. No one was up when they left the inn. There was a light drizzle, and Riley put the heater on in the Land Rover.

The fastest route to London was A 74, which was a green-marked interstate. They stayed on the interstate and wove their way through Carlisle, Lancaster, Manchester, and over to Sheffield. They were in the counties that the queen's captivity route followed, and this was enough to see the country that she had to travel in. In the eighteen years that the queen was held captive, she had been moved from Sheffield Stafford, Derby Shrewsbury, and Coventry England until the fateful day she was taken to Northampton and to the infamous Forthinghay castle where she was tried and beheaded. It was enough for them to imagine the horror of her imprisonment without touring each and every place she had been taken.

They followed the M-1 from Northampton straight into London, and it was nearly six o'clock when they drove to the famous Brown's Hotel where Lily and Ariel had broken their trip on the way to Scotland. It was a wonderful place, and Ariel was glad that they had returned to the comfortable old hotel. The desk clerk greeted her like an old friend and gave Ariel the same suite that she had shared with Lily.

As soon as they stepped into the suite, they were treated to a level of comfort and elegance that Riley had never experienced before. It made the cutting short of their trip less disappointing, and Ariel enjoyed pampering Riley. The luxury was wonderful, especially having breakfast in the suite served with hot steaming coffee in a shining silver coffee pot. By now, they were used to staying together. The large suite had a bedroom and a sitting room. Lily had had to order a portable cot and had given Ariel the big bed. Now Riley and Ariel shared the bed just as they had been doing throughout their tour. The bathroom was marble with heated towel bars and a long tub that Ariel filled with scented bubble bath.

She still had a couple of days before her June 4 deadline to take an airline trip. They had just made it in time, and her doctor's note would get them on board tomorrow at noon. The long soak in the tub restored Ariel, and she suggested they dress and go down to dinner. Ariel had a soft gray maternity dress of velvet and black boots. She wasn't going to go dancing, but the dress was warm and serviceable and was of a stretchy material that definitely showed her body. Showing your bump was the fashion, so Ariel was only a little self-conscious when the two of them walked into the restaurant. Riley was in a beautiful gray suit, and the two looked splendid as he held her arm and escorted her into the restaurant. They chose a table with upholstered chairs rather than a booth. Ariel didn't think she'd fit in one while the chair could be adjusted for her girth.

Riley ordered lobster with drawn butter for both of them. It was a wonderful evening, and when they were finished and back in their room, they called Sibyl and Robyn to let them know where they were and to say good-bye again.

"Be sure and call me when the babies are born, won't you dear. We are thrilled for you and wish you all the blessings for you and your little ones." Sibyl and Robyn shared the phone ear to ear.

Riley got on, described their trip, and told why they had cut it short. By the time he got off the phone, Ariel was already in her nightgown and had turned down the huge bed comforter of down. There was an elegant canopy on the bed and big thick columns on the bedstead. Riley slipped in beside her, and they kissed each other good night. Riley laid in the dark for over an hour, listening to Ariel's breathing, soft though occasionally she would make a small snore. The babies were taking up so much of her lung capacity that he was amazed that she could breathe at all. Riley turned his thoughts to their arrival in California then to how they could protect her until the babies were born.

Finally, Riley fell into a restless sleep and had already awakened when the telephone rang with their wakeup call at 7:00 a.m. Shortly afterwards, a knock on the door brought them breakfast of coffee and juice with scones and bacon and eggs. It was wonderfully relaxing not to go down to breakfast but to sit by the window and watch the bustle of London. It was a shame that they didn't have time to explore the city, but Riley promised himself that they would come back and explore the country properly when Ariel had delivered the babies, and they were able to be married. Riley promised himself that too. They would be married. Now he just had to get her home and safely delivered of the twins. Zoe was going to meet them and fly them home. Plans were in the works for a twenty-four hour guard at the farm, and if need be, he knew Zoe, she'd move in with Ariel until the babies were born. It would all be fine. It had to be!

The ten-hour flight got them into New York by 10:00 p.m., and they stayed at the Plaza to break their flight as they promised Dr. Forbes that they would. Finally, though, they were on the final leg of their journey, and the big 727 United jet swooped out of the sky and treated them to a scenic view of the city of San Francisco. Ariel was so happy to be home that if she could have, she'd have kissed the ground, but she wouldn't have been able to get up if she'd tried.

Zoe, good as her word, was waiting at the gate and had a wheel chair with her. Ariel protested. "This is silly, I can walk. People will think I'm an invalid." However, Zoe insisted, and she drove the chair as efficiently as her plane. They whizzed through the concourse and into the area for small aircraft departures and arrivals. It was quick and smooth and before Ariel knew it, she was tucked into Zoe's Cessna, with Riley behind her in the back seat.

The Cessna taxied onto the runway and waited for tower instructions. In only a few minutes, they got the okay for runway 32. Zoe powered up, and they were off.

Zoe had kept the surprise of Lily's early return to herself. Ariel and Riley were so busy telling her all about their trip that it was easy to listen to them as they flew across the Central Valley and headed due east to Columbia. As much as Zoe was frightened for Ariel's safety, she was also delighted to see them both. She had a patrol car stationed around the clock at the ranch for as long as the office would let her. They had turned over every rock in this investigation, and they were beginning to zero in on one of the doctors at the clinic. The lab tech, George Warner, had worked almost exclusively for Dr. Hillerman, who also was Ariel's doctor. So far, they hadn't turned up the computer from George's home or anything at all at the clinic. They had looked at all of the computers at the clinic, and there was nothing on Ariel other than just what they all knew--that Dr. Hillerman had done a routine in-vitro fertilization procedure on her, and the results were two viable embryos implanted last October. Ariel's file was the only one they could get a court order to look at. If there was anything else done to Ariel, it wasn't in her file.

The next step was to get a court order to look at Dr. Hillerman's home computer as well. So far, the judge had deferred the order, and they were in limbo. They couldn't move forward, except to harass the doctor by pulling him in for questioning about his technician's horrible murder. Zoe knew he had something to do with Warner's murder and maybe Sarah's and Morgan's as well. Sarah's injuries had been done by someone who knew just where to go in to hit the spinal column and cause her instant paralysis. Zoe and David knew he was involved, but he had lawyered up, and they couldn't touch him.

The vagrant Davidson, who had attacked Morgan and Ariel and killed Morgan, had had too much money on him, out of proportion to his usual hand-to-mouth existence. The doctor could have paid him to kill Morgan, but if he had, there wasn't any evidence of it, and they couldn't get access to the doctor's accounts without that darn court order. Zoe was so busy thinking about the case that she was barely listening to Ariel and Riley, except to go "uh huh" periodically as they flew along the last leg of the trip up 120 to the Columbia airport.

When they taxied into the little airport, they were surprised and happy to see Lily and Mark waiting for them in the small lobby. The old regulars were lined up on comfortable chairs outside, just on the edge of the tarmac and under the eaves of the building--old flyers who spent their days gabbing about their experiences. Most of them still had small planes stored at the airport, but they spent more time talking about their flying days than actually flying. Zoe stopped and chatted for a minute with her father's friend Bud Masterson. He and her dad had been schoolmates and remained close all these years. That was what Zoe liked so much about the Columbia area. Everyone knew each other, and though Sonora had the bulk of their shopping dollars, the small community of Columbia had their neighborliness. Ariel and Riley waved at Bud and his cronies chewing the fat with Zoe as they walked into the lobby.

When Ariel saw Lily, she burst into tears, and the two sisters hugged each other, bringing Riley and Mark into a group hug.

"Lily, how long have you been home? I didn't expect you till September."

The group moved toward the two jeeps parked in the airport parking lot, just really a big empty field that adjoined the small tower and airport office. Mark piled the luggage into Zoe's jeep, and the four climbed into his wrangler. Zoe was just coming out of the building when Mark hollered at her to hurry up and follow them. Mark started asking Ariel and Riley how their trip went, and Ariel's question to Lily was slid over and ignored. They got to the farm, unloaded the baggage, greeted Ben and Julie, and admired Sofie's puppies--only two little females left, which Ben thought might make a nice start for a kennel that Ariel had been thinking about starting.

The group trooped up the stairs, and Riley and Julie beamed when Ariel went into the newly painted and furnished nursery. Ariel sat in the rocker and looked around at the little lamb lamp and the new white cribs with Julie's newly crocheted baby blankets in soft pink, blue, yellow, and green squares that covered the beds. Ariel got up and opened the white wardrobe that Ben had painted and admired the tiny little sleepers and stacks of infant, birth-size disposable diapers.

"Wow! Everything is ready to go! I'm amazed that you did all of this, and nobody said a word. I was worried that I had that all to do. To tell the truth, I'm very, very grateful that I don't have to even think about it. You've taken a load off my mind." Ariel's eyes filled with tears, and Lily came up to her and gave her a hug.

"Come on, sis, let's go down and get a bite to eat. Julie's been putting together a feast for us." Lily handed her a handkerchief, and the two sisters went down stairs arm in arm.

"I don't know why I cry so easily. This is a wonderful surprise. I'm so happy to see you, but, Lily, you're so thin. Are you all right?"

Lily hugged her tightly. "I'm going to be fine. Let's go eat, and we'll talk when we are through. I have a lot to tell you too."

Julie and Ben were pulling a big rack of ribs off the barbeque. They piled them up in the center of the round kitchen table. Julie put a big bowl of potato salad and one of coleslaw with apples and raisins beside the ribs. She was just taking out the French bread when they came into the big kitchen.

"Folks, sit down and eat. You must be starving after that long trip. Here, Julie, I'll get the Jell-O; you just get everyone started. " Ben urged Julie.

So Julie sat down and let Ben get the avocado Jell-O that made any meal special. It was an old family recipe and included lime Jell-O, mashed avocado, crushed pineapple, and whipped cream. It was delicious. Sarah had served it often, but in the interests of their waistlines, they had substituted Cool Whip for the whipped cream, and it tasted just like Sarah always made it.

The evening moved along swiftly. Dinner was devoured, and there was nothing left but rib bones and scrapped bowls. Dessert was strawberry shortcake, and this time real whipped cream was generously applied. Julie made individual shortcakes with Bisquick, and the strawberries were from their own patch.

Ariel sat back and looked at her family, so grateful for them all. The three siblings were alone, without their parents to draw them close, but Ben and Julie had stepped right in and brought them together. Riley and Zoe were family too. They'd all known each other all of their lives and as the tragedy in their family made spaces at the table, they had come in and filled them. Riley caught her eye and smiled, and Ariel smiled back. Riley was going to spend the night in his apartment and go see his landlord tomorrow to give notice. Then he would move into the big yellow house to help protect Ariel during the night, and because they had gotten used to being together and couldn't bear to be apart.

It wasn't until breakfast the next day that Ariel got Lily to tell her what had happened to her. The two sisters sat at the round table over coffee, and Lily told her story.

"After Matt died, I just fell apart. I was just devastated, and I knew that I wouldn't be able to stay till the end of my tour. The doctors who treated my shrapnel injuries were very, very kind, and they intervened and got me deferred on medical leave. Matt had asked me to marry him only minutes before the bombing, and I had said yes. We had that joy for only a few minutes when all hell broke loose, and I was holding his body in my arms. Oh, Ariel it was horrible! He was killed instantly, and I was knocked to the floor with his body on top of me. They told me later that his body was what had shielded me from instant death."

Lily sat stirring her coffee with a faraway look in her eyes that Ariel was to observe in her whenever she came upon her as she helped Julie with the summer freezing of all of the fresh foods the farm grew.

Ariel had come home right in the midst of the canning season, though Julie and Lily weren't actually canning--they were freezing the farm's bounty. The first day Ariel was back, there were delicious Gravenstein apples that would make wonderful winter pies and cobblers to prepare for the freezer as well as fresh green beans that Ariel snapped and put into boiling water for a second or two to blanch before putting them in freezer bags. The tomato harvest was abundant, and Julie made pots of sauce that went into the freezer in quart size plastic containers to be made into pizza sauce and spaghetti sauce as well as lasagna sauce. It was a busy day. Lily worked right alongside Julie and Ariel until they had processed it all.

Ariel's back ached from the long day of preparing the fresh fruit and vegetables for the winter. It was satisfying though, and Ariel sighed happily, as she took a cool shower. Riley was coming for dinner, and she was a mess. Her shirt was filthy with fruit juice stain, and it was a relief to get into white cotton maternity chinos and a loose gauze blouse the green of her eyes.

Chapter 36

iley took the back stairs two at a time and knocked quickly on the door before peeking inside. His mother, Julie, was at the range, and the kitchen smelled wonderful. He went to his mother and grabbed her from behind, startling her. "Oh, Riley, stop that, you gave me a fright, for sure you did." She turned and looked at her son and put her hand to her mouth. "What's the matter, son?" Riley shrugged and motioned for her to come and sit down.

"Ma, I found out something today that has shocked the life out of me. I have both some bad news and maybe some good news too. Time will tell. Brace yourself. Where are Dad and Ariel? I want them to hear this too. I'll go get her. Could you call Dad in?" Julie called Ben in and in trod Riley's Brittney Spaniel, Freckles, along with Sofie and her pups, Daisy and Ruby. Ben wanted to know what was up, and Julie just shrugged.

Riley was going up the back steps to the second floor when he saw her at the top of the stairs. She looked clean and fresh and huge in her maternity pants and loose blouse. He reached her quickly and hugged her, as well as kissing her soundly.

"Wow! Riley, did you miss me that much today?" Ariel smiled up at him and then saw the serious look on his face. "What's the matter, Riley? You look like you've had a rough day."

"Come down with me to the kitchen. I've something to tell you all, and I want you all together when I say it." Riley held her arm and helped her down the stairs, which were getting harder to navigate with her huge stomach. They reached the bottom step just as Ben came in and looked puzzled at Riley.

"What's up, Riley?" he said as he joined the others in the kitchen. The big round table was where all family discussions had taken place ever since Ariel was little and that continued to the present.

Riley brought out the lemonade and glasses and poured them all a drink.

"I've just learned that I have a son. When I went to the apartment, there was a message from Meredith Campbell. When I called her back, she floored me with the news that Rachel died of cancer and left a ten-year-old boy. He doesn't have anyone, and apparently, the boyfriend Rachel was with doesn't want him. The date of his birth is August 4, 1998. That could be just about right. Rachel left me just after Thanksgiving. I didn't know she was pregnant. She might not have known yet either, and when she found out, she chose not to tell me. I don't know; it's all up in the air. Meredith said the boy's name is Jonathan Stuart Roberts, and I could take a paternity test if I want. Well, folks, I went down and had the test today. I should know something soon. If this is my son, I want him. Meredith said that they would test him and have the test compared. If he is my son, I might have him before the month's out. It's amazing and scary, but I couldn't turn my back on him if he's mine. The thing is what would I do with him during the days?"

Ariel had listened carefully and immediately said, "Have him here with us." Julie and Ben nodded their assent.

"We are here at the farm. He could be with us. Ben could keep him pretty busy, and we could keep him for you when you're at the office." Julie said. It was that easy. Riley couldn't believe how generous Ariel and his folks were. The truth would come out with that test, and then they'd go from there. Riley told them that Meredith wanted him to go to San Francisco to meet Jonathan just as soon as the tests were verified.

The week went by in a whirl of activity. Ben and Julie cleaned out a spare room in the big house where Mark had bunked as a boy. It was a little room right off the kitchen and with a new blue woven bedspread and crisp white curtains, it looked fresh. There already were shelves and a student desk with a gooseneck lamp where Mark had done his homework.

Chapter 37

The phone rang early Monday morning, and Julie was in the kitchen making breakfast for everyone. "Frazer farm, Julie speaking!"

"Oh yes, Meredith, how are you, dear, and your parents?"

Finally, Meredith got to the purpose of her call. "Is Riley there? This is the number he gave me to call him at."

"Yes, he just came in to the kitchen." July turned to Riley. "Riley, for you." Julie put the phone down, and Riley picked it up. She couldn't help listening, and she waited with her lips pursed.

"Okay, that settles it, Meredith. I'll meet you at your office at eight tomorrow. Thank you for calling and letting me know." Riley put the phone down with a stunned look on his face just as Ariel walked in looking for her first cup of coffee.

"I'm a father!" He went to his mother and hugged her. "And you and Dad have another grandchild!"

He reached Ariel and gave her a huge hug and kiss too. "I'm to go to San Francisco tomorrow with Meredith, and we're going to bring him home tomorrow. Oh my gosh! I've got to sit down." Riley plopped down in the kitchen chair, and Julie, with tears in her eyes, poured them all a cup of freshly ground coffee.

They were all so excited, and yet Ariel was a little worried too. She knew that the poor kid had had a difficult time of it. She had talked with Meredith cohort to cohort, and though she couldn't give any particulars, what she did give her was enough to get the picture of a little boy who had been taking care of his mother for the past year during her illness. The boyfriend had been abusive, and they had ended up in a shelter for mothers and their children who were fleeing from abusive situations. Her heart went out to Jonathan, and she hoped that he would adjust to living with a father he had never known he had. Thankfully, from her experience with foster placement, she was aware of how fast children responded to loving caretakers. That didn't mean there wasn't plenty of work to do to get them to the place where they could trust that no one would hurt them or that they'd have to leave again.

The day was a blur for everyone. Riley was seeing patients all day and got back to the farm after eight that night. The rest of them went through the day anxious and hoping that Jonathan would fit in at the farm. They all pledged to do everything in their power to help him. Ariel felt the waiting the keenest, because she was such a whale that she couldn't do much to distract herself from thinking about the changes that were coming to them all. There would be three children at the farm by next month. What would this be like and would they be able to reach Jonathan and bring him into this bustling growing family? How would this impact Riley and Ariel's life? Would they get married as they had talked of? Would this upset a life of their own? Ariel was exhausted when Riley got home and had already gone to bed propped in her lounge chair. The babies made it hard for her to breathe lying flat, so this lounger was her bed until they were born.

Riley peeked into the room, tiptoed over to her, and covered her with a light cotton blanket. It was over a hundred degrees outside, and the swamp cooler was working overtime to keep the house a cooler eighty degrees.

Ariel stirred as she felt the weight of the blanket and

opened her eyes. "Riley, how are you doing? Are you ready for tomorrow?" Ariel reached out and pulled his face down to her and kissed him gently. It was a reassuring gentle kiss, and before Riley could answer her, he saw her eyes close and send her back into her dreams.

"Good night, my dear. Golden dreams. I'm fine. I'll talk to you in the morning." Riley tiptoed out and went downstairs. The house was dark. Lily was in her cottage, and Julie and Ben had gone out to their apartment, so Ben could watch the Oakland Athletics' baseball game.

Riley walked quickly to the little bedroom that was once Mark's and would now be Jon's and looked at it. He had made sure there was new play equipment as well as a small television set with a Game Boy. Ariel had suggested that, saying, "It gives him a break from the strain and stress in the early days as he becomes accustomed to his new home. Don't worry, we'll limit it, but in the beginning it can be helpful in his transition process."

Riley looked in the closet at the empty hangers and visualized boy clothes hanging from the wooden clothes hangers. *My God, my life has certainly changed, but I'll do my best for him and for Ariel too*, he thought as he quietly closed the door. The room would do, and he would be with him every evening. Somehow, this would all work out.

Chapter 38

The alarm jolted him awake at six thirty in the morning. Thankfully, when he peeked in at Ariel, she was still sleeping soundly. He'd let her sleep. She'd been up and down half the night going to the bathroom. His mother was already in the kitchen when he came lightly down the back stairs. She smiled up at him and handed him a cup of black, fresh-brewed coffee. Julie was excited. It wasn't every day you met your first grandson. Julie had made him eggs and bacon and was just buttering some toast.

"Ah, Ma, you didn't have to go to so much trouble. I'd have gotten something on the road."

Julie put the plate down briskly. "I was wide awake at five. Might as well do something as to lay there worrying how he's going to like us and us him."

As usual, Julie hit the nail on the head. Riley dipped into his eggs with his toast and smiled up at her. "It's going to be fine. You're going to charm him like you do Callie, and I expect he's just as worried himself today on whether he'll like me or not. I'm going to do everything I can to help him adjust, and I know you and Dad will be just what he needs."

Riley looked at his watch and scooted his chair back. "Well, I'm off. We should be back here after dinner. Don't wait for us. I'm going to take him to his favorite grease pit. Nothing like a juicy hamburger to help bond, especially if we top it off with a big chocolate shake and French fries. Gotta go, Meredith is waiting for me." At that, he reached over, gave his mother a hug, and held her for a moment. "Thanks, Ma. I don't know what I would have done without your support and Dad's too."

"Oh, go on with you now. I'm busy, and the sooner you go, the sooner I get to meet him."

Riley laughed and bound out of the house and down the stairs. Meredith was driving, and it was just eight in the morning when he drove up to her office. She was waiting for him in her car, and she gave the horn a tap to alert him to her presence.

"Come on now, Riley, don't let anyone see me. If I go into the office, I'll get all tangled up in everyone's cases, and I'll never get out of there." The two sped off in her big county-issued sedan. Gray, like them all, without any markings identifying it as a county car except a number on the back rear bumper. Meredith drove fast and kept a stream of conversation flowing. By the time they reached the Bay Bridge three hours later, they'd caught up on their lives from their school days. Riley was grateful for the diversion that reminiscing about school days caused. It was only about fifteen minutes later that they drove into the parking lot at the social services building. Meredith went into short-term parking and grabbed her briefcase. The two hurried into the building, the guard called up to Ashley Harper, and they were sent up to the fourth floor, room 207. Ashley met them at the door and ushered them into her small office. At least she had an office, so she was a senior social worker; otherwise, she would have just had a cubicle to squeeze them all into.

"We'll be meeting Jon and his foster mother in a half hour in the play room. You made good time. How was your trip?" She was busy gathering the case file together and as they were answering her, she hurried them down the hall into the small lunchroom for a cup of coffee. "As soon as they get here, I'll be notified, but we might as well have some coffee, and I can answer any questions you might have." She looked at Riley and waited. She was small and plain with short cropped gray hair. She wore no jewelry except a wide wedding band.

The silence lengthened, and she let it, until finally, Riley cleared his throat. "What can you tell me about his life?"

Ashley looked steadily at him before she flipped open the case file and began to read. "The hospital social worker called us when they found Jon in Rachel's room. That was on May 10. The boy was wearing old dirty jeans and a very dirty tee shirt. His shoes didn't have any laces. Apparently, when his mother got so sick, and they brought her to the hospital from the shelter, Jon slipped away from the caseworker and hid until they gave up searching for him. He then made his way to his mother's room and subsisted on leftovers from people's trays. There were two another women in the ward with Rachel. They befriended Jon and shared their meals with him. He hid out every time someone came to check his mother, and when she died, he hid in the bathroom.

"The caseworker told us that Jon and his mother had been at the shelter for about a month, and they had come from a very bad situation. Jon was beaten pretty badly by the boyfriend when he got between his mother and the man. His mother finally got the courage to call the police when she saw the condition that Jon was in. The police brought them to the shelter and that was where they were when Rachel's condition got so bad she had to be hospitalized."

Just then, Ashley's cell phone rang, and she excused herself and answered it.

"Okay! Jon and his foster mother, Mrs. Martinez, are here. Shall we go meet your son, Dr. Roberts?" Suddenly Riley's mouth went dry, and all he could do was nod.

The playroom was on the second floor, and it only took them a moment to reach it by the back steps. The workers used the steps instead of the elevator, because they could get there much faster than the elevators could. Ashley led the way into a big room with lots of stuffed animals and games. There was a Hispanic woman and a small slim boy playing checkers together in the back of the room. It seemed to take forever for Riley to cross the room, and then he and Jon were face to face.

"Jon, I'd like you to meet your father, Riley Roberts. Riley, this is your son, Jonathan Roberts."

Everyone sat down, and father and son stared at each other without saying a word. Meredith was amazed at how much they looked like each other. The same dove brown hair and deep blue eyes. Jon was thin and so like Riley when he was ten. Meredith remembered him from her fourth grade class. They were almost carbon copies of each other. Riley saw the resemblance too. It shook him up, and he had to clear his throat before he could say anything.

"Jon, I'm so sorry about your mother. She didn't deserve to have to go through so much. I hear that you did your best to protect her, and I want you to know I think you are a very brave young man." Riley paused and waited for Jon to speak.

"I miss her so much. Are you really my father?" He looked up at Riley as he tried to fight the welling of tears in his eyes. Jon was curious about Riley. The workers had told him he had a father, but he didn't understand why he had never known about him. He didn't want to like this big tall man who had his coloring and eyes. He didn't want to like someone who would leave his mother the way he did. At least that's the story his mom had always told him. He heard from the worker that his father hadn't known about him. He could believe that because his mom didn't always tell him the truth. He knew that about her, but he couldn't believe she'd keep such a big thing as a father from him.

Riley nodded, and reached out to take him in his arms. Jon hesitated, and the hug turned into a quick shoulder hug. Both Jon and Riley looked at each other, and Riley smiled at him.

Riley decided to be straight with him, and so he told him. "I'm sorry, Jon; Rachel left me and never told me that she was expecting you. I was working long hours, and I'd be called out at all hours. Sometimes it would upset your mom, especially if she had made plans and I had to go deliver a foal or calf. It just got so she didn't want to be with me anymore. I tried to find her, and then when the divorce papers came, I didn't fight it. We never spoke or saw each other after she left, so I never knew about you, and I am very sad and sorry about that. Will you come and live with me and give me a chance to make it different for you?"

Riley held his breath as he waited for his answer. Jon hitched his shoulder, nodded with his chin, got up, and picked up his backpack. Things moved quickly. Jon said good-bye to Mrs. Martinez and endured her hug and kiss. Meredith and Ashley went back to Ashley's office and signed off on all the paperwork. Meredith would be Jon's social worker until the judge turned him officially over to Riley after several home visits to see how they were adjusting to each other. Between Meredith and Ariel, Riley had all the experts around him he needed to be the best father that he could be to Jon. It would take time, but he saw in Jon a strong little boy who also loved his mother, and Riley hoped he could bring some hope, trust, and love into Jon's life for both of them. Meredith came down to the playroom, and it was time to go. It was close to noon, and Riley asked Jon if he wanted to stop for a burger. It just took him a minute to ask for a McDonald's meal. Riley gave him the job of finding the first golden arches they could as they drove on Highway 580 toward the farm. It was only a minute before Jon saw golden arches at the Tracy turnoff and hollered and pointed.

"I see it, Jon, hold your horses. I have to get over to the off ramp."

Meredith expertly stirred the car to the off ramp and in seconds, they were pulling into the familiar eatery. Meredith spent a lot of time in McDonald's, as did her other workers, because this was one of the best places to meet a biological parent for a visit. It was a public place and therefore safer. The ones they went to had the playrooms, too, so that when the workers had to discuss anything with the mom and dad during a supervised visit, the kids could be off playing and wouldn't have to hear the conversation between the worker and his parents. Most of the foster kids she dealt with were super sensitive and protective of their parents. They might have abandoned them or beaten them, but they were their parents, and that was that. It had always amazed Meredith--the fierce loyalty--and she hoped that when Jon got to know Riley, that bond would develop for them too. Both of them had been hurt by Rachel, and Meredith hoped that Jon would give Riley a chance, and that Riley would be patient with this young child. There was a lot of good in Riley and in Jon too. Meredith had seen a lot of kids go through the system, and she could tell when they were salvageable. Jon, she hoped, was one that was.

The three ate their burgers and slurped their shakes and when Riley made a big slurping noise, Jon laughed and slurped his too. Meredith looked sternly at both of them, and they giggled at each other. Riley would get down to Jon's level to reach his playfulness. Ariel had often told him that if she could get a kid to giggle and act like a kid, she could win them over. It was the "old souls" she'd see that had been so hurt that they wouldn't risk any communication that she worried for. Give Jon a few weeks, and she just bet that the two would be comfortable with each other.

Riley had his heart set on it.

Riley and Jon said good-bye to Meredith at the office, and they set a date for the next week for her to come by and see them at the farm. It was only a short drive to the farm, and Riley took the time to tell him that he would be meeting his grandparents there as well as Ariel and Lily and Mark. Riley told Jon all about the close group of friends and family that would be sharing the ranch with them all, and Jon listened, wide eyed and quiet.

When they turned into the farmyard, it was already dinnertime. Ariel heard them coming and met them at the door.

"Riley, you made good time!" Ariel looked past Riley at the small thin boy, and her heart went out to him. "Just in time for supper." She smiled at him and opened the door wide. "Welcome Jon, I've heard so much about you."

Though he'd told his Mom not to wait for them, they found two places set at the table, and a big meat loaf with baked potatoes and green peas waiting for them. Riley introduced Jon to everyone and even Sofie and her pups, Daisy and Ruby, were there. Jon smiled shyly at everyone, but when Ruby bound up to him and jumped into his arms, he dropped to the floor and let her lick him all over. The adults all looked at each other and smiled. It would take time, but that boy had a friend already who could heal his heart better than anyone else could.

Dinner was over, and Jon's eyes were drooping. He and Ruby had found a ball and had played fetch until Ruby dropped down beside him. "Hey, Jon, let's show you where you're going to bunk, and if you'd like, Ruby can bunk with you too." Riley opened the door and turned on the light to the little room, Ruby raced ahead and jumped right into the middle of Jon's bed. Everybody laughed, and when Jon had gotten into his to small pajamas and brushed his teeth, Riley tucked him in.

"Good night, Jon, hope Ruby leaves you enough room on

the bed, but if she doesn't, show her who's boss and make her sleep at the foot of the bed. Golden dreams, Jon." Jon waved goodnight, and his eyes closed before Riley had the lights out and the door closed. A small night light shone on the boy and the dog snuggling up to each other, already drawing comfort from each other.

Ariel and Riley were surprised at how quickly Jon fit into the family. Jon and Ruby were constant companions, and if they weren't in the kitchen bugging Grandma Julie for snacks and treats, they were out in the barn and orchard following around behind Grandpa Ben. There was a lot to do on the farm, and Jon had never had such an interesting, fun place before. When he lived with his mother and her various boyfriends, he spent most of his time watching television in his room, hiding from interactions with his mother or the fellows she ran with. He never knew whom she'd bring home with her. After one of her "friends" tried to get into his bed with him, and Jon was able to get away from him, he insisted on having a lock on his door. Even with the lock, he was super careful of going out to the kitchen and even the bathroom if one of his mother's friends was around.

Every morning, Jon was awake and waiting for his father to come down to breakfast, already at the table and eating Grandma Julie's pancakes and eggs. Riley would wash his hands and sit down to eggs over easy and wheat toast down with black coffee. The two would discuss Jon's plans for the day, and if his father had a slow day without surgery, Jon would often tag along with him to the office. Jon learned how to put fresh water in the pens, and if there were kittens, he'd often have one or two purring contentedly in his arms.

Riley enjoyed those days when there was time for Jon and Riley to sneak off for lunch, and they always ended up at the covered wagon hot dog stand that Larry ran. They always ordered the colossal hotdog with everything on it and chips and a soda. It was fun to walk around the historic town of Columbia and saunter over to the park with their food. It was hot one day when the two picked their favorite tree and settled down to eat their dogs. Jon wolfed his down and tackled his chips. He was just finishing his soda when he looked up and met his father's eyes with a questioning look.

"What's on your mind, Jon? I can see the wheels spinning in there." Riley smiled at him and waited for him to get it out.

"I just wondered if you were going to marry Ariel? She's going to have those babies and all." Jon trailed off and looked off at a tour bus full of kids who had come to Columbia to learn about California gold mining history.

Riley gave him a hug and thought how to best answer him. "We've talked of marriage, and I want to marry her. These babies are from her husband, Morgan, before he died, and she wants to wait until they are born before she makes another commitment to me and our marriage. I told her I'd wait. Ariel and I also talked about how now that you're with us, we would adopt you. I want you to know that you and I are a package, and just as I will take Ariel and her babies, she is committed to taking you and me too.

"You're not to worry, Jon, it's going to all work out. I have already told Meredith to get the paper work for your adoption to the judge as soon as it can be put on the court calendar. Your mother did not name me as the father on your birth certificate, so even though the DNA has come back a positive match, we have to legally adopt you. It's confusing I know, but I'm trying to hurry everything as fast as possible, so that you know you aren't going anywhere but with me. Ariel has only a very few weeks to go before the babies are born and when they are, we will be free to make us all a family. I promise you, Jon."

Chapter 39

June went by in a rush, and Jon was happy with his new family. Grandma Julie was busy every day preserving the harvest from Frazer Acres.

The only thing they didn't preserve was the strawberries. They ate fresh strawberries for breakfast in fresh fruit compotes and for dinner as strawberry shortcake and strawberry pie until the little patch had finished producing.

No one got tired of the fruit.

Riley was eating dinner every day with Ariel and Lily and Mark and Jon whenever he was home. Zoe would drop in after her shift was up and check in with the patrol who was watching the farm from their patrol car. Often, they sat under folding chairs in the shade as they listened to the radio. Zoe was always happy to sample the daily fare, eating her portion with gusto. Ben rigged up a canvas covering, and the officers were as cool as it was possible to be. It was beginning to feel like they weren't necessary, and finally the day came when they were pulled off the stakeout.

It made Riley nervous, and he made sure that the front gate was locked whenever anyone left the farm. At night, Ben and Riley both slept with pistols at easy reach. Everything that could be done was being done. It was a nuisance to have the house locked up both front and back. Carrying their keys became the norm.

Ariel felt like a prisoner in her own home, and nothing could change the fact that she was. The days of June dragged hot and long, and it was a relief for everyone when the end of the month came. The month had slipped by with temperatures in the nineties, and then it was July, and the heat wave reached one hundred and ten degrees. No one could do much, and the house was shadowed with all the shades down and fans blowing throughout the rooms. The swamp cooler worked overtime keeping the inside temperature a cool eighty degrees. It was a time of quiet enduring.

Ariel got up early when it was still cool, and by noon, everyone who could was taking a nap, stripped of clothes, and laying out flat on their beds. Ariel's huge mound made sleeping impossible, and she put a white sheet over the lounger that Riley and Ben had moved into her room. This is where she slept the month of June and where Lily found her barely covered in a cotton shift, her feet swollen to twice their size. It was the morning of July 3.

Ariel hadn't taken Dr. Forbes advice and gotten a room near the hospital two weeks before the birth was expected, and she hadn't said a word about it to anyone at the farm. Ariel had her sister with her, and if anything were to start, Lily would be able to tell her in plenty of time for them to get to the hospital. Ariel wasn't worried, and she would much rather sit it out at home in reasonable comfort than in a motel room.

Lily and Ariel were having coffee together in Ariel's makeshift bedroom on the summer porch. Lily had just been telling Ariel how she was going to take a hike up Silver Creek to get some good exercise when she looked down at Ariel's ankles and frowned at their puffiness.

"Ariel, let me look at you." She pushed her fingers into Ariel's ankles and put her stethoscope on Ariel's mammoth stomach to listen to the twins' heartbeats.

"Sis, I think you should get your bags packed. I don't like the looks of this swelling, and I think you should check in to the hospital in Modesto today."

"I know, Lily. I've called the doctor, and he's trying to get me a bed, but so far they haven't had one. He said to call him tomorrow, and if he had to, he'd put me in the hall in the maternity ward until a bed became available. I was going to tell you at lunch. I'll be glad when it's over, and I wouldn't mind the hallway at all if it meant that I'd be done with this pregnancy. It's the heat that really has gotten to me. I begged him to induce me, but he's not seen me for my whole pregnancy, so he's extra cautious and wants to wait until I show definite labor pains." The sister's were agreed that if there were any change at all, they'd head for the hospital.

The telephone call came that night. Ariel's doctor had found a room for her, but it wouldn't be available until afternoon the next day. Lily was relieved, and she told Ariel to get ready and she'd drive her down to Modesto. Because she knew she would be confined until after the birth, Lily decided to take a short hike at her favorite creek.

Chapter 40

Lily left the farm at dawn. It was the Fourth of July, but no celebration had been planned except Riley's birthday party was to be that night. Even that might be postponed if Ariel was in the hospital today as Lily hoped she'd be.

Lily had her hiking shoes on and a frozen bottle of water in the side pocket of her hiking shorts, an old trick to keep water cold; by the time she needed it, it would be thawed and frosty. It was still damn hot, and she was glad to have an early start. Silver Creek was one of her favorite hikes. Ariel and Mark had climbed up that creek every summer with her. As she walked through the wild grapes that covered so much of the entrance to Silver Creek, she thought back to how they had played up here climbing the steep rocks up to the top where the road met the creek causing a break before running under the road and cascading down again at almost a 25 percent grade. The climb was a good test of her strength, and she welcomed the energy it took. She was out of breath by the time she reached the top. There were great holes in the dried up creek bed with tools strewn all around. Someone was working the creek, digging deep into the bedrock to scrape the gold out of the cracks and crevices.

Lily welcomed the mindless climbing. It helped her to escape the pain of the memories of Matt. This place had so many memories of her childhood jaunts with her siblings and

Riley that for a while she could forget the horror of Matt's death and concentrate on the fun times they had all had during their summer breaks from school. At the top, there was an old wall built by the Chinese miners in 1849. Lily examined the wall and marveled at the skill that they had used to hone the rocks and make a wall that stood the test of time. Lily was mentally refreshed and relaxed. She finished drinking her water, turned back, and walked down, down, down, over the rocks and past the miners' excavation. The miners today used fancier tools, but their goal was the same as those ghostly images of small men who had left their mark on the creek with their timeless wall, yellow gold!

Lily slipped back into the house before Julie had gotten over to start the coffee and started it herself. The coffee perked quietly as she went out to the front gate and brought in the *Union Democrat,* and she sat and read it while drinking her coffee.

Riley and Jon joined her, and Riley asked her what she thought about just driving Ariel down to Modesto and throwing themselves on the mercy of the emergency room. Lily laughed. "Riley, I'd love to do just that, but you know Ariel. She's arranging for a bed, and it is supposed to be this afternoon. If the hospital doesn't call by noon, I'm going to get pushy. I don't have patient privileges at that hospital, but I can pull some strings as a navy physician. It will be today, I guarantee it. As soon as we get an okay, I'll call you."

Riley finished his coffee and muffin, ruffled Jon's hair, and hugged Lily. "Okay, guys, I'm going, and I'll be waiting for your call." Riley bounded out of the room and gave his mother a kiss on the way out. He stopped to rub Sofie's head as his father met him in the yard. They stopped for a minute to chat, and then Riley patted his father on the shoulder, got in his Tahoe, and took off with a peal of tires. Riley worked half days on Saturday to give his working clients an opportunity to see to their pets' care.

The sun was already high when Ariel crawled out of the lounger she was sleeping in, and she'd had it. Riley had put the lounger on the screened porch to catch what cool breeze she could. Today was supposed to be a scorcher over one hundred five degrees, Ariel was exhausted already. The doctor hadn't called yet and that was the first thing she was going to do when she had the energy to get up. The squirming infants had kept her awake most of the night. Sleep was impossible, and as soon as she'd dose off, one of the twins would start moving around and waking her up again. Her back ached, and the only thing that helped was an ice pack and sitting in the lounger that had been Morgan's. The only thing on television in those wee hours were info commercials. Ariel had taken to walking around the house, straightening things, and even doing the laundry. Julie complained that she didn't have anything to do in the morning when she came. Ariel grumbled that she'd have plenty to do when the little guys came and to appreciate the "vacation."

It was a difficult time with Ariel's irritable mood, and everyone shied away from her. They called and stopped by, of course, but even Zoë, Mark, Riley, and Jon knew when to shut up and have important business elsewhere. The babies were due any day now, and she'd be so relieved to be released from this weight. Her ankles stayed swollen, and she couldn't put on shoes except her flip flops. She hadn't been able to walk up the stairs for over a month. For the present, her bedroom was the porch. She had Julie move her maternity clothes and underwear into a makeshift closet at the end of the porch. There was room for a short pole in the built-in cupboard, and her sparse wardrobe hung there. The underwear and stockings slipped easily into a single drawer in the built-in desk that had been in the house since Sarah and Paul had lived there. Sarah used to write her case files here, and Ariel and Lily had used the porch to play house. Ariel was the mother, and Lily was her child. Ariel smiled when she thought of the time when Lily was little. Lily was a beautiful child with black hair and green eyes. Ariel wondered if she would have a little girl like her. She wondered if her children would use the porch this way and thought that it would make a great play area with a gate across the door when they were in the toddler stage and pulling everything out of drawers and playing with whatever they found. The porch could be baby proofed, and toys, little chairs, and a tiny table could be brought in. Ariel still had the alphabet rug that Sarah had bought for Lily and Mark to play on. Now it was faded to a soft patina of colors that would be perfect for the play porch. Ariel had it ready, cleaned, and wrapped for when they would be old enough to be put out here for a few hours to play while she worked nearby on the book she had wanted to write ever since she had become a social worker.

Ariel knew with two infants that she would be both father and mother to, that she wouldn't be working outside as a social worker for quite a while, if at all, but there were other things she could do to keep active, and one of them was to write. Truth to tell, she had already written the equivalent of several books with the eight and one-half by fourteen inch, single-spaced reports she had kept on each child. Now she just had to pick a situation and use that to get started.

Thankfully, it would be over soon. She walked heavily into the bathroom and stripped off her tent-size nightgown. Ariel avoided the mirror; she already knew she looked like a beached whale. The tepid shower felt wonderful and gradually she increased the cold water until it cooled her all over. The babies were wedged in tight now, and all they could do was stick an elbow or foot out to move the other twin out of their way. As Ariel dried herself, all of a sudden, there was a great heave and a foot stuck right out. Because she was thin, it was all babies. She could grab the foot through her skin and hold it for a bit before it eventually slipped away again. It was like a game between mother and infants. They'd stretch out, and she'd grab their foot, wiggle it a bit, and talk softly to them.

"Hey, little one, Mommy's going to see you soon." Just then, the phone rang, and irritated, she pulled a clean Muumuu over her head. Ariel debated whether to leave the phone on voice mail, but if she did, it might be the doctor, and if it were Zoe, Mark, or Riley, they'd think she'd gone into labor. So with a heavy sigh, she walked into the kitchen and picked up the receiver.

"Hello?" she said.

She was wary and annoyed, defensive. She thought it was her friends bugging her on whether she's had any signs of labor starting, and she was prepared to bite off their heads for pestering her.

"Hello, Ariel."

"Yes?" she said.

The caller gave her the code that he had suggested to her months ago. A post-hypnotic suggestion that sent Ariel into instant obedience.

Ariel put the phone down and walked purposefully toward the front door. Julie was just coming up the back stairs and heard the front door click shut. Ariel must be going to get the mail. Julie sighed in relief. It was hard to be around a late pregnancy, and Julie would get busy with the vacuum, so that she wouldn't be expected to talk to Ariel right away. It was their pattern for the last few days. After she was done and had gone into the kitchen to make them both a bite of lunch would be soon enough to talk. She felt so sorry for Ariel. The heat was miserable for them all, but for her she could just imagine. When she'd had Riley, on July 4 for a present, Ben brought a fan and ice he'd filled into a big bowl from the hospitals ice machine to her in the hospital. She smiled as she remembered how nice it was, and she was the only new mother to have a fan.

Well, it wouldn't be long now. Julie hoped it would be today, but babies had their own agenda and wouldn't be rushed. Julie had bought an ice cream cake for Riley's birthday, and she'd planned a crab Louie salad that was his favorite and perfect for the hot day.

Julie was hoping that the babies held off until after the party tonight. No real urgent symptoms, just that pesky back ache that had started yesterday. As much as Julie wanted Ariel to start her labor too and have the little ones, she hoped that they'd be able to do the birthday dinner. Ever since Riley and Ariel had come home from Scotland, she'd noticed that they were very fond of each other and seemed to have reached some kind of arrangement that worked for them both. Julie sighed and turned on the vacuum. Because they were an hour away from the hospital in Modesto, Lily was going to drive Ariel to the hospital today as soon as they called her with a bed. In case she started labor, she would be staying at the birthing center at Doctor's Hospital in Modesto. Her doctor would be able to monitor her, and if things didn't start up on their own, he'd start her on a Pitocin drip.

The patrol car was long gone, Zoe couldn't get any more coverage, and Ben and Riley slept with their guns beside them. Riley had moved in and was sleeping in Ariel's room while she took the lounger, but he was long gone to the office, and Ben was hard at work spraying the orchard. Lily was in the shower so for a short time, there wasn't anyone actually on watch.

Jon and Ruby were in the almond grove picking at the almonds. Grandfather Ben had sent Jon to bring him a handful of the almonds to see if they were ready yet. So much could be told of the condition of the crop by checking the almonds. The first harvest would be the nonpareil almonds. These, Grandpa had told Jon, were the premium crop, and Grandpa Ben hoped to get eighty cents a pound for them once they'd been to the huller. Jon would bring his grandfather the almonds he'd picked, and he'd be able to tell when to call for the irrigation water. Then about a week later, they would start harvesting them. It was interesting on the farm. There was so much to learn, and his grandpa was patient with him. It made him feel good to be trusted to bring the almonds to his grandpa.

As Jon climbed to the top of the tree, he saw Ariel coming down the driveway. He watched her without calling out to her. Ariel had been so moody lately that he didn't want to say anything to her.

Ariel walked out the long drive. The hot sun beat on her head, but she didn't even notice it. She unlocked the gate and walked to the mailbox and then past it and down around the curve of the country lane. The big black Suburban was by the side of the road pointed toward the canyon. Ariel walked up to the car and opened the front door. The man started the motor, and the car moved swiftly away from the almond farm and down, down the gravel road into the canyon.

When Ariel got into the car, Jon scrambled down from the tree and ran back to the house.

"Grandma, Grandma, Ariel got into a car with a man and went down the canyon."

Julie was drying dishes, and she turned and stared at Jon.

"Oh my God, no." She turned and grabbed the cell phone and punched in Riley's office number.

"Grace, get Dr. Roberts for me. This is his mother, and this is an extreme emergency." Grace, who had been Riley's office manager ever since he opened his office, could hear the urgency and immediately went to get Riley.

Riley listened as his mother described what Jon had seen and then hung up and called Zoe.

Thankfully, he reached her right away.

"Zoe, Ariel is missing. Jon saw her walk to the road and get into a black Suburban. Jon saw a partial license number, VIP something, and saw the car go down the canyon toward the bridge over the South Fork of the Stanislaus River. Jon said she got in of her own will and didn't seem upset. Zoe, what are we going to do?"

"Okay, Riley! I'm going to get the helicopter. We'll find her. David's been listening and has already called for cruisers to go down the canyon and look for the Suburban.

"You go to the farm and see if Jon can remember anything else. I'll send a detective to interview him right away." Riley hung up and rushed to his truck, spraying gravel as he drove off toward the farm.

Chapter 41

Lily was staying at the big house until after the babies were born. She turned off the water in the cool shower and heard a siren close by. She hurriedly toweled her hair and climbed into shorts and a tank top. She'd just slipped her flip-flops on when she heard the siren cut off right out in the farmyard. Quickly she checked Ariel and discovered the room was empty. Lily knew that something bad was happening, and she ran down the stairway as fast as she could. When she reached the kitchen, a detective was already sitting at the table with Jon and Julie and was taking notes. Lily rushed into the room. "Where's Ariel? She's not upstairs."

The trio at the table all turned to look at her, and Jon stammered, "I saw her go and get into a big black Suburban." Suddenly the yard was full of patrol cars with red and blue lights flashing. Ben hurried in from the ranch and stood by Julie as the detective questioned them.

When Lily heard that Ariel had climbed into the car of her own free will, a memory of what Ariel had said at her doctor's office in Scotland flooded her mind.

"Hypnotism!" she yelled."

"What?" the detective asked.

"When we were at her doctor's in Scotland, she asked the doctor if she used hypnotism for the delivery. I asked her how she knew about that technique. Some people find it to be very helpful for their delivery, and she didn't seem to know, but I'll bet you that the doctor who was treating her here did some kind of hypnotism, so he could control her and do what he wanted with her. I heard the phone ring just before I got in the shower. Who was that?"

Julie looked at Lily, turned, and put her face in Ben's shirt.

"I didn't answer the phone. Ariel did. Oh my gosh, did he reach her by telephone?"

The detective had the Department of Motor Vehicles put a trace on all Suburbans that had VIP on their license plates. Jon had said it was a name, so it was a vanity plate. *There shouldn't be many of those with those initials*, he thought as he gave the clerk the information.

The clerk got back on the line and said there was only one vanity plate in the Columbia/ Sonora area with those initials. It was a vanity plate named "Viper" and the black Suburban was registered to Dr. Richard Hillerman at Parrotts Ferry Road, in Columbia. That was right off Highway 49, and the detective thanked her and barked the information into the radio. A car would be sent to that address immediately.

Detective Dan Goodnow hung up the phone and immediately asked to be patched to Zoe Clayborn in the helicopter.

In just a minute or so, the radio crackled, and Zoe answered, "What have you got, Dan?"

The detective filled her in, and she barked orders for him to check the doctor's house and to see if he owned any other houses in the area.

Detective Goodnow called the clinic and asked to speak to the director.

"Dr. Salter, we have a situation involving one of your doctors, and we don't have any time to lose. Does Dr. Hillerman have a second house in this area, somewhere he goes to get away from his routine?"

Dr. Salter listened carefully and then with a sigh answered the detective, "Dr. Hillerman has a cabin he and his wife own in the canyon off Italian Bar Road near Valleycitos. I don't have an address, but it's white with a red tile roof, and it's on the left hand side of the road. I was there once for a weekend." The detective hung up and again patched into the helicopter. Zoe answered immediately.

Chapter 42

It took about ten minutes to drive to his hideaway where his wife Muriel was waiting and had the birthing room ready. The man didn't speak again to Ariel until they drove into the driveway of the isolated house that was tucked onto the top ridge of the canyon along the south fork of the Stanislaus River. He warned her to watch her step as she stumbled along the rocky trail to the house. "Careful, we don't want any accidents now. It's time to see our creation!"

Ariel nodded, and he gripped her elbow to help steady her progress to the house. The house was a two-story Mediterranean with a red tile roof and white painted stucco. A veranda gave sweeping views of the rugged Knight Mountain to the east of them. The river had slowed to a trickle, and he could hear the whine of dredging equipment vacuuming the floor of the river for the sought after elusive gold nugget.

The door to the cabin opened, and a stringy haired woman with jet-black hair and a sallow complexion stood waiting at the door. It was the nurse, Muriel, from the clinic. She was Dr. Hillerman's wife too. The man took Ariel's arm and walked her up the steps into the cabin. Then the man spoke softly to Ariel and gave her his last instructions. She was to walk to the bedroom reserved for her and lay on the bed. Muriel would help her. It would all be over soon, and she would have her babies.

Muriel ushered her into the bedroom and helped her strip out of her muumuu, all that she could wear in heat like this. Ariel was docile and let Muriel undress her and put a white hospital gown on her. When she was ready, the man came back into the room and snapped his fingers. Ariel was instantly asleep. The pair worked together getting Ariel's feet into the stirrups and raising her gown, exposing the huge mound that was her stomach.

Working quickly, the man and his wife proceeded with the cesarean section. Ariel slept on with only the hypnotic suggestion that she would feel no pain for anesthesia. Baby A came first, a big healthy girl who, when Muriel put her on the scale, weighed in at six pounds, big for a twin. Baby B showed her face three minutes later, as the doctor carefully lifted her out of Ariel and put her in his wife's arms. She quickly weighed her. She topped her sister's six pounds by three ounces. Muriel wrapped her in a receiving blanket and then looked up at her husband with a wide grin. Their eyes met, and he nodded. Muriel took both baby A and baby B quickly out of the room. She dried them quickly and put tiny newborn diapers on both of the girls. Then she picked up the layette nightgowns she had lovingly made for "her babies" and dressed them both alike. They slept wrapped cocoon style side-by-side in a new white crib that had been waiting just for them.

Ariel opened her eyes and stared in confusion around her. The clean bedroom where she had been taken was now a dusty grimy storage room. She was lying on a mattress that smelled like old blood. "Where am I? How did I get here?" Ariel tried to move and discovered that her arms were bound at the wrist with white plastic strips like riot squads used. Frantic she looked down towards her stomach, and the huge mound that had been part of her for the past five months since she began showing wasn't there. Her stomach was flat, and she could see her feet for the first time in months. "My babies, where are my babies!" she began to scream. "Help me, please somebody help me!"

Scattered about the filthy floor inside the small filthy room were magazines. She could barely make out the pornographic covers. Just then, the door opened, and Muriel came in, her eyes flashing angrily. "Shut up! Just shut up! She held up a needle and plunged it into Ariel's arm, turned and left the room. Ariel heard the door lock and just before the drug started to pull her down into a swirling black hole, Ariel screamed again, knowing that there was no one to help her.

She didn't know how long she slept, but her mouth was dry and her breasts were hard with Colostrum. "Where are my babies?" The morning sunlight filled the broken window on the other side of the room, and she saw a tiny glimpse of the sun. She didn't know what they have done with her babies. She dimly remembered the first minutes, those unreal minutes when she thought she saw Muriel taking her babies out of the room away from her. She remembered pleading for a look at them. *Ariel, you must get yourself together. Think, Ariel*! She looked around the storeroom and behind her on an ironing board sat a shiny iron. Nothing else in the room would be heavy enough. Could she get to it? Ariel listened and heard voices coming through the heating vent. They were arguing.

"You promised me these babies! You can't take them; they're mine! I've done everything you wanted, and all I wanted was children. You and your fancy ideas. You murdered that doctor and tried to kill her too! Just get rid of the mothers, and no one will be the wiser. I've been out in this god forsaken spot for the past year without any contact with anybody, just so I could say I'd been too ill to see anybody so that they wouldn't suspect. These babies are mine, and I won't let you experiment on them." The dishes clattered as she dumped them into the sink.

Another familiar voice talked soothingly to her. "I just want to take some samples to make sure that they are DNA replicas. I have to keep the mothers until I've done my experiments. Muriel, you must be patient!" The voices trailed off and from somewhere upstairs she could hear the tiny cry of an infant. Ariel felt her body respond and fluid gushed from her breasts. "Riley, Zoe, how are you ever going to find me?"

Ariel struggled to sit up, and her stomach felt like a red-hot poker had seared across it. "My God, they've cut them out of me!" Just then, she heard a car start up and drive off slowly down a gravel-sounding road. She listened carefully, then she heard her babies crying again, and the woman Muriel cooing to them. She felt vomit rising in her throat. She turned on her side and inched her body toward the edge of the mattress. The stinking mattress was horribly stiff and stained black, and she finally reached the edge of the bed. Slowly, she put her feet on the floor and using her hands and elbows, she braced herself, turned, and pushed with all her strength into a sitting position. Escape was the only thought in her head but with a locked door and plastic bracelets, she was helpless. Then Ariel saw the wall plug right by the door.

Slowly, she inched her body to a standing position and shuffled toward the iron. The iron felt so heavy, she wasn't sure her idea would work, but it had to. It was her only chance. Picking up the heavy iron, she shuffled toward the door and the electrical outlet. Quietly, she plugged the iron in and moved the setting as far to the right as it would go to LINEN, the hottest setting. Ariel placed the iron on the counter, and when it was as hot as it would get, she placed her arms close to the red hot edge of the iron and forced herself to put her wrists with the heavy plastic ties right on the iron. The plastic sizzled as it heated up, and Ariel felt the burning of her skin. She pulled with all her might, and the hot plastic oozed apart thinner and thinner until it finally broke. She was free. For a moment, she felt panic. What if they came before she was prepared? Her muumuu was lying on the counter. Quickly Ariel took off the hospital gown and pulled the muumuu over her head. What if there is more than one person still in the house? Everything depended on only Muriel answering her calls. Ariel prayed, "Help me, God," as she began banging on the wall next to her bed and hollering into the heating vent as loud as she could, gripping the handle of the red hot iron.

She didn't know how long she yelled and pounded, but finally she heard Muriel coming down the stairs muttering, "That damn fool woman is too much trouble; this time I'll give her a dose that she'll never wake up from."

Muriel unlocked the door and stepped into the dim storage area. Ariel stepped from behind the door and pushed the iron into Muriel's face, surprising her. She lost her balance and fell on the full syringe. Ariel brought the iron hard down on her head. Muriel's head made the sound of an egg cracking. Ariel jerked the iron cord from the wall and tied Muriel's hands behind her back. That done, she slowly made her way to the door and to her babies.

Ariel followed the faint cries, and when she slowly climbed the stairs as silently as she could, she worked her way down the hall and into a little nursery carefully prepared for her babies.

The two infants are lying next to each other in a white crib. Ariel quickly looked at them and at the little wrist bands that they both wore. Baby A, female, born July 4, 2009, at 10:00 a.m. Ariel moved to the second infant and read her band--Baby B, female, July 4, 2009, at 10:05 a.m. The babies were born five minutes apart. Her last name, Houston, was on the band. Muriel was a well-trained nurse for her husband and did everything according to the book. Thankfully for Ariel, she would know which little girl was which. Quickly, Ariel looked around her and took a large soft comforter off the day bed. That would have to do. She picked up her daughters one at a time and laid them together in the comforter, and then she picked up some newborn diapers and folded them into the comforter, making a bundle of babies and diapers. Ariel, listening carefully, started toward the kitchen.

When she reached the country kitchen with all of the fancy stainless steel appliances and granite counters, she saw Muriel's purse sitting on the island. Rummaging inside, she found the keys and her cell phone. With the babies wrapped securely in the comforter, she slowly made her way through the back door mudroom and outside to the red Jeep Cherokee she had seen out the kitchen window. It seemed to take forever, moving so slowly and holding her new baby daughters, to get out the kitchen door and down the side steps to the driveway where the car stood waiting. Just as she opened the car door, she heard a baby cry. She looked down at her sleeping twins and realized that there was another infant in the house. Quickly and carefully, she laid the babies on the floor of the jeep on their backs snuggled together with the comforter cushioning them. Everything was going in slow motion though in her mind she was going as fast as she could. Then she heard it again, a soft wailing that made her breasts ache. She couldn't leave the infant all alone in the house with no one to care for it. As fast as she could, she worked her way back into the house and followed the soft cries. The sounds were coming from the basement where she had tied up Muriel, but as she carefully walked down the stairs, she heard the crying coming from the end of a short hallway. The door was unlocked, and Ariel pushed it open. At first, in the dim light all she could see was the shape of a person lying on a cot with a sheet tucked around her. Ariel yelled for the woman to wake up and cautiously walked toward her.

"Hey there, come on now wake up. You're in danger here. I

need your help! Please wake up!" As she came to the head of the cot, she saw a small Hispanic woman with long brown hair. Her eyes were open, and they were staring up at her. Ariel caught her breath as she looked closer at the too-still woman. She put her hand on her arm and felt the cold skin; rigor mortis was already stiffening the body. Ariel pulled her hand away, shocked at the sight of the dead woman.

It was then that the crying baby started up again, and Ariel looked around the room. In the corner was a white crib, and when Ariel walked over to it, she was stunned to see two more babies. The little arms were flailing, and the infants' mouths were quivering. Ariel looked at the bracelet and for a moment didn't believe what she saw. The tiny wristband gave the name of the woman as Emanuella Rowena Rodrigious, and after that was her name, Ariel Houston. She didn't understand, and she frantically looked at the date of birth. It was nine o'clock in the morning. Just then, a smoke alarm went off, and Ariel picked up the babies. Ariel checked the wristband on the second infant, and she thought there must be some mistake as this baby too had Emanuella's name and also her own. Frantic, she looked around the room and saw a blue blanket that she quickly spread open and wrapped the two infants in, just as she had the two babies alone in the Jeep Cherokee. Slowly she walked back along the hallway and noticed the smoke curling up from under the doorway. Ariel hurried past the door, and as fast as she could, she left the house. The walk to the jeep was exhausting her, and she was afraid she wouldn't make it. Grimly, she clutched the babies tight against her and finally reached the jeep. She put the two infants on the floorboard of the back seat.

There must be some explanation. What she had seen wasn't real. Ariel closed the back door to the jeep, opened the driver's door, and eased her way in. The car spit gravel as she drove out the driveway, but she didn't know where she was! Should she turn left or right? The cell phone was still on the front seat where she had laid it while settling her babies into the car. Ariel grabbed the phone, switched it on, and dialed 911. "Oh please, please, work," she cried as she waited for the roaming signal to locate a cell tower. She held the phone to her ear as she started driving. Finally, the phone began to ring and blessedly was answered.

"911, what is your emergency?"

"Hello, my name is Ariel Houston. I'm driving a red Jeep Cherokee. I was kidnapped by my doctor and his wife; they took my babies from me. I don't know where I am. I'm driving somewhere on Italian Bar Road, but I don't know where I'm going. Please call Zoe Clayborn at the Tuolumne Police Department, and please someone find me. I don't know where Dr. Hillerman is, and I think I've killed his wife, but thankfully I'm alive, and my babies are alive and with me." Ariel hesitated and then said. "There's a fire at the Hillerman's house. It's on the top of the ridge. Get help. I couldn't do anything for her, but I saved four babies. Please call Zoe Clayborn."

"Mrs. Houston, keep your cell phone on, and we will track it. I'll call Detective Clayborn right away but don't turn off your phone. Keep listening, and I'll get back to you as soon as I've reached her."

Just then, a black Suburban came up behind her and crashed into the back of her Cherokee, trying to knock her off the road and deep into the steep canyon on her right. Ariel screamed that she was being forced off the road, and then she dropped the cell. She put her foot on the gas and fishtailed around the corners of the narrow one lane road, racing to outrun the Suburban. The jeep climbed up and up higher and higher; Ariel kept her foot hard on the gas pedal. The suburban caught up to her and rammed her again, sending the Cherokee close to the edge. Her back tires tipped off the road, and it was only Ariel's driving that got her back centered again. Again and again, the Suburban rammed her. She focused on driving down the center of the one-lane road, holding the wheel and giving it gas whenever the Suburban rammed the car. By the grace of God, she kept ahead of it so that it couldn't force her over the cliff.

Again and again, the Suburban pounded her back end. The big SUV had a pushing bumper that kept the driver from disabling his vehicle while he rammed into her. Ariel was having a hard time keeping the car on the road. The road curved sharply, and Ariel lost control of the jeep, careening from side to side, she hurdled up the narrow mountain road. The babies were crying lustily, and Ariel couldn't do anything for them except talk to them in a soft voice while inwardly she was screaming.

"I'm sorry, little ones. I'm doing everything that I can to outrun him. This is a terrible way to start your first days of life. Mommy will make it up to you, I promise. Oh God, help me, please help me." Just then, swooping out of the canyon and on Ariel's immediate right, a big Blackhawk helicopter swept right to the edge of the road and kept pace with the jeep. Ariel could see Zoe and David inside. David was leaning out the side with a rifle. Ariel couldn't do anything but keep hugging the mountainside of the road, praying that there would be no one coming in the opposite direction. Ariel heard a burst of gun fire and looked back just in time to see the right front tire of the Suburban shot out and an enraged Dr. Hillerman wrestling the steering wheel. He lost control of the big car and was swept right off the road, plunging down into the canyon five hundred feet below.

A huge ball of flame rose up from the spot the Suburban had landed. Ariel eased her foot off the gas pedal and brought the jeep to a stop. Directly in front of her was a Tuolumne sheriff's car, lights blazing blue and red, and an ambulance huddled by the side of the road. Ariel was stiff with fright. Suddenly a car door slammed shut, and Ariel looked up to see Riley running toward her. She opened her door, and the two fell into each other's arms. "My babies, please, please help me save them.

Riley yelled for the paramedic and jerked open the front passenger door. The babies were purple with crying, and their mouths trembled. Ariel reached in to pick them up, but Riley held her back. "Let them check them out before you move them."

"There are two more babies in the back. Ariel had turned toward the back door of the jeep and didn't see the shocked expression on Riley's face. One twin had a gash on her forehead that was bleeding and was already a deep purple blue from crying.

"Here, ma'am, I've got to take a look at them. You go with Dr. Roberts to the ambulance, and we'll bring the infants in a minute." The paramedic looked into the jeep and put his stethoscope on the chest of the first baby. His partner came running, carrying four clear plastic carrying beds for the infants. Gently supporting their heads and backs with rolled towels, the paramedics laid them in the carriers. Ariel leaned down and kissed them. The babies were tucked into the ambulance and strapped to the gurney. Riley helped Ariel climb in after them. It was a bumpy ride to the main Italian Bar Road where the dirt and gravel gave way to smooth asphalt. Riley held on to Ariel as she kept vigil over her infants, cooing to them softly and sobbing into Riley's shirt. The ambulance put on the siren as soon as they hit the pavement and drove through the edge of town, turning carefully onto Pacific Street and then left on Broadway to Highway 49, hurtling toward Sonora Regional Hospital.

Ariel couldn't speak, and Riley used his hands and arms to comfort and protect her from the swaying ambulance ride. It seemed like hours but was only about seven minutes before the ambulance was turning into the emergency entrance. A nurse came out with a wheel chair for Ariel, and Riley helped her into it as the paramedics carefully carried the babies inside. Ariel refused to be seen by the emergency room staff and insisted on accompanying her babies as the staff ordered CT scans and did a through physical checkup of the infants. Riley and Ariel were sitting together waiting for news when Zoe and David arrived.

"Zoe, I saw you and David. You were magnificent. You saved us. Thank you, thank you, my friends." Ariel began to sob again, and Riley went in search of a nurse. Ariel was whisked into a cubicle, and nurses were taking off her horribly soiled muumuu, the same one she had worn that morning when she stepped out of her house and walked toward the mailbox to be taken away by Dr. Hillerman.

Zoe hugged Ariel and explained. "David and I were searching the canyon for you in the copter. I got the call from the 911 operator, so we were able to look for you on the road. I saw the black Suburban chasing the red jeep, and I knew we had to do something drastic. Thank God, David's a fantastic marksman!" Zoe stood at the door of the cubicle, and when she was done explaining, she gulped her water and marveled that Ariel and the babies were all right. She was so sure that they'd all be killed. It made her legs jittery, and she looked for a place to sit down. Just then, the emergency doctor, a young intense man with a slim, almost gaunt, body and straight black hair, slipped into the cubicle and peering over his horned rimmed glasses, he asked quick questions to Ariel.

As he listened to her story, a look of horror came into the doctor's eyes. Ariel told him all she knew. "Mrs. Houston you're a very, very lucky lady, and your babies are too. The CT scans ruled out any concussions, and from what I heard, you had protected them as much as possible by bedding them on the floorboards of the car. The one baby has a small wound that I put a butterfly bandage on to keep the skin together. She'll be fine, but I'm sorry that there might be a tiny scar, though, of course, it will fade as she grows older. The comforter helped keep them from flying around the car. Your babies are fine, and once we get you checked out, I'll take you to them.

The doctor removed the bandages from her abdomen and gently probed her stomach with competence. "Well, Mrs. Houston, you were given a traditional caesarean section, and it was done with all the professionalism I would expect to see from a board certified ob-gyn. As for the rest of it, I'm appalled that you were treated in such a terrible way by a colleague of mine. I knew Dr. Hillerman, and I knew him to be competent, but something changed him, and we no longer saw much of each other. I'd like your permission to do a DNA test on the infants and on you. I think it will answer any lingering questions you might have as to why Dr. Hillerman became the monster he did."

Ariel nodded her agreement, and a nurse handed her a consent form to sign. Then, after putting a clean hospital nightgown on and using one as a robe, the nurse took her to Admitting to sign herself and her infants in for observation.

Chapter 43

Riley walked beside her as she was escorted to the maternity ward and taken to the glass enclosure where she could see her twins being bathed, diapered, and put in clean nightgowns. They were wrapped like papooses and tucked back into the clear plastic bassinets. The nurse tending them saw them and walked to the door to tell Ariel that as soon as she was settled in her room, she would bring the babies to her for nursing. Ariel burst into tears, and Riley wheeled her out of the glass-lined hallway and followed the orderly to her room.

Riley left Ariel with the orderly and a nurse at the door to her room and quickly walked to the waiting room. He was filled with thanksgiving and yet also a rage so deep, he was stunned by the savagery of his feelings. He stood by the window and rubbed his hands over his face, looking out the window at the normalcy of the view of Sonora, where people were going about their daily errands oblivious of the drama he had been witness to. Suddenly he was sick of the savagery and greed of the world, sick of the Hillermans of the world who took what they wanted without consent and no conscience. The sickness raised bile, and he leaned over just in time to puke the thin trickle of vomit into the plastic garbage can, which was thankfully right beside him. He hadn't eaten since breakfast and when his mother called him, he was so caught up in trying to find Ariel that it amazed him that it was only a little after noon.

The detectives knew there was a house that Dr. Hillerman and his wife owned, but it took almost an hour for them to look up the address. They were on their way there when Ariel was being chased up the mountain, and the officers were told to stand down and let the helicopter handle it. The best they could come up with was that Ariel had left the house at nine thirty in the morning and within a half hour, she had had her twins removed from her abdomen by cesarean section. The doctors at Sonora Regional were amazed at how alert and awake Ariel was and how she was able to save herself and her babies. There was no anesthesia used except the hypodermic afterwards. They were intrigued that the hypnotism allowed her to undergo the surgery without pain. Riley was still in shock that so much had happened so fast. He was reeling, and yet he was so grateful that Ariel was alive and had survived, as well as her twins.

Chapter 44

Zoe slipped into the room and stood beside him as he finished heaving his guts out. When he was done, she was there with a cold damp paper towel and helped him wipe his face.

"Riley, I need you to be strong and brace yourself, it's not over yet."

Riley finished drying his face, and he looked at her with a wary stare. "What do you mean, Zoe?"

"I just got word from the fire department and David that they found the house that Hillerman hid Ariel in. Riley, there was a body there of a young woman and the body of Hillerman's wife was just where Ariel left her in the utility room down stairs. I don't think Ariel killed her, but an autopsy will give us cause of death. The hot iron had started a fire in the utility room when it fell on some magazines. Hillerman's wife was dead, however. When the firemen moved the body, they found a hypodermic needle plunged into her stomach, and she was laying on it. The door was closed to the utility room, so the fire snuffed itself out due to lack of air. It was only when the firemen were mopping up, and the coroner had come, that David, who was searching the rest of the house, came upon the body of the other woman. She had had a cesarean as well."

"Well, I'm sorry as hell for the women, and it's a bad break for the kids, but what does that have to do with Ariel?"

Zoe moved over to the waiting room chairs, sat down, and beckoned Riley to join her. "The babies' bracelets say Houston on them."

Riley looked at Zoe in disbelief and put his hands across his eyes. "For the love of God, what the hell is going on?" he cried. "Does Ariel know about this?"

"Not everything; she's puzzled and confused. She read her name on their wristbands when she heard the infants crying and went and got them. They are still investigating, but the babies are in the hospital and are being examined. Social services has been called for an emergency foster home." Zoe started to say more, but Riley interrupted.

"No, no foster home. If they are Houstons, they are coming home with their sisters. Do whatever you need to do to prove their paternity."

Riley got up and started down the hall toward Ariel's room. Zoe ran behind him, but his long legs covered the distance twice as fast as she could go. "Riley, wait a minute!" But Riley kept walking and went straight into Ariel's room where he stopped short. Ariel was sitting in the big lounge chair nursing both twins at once. She looked up and grinned at Riley. As Zoe came into the room, she saw Riley bending down on one knee and smiling at Ariel. She looked radiant, and Riley didn't have the heart to disturb the happy family. It was hard to keep the secret, but both Zoe and Riley put aside their mission and joined in Ariel's happiness, cooing and exclaiming over the babies. Finally, both babies were asleep, and Ariel's baby nurse came to claim them and put them in the nursery so Ariel could get some sleep.

Just then, Dr. Stevens came in. Riley and Zoe looked him in the eye, and Riley nodded. Ariel was about to get the shock of her life, and Riley couldn't do anything to help her except to be there and hold on to her. Zoe, Riley, and Dr. Stevens sat wherever they could find a perch. Zoe sat on the bed, and Riley stayed where he was beside Ariel, holding her hand. Dr. Stevens perched on the wide window ledge. The moment had come to tell Ariel the latest in this never-ending saga.

Zoe cleared her throat. "Ariel, we've some news that is absolutely astounding, and we need to know what your wishes are. At the house where the Hillerman's held you, they found two dead women. I presume one is Hillerman's wife and the other is the other infants' mother, dead of a lethal overdose of Diprivan, a potent anesthesia only available to hospitals and clinics."

Ariel's eyes got huge, and she shuddered. "Oh my God, that poor woman. Hillerman's wife got her, and she was coming to give me an overdose too, but I hit her with the iron." Ariel began to cry, and it took a few minutes before she was able to listen to what Zoe said next.

"Ariel, the woman was a surrogate. Those babies weren't of her genes. We will need to test their DNA, but the evidence is pointing to the babies coming from extra eggs that Dr. Hillerman harvested from you. Ariel, the name bands on their wrists say Houston."

Ariel, looked from Zoe to Riley, and he held her close while Zoe continued, "Dr. Hillerman was experimenting with cloning, and the documents on his experiments were all at his house where you were held. We will have to get a court order for DNA testing of these babies and compare it to you and your twins DNA. The evidence so far leads us to the very strong possibility that these are your twins as well."

Ariel stood up and leaned on Riley. "Riley, take me to see them please, right now."

Dr. Stevens addressed the group. "While we are waiting for the court order, Mrs. Houston, I need your permission to compare your DNA and your twins' with these other babies." He reached into his pocket for his pen and slid the paperwork over to Ariel. Ariel signed the papers and then slowly walked with Riley down to the nursery.

Chapter 45

The babies were in isolation on the other side of the nursery from Ariel's twins. Dr. Stevens opened the door and requested that the babies be brought to the window. The nurse quickly brought the clear plastic bassinets to the window, and, at the doctor's nod, picked up the closest baby and brought her to the viewing window. Ariel stared and collapsed against Riley. "They're mine, dear God, they're mine!"

Riley held Ariel up, and Zoe ran to get a wheel chair. Ariel looked up as the nurse picked up the second baby and brought her to the window. The infant was an exact copy of Ariel's twins, and Ariel was overwhelmed with emotion. She grabbed Zoe's hand and as she was gently settled in the wheel chair, she looked up at Zoe. Without a moment's hesitation, she told Zoe to get her Meredith Campbell, her boss at the social services. There was no doubt in Ariel's mind that these babies were sisters to her twins. As a social worker, she knew how complicated this situation could become, and she wasn't going to let that happen. Meredith could make Ariel an emergency foster placement. These babies were not going to go anywhere but to her home. She'd wait till the DNA test was complete, but she already knew that these twins were hers, and damn if she was going to let Hillerman mess with her life anymore. This was the most outrageous crime that could be done to such innocent children. They needed protection,

and no one was going to take them away from her. And it was
a crime! Hillerman had stolen her eggs and used her DNA to
replicate her.

Hillerman had messed with the wrong woman, and this was
going to stop right here, right now.

Zoe called Meredith at home. She told her the incredible
story and what was transpiring. It was less than an hour later
that Meredith walked into Ariel's hospital room. Ariel looked
her straight in the eye and told her what she planned.

"I've been fingerprinted and was investigated when I became
a social worker. Do you remember when I had little Ashley
Bennett for a month and my house was given a home study and
clearance for emergency foster care placement? Well, get my
foster parent file and give a copy to the judge. I want those babies
to come home with me when my twins are released. I'll not have
them with strangers. I have plenty of help and room."

Meredith shook her head in disbelief. "Ariel, I can't begin to
know what the court is going to do. But if you will wait until the
DNA comes back, and if it's your DNA, I don't see how the court
can refuse your fostering them until they can be legally turned
over to you. But, Ariel, are you sure you want to do this? You've
just had a cesarean section, and four infants are a huge amount
of work."

Ariel nodded. "Just do it, Meredith. I have help, and I
can afford to hire more. When will we have the results of the
DNA test?"

As Ariel looked up, Lily, along with Julie and Ben walked
into the room. Lily put her arms around Ariel, and the two
sisters sobbed. It took a few minutes to mop up the tears. Ariel
introduced Lily to Meredith and pretty soon the whole story was
told again, and Lily, holding Ariel's hand, looked flabbergasted.
Lily turned to Meredith and told her that she was an MD, and she

would be assisting her sister with the two sets of twins. She put on her professional demeanor and demanded to see the babies. Meredith escorted her to the nursery, and Julie and Ben with Riley explaining what had just happened, followed behind. Ariel had been put to bed and given a light sedative. It would soon be time for the twins next feeding, and Ariel was emotionally exhausted by the amazing news that there were now four babies to care for. Ariel's last thought before she slept was that she'd have to get the extra bedroom next to the nursery set up for the second set of twins. "My God, thank you for saving them. I'll raise them all together."

Chapter 46

The DNA tests would take time, but the results wouldn't surprise anyone. These babies were all sisters, of that there was little doubt. The test would just confirm what anyone who had eyes could see. These babies looked identical. Ariel and the four infants all came home together. It was a quick job of converting the extra room into a make-do nursery. Riley and Julie went to Modesto and got two white cribs and a wardrobe and changing table identical to the ones in the yellow nursery. They didn't take time to paint, but Julie and Lily scrubbed the walls and washed the curtains. The Wedgwood blue walls looked clean and bright with the white sheer curtains and new white furniture. A big white rocking chair was bought for the blue nursery, and Lily arranged for twenty-four hour a day nursing for Ariel and the four infants.

Ariel and the infants were released from the hospital. Meredith had gotten a judge to release the two infants that Emmanuelle had carried into Ariel's care while a complete investigation was conducted. It was quite a sight when Riley and Ariel drove up to the farm with four infant seats lined up on the back seat of the farm van, the only vehicle big enough to hold the infants, Ariel, Jon, and Riley. Ariel made a mental note that they'd have to go shopping for a new SUV.

Ben and Julie helped them bring the babies inside, and Riley carried two babies straight up to the yellow nursery while Ben and Julie carried up the other twins to the blue nursery.

Ariel, with Lily's help, walked slowly up the stairs and peeked into both nurseries at the sleeping infants. The extra-duty nurse, Serena Foster, met her in the hallway and helped her into bed. Ariel was exhausted from the effort and was soon fast asleep. Incredible as it seemed, Ariel was able to nurse all four infants with supplemental bottle feedings done by the nurse. It was an amazing sight. The only feeding that Ariel was grateful to leave to the nurse was the 2:00 a.m. feeding. Ariel slept through the night soundly and didn't even hear the infants as they woke for their feedings. Lily had put a fan in the hallway and ran it all night. The white noise it made blocked the noises in the nursery, and so the family was relieved of the late night feedings.

Chapter 47

riel greeted Lily who brought her the first twin, Kendall Rae. "Ah, there you are Kendall, here let me have her, Lily. Come and sit with us a bit." Lily brought two cups of coffee and set them down by Ariel's nightstand. Ariel was nursing Kendall in bed, propped up with pillows. Kelsey Rose was in Lily's arms having a quick sip of a bottle while waiting her turn with her mother. Kaitlain Renee and Kelly Rowena were having bottles with Julie and Serena, the day nurse. At the next feeding, Kaitlain and Kelly would be nursed by Ariel. The routine was working well. By nursing all the babies, Ariel was able to bond with them all. It was amazing that though they were identical, except where Kendall had a small scar on her forehead from the mad race down Italian Bar Road, the girls each had their own uniqueness as well. Kendall was quiet and solemn and watched her mother's face while she steadily nursed. Kelsey was a fussy eater who was forever latching on and then frustrated that she couldn't get enough milk fast enough. Kelsey preferred the bottle, and Ariel knew it, but it was important to Ariel that she have a few minutes to bond in this special way. Kaitlain was like Kendall--another solemn, quiet one. She preferred to sleep, and Ariel had to keep nudging her awake to eat. Kelly was the most wide-awake, and her green eyes never left Ariel's face. Kelly liked to pat Ariel's breast while she nursed, and she nursed a solid steady twenty minutes before she turned away, full and ready to nap.

The girls all wore their wristbands, and Ariel was worried that they would fall off. Something more permanent would have to be done until they were old enough to tell her who they were. Ariel was toying with the idea of having a tiny letter a, b, c, or d tattooed on their feet. It would keep them from being mixed up. But until the judge ruled on the parentage of Kaitlain and Kelly, she would have to make sure the wrist bands didn't come off. For now, Ariel had put the letters on with black markers to their heels, and after each bath, she refreshed the letters again.

Chapter 48

oday Meredith was coming by. She was acting caseworker for this case, and so far everything was going smoothly. Lily was thankful for all of the commotion and that she could keep busy with the four babies. She sighed as she sat and rocked Kelsey.

"Ariel, who would have thought that your world and mine would have changed so quickly?" Lily had told Ariel, Riley, Julie, and Ben about the death of Matt by the suicide bomber and of her shrapnel injuries that, thankfully, had healed up clean and with minimum scaring.

"I know, Lily! Six months ago, I thought that my life had ended of any happiness. And now I have Riley, Jon, and these four rascals." She looked at Lily with concern. "Lily, what are you going to do?" Lily burped Kelsey and adjusted the blanket. It was July 14, and the twins were ten days old, give or take a few minutes.

"I'm going to stay here and help you for as long as you need me and when you're all healed up, I'm might go to Scotland for awhile and visit the greats, Sibyl and Robyn. With all that's happened, it would be so easy to stay here and be absorbed into your household. I already love my little nieces, but I'm not going to. I have to come to terms with Matt's death, and these little cuties keep me from doing that. I'm grateful for the distraction they bring, but they're not mine, and as much as I love being here, I need to find my own life."

Ariel looked at her sister and understood. Scotland would help her to find peace and healing as it did her. It was the best thing she had done, and she was grateful that Riley didn't give up on her and had insisted on the trip through Scotland and England to follow the queen's trail. It brought them so close, and she knew it was the magic of the stones that merged their hearts. By the time the journey was over, Ariel and Riley had fallen deeply in love.

Chapter 49

Zoe

Zoe drove steadily up the mountain toward Rose Creek. She stopped at the bridge and made a left turn onto a road that had prominent signs reading private claim. She got out of her jeep and quickly opened the barrier protecting the road from uninvited guests. Using her key, she unlocked the Masters lock. She drove for another quarter mile to the camp and parked her jeep. There was another Jeep Wrangler. Mark was here. Zoe walked along the trail to the dredging site and stripped off her jeans and shirt. She was wearing a plain black bikini. She put on her facemask and snorkel and walked into the water toward the dredge.

Mark had his back to her and, using a Huka breathing device, was completely underwater. Zoe moved next to him and put her face under the water to see what progress he was making. Mark had cleared a lot of the rocks away and was vacuuming the silt and gravel in with the four-inch nozzle. The dredge was loud, and as the material flew up the nozzle, some of it stuck in the grooves and traps as it was designed to do. Hopefully, by the end of the day, there would be gold trapped in the miners moss too. Zoe reached over and tapped Mark on his back. He looked startled and turned toward her. A big grin lit up his smile, and he motioned for her to go tap the kill switch on the dredge. Zoe moved over to the dredge and using a wooden pole, tapped the metal kill switch, and it was blissfully quiet.

"Hey, Zoe, glad you could come play with me today. Do you want to do some dredging?"

He looked puzzled as she shook her head no and said, "Later, let's talk a bit." Mark took off his weight belt and wet suit hat and walked with her through the four-foot pool of water to the bank.

Zoe didn't waste any time. "I've heard from the doctor. We have the results of the DNA test on Ariel and the twins." Mark waited for her to finish.

"The twins' DNA are exact copies of Ariel's. It's just as we feared, Mark. The twins are the world's first known clones. Dr. Hillerman's paperwork on this case leaves no doubt, and the DNA study confirms it. I came to get you so that we can be there when the district attorney holds a press conference. Mark, I'm so sorry. I tried to stop it but after the DA talks to the press, it's going to be a media frenzy."

Zoe knew with the investigation of the death of Dr. Hillerman and his wife, Muriel, it would all come out. Zoe had sent a patrol car to Dr. Hillerman's weekend house off the main road to Vallecitos, and they combed the doctor's study for any information on what he was working on. It was all there. Hillerman was experimenting with Ariel's eggs and not only had he implanted Ariel with the two ovum that he had altered, but he gave the other woman cloned eggs from Ariel. This was such a huge story for this tiny community that there was no way to keep this quiet.

"Damn it, Zoe, hasn't Ariel the right to some privacy? What

the hell, let's go. I want to be there."

Mark with Zoe right behind him, zoomed down the mountain toward his cottage at the farmhouse and Mark changed into light chino pants with a polo shirt and loafers. Zoe changed into her standard black jeans and black shirt, adding a lightweight tan linen blazer to look more like the detective she was, and they went roaring off in Mark's jeep to the Sonora District Attorney's office. Ariel was blissfully unaware of this latest invasion of her privacy.

Chapter 50

Zoe and Riley reached the Sonora DA's office just minutes before District Attorney Sloan Carpenter announced that there had been four babies born with identical DNA to the mother. These were the world's first clones. Like Dolly, the sheep that had given birth a few years ago to worldwide attention, this story would be even bigger. There were over fifty microphones set up, and the room was jam-packed.

Zoe worked her way to the DA's side and when someone asked her for details of the murders and the discovery of the babies' birth, Zoe spoke for the first time. "This is an ongoing police investigation, and I can give you no more information than that. I ask you to respect the privacy of the mother and her infants, and I warn you if anyone tries to take pictures or trespasses in any way, I will make sure they are prosecuted to the full extent of the law."

Zoe turned and left the room with Mark right behind her. Zoe drove fast, and the two took the old Sonora highway toward Columbia and the Frazer farm. They wove their way through old Columbia with Zoe watching behind them to make sure no one was following them. Zoe drove into the ranch yard, and Mark hopped out and secured the gate. Thankfully, it was an automatic electric one that would offer some protection from intruders. The problem was that the farm was so big that anyone who really wanted to get in could by going to the end of the property and climbing in from the canyon side.

The story made all the networks, and Ariel listened to the news in shock. Riley and Mark sat with her, and Zoe and Lily were squeezed together on the carpenter's bench at the side of the couch. This was the first that Ariel had heard of the cloning, and it devastated her. Not only was she robbed of her privacy but she was robbed of Morgan's heritage. The babies were only made up of her DNA and were an exact copy. It would be like looking at herself growing up. Everyone was quiet after the television was switched off. They were all in a sort of shock.

Riley and Ariel talked long into the night. The result of their long evening was that Riley and Ariel would be married as soon as it could be arranged, and everyone would then carry the Roberts' surname.

"I am honored, Ariel, that you and the babies will bear my name. I love you, and I already love the little mites too. Thank you for your trust and love."

Ariel and Riley stood on the porch and listened to the crickets. She was facing the back of the property, but even with the farmhouse between them and the front gate, they could see the glow of the lights and hear the crowd of reporters and newscasters trying to get a peek at any activity within the farm compound. It was four o'clock in the morning, and they were all still there making up sound bites and stories to satisfy their editors and producers. It had only been seven months ago that Morgan and Sarah had died. Their deaths were directly related to Ariel, and she bitterly regretted their loss. What would happen to her and her babies and would this be the end of it if she and Riley married? Ariel loved Riley, but it felt like she was dishonoring Morgan to marry so soon after his death. If they married, would Riley regret the decision when they were hounded by the media ?

Ariel looked up into Riley's earnest face and knew that he was giving her a tremendous gift of himself. She knew he would honor and cherish her as well as her infants. Finally, the decision was made, and she looked up at Riley and grinned. From now on, she and Riley would be forever together a safe port for her babies. She looked into his face and the huge grin on it, and they both laughed and kissed.

"Oh, Riley, I love you so much. I'd be a fool not to grab you before you can think about it. Yes, yes, my darling!" She reached up and pulled his head down to her.

Then his mouth was on her, sucking her in with a desperate hunger that threatened to consume them both. He dragged her up, his mouth streaking down her neck to her breast. Eagerly Riley kissed the deep cleft between her breasts, teeth scraping, until gasping he pulled her shirt up and released her from her bra. Then he was sucking and the blue white milk filled his mouth. Riley and Ariel clung to each other, oblivious of the media outside their gate, lost in the raw, sweet excitement. They loved each other and couldn't get enough of each other.

Riley moved her onto the day bed and quickly in the dark, with only the moon as witness, plunged his fingers inside her. She bucked, cried out, came. He watched her eyes go dark green, her head fall back so that the long line of her throat was there for him to feast on. He freed himself from his jeans and slipped into her. She cried out again, her muscles clamping in orgasm tight around his cock.

Down, down he went, lost in the smell of her, a delicate vanilla scent that seemed to envelop him. He shoved her knees up and stroked deeper, harder, darkly thrilled when her teeth bit into his lip. He plunged inside her, quivering with raw, blind want. Sensations swamped her, clawed at her; the orgasm slammed into her, a hard, hot fire, deep inside of her. She went limp, her hands slid from Riley's shoulders, sated, out of energy, she lay under him exhausted. Riley groaned, and his body shuttered as he plunged then stiffened. When it was over, he collapsed beside her, and Ariel smiled, her lips curving in deep female satisfaction.

Chapter 51

Late August

The almonds were ready! Ben organized the crew and starting at dawn, he went down the first row. There was quite a procedure to harvesting this versatile nut. First, they trees had to be shaken with a Shock-Wave shaker machine, and when all the almonds were off the trees in one row, the Flory Pick Up Harvester sweeper came along and pushed the almonds into rows. Then at the end of the row, there were always a few left as the big machine turned to the next row. It was Jon's job to take the Rhino quad and pick up the end of the row nuts with a shovel and a rake.

Jon loved driving the Rhino and at the end of every row, he'd jump off it, sweep the nuts up with the rake, and shovel them into the back pickup bed of the Rhino. It really was an efficient operation. Standing by, in front of the gate, was a huge double trailer semi that received the nuts and took them to the huller for processing. It took almost a week to shake the trees and gather up the nuts. As Curt and Denny took the big sweeper and tipped the nuts onto the conveyor belt, Jon came up behind them.

Maneuvering the Rhino quad, he tipped his little pickup bed onto the conveyor belt and watched his nuts climb up the belt and fall into the semi. When one of the big trucks was full, another one fell into place as the full truck drove off to the hullers.

Even Riley took a week off from his practice and joined the pickers, his father, and Jon operating the equipment and sweeping the orchard clean of nuts. It was amazing that there was little waste. The nuts had always earned premium ratings, and Ben always got the highest price for the nuts, which were already pre-sold and shipped directly to China after hulling and packaging. Ben's job was over as soon as the semi took its load to the huller.

When the last truck left, the crew gave a high five, then laughing and joking, they headed for the showers. Ben would take them all out to dinner to celebrate.

"Jon, how did you like harvesting almonds?" Ben asked as he walked with him to the house.

"That Rhino was neat! I'd like to help with the second harvest in September too." Jon called Ruby and Daisy and turned the hose on the dogs. The heat was in the 90s, and the pair scampered through the sprinkler, soaking Jon's clothes and Ruby's and Daisy's fur.

Ben watched his only grandson and smiled. He had time now to take him fishing. It was a rowdy bunch who went to the big all-you-can-eat buffet restaurant. Riley, Jon, and Ben piled their plates with ribs, chicken, and everything that could fit on it in the way of side dishes. The dessert bar beckoned, and Jon filled a bowl with soft serve ice cream covered in M & Ms and nuts. There were pies, cakes, and cookies to choose from too. Jon settled that by taking one of everything and when he went back to the table, Denny and Curt kidded him about having eyes bigger than his stomach.

Riley smiled at the motley crew and looked wistful for a moment. "It's too bad that Ariel and Lily weren't able to come. Next time, the babies will be three months old, and Ariel can probably get away for a few hours."

Ben tucked into his dessert, a huge slice of blackberry pie with ice cream on top. "You've got yourself a big commitment, son. With Jon and Ariel and the four babies all at one time, my gosh, I don't know how you're coping, but you and Ariel sure are doing a hell of a job with all of them."

Ben chewed his food and slurped his coffee while Riley thought about what he said. "I know Dad, it has been a lot, and I'm not sure either Ariel or I have really dealt with everything completely. It's only been seven months since Morgan and Sarah died, and here we are with these five children. Jon's great, and he seems to be settling in okay. Ariel and Lily are handling the babies just fine. I keep looking for the roof to fall down or something. Is it really over? After all of the terrible things that happened this year, I really haven't relaxed my vigil, and I can't believe that we are all going to be okay, but I certainly am doing all I can to keep it all together. I think when we marry, it's going to all come together."

Just then, Denny and Curt came back with second helpings that heaped their plates with more ribs and chicken, and Riley and his Dad just laughed at them. It was going to work. It had to. The men chatted about the second harvest coming in late September when the trees would be shaken again, and the whole procedure repeated. It was after 11:00 p.m. when Riley, Jon, and Ben got back to the farm and tiptoed to their beds, exhausted and sated with a job well done and a meal fit for a king.

Chapter 52

Ben got up at the first light of dawn and quickly dressed, tiptoeing around so he wouldn't disturb Julie. Today was a day he had been looking forward to for months. So much had happened since Jon had arrived, and Ben couldn't take him fishing until the harvest was over, but now it was. Ben was smiling broadly as he rummaged around the kitchen and got fresh coffee perking. He made big sandwiches of peanut butter and jelly and when he had drunk his coffee and finished off a couple of pieces of peanut butter toast, he tucked everything in his knapsack and walked over to the big house as dawn broke. Ben was glad when he and Julie had moved back to their small apartment above the barn, after Ariel and Riley came back from Scotland. It was cozy and quiet and with five children in the big house, there was way too much noise for him to deal with.

He'd quietly unlocked the kitchen door with his keys and tiptoed to Jon's room. Ben opened the door, and Ruby opened her eyes and looked up at him before closing her eyes and snuggling down against Jon.

"Hey, Jon, come on wake up! It's fishing time, buddy." Jon stirred briefly and then burrowed down in the covers. He was still tired after helping to harvest the first half of the orchard. It took another five minutes of shaking him and pulling the covers off of him before Jon was awake enough to get excited about the fishing trip. Ruby jumped off his bed as Jon pushed her. He was up!

Ben told him to hurry and went into the kitchen while Jon went to the bathroom and combed his hair. There was a big glass of milk and a couple of pieces of peanut butter toast with a sliced banana waiting for him. Jon ate quickly, and they were soon out the door. Ruby was left home, looking dejected as Ben and Jon climbed into Ben's old red pickup and headed down to a favorite fishing hole at the bottom of the canyon on Old Italian Bar Road. They parked the truck, and Ben carried the fishing gear and gave Jon the tackle box. Just as the sun came down into the canyon, Ben and Jon were set up, hooks baited, and poles in the deep pool of water. All of a sudden, Jon's line went taut, and Jon was battling a fish bigger than any he'd caught before. Truth to tell, he'd never gone fishing before, so this was his first. Eyes shining, Jon pulled the big brown trout out of the hole and proudly showed it to his grandpa. Ben was so excited he walked right into the pool and caught the fish in his net.

"Hey, look at the size of this one! Wow, Jon, you keep this up and we'll have a fish fry tonight!" Just then, Ben's line went taut, and he had a fish on too. "Okay, Jon, you take this one out of the net, and I'll just see what we've got here." The man and the fish battled until the trout was finally tired out, and Jon could lift him into the net.

It was a couple of happy fisherman who finally sat down to lunch, their creel full of fish. "Grandpa, I wondered ever since I came. What was my Dad like when he was my age?"

"Well, Jon, have you looked in the mirror lately? You're a spitting image of him. You walk like him, and you talk like him. You slick your hair down just like he did, and the way you take care of Ruby and Daisy, I wouldn't be a bit surprised if you became a vet too!"

"Really, Grandpa, do you really think I'm just like he was at my age?" Jon beamed, and Ben hugged him tight.

"Jon I'm so thrilled to have you as my grandson, and I know your grandma Julie feels the same. You are a joy and a blessing to this family and don't you ever forget it."

After this speech, Ben and Jon gathered up the fishing gear and headed back down the river to where they had parked the pickup under a big laurel tree. That night, the fish were cleaned and breaded with flour and corn meal, and Julie fried them golden crisp. The big green salad and fresh crisp bread were so filling that Jon was stuffed. Everyone was so proud of him that the compliments flew, and they asked him when there would be fish on the table again. Jon smiled, shy with the attention, and his grandfather Ben winked at him.

Riley tucked a tired and sleepy Jon in and then leaned over and kissed him gently on the forehead. "Great dinner bud! Next time how about if I come along? I haven't been fishing in a long time." Jon smiled at his dad and fell instantly asleep, even before Riley had tiptoed out of the room.

Chapter 53

The household was bustling with babies crying and last minute nursing so that Ariel would have a chance of getting through her wedding ceremony without leaking milk all over everything. She had purchased nursing pads that were lined with plastic to keep her dress free of overflow. It was amazing. She was nursing four babies, and her breasts were overflowing with abundant milk for all of them. Truth to tell, it was getting to be a bit embarrassing when she'd wake up in the morning and turn over and milk would stream out. Riley would lean over and let the milk run into his mouth. He said it was strength giving, and then he'd turn to her, and they'd kiss, and if the house was still quiet, they'd make slow sweet love.

Riley had moved in when the twins were a week old, and now it was the end of August. The judge had ruled in Ariel's favor and had decreed that Kaitlain and Kelly were indeed the property of Ariel Houston. The cloned eggs that had been implanted into the surrogate who had died after giving birth were the unlawfully stolen biological property of Ariel.

It was a hot day with a clear blue sky, a perfect day to get married, Ariel thought as she fed the babies. By now, it was a routine that took about an hour, more if one of them was too sleepy to eat. Usually it was Kaitlain, and today was no exception. Ariel coaxed Kaitlain awake to nurse, and she would for a few minutes and then go back to sleep. After about ten minutes of trying, she gave Kaitlain to Lily, and an eager Kelly latched on. Kelly made up for Kaitlain's laziness. She slurped and sucked and made all kinds of little noises, as if she was enjoying the experience immensely. Ariel looked down at her and a warmth went through her. Kelly and Kaitlain were as much hers as if they had come out of her body too. Kelly was such a little glutton that she hardly left any for the last two to nurse. Kendall was the last one, and she protested when the well went dry. Ariel quickly switched to a bottle for the thriving infant. The twins had gained almost three pounds since their birth and weighed a whopping nine pounds plus a couple of ounces each. They were within an ounce of each other's weight, and now their faces were filled out, and their eyes were becoming their true color of emerald green. The thatch of red hair that covered their heads was about an inch long and curly. Ariel couldn't tell them apart, so the black pen initials on their heels were still necessary. It was working well to bath one infant at a time, making sure to put the correct initial on their heel as soon as they were out of the sink. It was a routine that Ariel supervised herself.

The wedding was going to be at 11:00 a.m. in the cool of the morning under the almond trees and within the circle of stones that had such a look of the stones on the Isle of Lewis where Riley had proposed.

Ariel slipped into the soft white cotton dress. It was simple yet elegant and just right for a hot summer day. The sundress fit her perfectly and with all of the nursing, she had lost her post-pregnancy fat quickly. Her breasts were larger than they were before. Peeking over the top of the sundress, they were creamy mounds, and the tiny diamond that was cut like a heart lay nestled between them. Riley had given her the gold and diamond necklace when the twins came home from the hospital. Riley had slipped the necklace around her neck in celebration of the event. Ariel looked in the mirror one last time before she walked out to the orchard to meet Riley and become his wife. Lily stood next to Ariel, admiring her sister's slim figure and radiant smile.

"Ariel, you're a vision! I would never suspect that you had had twins only six weeks ago. Here's something borrowed, and it's blue too so you can get away with one less trinket on this hot day." Lily slipped a little gold ring with a stone of a deep blue sapphire on her baby finger. It was Lily's confirmation ring from when she was thirteen and confirmed at the little Red Chapel in Sonora. It still fit her but only her pinky finger, and Ariel smiled and hugged Lily.

"Thanks, sis, it's perfect!" Ariel turned and smiled at her. The sisterly hug was heartfelt, and Ariel clung to her for a moment. She wished so much that Lily could have the happiness that she had. The two sister's broke apart, and Lily quickly wiped her eyes and then briskly reached over and handed Ariel her bouquet. It was too late in the year for spring flowers, but Ariel's rose garden had come through royally, and her bouquet made by Julie was an elegant assortment of just opening buds. There were white and lavender roses with very pale yellow baby roses still buds. Julie had expertly wrapped the stems in florist tape and the roses trailed down from the main bouquet to nestle among the ribbons of white that were attached.

The flowers were beautiful, and so much a part of her home that Ariel felt cherished and loved by the small group that gathered with her and Riley to witness their vows. Ariel was so happy that the greats--Grandma Sibyl and Grandpa Robyn--had arrived yesterday in time to witness their vows and welcome their new great-granddaughters as well as Jon into their hearts.

Riley met her in the circle of stones, in a black, short-cropped tuxedo of thin summer weight linen with a snowy, pleated front shirt, black bow tie, and a cummerbund of discreet moss green. Ariel caught her breath as she walked slowly toward him with only Lily as her attendant. Lily had picked out a long flowing sundress in a color that went so well with the lavender roses in Ariel's bouquet. The color was called sterling silver and was a soft gray lavender that complemented her long black hair. The most Reverend Tom Bender presided in his long black robes, looking hot and somewhat flushed in the face.

Zoe watched from the white chairs set up for about twenty-five close friends and relatives. Mark was acting as Riley's best man, the two having grown close within the past year as they struggled to deal with the tragedy of the loss of Sarah and Morgan and the near tragedy of Ariel and her babies. Jon, as the only groomsman, stood next to his father and Mark in a black tux with a moss green cummerbund identical to his dad's and Mark's.

Robyn and Sibyl were resplendent in their finery. Robyn wore his kilt and was freshly shaved. Sibyl was in her coolest dress-up dress of soft blue silk. It was light and airy and flowed straight from her shoulders. She wore a corsage of white roses with blue irises that Julie had made especially for her. Julie and Ben were both spruced up with Julie in a pink cotton sundress with a corsage of white roses and pink carnations that she had sent over from the local florist in Sonora. Sibyl had brought some heather from Scotland and a sprig was tucked into the white rose boutonnieres that all the men wore and also into Lily's and Ariel's bouquets. Everything went like clockwork, and the ceremony was so beautiful that there was hardly a dry eye among them. After Rev. Tom led the couple out of the stones and introduced them as Mr. and Mrs. Riley Roberts, the bride and groom led the way to the house where a luncheon of poached salmon and a selection of salads was waiting for them. Julie bustled about overseeing the caterers who didn't need any help at all. Mark and Ben were busy pouring champagne that Ben had picked up personally the day before from the local Ironstone Winery.

Ben was the first to toast the bride and groom. "My son, you have been a joy and a blessing to your mother and me, and we rejoice in your happiness with Ariel. Ariel, we welcome you to our family, and though we have always felt part of your family, we now rejoice that you are also a part of ours. May you and Riley, Jon, Kendall, Kelsey, Kaitlain, and Kelly be a loving joyful family, and we wish you all the happiness God can bestow all of your days ahead."

Riley hugged his father and mother, and then he turned to Ariel and kissed her as they listened to the rest of the toasts. Mark and Robyn concluded the toasts, and all of the guests swept into the house, grateful to be out of the hot sun. Riley's sister, Melonie, and her husband, Greg, were there, and there was a great deal of joking and bantering going on. Melonie could have been Riley's twin, the two looked so much alike. She was long legged and tall, with his sandy hair and deep blue eyes, a vision in a light blue sundress that had wide straps.

The reception was perfect, and with the heat, the cold poached salmon was just the right entrée. The salads were delicious, especially the sugared walnuts and raspberries with romaine lettuce and a light raspberry vinaigrette. The four-tier wedding cake took pride of place in the center of the room. It was a special carrot cake recipe from Sibyl, just like the cake that she had made for Robyn's birthday. Riley loved her carrot cake. Julie had made enough for the four tiers. There was a cream cheese frosting that was delicious with the towering confection. When everyone had finished with their plates and the cake, Riley and Ariel stood up together and thanked everyone for supporting them and being their friends through this long past seven months. Ariel nearly broke down as Riley explained why they decided to marry so quickly.

"I talked her into this marriage when we were in Scotland. She kept refusing, but I wore her down. When the twins came, and we discovered that there were two more, we knew we would be better off together than apart. An instant family is what we have formed today, and to seal the deal, we are having the girls baptized today as well. My son, Jon, was officially adopted by me, and the papers signed last week. Ariel and I welcome him officially today as our son, and we rejoice that he has become part of our family for all time. Jon was baptized a Lutheran and will keep his faith denomination. Rev. Tom, we're ready. Will you do the honors?"

At that, there was a commotion at the top of the stairs. Down came Mark with Kendall and Zoe with Kelsey. Lily and Melonie brought up the rear with Kaitlain and Kelly. Everyone clapped, and the infants were wide eyed, their green eyes round with interest. Their flaming red hair, short and curly, stuck out of the tops of the little, white lawn, christening caps that Lily had bought to match the christening gowns from her and her brother and the ones that Sibyl had brought with her of Paul's and Jackson's from the attics at Brindle Hall. The long dresses were all nearly identical, which surprised everyone. There was almost fifty years difference in the dresses, but the style hadn't changed a wit. Julie had washed and bleached them and put a light starch in them, and they ironed up beautifully.

The four godparents gathered in the living room in front of the fireplace where a baptismal font had been set up using a Waterford crystal punch bowl of Sarah's. Rev. Tom followed the ancient ritual and intoned, "Kendall Rae Roberts, Kelsey Rose Roberts, Kaitlain Renee Roberts, and Kelly Rowena Roberts, I baptize you in the name of the Father, Son, and Holy Ghost."

Rev. Roberts sprinkled each baby with the holy water and then turned to the witnesses and presented the children to them.

"You godparents have been given a special task of praying for these children and making sure they are brought up in the family of God. You parents will instruct them and teach them of Jesus and make sure they have been raised in the Christian faith."

When Rev. Tom had finished, the room burst into applause, and the babies were passed around to admiring hands until they had had enough and started to cry. The day ended with hurried good-byes, and all but the immediate family left. Everyone helped with the feedings of the four hungry girls. Ariel nursed Kaitlain and Kelly, and then Kendall and Kelsey, passing each to Lily and Melonie to finish feeding with a bottle. Robyn and Sibyl were amazed at the routine and how efficiently the feedings went. Sibyl held Kendall, and Robyn held Kelly when the feeding frenzy was over. The infants were so used to extra people holding them that they slept quietly on their laps.

"Well, Ariel, you've certainly gotten an abundant blessing in your life! These little ones are going to help fill your life with wonder as you watch them grow and become the people they are meant to be. It is quite a responsibility, but I know you and Riley will grow to be great parents for them," said Sibyl as she nuzzled Kendall and smelled her sweet smell of well-powdered baby.

Chapter 54

It seemed to take forever for the house to settle down, but finally everyone went to his or her beds. Lily and Mark left together, walking to their cottages.

"Mark, I think we saw a little miracle today. After the pain of Morgan and Sarah's death and all the trauma that Ariel went through with that insane doctor and almost losing her and the babies, I am so happy for Ariel and Riley. They give me hope that I'll get through the loss of Matt. Right now I needed to see a happy outcome."

Lily and Mark had reached her cottage, and he drew her into his arms. "You'll be all right, sis. You're strong, and we are here to help you. I'm just so thankful that you weren't killed as well. Matt did a heroic act when he stepped between you and that bomb, and I'll be forever grateful to him. I wish I had been able to meet him." The two drew apart, and Lily smiled at Mark then turned and walked briskly into her cottage. Mark looked up at the stars and as they always did, they comforted him. They were huge up here in the darkness, and with no competition from city lights, they looked like millions of diamonds. Age old, they've been out there ever since he was old enough to notice them, and he'd learned the names of all the stars and constellations. Someday he would show his nieces the stars. Mark walked on to his cottage and went straight to bed.

Ariel and Riley were the last to retire. They sat on the front porch looking at the stars. Everyone had gone to bed, and the house was quiet as they tiptoed up to their room. The honeymoon would have to wait until the babies were older, but the loving was not dependent on an exotic location.

Ariel had a simple cool nightgown of cream that Lily had bought for her as a gift. She slipped it on and lit a vanilla candle that Lily had also bought for the occasion. Ariel giggled. Lily was quite the romantic, and Ariel was glad. With the babies taking so much of her time and energy, she hadn't even thought about a special new nightgown. The creamy lightweight silk clung to her body and with her newly enhanced breasts from the breast feedings, Ariel looked sexy and also demure, a fetching combination. Riley was waiting for her already in bed as she walked across the rug, turning lights and lamps off as she went. The candle cast a soft glow to the room that felt like a safe snug cocoon. Ariel went to Riley and kissed him gently on the lips.

"My, Riley, you feel so good, and I'm so glad that you kept after me to marry you, my dear sweet husband." Before long, their kisses turned to urgent need, and Riley and Ariel responded with age-old ritual of loving. This time Riley was gentle and sweet. The two made sweet love by the light of the moon in the big bed that Ariel and Morgan had inherited from Sarah and Paul. Now it was theirs, and it felt so right.

Chapter 55

In the morning, Ariel woke before Riley, her breasts bursting with milk. She tiptoed from the room in her robe and went straight to the nursery. She could hear the wailing as soon as she got into the hallway. Ariel was so thankful for the nursing staff that took care of the feedings in the night, but she loved the first feeding of the morning when she'd pick up one of the infants, usually the one wailing the loudest who had had to wait for a bottle and put her to her breast. Instantly the wailing would stop, and peace would be restored in the nursery. Ariel greeted the nurses--Serena, who had been up all night, and Peggy, who had arrived for the day shift. The three chatted together while feeding the infants. Ariel shooed Serena, a tiny little woman who was almost mouse like, off to bed. She was only about five feet tall and didn't weigh more than ninety-eight pounds soaking wet. She wore her mousey brown hair in a pixie cut, but her huge blue eyes made up for her lack of statue. Peggy was just the opposite--tall and buxom with ample hips. She was a dishwater blonde who looked like she had been through a lot in her life. She was in fact a single woman who had raised her daughter alone. Now that her daughter was in college, she worked in private nursing to help with the expenses as well as taking a swing shift at the hospital. There were a couple of lounge chairs in each room for the nurses to use when their charges were asleep. The infants were almost sleeping through the nights, and when they finally did, Ariel felt she could do with an au-pair girl in the day to help her. Peggy was the day nurse. She took over promptly at 8:00 a.m. while Serena slept the day away.

The days were routine with feedings every four hours and daily baths and diaper changes every few hours or so. The rest of the household took a turn as well. When Julie finished with her tasks for the day, she'd slip in to help with the afternoon feedings, cuddling her "grandchildren" and tweaking their cheeks as they nursed from the bottle. Ariel didn't know how long she was going to nurse them, but she found the nursing a lot easier than bottle feeding. She'd know when she'd had enough, she thought. Sibyl and Robyn took a turn at feeding them too. Robyn adored the infants and held one whenever he could. Sibyl would sit with Ariel and feed whichever child needed it. Sometimes she spent the entire morning in the nursery, and Ariel had to shoo her out for lunch. It was quite a household to feed, and Julie was kept busy with meals for at least eight adults at a time. They loved her clam chowder and big crusty sandwiches. Julie beamed at all the activity in the house. With the Scotland great-grands, the nursing staff, Ben, Ariel, and Lily, there was always someone to talk to. Riley went back to his practice every day for about six hours, and then he'd be back to hold, cuddle, and feed one of the infants.

The babies were growing so fast now, and they smiled when Ariel talked and cooed at them. It was definitely going to be a full-time job for her even when the nursing was over and they started on solid food. So far, the formula and breast milk was enough, and they were able to sleep through the night. Lily was supervising their care. Truth to tell, it was great having a resident physician, though so far all Lily had to do was weigh and measure the girls. At six weeks, the girls were at nine a half pounds, give or take a few ounces, and were twenty-one inches long. Lily measured their heads and declared that they were growing at a normal rate, and everything was fine. If everything progressed on schedule, they would start introducing solid food to the infants in the next day or two. Lily recommended mashed fresh bananas as their first solid food.

Chapter 56

"Ariel, look at Kendall. She's grabbing for my fingers when I wiggle them right by her." Ariel was nursing Kelsey, and she looked up to see Kendall earnestly reach for Lily's finger and try to put it in her mouth. Kelsey was watching as she sucked at Ariel's breast and rubbed her tiny hand over Ariel's breast to try and hold on to it. It was a contented scene in the nursery with the sun hot, and the air was so dry that Lily walked over to the window to peer out at the hot relentless sun. The swamp cooler kept the house a cool eighty degrees. Ariel hadn't noticed the heat and dryness, as busy as she was inside with the babies, but Lily walked to the big house every day from her cottage and was beginning to be concerned when she saw the dry shrubs all around the house. There was a warning posted by the Columbia Park District Rangers--no fires, not even charcoal was allowed during this heat wave. It was a hundred five on the porch this morning when Lily walked over.

Lily was emptying out her mother's surgery and repainting the walls a cool light green with white trim. Since Lily had gotten back, she had decided to open the surgery as a free clinic for the farm, and she would be the sole physician for the babies. It would save Ariel from having to drive them to town, and besides, she needed something to keep her busy. Word got out that Lily was open for business, and before long, there was a steady stream of patients with cuts, bruises, burns, and fevers. The neighbors came to Lily, just as they had come to see Sarah when there was an accident or sickness. Lily had often helped her mother while she tended the prospectors, many who were without medical insurance. There was always someone getting hurt on the river, like crushed fingers from moving heavy boulders in search of the gold nugget that they were sure was just under the big boulder. Lily cheerfully bandaged their hands and warned them to stay out of the river until they were healed up, but the next day they were back to the search, moving rocks and dredging with a protective latex glove over the injured hand. Lily just sighed and waited for them to come again.

This morning though the air was hot at 8:00 a.m., and it was over a hundred and ten by eleven o'clock. Lily was between patients and looking out the window that had a view of the canyon and the Stanislaus River snaking below. It was Lily's favorite view, and she often stopped and looked out at the ancient river and deep canyon that had resulted from the relentless water carving the canyon deeper and deeper over the millenniums. Today, however, she noticed a plume of smoke curling up the canyon. Lily ran to her cell phone and dialed 911.

"There's smoke in the canyon along the Middle Fork of the Stanislaus River; I'm calling from Frazer's Acres. We're right above it." Just then, a puff of flame flared up, and Lily could see the flames claiming a tree crown. What was a plume of smoke was now a raging fire. Lily finished with the operator and ran to the house to let Ariel know. Frazer Acres was often used as a staging area for the canyon fires, because it had a large open fields with room for equipment and men.

"Ariel, there's a fire in the canyon. I've called the fire department, and they're sending trucks and helicopters. We're to stand by until they arrive." Lily ran out to the barn where Ben and Julie were having lunch in their small apartment over the barn office.

"Julie, Ben, we have a fire in the canyon. The fire department is on its way. We're going to be hosting the firefighters, and in this hot dry heat, it's bound to be a bad one. Drag out the big coffee urn. I'll check our store room."

Lily turned and headed back to the house. Julie left her sandwich and ran after Lily. With the farm used as a staging area, they would be safe enough unless it got out of control big time. Lily rushed into the house and up the stairs to the nursery where she found Ariel already stuffing damp towels around all of the windowsills to keep the smoke out. The two sisters worked together putting the damp towels around all the windowsills on the second floor, and when they were done, they started on the lower floors as well. They ran out of towels, so they used sheets, rolling them and cutting them the width of the window. They shoved the sheets around the front and back door sills as well. They had just finished when the yard started filling with fire trucks and park personnel. With such steep terrain and dry vegetation, a mixture of dry grass, heavy brush, and mixed-conifer, they weren't taking any chances.

As the fire departments coordinated their services, Lily saw more trees exploding into flame, and she knew it was going to be a long night. Frazer Acres was about a quarter mile from the fire's perimeter. The U.S. Forest Service Manager, Bob Turner, a big, hard-bellied farmer's son, was a fellow that Lily had gone to school with, and he was a friend of Mark's too. Lily rushed out to Bob and listened as he instructed the men and women gearing up for a hot, dirty job.

"If it runs up the canyon, we'll have a little bit larger fuel break. The helicopters are dipping into New Melones Reservoir and dumping their buckets as fast as they can. The plan is to keep the fire south of the river, north of Contention Ridge, and west of Sandbar Flat Campground. I'm hearing reports from the first copters that about a quarter mile up the river canyon from the fire, the smoke is so thick the helicopters making water drops disappear and reappear on the other side. We've got ground units fighting it on foot. Go to it, and for heaven's sake, be careful. This is a hot one!" Bob turned and switched on his radio.

The *whump, whump, whump* of the helicopters passing over the farm all day and into the night with their water buckets brimming with water unnerved Lily and brought back the war in Iraq and the bombing of the restaurant where Lily and Matt were eating. Lily steeled herself against the overwhelming feelings that threatened to overcome her and focused on first aid supplies. She had lots of gauze and bandages, and all she could do here was treat minor burns and cuts. Anything else would have to be taken by helicopter over to Sonora Regional where they had a heliport on the roof of the hospital. Lily was busy and already treating some of the firefighters who had gotten burns on their faces when a tree flared up in front of them. All the while, she was worried about Mark who she knew had been called up as a first responder. Lily and Ariel did what they could as the exhausted firefighters trickled in for breaks and sleep. They bedded down under the almond trees. Ben was busy helping Julie keep the big long tables filled with bottled water and endless gallons of Julie's homemade stew with green salad and crusty garlic bread that was gratefully accepted by the men and women who had been out on the lines all day and into the night.

Ben was never as tired as he was helping Julie. Thankfully, he'd just finished the second harvest of the Carmel Almonds the day before this inferno started. The Carmels were the pollinator almonds and were grown on alternate rows between the nonpariels. The only difference in them was that they had a harder shell, and Ben always thought they were oiler. They fetched forty cents a pound, half of what the nonpareils fetched, but they were necessary as pollinators, and they were good for cooking too.

"Ben, can you get me some more napkins and silverware, please," Julie hollered over to where Ben had been sitting on the edge of the table, kind of daydreaming and remembering what fun Jon had using the shaker on the trees. *That boy was a pure pleasure*, he thought. Ben hurried over to the kitchen storeroom and grabbed a bunch of silverware and napkins, chuckling to himself all the way back to Julie.

Chapter 57

no one had heard from Mark, and they knew that they wouldn't until he came in. Every truck that rolled into the yard caused them to look up from whatever they were doing and hope it was Mark, but it wasn't.

Zoe showed up after work and pitched in as well, ladling stew and sharing wise cracks with the crew.

Mark was on the south side of the river when a conifer burst into flames in back of him. Suddenly his clothes caught fire. He struck out blindly away from the core of the fire, not sure if he was heading in the right direction away from the flames and toward the river, until he stumbled and fell right into the river and submerged as quickly as he could. It happened so fast that all he could do was keep under the water as the fire roared across the river and jumped over to the other side. His partner, John Carver, saw him go into the river and jumped in right behind him. The two stayed under as long as they could before coming up for air. Barely breaking the surface, they kept submerged with just their mouth and nose clearing the water so they could breath. It seemed like hours, but was only a minute before the fire had jumped across them. John helped Mark go down river, keeping to the center of the river. Mark's clothes had smoldered, and he knew he was badly burned. The two kept moving. Mark wasn't going to stay and die in the fire. Finally, the two were clear of the flames, and John was able to carry Mark out of the river to the clearing where a helicopter was parked at the ready to transport casualties. The helicopter Medivac went straight to Sonora Regional where Mark was admitted with second-degree burns on his back and legs. The call came to the ranch shortly after midnight. Lily picked up the phone and listened as someone on the other end told them that Mark had been injured and was asking for Lily. Lily barked questions to the nurse at the other end and was told that Mark was in the burn unit but that his injuries weren't serious. Lily dropped the phone back in the cradle and ran to tell Ariel and Zoe who were sitting together in the kitchen taking a break from serving food to the endless line of firefighters.

"Zoe, Ariel, it's Mark; he got caught in a flare-up and is in the hospital at Sonora."

Zoe stood up and grabbed her coffee. "Come on Lily, I'll drive."

Lily and Zoe drove into Sonora with lights flashing. They reached the hospital in record time, and Lily and Zoe found Mark lying on his stomach, his back a flaming red. He was doped up good with morphine, but he was awake. Zoe reached over, held his hand, and softly talked to him. The nurses said that the burns were second degree, and if they wanted more information, they should talk with the doctor. Lily called Ariel and told her.

"It's not as bad as it sounds. They'll keep him for a few days, giving him fluid, and if all goes well, he'll be home soon. No, I don't think you should come right now. He's all doped up and won't even know we were here when he wakes up tomorrow."

Lily ended the call and went back into the room. Lily's professional eye assessed his condition. He had second-degree burns on his back, arms, the back of his legs, and even his butt. Thankfully, he wasn't going to need skin grafts, although the doctors said that had he been exposed to such extreme heat for another few seconds, he would have probably been in and out of hospitals for the next year. He was a lucky man.

"Here, Mark, drink some water, I want you to have as much water as you can hold. It will help to flush your system." Lily held the glass with the flexible straw, and Mark, to save her nagging at him, slurped the water up through the straw, making terrible noises to annoy her as he did. He was in the process of making offensive noises when Zoe walked in and when he saw her, he nearly choked.

"Hey, Mark, do you need artificial respiration? They say I'm the best on the Heimlich maneuver." Zoe laughed at his embarrassment, looked up at Lily, and smiled.

"I was just giving Lily a bad time; she's acting like Nurse Ratchet," he said with dignity. The sheet slipped and exposed his bare butt for the entire world to see, and neither Zoe nor Lily took pity on him and covered him up.

Chapter 58

Lily and Zoe stayed by Mark's side around the clock except during his extensive skin treatments where the nurses had to keep taking off the burned skin. Even with the morphine, Mark screamed in pain. Zoe was close to losing it when he screamed like that, and the two old friends clung to each other in the waiting room and sobbed together. Zoe had to go back on duty, having begged as many of her cohorts as she could to cover her shifts. Mark wasn't family to Zoe in the eyes of the law, but Zoe saw it differently, and Lily watched the way Zoe helped Mark to drink from a glass, holding the glass and straw for him. Lily could see that there were a lot of feelings for Mark that Zoe herself didn't realize. Lily hoped that her brother, who was known to be gun shy with women, would not push Zoe away when he was conscious enough to know how she felt.

It was the better part of a week before Mark was released. Lily was waiting for him after she paid his bill and got his release orders. She took over from the nurse who would not allow Mark to get out of the wheelchair until he was actually outside the building. "You look a hell of a lot better this morning than when they brought you in," Lily said. Mark laughed.

"I wouldn't recommend this place as a vacation destination."

"Next time watch your ass, Mark." Lily gulped to keep the tears from gushing.

"I'll keep that in mind," Mark said. It really was good to be getting out. "Where's Zoe?" Mark said looking around the lobby.

"She had to pull an all-nighter to pay back some of the folks who worked her shifts for her when you first came in. She'll be at the farm later."

Mark looked disappointed, and Lily grinned. *Well, well, little brother was smitten.* Lily hoped that it would stick. Zoe was a great friend, and she didn't want her hurt.

"Did someone bring my car over?" he asked.

"You've got curb side service, little brother, and I'm the chauffer."

Lily propelled the wheel chair out to the curb and helped Mark into Ariel's Buick. It was a lot softer ride than her jeep, and Ariel hadn't driven it since way before the twins were born. In fact, Ariel and Riley were starting to think of a new car that would be big enough for their instant family. Julie was in line for this car as soon as they could find the perfect SUV.

Mark stayed at the big house, which added considerable commotion to Ariel's days. He had constant company, and Ariel began to feel that she was hosting the entire Tuolumne Fire Department and Forest Service. It was like a party every day.

The greats, Sibyl and Robyn, helped her as much as they could. Coffee and homemade Scottish shortbread, from Sibyl's recipe, was very popular, and Sibyl was making batch after batch. Finally Zoe and Lily moved Mark to Lily's cottage, and Lily hosted the hordes, showing everyone out by 10:00 p.m. when she declared visiting hours were over. Zoe was the exception. She'd come and play cards with Mark until she too had to go home in order to get some sleep.

When the doctor okayed it, Mark began to walk around the farm and spent a lot of time with Ben. It would be months before he would be able to go back to work, and he was going stir-crazy watching television and reading. Ben was able to use him to order supplies on the computer. He even gave him the books to keep updated. Mark found that he liked the work, and he began to toy with the idea of getting out of the fire department when he vested in his union.

Chapter 59

The days moved along, and everyone at the farm was busy in one way or another, especially Ariel with the babies and Riley with his vet office. Lily had a thriving practice of neighbors and even had some of the foster kids that Ariel supervised when she was working. Lily donated her services for their care. Ariel loved it. She was able to visit with her former cases, and she even shared her babies with them. It got her to thinking that when the babies were older, maybe there would be a way that she could use the farm for special events to enrich the foster children's lives. She visualized a Ranch Day, where the children and their foster families could come and swim in the pool, and she'd have a picnic for them. There was the canyon with the fishing as well. It was something to think about but not for a while yet. It was all she could do to get through the daily feedings.

Now that the babies were almost five months old, she was seriously considering weaning them. Though they didn't have teeth yet, Ariel could feel the tiny teeth under their gums as they sucked at her breasts, and sometimes Kelly especially would bite down hard on her nipple, and it hurt. Ariel would have to tell Kelly "No!" and stop her from nursing, only letting her latch on again when she acted gentler.

Meredith was thrilled with Lily because with Medi-Cal, the

providers who were authorized to treat the children, though acceptable, weren't always willing, and there were less and less of them willing to accept the low service fee. Lily wrote out prescriptions, and they used their Medi-Cal to pay for the drugs that were needed. It worked for all of them. Zoe and Mark were becoming closer and closer, and Lily worried that Mark would break her heart, but all she could do was watch and hope for the best.

Mark was back in his own cottage, and Lily could see Zoe's jeep there far into the night on the weekends and sometimes still there in the morning. No one commented except to raise their eyebrows at each other. It seemed that the whole farm was holding its breath to see what happened next.

Chapter 60

november was cold, and there was heavy rain the week before Thanksgiving. Sibyl and Robyn were planning on staying through till the New Year, and Ariel and Sibyl were planning a big family Thanksgiving, with Zoe and Lily's input when they had the time. They would be eleven for dinner. Julie was busy polishing up the house, and there were wonderful smells coming from the kitchen the week before Thanksgiving. Dinner would be at four o'clock in the big dining room where Ariel, Lily, and Mark had always done their schoolwork.

Sarah's presence in the house was palatable, and there were warm stories of her fabulous Thanksgiving dinners, especially when Paul was alive. This year there would be two places at the table that would never again hold Sarah or Morgan. Ariel felt their loss keenly, especially when she wanted to tell Morgan or Sarah something the babies had done. There were still raw feelings over their loss. Riley comforted Ariel when she couldn't hide her tears, and Ariel was thankful that Riley truly understood and didn't have any jealousy over her memories of Morgan. Riley had loved him too.

It was Thanksgiving Day. The house had never been so full, and the big table was stretched to fit them all. Julie had starched and bleached a thick white damask tablecloth and napkins that

Sarah had used every holiday. There was a cornucopia of fresh fruit and nuts on the sideboard, and on the table were Ariel's pewter candlesticks with cream-colored beeswax candles. The centerpiece was a handcrafted, old, chuck wagon model without a cover, filled with nuts and red grapes and persimmons pulled by a hand carved turkey that had graced the Thanksgiving table since Ariel was a little girl. It had been her mother's, Kate's, and now that she had gone back to Scotland and visited her mother's grave and met her Aunt Claire and Jackson, she loved the turkey even more. The table was set with Sarah's china, a wonderful pattern that brought out the rust and autumn colors of the season with a rim of fall designs on white plates. Sibyl made her famous dressing with giblets and celery and onions. The pumpkin pies were Julie's contribution and were from the garden where Julie had been nurturing some big sweet pumpkins. There were the traditional side dishes of mashed potatoes and green bean casserole with mushrooms and water chestnuts. Lily had made a cranberry relish that Sarah had always made, and there were homemade yeast rolls and fresh butter too.

Everyone was stuffed, and when the babies were brought down after their naps, everyone took a turn holding them. The babies spent the hours after dinner in front of the fire nestled in Ben's, Julie's, Sibyl's, and Robyn's laps as part of the family festivities. And when one of them woke up, Ariel would feed the hungry mite with a light shawl thrown over her shoulder and across her front. Everything was relaxed and a fun game of Texas Hold'em was being played in the family room. Riley, Mark, Zoe, and Lily, as well as Ben and Robyn, vied to beat the others and be one of the winners.

The day was too soon over, and Zoe had to go on duty at 8:00 p.m. The rest of them pulled out leftovers and made huge turkey sandwiches and went back to the game. Finally, Robyn came in first place and Ben second. Lily was happy to get third. The pot with six of them playing wasn't big, but the winnings were all the sweeter when they saw the pleasure Robyn and Ben had when they beat the young ones!

Chapter 61

Thanksgiving was barely over when it seemed the household was busy getting ready for Christmas. Everyone tried to get the perfect gifts for each other without anyone finding out. Ben worked long hours in his carpentry shop. With winter winds blowing, there wasn't anything to be done in the orchards, so he spent the time making cedar jewelry boxes for all of the women in the family. For the men, he made pocket change and watch holders for their dressers. Julie was busy making sweaters for everyone from the fine wool that Ariel had brought her from Scotland, and Sibyl made fruit cakes and truffles that she sealed away until Christmas to meld the flavors.

Riley was at his office the Friday after Thanksgiving, the biggest shopping day of the year. He was glad that he'd had an excuse not to go with Ariel and Lily, who had made that day a special gal's day out ever since they were little and Sarah would take them to San Francisco for a weekend shopping frenzy. Now they stayed closer to home, going only as far as Modesto to pick up the bargains that had been advertised Thanksgiving morning in the Union Democrat.

The phone rang, and since it wasn't an office day, he let his answering service pick it up. They would call him if it were important. It was quiet in his office and he used the time to catch up on his paperwork. He'd given his staff the day off as well. He was a little surprised when his emergency number, that only the answering service had access to, rang shrilly. Riley picked up the phone on its first ring.

"Dr. Roberts, there's a call from Zoe Clayborn for you; she says it's an emergency."

"Okay, Anne, thank you." Riley punched the blinking light on his phone and answered, "What's up, Zoe?"

"Riley, we have some horses that we are rescuing, and I'm looking for spots for them."

"How many do you have?"

"Thirty-five. I wonder, there's a cute newborn filly looks about a day old, still has the umbilical cord attached. It needs round the clock care, and I wondered if Jon and Ben might want to take her on. Her mother's in fairly good shape, and she's nursing the filly, but we've got to get some help for them right away. What do you say?"

"Absolutely, bring them straight to the farm; I'll call Ben and have him get the birthing stall filled with bedding. I'll meet you at the farm in--what do you think? Two hours do it?"

"That's fine. I'll have them out to your place as soon as possible. Thank you, Riley; I hope I can get as good a response from the rest of the community."

"Call Harry Blackstone and have him put out an urgent radio message. I'll bet that will do it."

After listening to Zoe regarding the horses and how they had gotten the call that they had been abandoned and were left starving in a corral without food or water, he couldn't keep the anger down as he hung up. He slammed his fist onto the desk and swore. He'd seen this all too often in this terrible economy. It wasn't just horses that were abandoned, but dogs, cats, cows, and pigs had all had their share of neglect and abandonment. Riley sighed and knew he couldn't change the situation, but maybe they could be a part of saving this mare and her new filly. Riley reached for the phone and called his father.

"Thanks, Dad, for taking this on. I'm on my way home, and I'll stop and get some feed and some formula for the filly. The mare is going to need to get nourished before she'll have much to offer her filly."

Riley drove into the farm and was surprised to see the police horse trailer already there. Zoe was leading out a pathetically thin roan mare with a white star on her forehead and four white stocking feet. The filly came out next from the two-stall carrier, wobbly, with four white stocking feet and a blazing white star just like her mother. Ben had the birthing stall full of soft bedding and stood by as he watched Jon, with a big grin on his face, lead the filly. Riley grinned back and followed Zoe and Jon into the barn to the birthing stall. Riley looked over both horses. He ran his hands over the mare's neck and felt the swelling. Jon was watching him.

"What's wrong with her?" Jon asked, standing quietly beside his father and still holding the filly's bridle.

"This mare's got laryngitis."

"Laryngitis? Horses get laryngitis? How can you tell?"

"See here." Taking Jon's hand, Riley guided it over the throat. "Can you feel it's swollen?"

"Ah, that sucks, you poor thing." He made soothing noises as he patted it gently. "Is she going to be all right?"

"She will when we get done treating her, but we have to watch that her air passage doesn't swell shut, or she'll choke."

"You mean she could die?" Jon pressed his cheek against the mare's cheek. "But, Dad, it's just a sore throat."

"In you, but in her it's different. I don't think it's too serious. She can't eat yet, but gruel and some linseed tea will help keep her strength up. We'll keep her warm and treat it with eucalyptus inhalations and smear camphor on her tongue three or four times a day. The mare's knee needs tending. I'll apply a non-irritating blister to her knee sprain." It made Riley boil to see how the horse had been neglected.

Riley continued to run his hands over the horse and found a knot on the mare's back. "She has a small abscess here. We'll want to bring this to a head." Riley went to the back of the barn, filled a bucket with hot water, and brought it back to the stall. He took a thick piece of flannel, dunked it in the hot water, and rung it out. The steaming cloth he placed over the abscess would draw it out and bring it to a head.

Riley finished his exam by looking at the mare's eyes and teeth. She was only about three years old, and if they could get her healthy again, she'd have more pretty fillies and colts. This was a thoroughbred horse, and the filly looked to be too. Riley fed the gruel and tea to the horse and prepared formula for the filly. He showed Jon how to hold the nipple bucket, and Jon smiled in delight as the filly latched on to the nipple and sucked and nursed its fill. She was a delight, and Riley thought of naming her Star Delight and her mother Blazing Star, once he saw how she healed up. For now, it was okay to hold off naming them and just talk gently and softly to them both.

Ariel walked out to the barn, bundled up against the sharp air. It would be less than thirty degrees tonight. She opened the big barn door and peered in. There was a light at the end of the stalls where the birthing stall was. Ariel headed for that one and came upon father and son bending over the filly stroking and admiring her.

"Riley, Jon, the baby's beautiful and look how she nurses from that bucket. That's precious. You both did a great job, and I just know they're going to be fine. I've held the soup hot for you. Are you about ready to come in?" She leaned over the stall and watched as the filly drank the last of the formula. The three closed up the barn and left a small light burning, so they could find their way in later before Jon's bedtime when it would be time for another feeding for the filly. Arms around both Ariel and Jon, Riley felt his world was complete.

Lily came back from Mark's house where she'd gone after dinner. The two were plotting their Christmas presents. Mark wanted to get Jon a saddle, but Lily thought they could wait on that and give him one for his birthday in August. The filly would be eight months old then, and Jon could put the saddle on her to get her used to it before he put his weight on her after her first year. They had made a big long list, and Lily agreed to start shopping for the presents, since she had more free time than Mark did. It would be fun to see all of their faces when they opened them.

Lily slipped into the barn, went straight to the birthing stall, and stood leaning against the stall, peeking over the top at the two horses. "Oh my, you're a cutie!" she said as she looked at the filly that was looking straight at her. She saw the flannel on the mare's back and knew that there must be an abscess under it. Riley had done a good job, and the mother and her filly looked comfortable, but the mother was skin and bones, and Lily knew she'd need lots of tending. "Well, it looks like I've a volunteer project in front of me. I need you as much as you need me." The mare looked up and stared at her, and Lily turned and went into the house to offer her help with the horses.

The next morning at breakfast, Lily spoke before she could rationalize her way out of it and cornered Riley over coffee.

"Riley, I can take care of the mare and help Jon with the stall mucking and feedings. We can work together. Okay by you, Jon?" Lily smiled and tousled his head.

It only took a minute for both Jon and Riley to agree, and Riley quickly wrote a feed and treatment schedule for the mare. Jon knew what to do with the filly, but with Riley having to be at the clinic, he welcomed Lily's help.

"With you and Jon working together, I know I don't have anything to worry about, and Ariel and I have our hands full with the babies upstairs.

Ariel smiled at Riley and then stood up. "Speaking of babies, I hear them now. I'll see you later, guys."

Ariel ran up the stairs, so happy to have her trim figure back and be able to run up the stairs again instead of plod like she did when she was carrying her twins. Lily followed behind her, and together they fed and changed all four babies. Ariel had put a refrigerator and a microwave in the nursery, and everything was close by. With the nurses gone till Monday, this was the first time Ariel and Lily had had the babies all to themselves. Riley came up just as they were changing Kelly, and Lily promptly handed her to him with a warm bottle of formula. Riley sat in the rocking chair and rocked her. It was a sweet scene of feeding babies with the adults talking softly to each other.

That evening, Jon and Riley were in the barn a long time. Riley dressed the mares abscess and treated her leg with a fresh non-irritating blister dressing. The filly was sturdy on her legs, and the mare was able to eat all of the gruel with the linseed oil that Riley was treating her sore throat with. Thankfully, there was no additional swelling, and he was hopeful that the mare was going to be all right.

It was past dinner when Riley and his son went into the house. Ariel had kept the turkey noodle soup hot for them, and they ate it with turkey and cheese sandwiches.

"Ariel, thanks for holding dinner. It's delicious, and I think the horse and her filly are going to be fine. It means that were going to have to hand feed the filly for a while until her mother's stronger, but I do want her to nurse a bit every day to keep the milk flowing. Jon, are you up to feeding the filly just before bedtime? Then we'll let the mother have her for the night feeding. I think that little filly is just your size."

Jon looked up with surprise. "You mean she's mine?"

"If you take care of her, muck out her stall, and feed her every morning and afternoon and just before bedtime." Riley said, smiling and ruffling his hair.

"Oh, I will. Thanks, Dad!" Jon and Riley embraced and hugged each other, and Riley knew everything was going to be all right with them both.

Chapter 02

he month between Thanksgiving and Christmas went by fast. Jon never missed feeding and caring for the filly and even her mother. He'd muck out the soiled straw and lay fresh sweet bedding in the stall. Star greeted him every time he came in to feed her and let him comb and curry her. He always brought fresh apples and carrots for both of them, and the horses thrived. The mare's abscess healed and her laryngitis as well.

The week before Christmas, everyone went to the woods with a boiling honor guard of excited basset hounds, Sofie waddling behind her brood. The two pups that had been saved from being sold were little females that Ariel and Lily hoped to use for future breeding. Sofie was from championship stock, and the pups' father was a champion as well. They wanted to have a kennel for the nurturing of the breed. The pups, Dixie and Ruby, were joyful additions to the farm. When the babies were older, Ariel felt that this would be a good job for them, and they would learn to care for the animals and train them too.

It was a wonderful day. They brought back tractor loads of pine and holly, silvery green moss, and rich brown buckeye nuts. The huge dense pine tree stood almost ten feet tall and had pride of place in the living room with barely room for the traditional star on top. It was only an inch or two from the ceiling. Ariel decreed no decorations on the tree except the silver green moss and pinecones and small clusters of holly berries. The lights were tiny clear crystal bulbs that looked like a thousand stars among the branches. Red velvet bows were tied among the branches.

This year, the house was truly transformed. Cleaned, shined, and waxed down to its rich pine floors by Julie, Ariel, and Lily. It bloomed with the bounty of the woods and smelled in the foggy twilights like the forest and the river combined. Frazers Acres encircled all who entered; the yellow farmhouse with its bright tin roof sheltered them all and helped heal the horror of the terrible, and yet wonderful, year they had all endured. Forever after, Ariel would remember that Christmas as one of healing and renewal--her newly forged family from infants to the greats, the mystery of Ariel and Riley's pairing, a miracle of life's ability to bring wonderful gifts, and surprises in the wake of such tragedy and pain.

Ariel lit candles everywhere in the evening: in the kitchen, the dining room, carefully placed in the front windows that were bare of curtains, and in their bedroom as well. Fires burned in both fireplaces, the pungent smell of fresh pine curling in the air.

On Christmas Eve, the family gathered at four o'clock. Ariel was wearing a long green velvet hostess gown with Morgan's emerald earrings in her ears. Lily had on a red wool dress with long tight sleeves and a long straight skirt. She wore her mother's ruby and diamond earrings. Her black hair swept up in a chignon fastened with a gold and diamond barrette. Sibyl wore a striking tartan Stuart plaid long wool skirt with a red turtleneck sweater. Zoe was in a black velvet pantsuit with gold studs in her ears. Her blonde hair had grown long, and she wore it loose over her shoulders, a change from the pinned-up, daily look of the cop. She looked elegant and feminine as she bustled about the house helping with an extra pair of hands wherever she was needed. The men all wore soft sweaters and slacks of soft wool. They wore a variety of Bay Rum-type aftershave that went from woodsy to spicy and added a masculine spice to the air.

Earlier in the day, Ariel and Sibyl had gone off by themselves armed with popcorn and seeds rolled in peanut butter as well as pinecones, small ears of dried corn, whole apples, and oranges. They found the little tree by the edge of the farm in view of the windows of the living room and trimmed a tree for the critters. They strung the tree with the popcorn and cranberry strands that they had carefully threaded by the fire the night before. Throughout the day, as they put the beautifully wrapped presents under the tree and Ariel sat and nursed the babies, they watched the deer and the squirrels and the winter sparrows flock to the tree, tentative at first and then more boldly nibbling on the trimmings.

Christmas Eve was when traditionally the family had gone to St. James for the candlelight service before they opened their presents. The babies made this ritual difficult to do this year. For Ariel, the tradition was keenly missed, but she looked up at the stars and said a prayer for the safety and well-being of her family; it was enough, and her heart was filled with gratitude.

Because there was such a big dinner planned for Christmas as well as a huge breakfast, Christmas Eve was simpler fare with oyster stew and French bread. A plum pudding was lit, and a hard sauce was poured on each slice. Ariel liked vanilla ice cream and offered it to all who wanted it. After the dishes were put in the dishwasher, the family gathered around the huge tree and admired the simple decorations. Lily and Mark distributed the gifts as they had since they were toddlers.

Ariel and Riley had the bulk of the packages as they were opening the babies' gifts as well. There were silver cups with each girls name on it and silver spoons as well. Julie had managed to knit them all sweaters and warm stocking hats of pink yarn with a great tassel on the end. Lily had gotten them silver rattles with their names engraved on them, and Mark and Zoe had given them gold lockets with an A, a B, a C, and a D engraved on the back of each one. Ariel and Riley had given each other new ski parkas and warm mittens. Sibyl and Robyn got new warm mufflers and warm leather driving gloves as well as hand-knitted hats from Julie and Ben.

Right after opening their presents, stuffing all the wrapping paper in big red Santa sacks that had held the gifts, and straightening up the living room, they watched a wonderful Christmas concert on the television featuring Celine Dion and Josh Groban. They were wonderful, singing all of the holy sacred music with their clear beautiful voices. Everyone enjoyed it, and then after stuffing themselves with fruit cake and truffles with fresh ground coffee served in Sarah's white and gold Italian coffee cups, it was time for bed. Every bed was full, and everyone stayed at the big house, including Julie and Ben. The house just expanded, spread, and embraced them all. It was a wonderful evening, and it was long past midnight when all the lights were finally out and everyone was snug in their bed.

The nurses, Serena and Peggy, had been given both Christmas Eve and Christmas Day off to be with their families, and everyone helped with feedings and diaper changing. The babies slept all night and when they woke up, they cooed to each other in their cribs. It was quite a trick to get them diapered and fed and when they had, they brought them down to breakfast with the rest of the family. Lily and Zoe fed them mashed bananas in rice cereal while Ariel and Julie made pancakes and thick sliced ham. Ariel made a green chili oven-baked egg casserole that went well with slabs of ham and pancakes with pure maple syrup.

After breakfast, the dishes were done, and then it was time for the prime rib to be rubbed and left out to meld its flavors and seasoning. At about two o'clock, it was popped into the oven, and au gratin potatoes and Waldorf salad with fresh green beans and homemade rolls were prepared. When the prime rib came out at four o'clock, it was covered to set before it was carved and the wonderful drippings were made into a thick, rich gravy. The au gratin potatoes and rolls were popped into the oven to bake. Everyone helped with a small part of the dinner preparation. Sibyl arranged sliced fruitcake and truffles on the special Christmas plates and then covered them with plastic wrap to keep them fresh. Colorful Christmas cookies were put on crystal plates and covered for after the dinner. There was eggnog and sherry as well as sparkling ciders for the table.

The dining room had been shut off from prying eyes all day and Lily and Ariel had covered the table with a red tablecloth and napkins and strewed the gold covered chocolate coins that had been a tradition from their parents' day. The silver candlesticks were beautiful in their simplicity with the creamy white beeswax candles. They placed boughs of greenery in the center of the table and used Sarah's gold-rimmed plates with the large crystal goblets that Paul had ordered for their first Christmas as a family. All around Ariel and Lily were the memories of their father and Sarah. Ariel was so happy that Lily enjoyed keeping memories of their family alive through the beautiful things that their parents had bought and used for the holidays.

Finally, everything was ready. The doors to the dining room were thrown open, and the family sat down to eat. The sideboard was groaning with food, and everyone helped pass it. The family, including infants on four laps, talked and laughed together. Ariel looked around the room and caught Riley's eye, and they both smiled broadly at each other. This was their family. All around them were the memories of Paul and Sarah and Morgan, but the new memories being formed and the new families growing out of the old was truly a blessing that a year before would have been difficult to imagine. Ariel lifted her glass, and everyone around the table did the same. The toasts were short and heartfelt; there was an air of true thankfulness that the family had survived.

The stars were out bright as only the stars on this mountain could be. Ariel and Riley walked out on the deck to look at them. They turned to each other, and Ariel reached up to Riley and kissed him. The kiss deepened, and with smiles, they turned and walked into the house now hushed with the late hour. They opened Jon's door and smiled as Ruby and Daisy looked up from beneath a nest of blankets to peer back at them. Jon had his blankets over his head, and Riley tiptoed over to his bed and straightened the covers. Jon opened his eyes, and Riley patted his arm and whispered. "Go back to sleep, son. I'm just tucking you in." Jon turned toward the wall and draped an arm over Ruby. Small sounds of snoring escaped from the bed as Riley and Ariel tiptoed out of the room and closed the door.

They walked up the stairs, peeking first into the blue nursery where Kaitlain and Kelly lay sucking their thumbs in their sleep and then into the yellow nursery where Kendall and Kelsey were doing exactly the same thing. The babies made sucking sounds, and Riley and Ariel tucked loose blankets before going into their room. After the terrible year they had survived and the wonderful Christmas, all Ariel could feel was grateful, and she spooned next to Riley and kissed his neck. For the moment, the house was silent and all were asleep. Tomorrow it would all start again, and Ariel savored the quiet and snuggled close to Riley.

"Golden dreams, Riley!" she said as she drifted off to sleep.

CPSIA information can be obtained at www.ICGtesting.com
Printed in the USA
LVOW072324060512

280504LV00004B/3/P